P9-BYG-983

LT
FIC
Wax

Rutland Free Library
10 Court Street
Rutland, VT 05701-4058

DISCARD

# A WEEK AT THE LAKE

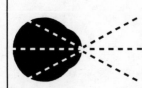

This Large Print Book carries the
Seal of Approval of N.A.V.H.

# A WEEK AT THE LAKE

## WENDY WAX

**THORNDIKE PRESS**
*A part of Gale, Cengage Learning*

LT  FIC Wax

Rutland Free Library
10 Court Street
Rutland, VT 05701-4058

DISCARD

GALE
CENGAGE Learning·

Farmington Hills, Mich • San Francisco • New York • Waterville, Maine
Meriden, Conn • Mason, Ohio • Chicago

Copyright © 2015 by Wendy Wax.
"Readers Guide" copyright © 2015 by Penguin Random House LLC.
Thorndike Press, a part of Gale, Cengage Learning.

**ALL RIGHTS RESERVED**
This is a work of fiction. Names, characters, places, and incidents either
are the product of the author's imagination or are used fictitiously, and
any resemblance to actual persons, living or dead, business
establishments, events, or locales is entirely coincidental. The publisher
does not have any control over and does not assume any responsibility
for author or third-party websites or their content.
Thorndike Press® Large Print Romance.
The text of this Large Print edition is unabridged.
Other aspects of the book may vary from the original edition.
Set in 16 pt. Plantin.

LIBRARY OF CONGRESS CATALOGING-IN-PUBLICATION DATA

Wax, Wendy.
    A week at the lake / Wendy Wax. — Large type books.
        pages cm. — (Thorndike Press large print romance)
        ISBN 978-1-4104-8342-3 (hardback) — ISBN 1-4104-8342-8 (hardcover)
        1. Female friendship—Fiction. 2. Interpersonal relations—Fiction. 3. Large
type books. I. Title.
PS3623.A893W44 2015b
813'.6—dc23                                                    2015024149

Published in 2015 by arrangement with The Berkley Publishing Group,
an imprint of Penguin Publishing Group, a division of Penguin Random
House LLC

Printed in Mexico
1 2 3 4 5 6 7 19 18 17 16 15

# ACKNOWLEDGMENTS

Every book leads in many directions and can require a surprising amount of information. This time, I'd like to thank:

Nettleton Payne II, MD FAANS for not running in horror when I (who barely made it through math and science) asked for help and for patiently (and repeatedly) explaining the brain and its reaction to trauma. He did his best. Any mistakes are my own. This might be the place to mention that this is a work of fiction.

Mary Alice Kellogg who shared her slice of New York courtesy of Big Apple Greeter, a network of more than three hundred volunteer Greeters who will show you New York's diverse neighborhoods through the eyes of someone who lives there.

The staff at the Inn at Erlowest, former Millionaires' Row mansion turned spectacular B-and-B, where I had the great fortune to stay while researching this book. I hope you enjoy the scenes that take place there.

5

Area native Nancy Jefts of Davis Realty for showing me some great houses, helping me pinpoint Valburn's location on Lake George, and for answering questions as I wrote. This might be the place to mention once again that this is a work of fiction as are the characters who appear in it.

Marcia and Sam Kublanow for sharing their love of New York and drinks at the Carlyle.

My critique partners and BFFs Karen White and Susan Crandall, charter members of The Nittie Club, who understand that sometimes you just have to "cue the tarantulas. . . ."

Thanks, too, to Wendy McCurdy for her ongoing editorial input and to my agent Stephanie Rostan for her ability to explain a business that defies explanation and for always telling it like it is.

# PROLOGUE

The thirty-room mansion that had once stood at the center of twenty acres overlooking six hundred feet of prime waterfront along Lake George's famed Millionaires' Row was long gone. Built by a young financier named Michaels as a testament to his success and a proclamation of his love for the young actress with whom he was besotted, Valburn had once sparkled as brightly as the young Valia's diamonds. A perfect stone in a perfect setting, it had glittered in the summer sunshine and glowed under the moonlight. A beacon that attracted others with talent and/or money up from New York City.

But great houses, like great loves, don't always stand the test of time. Valburn survived fires and infidelities, but was ultimately done in by indifferent heirs. More exotic locales. Descendants who "trod the boards" and preferred spending money to sitting in wood-paneled offices making it. Over time its wooded acres were divided up and sold off until only the guest cottage remained.

Of course, "cottage" is a relative term; in certain circles it has nothing to do with square footage and everything to do with feigned modesty. The Michaels cottage, which sat atop a lush rise of land and overlooked its own small beach in a quiet rocky-edged cove, was far from tiny and it most definitely was not roughhewn. A sprawling white clapboard, it had walls of windows that framed the deep blues of the spring-fed waters of Lake George, the green tree-covered tip of Hemlock Point, and the rocky shoals that were all that remained of Rush Island. Pilot Knob sat on the eastern shore, wrapped in soft blue sky. Its roof was pitched, its gables peaked, its shutters black. Stacked stone fireplaces rose from either end.

It had become a place of refuge for certain members of the Michaels family, whose DNA had been stamped more by the young wife's talent for acting than by her husband's for making money. They were almost never without means, but that desire for acclaim, the drive to perform ran thick through their veins for generations to come and through many branches of their family tree. The cottage now belonged to Emma Michaels, who had sought refuge there after both of her high-profile divorces. The last had taken place sixteen years before when she'd left her movie star husband and arrived with her newborn daughter in tow. The first had taken place long before that. When she was only fourteen. And the people she'd divorced were her parents.

# ONE

During her formative years in the booming metropolis of Noblesville, Indiana, Mackenzie Hayes never once heard the term "love at first sight." As a member of an extended family that prided itself on practicality, she had no doubt that if such a fanciful form of affection ever presented itself, she would be expected to stamp it out.

Not that this was an issue when you were freakishly tall and skinny and shaped way more like a pillar than an hourglass. When boys called you beanpole and skyscraper, and you were expected to go out for girls' basketball or track in order to utilize the ridiculously long legs and dangling arms that you would have happily traded in or had shortened if such things were possible. When you were plain and shy, it never occurred even to those who loved you that you might love pretty things, especially pretty clothes. Or that you might desperately wish you could wear them.

Under the guise of practicality Mackenzie

learned to sew. Then she learned to adapt patterns to fit and suit her. Though not strictly necessary, she began to sketch her own ideas and designs — beautiful things that flattered the figure or, in her case, created an impression of one. And while she never developed the kind of body or beauty that attracted male attention, becoming comfortable in her clothes helped her learn not to slouch quite so much and to at least pretend that her physical deficits didn't bother her.

Her parents applauded this practicality. Right up until the moment she announced that she was moving to New York City to pursue a degree and career in fashion design.

No one scoffed at the idea of love at first sight in Mackenzie's first heady year in New York. Which might explain why she succumbed to it so quickly. Why she was struck by a lightning bolt the moment she saw Adam Russell; zapped like a too-tall tree in a low-slung field, her bark singed, her trunk split in two. How one minute she was standing in a neighbor's postage-stamp kitchen, the next she was toppling over, her entire root system ripped from the ground.

It had been glorious to surrender so completely. To give up rational thought. To be so blatantly impractical. At the time it hadn't occurred to her that love at first sight might not be mutual. That there could be a striker and a strikee. That the lightning bolt might

12

not feel the same as the tree. That just because someone was your grand passion, it didn't automatically make you his. And that you might have to work a bit too hard for far longer than you'd ever imagined to convince him you were meant for each other.

"Are you ready?" Adam strode into the bedroom. Even now twenty-two years after that first strike, her husband's physical beauty sliced through her. Five years her senior, his fifty-year-old body remained firm and well toned. The blond hair that skimmed his shoulders was still thick and luxurious — a person's hands could definitely get lost in it — and only lightly threaded with gray. A spider web of smile lines radiated from the corners of the clear brown eyes that had first rendered her speechless. Adam Russell had that indefinable something that could light up a room, command complete attention, inspire adoration. To this day he looked as if he belonged on a stage or in front of a camera, not directing others or penning the words that would come out of others' mouths. Certainly not running a very small community theater in Noblesville, Indiana.

"Almost." Butterflies flickered in Mackenzie's stomach as she considered her slightly battered and rarely used suitcase. She was not a happy flyer, could not come to terms with the science that allowed something as massive as a 747 to reach thirty thousand

13

feet and stay there. For a "practical" woman she had been saddled with a far too active imagination.

Determined to squelch the butterflies, she refocused on the suitcase, which sat open on the bed, then surveyed the piles of clothing she'd stacked around it. There was underwear that looked nothing like the lacy things she'd worn the first time Adam undressed her. Capris. Shorts and T-shirts. Two bathing suits and a pair of flip-flops. Several sundresses she'd whipped up the year before. A dressier pair of black pants and a lacy camisole in case they ended up at one of the fancier restaurants near Lake George that hadn't even existed when she, Emma, and Serena had first started going to Emma's grandmother's summer cottage there. A couple of long-sleeved tops. A sweatshirt.

She'd already tucked in playbills from her favorite shows that she and Adam had staged since she'd last seen the women who had once been her best friends. Along with photos of the costumes she'd designed for the two children's productions they did each year. It was, after all, Emma and Serena who had shifted her focus from haute couture to costumes. Or had it been Adam?

"Stop it." He gave her a mock-stern look.

"Stop what?"

"Worrying. Air travel is the safest form of transportation on the planet. You'll be way

14

safer once you're on the plane than you will be on the drive to the airport." Now he sounded like the instructor of the fearful flying class she'd failed so spectacularly.

"Gee, thanks. I feel so much better now."

He flashed her the dimple. "Do you remember those relaxation techniques?"

Back when they'd been with a national touring company whose travel budget had included puddle jumpers that looked as if they were held together with bailing wire and rubber bands, she'd tried everything from alcohol to hypnosis to take the terror out of what her husband insisted was no more than an airborne Greyhound bus ride.

"Oh, I remember them all right," she replied. "It's just hard to conjure the soothing sound of waves washing onto a white-sand beach over the whine of jet engines." Nor could she completely banish the certainty that any mechanical sound was a harbinger of doom, that the slightest relaxing of her guard or her grip on her armrests would allow any plane she was on to slip into a death spiral.

"You'll be fine."

"Absolutely." As she placed the clothing in the suitcase, she let go of the wish that they were flying together instead of in completely opposite directions. Better to focus on what would happen after she landed at LaGuardia than freaking out about whether she'd ever get there. Carefully, she visualized the cab ride to Grand Central to meet up with Serena Stockton and then on to Emma's hotel for what she hoped would not be too awkward a reunion. And finally, the drive out to Lake George to the cottage Emma's grandmother Grace had left her.

She'd printed out her favorite posts from her blog *Married Without Children* to share, but would hold on to the news until she could tell them in person that she'd been approached about putting together a book comprising her best posts. She, Serena, and Emma had achieved varying degrees of success and now lived in different parts of the country, but Mackenzie could still see them as they'd once been — more different than alike, more scared than confident, determined to realize the dreams that had brought them to what all three of them were convinced was the epicenter of the universe.

Twisting her hair into a knot at her neck, she blew a stray bang out of her eye then tucked her quart ziplock bag into her carry-on. She wore little makeup and should need even less for a week at the lake, especially since Emma and Serena, whose looks were such an integral part of what they did, would have every beauty product known to man plus a few that weren't. Even Emma's fifteen-year-old daughter would undoubtedly be far more skilled at face painting than Mackenzie, as she'd discovered the last time they'd held one of their retreats — and Zoe had only been ten then.

Adam zipped the leather Dopp kit he'd retrieved from the bathroom and placed it in the elegant leather duffel that already held what she thought of as his Hollywood wardrobe. For his flight to LA, on which he would undoubtedly be not only completely relaxed, but also pampered by every available flight attendant, male and female, he wore designer jeans, a crisp white T-shirt, and a perfectly tailored navy blazer. She wore one of her own designs — a wrap dress in a supple washed denim that created the illusion of curves and showed off the long legs that had once been her best feature. For the briefest moment she wished she looked as good in clothes as her husband did. Or out of them for that matter.

She watched as he considered himself contentedly in the dresser mirror. The call from his film agent had come unexpectedly the night before and he was flying out on standby today. "So what did Matthew say?"

"He said they were crazy about the treatment. That they thought it would be a perfect vehicle for an ensemble cast." The excitement in her husband's voice was unmistakable, despite his efforts to tamp it down. "But you know how it is out there. Great enthusiasm ultimately followed by the inability to remember your name."

"Maybe this will be it," she said. "Even if it just makes it to the next level that would be . . ."

"A miracle." He gave her the self-deprecating smile that along with the smiling eyes and flashable dimple had initially knocked her bark off. Her heart squeezed in her chest. That was the real miracle after all these years. That she'd not only managed to win him but that they'd survived so many disappointments and compromises. That their inability to have children did not define them. This was what she blogged about: How sweet a life could be even without children in it. How much more time and energy a couple could give each other when their family was composed of only two.

Adam lifted their bags from the bed and carried them out to the car while she did a last check for forgotten items. As she locked up the house she reminded herself that if they had had the children she'd once wanted so badly, they couldn't have both picked up and just left like this; that Adam couldn't have traveled back to New York as often as he did for an infusion of what they were careful not to call "real" theater. Or to LA, dressed as if he already belonged there, to pitch his latest screenplay and nurture the contacts that might help him break into the exclusive circle of successful screenwriters.

"Are you looking forward to the retreat?"

he asked backing Old Faithful, their ancient but mostly reliable Ford Explorer, down the drive.

"Of course. It's just . . . you know, having to get on a plane to get there." She reached into her carry-on to make sure the bottle of Xanax was handy. She needed the slight blur they provided to propel herself down the Jetway, onto the plane, and into her seat. "And we haven't been to the lake or anywhere else together for so long." Her stomach squeezed this time. She turned to look out the window. They'd always been able to pick up where they'd left off. But they'd never gone so long without seeing each other before. And their separation hadn't exactly been a mutual decision.

"It'll be great," Adam said as he took the ramp onto the highway and headed toward Indianapolis, but she could tell his mind was already elsewhere. "It probably won't even take a whole glass of wine before you're talking nonstop and finishing each other's sentences." He glanced into the rearview mirror and smoothly changed lanes.

"No doubt." She said this heartily, doing her best to sound as if she meant it. "And you'll be back with an offer."

But as they neared the Indianapolis airport, her eyes turned to the planes taking off and landing, leaving plumes of white across the bright blue sky. As Adam made his way to long-term parking, Mackenzie washed a Xanax down with a long sip from her bottled water. For the first time she could remember, she wished her nervousness were only about the flying. And not how things might go after she arrived.

Serena Stockton closed her eyes and attempted to think like an animated character. Or more specifically the cartoon version of herself that she'd been voicing for more than a decade on *As the World Churns,* a remarkably smart and astonishingly popular soap opera parody that featured animated versions of the cast coupled with their voices.

Part Miss Piggy, part Jessica Rabbit, part *Family Guy*'s Lois Griffin, Georgia Goodbody wore a southern belle's dress cut low over a too-ample bosom and carried a fan that she sometimes snapped open to fan her face and bosom or snapped shut to use as a weapon on some unfortunate, albeit irritating, member of the opposite sex. Georgia spoke with New York's take on a southern accent. Which meant you would have had to be out in the back of beyond off some dusty southern road to ever actually hear anything remotely like it. Developing Georgia's character had required Serena, who had spent years eradicating her own southern accent as a student at NYU's drama department, to create an accent far more appalling than the one she'd been born with. An irony she tried not to dwell on.

"Why, I can't imagine what would make you think that," she drawled, stretching out each syllable, opening up every vowel, as she watched the screen version of herself bat spidery black lashes and pucker bright red lips that were certainly far larger and plumper than her own.

"You know I think the world of you." The eyelashes batted again. Her cartoon hand landed on her Scarlett O'Hara–sized waist. Georgia had an exaggerated version of Serena's face as well as her dark wavy hair and bright blue eyes.

Following her script and the character on-screen, Serena sighed dramatically then mimed looking up into her character's current husband's eyes. Georgia had been married and divorced more times than Serena could count, while Serena had never actually made it all the way down an aisle. But then Georgia had also been charged with, though not convicted of, second-degree murder and vehicular homicide, come perilously close to death three times, and had amnesia every other year for close to a decade.

*As the World Churns* was a well-written, equal-opportunity offender that did not require a laugh track. Big-name stars fought and cajoled to be written into an episode. Even Emma had once played an overperky

21

version of herself.

Now in its eleventh season the series still pulled a hefty twenty share and could conceivably go on forever; a mixed blessing for someone who made a generous living off the role, but who could no longer speak in public without eliciting laughter.

Even without the overdone accent Serena's voice was instantly recognizable. The moment she opened her mouth to speak, others fell open in delighted surprise. Then came the laughter as they peered more closely to confirm that she was, in fact, Georgia Goodbody. Or at least Georgia Goodbody's prototype.

What had seemed like a well-paid lark a decade ago had turned into her seminal role, the part she'd be remembered for. The last part she might ever get. Irony sucked. But at least it paid the bills.

From the recording studio, she took a cab home and raced around her town house straightening and packing. She still lived in the West Village, where she, Emma, Adam, and Mackenzie had met fresh off the turnip trucks that had deposited each of them in New York City, though her current digs were as far a cry from the crumbling rent-controlled walk-up she'd first lived in as Georgia Goodbody was from her real self.

A little over an hour later she settled into the club chair in her therapist's office and crossed her ankles on the ottoman. "Maybe I shouldn't renew my contract. Maybe I should drop out of sight for a year. Have plastic surgery. Try to raise or drop my real voice a few octaves. I could come back under another name."

James Grant, MD, PhD looked at her and said nothing.

She tried looking back, but he had way more practice with waiting others out. "What?"

"These are things you should discuss with your agent," he said. "Or the friends you're going to spend the week with for the first time in five years, but whom I can't help but notice you haven't mentioned once during your last three sessions."

She sighed Georgia Goodbody's sigh. This was what happened when you paid someone to reach inside you and rearrange your guts. She arched an eyebrow dramatically just as Georgia often did. There was the barest twitch of amusement at the corner of his lips.

"I think it's a good thing it's Georgia and not you who owns the kick-ass lethal fan," he said genially. His face reflected no agenda, nothing to react to.

She settled back into the chair. "It's been five years since I've spent more than an hour or two with either of them. And a year since Zoe turned up on my doorstep while Emma was out of the country on location. I hardly recognized her — that's how involved a 'fairy godmother' I've been."

"Okay. Let's go with that. Why do you think Emma stopped inviting you to the lake house? And why did she invite you now?"

These were very good questions. To which she had no real answers. He watched her with a pleasant but unworried look on his face. As if he thought she could answer them if only she tried.

"I don't know," she said finally. "I don't remember anything in particular happening; she just stopped inviting us. None of us are the people we were back when we met. Not that we even knew Emma was Emma then."

"I'm sorry?"

"She introduced herself as Amelia Maclaine and she didn't seem to have any more money than the rest of us. She took classes at NYU like I did and waitressed while she made rounds. Nobody recognized her or had any idea who she was. Not until she started getting parts. I think it was *Starlight Express* or *Into the Woods* when she made it out of the chorus that she got outed. We were all kind of freaked out when that happened — I mean, she'd been a child star, a member of the frickin' Michaels family who divorced her parents and then just dropped out of sight. But she was so ridiculously proud of being hired on her own merit. It was only later that we met the grandmother she'd gone to live with, the legendary Grace Michaels who had the house out on Lake George." Serena smiled, remembering. "If it had been me I probably would have had *Michaels* tattooed on my forehead or shown up at auditions with a note from my famous mommy and daddy."

"But you were friends."

"Oh, yeah. The best." There was a time she would have sworn to this in a court of law; now not so much. "Emma named us Zoe's fairy godmothers and insisted we all spend a week at the lake house for like ten years running. It was a blast. I never saw myself having children but it felt like Zoe belonged to all of us, you know? And then all of the sudden Emma wasn't really available anymore." She tried to keep the hurt out of her voice. She had once considered Emma and Mackenzie sisters. "She had a big career and a child and Mackenzie was busy in the hinterlands with Adam, and well, I guess we didn't really have all that much in common anymore."

"So why now? Why did she invite you? And why did you say yes?"

James Grant should consider a career in journalism if this psychiatry thing didn't work out. "Honestly, I have no idea. But I'm more than a little ticked off that she thinks she can just disappear and reappear whenever she feels like it. I said I'd come, but I still have a good mind to back out."

The session ended and as she paid at the front desk, Serena told herself she could still cancel, could still change her mind. Shit happened. She could claim an emergency and just send a note with her apologies along with the gift she'd packed for Zoe. Wouldn't that just serve Emma right?

*Standing in the Hall of Fame.* Da-da. Da-da. *And the world's gonna know your name.* Unbidden, the lyrics from one of her daughter's favorite songs drifted through Emma Michaels's mind. The melody was catchy, the tone triumphant. It wasn't really about baseball as she'd thought the first time she'd heard it, but determination. Dogged persistence. Success. Fame and/or notoriety as the ultimate achievement.

Emma happened to know that having an instantly recognizable name was not all it was cracked up to be. She knew this because her last name was Michaels. As in the large and unwieldy theatrical family, all of whom were descended from actors, and who when left to their own devices found other actors with whom they ultimately created little baby actors. Kind of like a virulent strain of thespian rabbits.

Her particular branch of Michaels had once excelled at playing the perfect family. Put any or all of them on a stage, in front of a movie camera, or even out in public together and they could make you wish your family were even half as close as theirs. Unfortunately, their day-to-day reality was quite different. Which was only one of the reasons she'd legally detached herself, fled to her grandmother's, and ultimately pretended, at least for a while, not to be a Michaels at all.

Today she was in New York with hours to kill before heading to the lake. At her daughter's request they were having lunch at one of the fancier restaurants on the Upper East Side not far from the Carlyle, where her grandmother's apartment had been and where she and Zoe had taken a hotel room. Emma sincerely hoped this would be the last time she'd be required to dress up to consume food for the next week.

As they entered, there was a muted stutter of surprise followed by a brief pause before conversation resumed. The other diners pretended not to notice them as they were shown to a white-cloth-covered table overlooking a walled garden. But if there was anything Emma knew how to recognize, it was an audience.

"Ms. Michaels." The maître d' smiled and pulled out her chair.

"Emma." She smiled back, automatically mirroring his vaguely midwestern accent; she had been born and bred with a finely tuned ear and could do almost any American dialect, with the possible exception of the un-

27

named one on *Swamp People,* which even the locals required subtitles to understand. "Please. Call me Emma."

He nodded and smiled again as he pulled out the other chair for Zoe. Her daughter was fifteen and had somehow ended up with far more than her fair share of the Michaels gene pool. Her thick red-gold hair was straight and chopped in angled layers that Emma's curls refused to be ironed, blown, or wrestled into. She was even taller than her grandparents and aunts and uncles, and had the creamy skin, finely chiseled features, and gray-green eyes that attested to their English/Irish heritage. Emma's complexion was only partly creamy and was sprinkled with nutmeg-colored freckles that not even the best studio makeup people could completely obliterate.

Emma had learned to make the most of what she had. But when you were the runt of the litter and looked more Cockerdoodle than Great Dane, you didn't do Shakespeare. You didn't star with Humphrey Bogart or James Stewart like her grandmother had. Or take direction from Mike Nichols or Stanley Kubrick like her mother. You didn't even play the tragically damaged wife of an unfairly convicted murderer on death row, a part her sister Regan won an Oscar for. You played the girl who couldn't quite get the guy. Or the spunky heroine who picked herself up after her husband left her and somehow finds a modicum of happiness as a greeter at Walmart. Emma had made a great living playing those kinds of parts. At forty-five she didn't get quite as many romantic comedy leads as she used to, though it was possible she'd still be offered the occasional dimple-and-giggle part when she was white haired and stooped from arthritis. Not that her estranged parents and siblings would be any more impressed by her body of work then than they were now.

They looked over their menus, and Emma considered how best to say all the things she wanted to say to Zoe. Conciliatory things that would convince her once and for all that Emma loved her and only wanted what was best for her. Even though despite all efforts to the contrary, she'd somehow turned out to be almost as abysmal a parent as the mother and father she'd so publicly "divorced." Uncertain, she reached for the bread. If she kept her mouth full she wouldn't be able to say the things she needed to say. But she might not say the wrong thing, either.

In just a few hours the one week she used to look forward to most every year — her lake retreat with the two women she'd known longest and best — would begin. They were the only people on earth who really understood why she'd come to New York all those years ago. They were Zoe's "fairy godmothers." The only friends around whom she'd never needed to be "on" and who remembered Zoe as the little girl she'd carted from country to country and movie set to movie set. Her daughter's memory of those happy years seemed to have disappeared along with her chubby cheeks and angelic smile.

If Mackenzie and Serena were here with them at the restaurant, Emma was pretty sure the bread she'd just swallowed wouldn't be turning to lead in her stomach. She was counting on them to help her fix things with Zoe and then somehow, before they all went back to their real lives, Emma would have to find a way to finally share the secret she'd had no right to keep. Then she'd see her attorneys to finish off all the paperwork. Even a benign tumor made a person want to put things right.

They placed their orders. Their retreat, at which calorie counting had always been banned, hadn't officially begun so despite all the bread she'd already consumed, Emma ordered rabbit food. Zoe, who got the Michaels metabolism, which appeared to be unfairly tied to height, ordered a burger and fries.

"I spoke with Calvin," Zoe said after the waiter left. Calvin Hardgrove, movie heartthrob, got top billing as Zoe's father on her birth certificate but made only cameo appearances in Zoe's life. "He said that he'd be away on location all summer but that if I want to stay in his guesthouse while I work on *Teen Scream* I can."

"No."

Zoe's lips tightened, but not enough to prevent a response. "Why not?"

Another basket of bread arrived. Emma managed to ignore it.

"Because you're fifteen years old. You can't live alone in a Malibu guesthouse without supervision. And I read the script. It calls for nudity."

"But my character doesn't undress. And it's not *gratuitous* nudity," she countered. "There's a reason why the characters take off their clothes."

Emma tried to sound calm but firm, but it was a stretch. "Yes, I believe that reason is so that they can have sex."

Zoe quickly changed tack. "You've left me alone plenty of times when you've been on location."

"I've left you with a sitter and a staff when I've had to," Emma replied. And only after Zoe got too old to miss so much school. "That's not the same thing at all." It wasn't, was it? Her voice faltered as she realized she was asking Zoe to accept things she'd never forgiven her own parents for. If Emma hadn't had Gran, she would have been completely lost.

"You're always trying to hold me back."

31

Zoe's voice rose. It was a favorite complaint and one she'd clearly come to believe. She delivered it with conviction.

Emma knew her daughter could act. She was fairly certain she'd been emoting in the womb and she'd done really well at the Los Angeles County High School for the Arts. She just didn't think there was any reason to start a career so young. Nor did she think a teen exploitation film in which most of the characters would be screaming their heads off while naked was an acceptable first vehicle. And Emma should know. She'd walked away from childhood stardom, but that didn't mean she didn't remember every painful moment of it.

Their food arrived. She checked her watch and wondered if eleven thirty was too early for a drink.

"I'm trying to protect you, Zoe. If you decide you want to act, there's plenty of time for that. After you finish school. Not before."

"Sonya is tutored on set," Zoe argued.

Sonya Craven was sixteen and had a regular role on *Teen Bitch,* er, *Teen Witch.* From what Emma had seen of Sonya — and her mother, with whom Emma had had the "pleasure" of performing — this was a clear case of typecasting and required almost no acting at all.

"You're not Sonya. And I am not Sonya's mother." Their voices were rising.

"That's such a cop-out." Zoe quivered with

righteous indignation. "At least Sonya's mother nurtures her talent instead of trying to squash it." Zoe's eyes plumbed hers. She could feel her daughter's awareness of the scene they were playing. When you were born into a theatrical family, there was no escaping theatrics.

Zoe put her glass down on the table and crammed a French fry into her mouth.

As emotional earthquakes went this wasn't even a five on the Michaels Family Richter Scale. Compared to some of the rows that had taken place while Emma was growing up, it was barely a tremor. But there was something about the wrath of a fifteen-year-old girl to whom you'd given birth and loved more than you'd ever imagined you could love anyone, that could yank the ground right out from under your feet.

Emma glanced around the restaurant. At a Michaels family gathering this altercation would hardly be enough to make people stop chewing let alone end a meal. But the other diners had fallen silent and were no longer pretending they weren't listening. It wasn't every day you got to watch this kind of performance between two members of the Michaels family without buying a ticket.

"Oh, what's the point?" Zoe, who knew intuitively how to end a scene *and* make an exit, removed the napkin from her lap, dropped it on the table, and scraped back her chair. "I'm out of here."

"Zoe!" Emma put some bills on the table as she stood. Then she was speed walking out of the silent restaurant. The last time Zoe had stormed off she made it onto a cross-country flight from LAX to Serena's in New York City.

Emma's heart beat frantically as she shoved open the door. Out on the sidewalk she saw Zoe already across the street and two blocks down. This was the Upper East Side of New York not West LA, but Zoe was a fifteen-year-old girl and bad things happened in expensive neighborhoods every day.

"Zoe!" Her eyes on her daughter, who was studiously ignoring her, Emma began to sprint across the street. Which was when something hard slammed into her with the force of a freight train and sent her hurtling into the air. She flipped a couple of times, bounced off what might have been the roof or trunk of a car, and slammed into the concrete. Stray thoughts filtered through her head; she empathized with Humpty Dumpty. She congratulated herself for having on clean underwear.

There was no pain, which definitely seemed wrong. She heard feet running and voices and then a siren in the distance. It occurred to her that she could die, and regret flooded through her. She'd already cheated death once. Now she'd never get the chance to prove to her daughter how much she loved her. Never see Mackenzie or Serena again. Her last thoughts began to run together: She should have scheduled the attorney before they left for the lake. Should have confessed the secret she'd been carrying. Should have begged forgiveness. Should have . . .

Darkness descended. Panic came with it. There was something she was supposed to take care of. Something that would alter the lives of the people who meant the most to her.

Her world was going black. And she couldn't for the life of her remember what it was.

# TWO

Mackenzie emerged from Grand Central Terminal blinking in the sudden sunlight and staked out a spot on the sidewalk near the Forty-second Street and Park Avenue entrance where Serena was supposed to pick her up for the ride uptown to Emma. Her handbag balanced on the small suitcase beside her. Her mouth felt dry from the plane and the fear, not to mention the tranquilizer, and she reached for the bottled water she'd purchased on the way out of LaGuardia. The flight had been relatively smooth, thank you, God, and she had resisted the temptation she always felt to throw herself on her knees and kiss the solid ground when she'd entered the terminal.

It was mid-June, the air warm, but not yet oppressive, and filled with the pungent aromas of food, gas fumes, and the undulating sea of humanity — some more washed than others — that surged and receded around her. Clothing was summer weight and in rare cases light in color. She smiled, remembering Serena's dry observation that New Yorkers would undoubtedly keep wearing black until they came up with something darker.

Glancing down she checked her cell phone for the time and any messages. Nothing. She wondered if Adam had managed to charm himself onto a flight yet, whether Serena had been held up in the traffic that now clogged both Park and Forty-second as far as she could see, and how when she did arrive, the cab would get anywhere near the curb. Mackenzie had been fifteen minutes late getting to Grand Central and Serena still wasn't here. She took another drink of water and reminded herself that she'd spent enough mental energy keeping that plane in the air; she was now officially on vacation. New York traffic was not something she needed to worry about. And neither was the potential awkwardness on the drive up to the lake. Which would take some four and a half hours, depending on traffic.

"Mackenzie!" She looked up and saw Serena emerge from a cab. Serena's white halter dress hugged the luscious curves she'd bequeathed to Georgia Goodbody and played up her shapely legs. Her dainty feet were encased in high-heeled sandals that were undoubtedly designer. Her toenails were a deep red that matched her lips. Hanging with

37

Emma and Serena had sometimes left Mackenzie feeling invisible. Which was no mean feat for someone her height.

"I see you're still working on mastering the concept of traveling light," Mackenzie said as the driver pulled what looked like a mountain of luggage from the trunk, then began rearranging it in an attempt to make room for Mackenzie's carry-on.

"Packing light doesn't work for me," Serena said. "The one time I did I spilled something on the lone, yet versatile, skirt I'd brought less than five minutes after takeoff. And although I'd like to pretend my beauty is natural, I need a lot more beauty products than can be crammed into a quart-sized ziplock bag." She hugged Mackenzie lightly and kissed the air near both cheeks. "Anyway, Emma's arranged a car and driver, so I might as well have everything I'll need."

They contemplated each other for a long moment before Serena added, "I forgot how tall you are."

"And I forgot that you're practically a midget." The insult rolled automatically off her lips, though Serena was in fact slightly taller than average and was often referred to as "statuesque."

"Hey, I'd gladly borrow an inch or two so that I could wear lower heels. My feet are completely pissed off and I've only been on them for a matter of minutes."

Mackenzie laughed. "Well, we can't have your digits angry at you. I hope you have a pair of flip-flops in one of those bags."

"Of course I do. It's just finding them that might be a problem."

"Georgia!" Parts of the sea stopped surging to form a small crowd. "Miss Goodbody!" There was pointing and some laughter. Serena turned to smile and wave, but her body was as tight as her facial muscles.

"Where's your fan, Georgia?" a middle-aged man laughed.

"I seem to have left that at home," she replied in a teasing tone. "So you're safe for the moment."

"Where are you headed? To work out?" a middle-aged woman tittered, though Serena was clearly not dressed for the gym. Georgia Goodbody spent a lot of time with her private trainer maintaining her "good body."

"I'm done for the day, thank goodness," she replied in the drawl that had made Georgia and her famous. "You all have a nice day now, you hear?" Gently, she turned her back on her impromptu audience. "At home I could have added a 'bless your heart' and she would have known I was telling her to take a hike. Here I'm always afraid someone will think it's a religious comment." Serena kept her eyes on Mackenzie's face. Her shoulders and her smile softened as the crowd dispersed.

"That's what you get for being famous," Mackenzie said.

"I know. And I don't ever want to seem ungrateful. But let us not forget I'm famous for being a sexy cartoon character. It's kind of hard to take that seriously.

"So, how's Adam?" Serena asked as they headed back to the cab.

"Good. He's on his way to LA to pitch a new screenplay."

"That's great." Serena looked at her closely. "And you?"

"Good. Everything's good. The theater's . . . good. I brought pictures from our production of *Annie*. The kids were unbelievably adorable. And the blog keeps growing." Mackenzie shrugged. "Noblesville isn't exactly the fast lane, but it's fast enough for me." She immediately regretted her defensive tone. "Do you think one of us should text Emma and let her know we're on our way?"

"I'll do it," Serena said as the driver slammed the trunk shut and held open the door, perspiration dotting his forehead and his smile more than a little strained. She pulled out her phone. "Oh, my God!" she said, looking down at the screen, her face twisted into a grimace of surprise, which turned into an expression of horror.

"What is it?" Mackenzie asked. "What's going on?"

"There's a text from Zoe! Emma was hit

40

by a car earlier this afternoon!" Serena leaned over the seat. "We need to get to Mount Sinai Hospital as quickly as possible!"

"Oh, my God!"

Serena's thumbs moved over her phone's keyboard as the cab began to inch back into traffic. When she got no response, she dialed Zoe's phone and then Emma's. No one answered.

"Oh, God, please hurry!" Serena and Mackenzie reached for each other's hands, holding on as the cab picked up speed and began to cut and swerve through traffic for what felt like Mr. Toad's Wild Ride.

Emma:

Darkness surrounds me. Fills me. Cushions me. I float in it. On it. Only pinpricks of sound. Muted. Mechanical. *Where am I?*

*It's all right, darling. You had a bit of a tussle with a delivery van. The van won.*

Gran's voice. Calm. Steady. Like arms wrapped around me. *I'm fairly certain you were taught to look both ways before crossing the street.*

*Am I dead?* There are no trumpets. No tunnel of white light. No hovering above my body. *Are you here to escort me to the "other side"?*

*Don't be so dramatic, dear.* Gran's voice delivers the favorite joke. *It's all right. I'm here.*

*Just as I've always been.*

*Zoe?*

I hear footsteps. A voice. "Ms. Michaels?"

Panic wells up when I can't respond.

*It's all right, darling. Sleep. Gather your strength. Remember the show must always go on.* She launches into a campy version of Ethel Merman's "There's No Business Like Show Business." Another inside joke we've shared since I first found the original cast recording of *Annie Get Your Gun* at the cottage and practically wore a hole in the vinyl.

The footsteps retreat. I float in the darkness and realize that if I'm talking to my grandmother, I must be dead.

# THREE

The cabdriver kept his foot hard on the accelerator and a concerned expression on his face the entire drive, which passed in a nauseating blur. But all signs of empathy evaporated after he handed Serena her receipt, hauled the luggage out of the trunk, and set the whole collection of it on the curb. "Sorry. Can't leave cab. Hope everything okay."

Serena bit back a groan at the thought of dragging the hard-sided suitcases up the steps and through the hospital, but she'd spotted Zoe slumped on a bench near the entrance.

"Give me your makeup case," Mackenzie said as the driver made his escape. "The rest is up to you." She turned and rushed toward Zoe as only someone who'd traveled lightly could. By the time Serena had dragged and bounced her luggage up to meet them, Mackenzie had Zoe wrapped in her arms and was holding her as she sobbed. Zoe had shot up another couple of inches since she'd seen her a year ago and even in distress she was beautiful — an elongated, finely boned version of her mother. Or more precisely almost a clone of Emma's older sister Regan.

"Where's your mother?" Serena asked. "Can you take us to her?"

Zoe nodded and swiped at her tear-streaked face. "She's on the eighth floor. She's . . . unconscious. And she's hooked up to all these machines." She swallowed. "I could hardly understand what the doctor said. Except that her brain is all swollen."

There were more tears as Mackenzie stifled a gasp. Serena shivered slightly as the seriousness of the situation sank in.

"They called Rex and Eve even though I told them not to." Her grandparents' first names sounded odd on Zoe's lips. "But someone at the ranch said they're on a roundup out in one of the canyons and won't be back in cell range for a couple days." She sounded closer to five than fifteen. "Regan's somewhere in eastern Europe on location and Nash . . ." She named Emma's actor/director brother, who was known for disappearing while immersing himself for a role. "No one seems to know for sure where he is." She sniffed and swiped again at her eyes. "I'm not old enough to make decisions."

"Come on." Serena stuffed the garment bag under one armpit. Her hands clenched around the suitcase handles. She wasted a couple of seconds wishing that hospitals had bellhops and luggage carts as they strode through the lobby.

"Should we call your father?" Mackenzie asked as they waited impatiently for the elevator.

"No." Zoe shook her head. "I hardly see him. And I don't think Emma . . . I don't think my mother would want him making decisions for her." Tears slid down her cheeks though Serena could see the girl trying to hold them back. They stepped onto the elevator, hauling their luggage in behind them.

"Well, we're here." Mackenzie had not let go of Zoe. She caught Serena's eye. Serena nodded her agreement. "We'll stay and make sure your mom is taken care of."

Serena had no idea if anyone would or could listen to them. Back when Emma had named them Zoe's fairy godmothers, she and Mackenzie had signed a stack of paperwork and agreed to be there should Zoe ever need them. But she had no idea where things stood in light of Emma's grandmother's death eight years ago, or Emma's virtual radio silence for the last five.

"Just take us to Emma."

"But I think only family is allowed."

"Then we'll be her step-sisters for the time being," Serena said. They might have lost five years, but that didn't mean they would leave Emma alone and unable to speak for herself.

Serena and Mackenzie piled their luggage in a corner of the family waiting room located just outside the entrance to the neurocritical ICU. Serena was practically vibrating with anxiety and could feel Mackenzie doing the same. But as they contemplated each other over Zoe's head, a nod from Mackenzie reassured her. Both of them had to do their best to present a calm, united, and hopefully comforting front for Zoe.

"Will you take us in to see her?" Serena felt an urgent pull to get in as quickly as possible and an equally desperate fear of what they would find when they got there.

Zoe nodded carefully. She hadn't shrugged off Mackenzie's arm around her shoulders and didn't look like she was about to anytime soon. Together they entered the ICU. No one stopped them as they left Zoe in the hall and slipped into the small glass-fronted room.

Serena had known it was serious. She knew they were entering a neurocritical ICU. Still she was unprepared for the sight of the woman she'd once considered her best friend.

Emma looked small in the hospital bed, dwarfed by the mass of machines and monitors she was attached to. They whooshed and beeped at regular intervals, their display panels glowing as numbers and graphs appeared and disappeared, the information no doubt feeding into the computers arranged on the other side of the plate glass windows that lined the hall.

Emma's head was swathed in bandages. Her eyes were closed. Mackenzie saw no sign of movement behind the lids nor any sign of awareness. Her chest moved up and down with mechanical precision, no doubt due to the clear plastic tube taped inside her mouth. A heavily bandaged leg was propped on a pillow.

"Em?" Mackenzie stepped closer to the bed, no longer able to hold back the tears she'd been so careful not to shed in front of Zoe. "It's us, Em. Mackenzie and Serena." They held their collective breath while they waited for anything that could be considered a response. But there was no indication that Emma could hear her. No sign that Emma was even there, inside the battered and bruised face, that horribly still body.

"Zoe's so beautiful, Em. You must be so proud of her." Her thoughts drifted back sixteen years ago to when she and Emma had been pregnant. They'd found out within weeks of each other and both of them had married during their first trimesters. But Emma had delivered a healthy baby girl while Mackenzie . . . She reached for the corner of the sheet and tucked it closer to Emma's side. She'd been too devastated, too jealous, too angry, too everything that first year to see Emma or Zoe. She hadn't even been able to look at the pictures of mother and baby that had appeared in all the magazines and tabloids. It had taken a full year for Mackenzie to be happy for her friend, to agree to be one of Zoe's fairy godmothers, a position only Emma could have thought up. Zoe had belonged to all three of them. And then five years ago Emma had stopped sharing her daughter, stopped inviting them to the lake, stopped pretty much everything except the odd holiday or birthday card. With no more explanation than she'd offered when she'd invited them this time. "You can't leave your little girl alone. You need to wake up."

Tears obscured her view as Serena stepped forward and took Emma's limp hand in her own.

"This is not okay, Em. You know if I had my fan with me I'd be rapping on your hand, not holding it."

"Good God, Serena!" Mackenzie whispered. "Have a little respect." She said this without much hope. Serena's worst jokes and most inappropriate statements had always occurred when she was the most worried or frightened. A fact she'd once had to explain at the funeral of a friend's mother.

"I'm just telling Emma that she's not allowed to give up. Not on us. And certainly not on Zoe." Serena held Emma's hand between her own as if she might somehow transfer some of her energy or will. "And while we're at it," she added, "I'd like to know what the hell happened five years ago that made you cut us off. We're not going anywhere until you wake up and enlighten us, Emma. No kidding."

Serena rearranged the sheet one last time, then placed Emma's hand back on top of it. "You remember all those episodes of *I Love Lucy* you made us watch? The fudge factory? All Lucy's failed attempts to get into show business? Well, as Desi would have said, 'You got a lot of 'splainin' to do.' "

# FOUR

The sun was coming up over the East River the next morning when Mackenzie entered the family lounge bearing two cups of coffee, and a bottle of orange juice for Zoe. Straightening slowly in the plastic chair in which she'd slept, Serena yawned and stretched, attempting to work out the kinks in her neck, her back, her . . . there were way too many locations to tally. "Bodies are not designed to mold to plastic. It's supposed to work the other way around." She spoke softly so as not to wake Zoe.

"Tell me about it." Mackenzie set the drinks down on the faux-wood table and rubbed the back of her neck. Her hair stood up in multiple directions and large dark smudges, which had once been eyeliner and/or mascara, had been rubbed beneath each eye.

"Wow, I hate to insult a gift horse," Serena said, reaching for the coffee. "But you look like shit."

"You too."

"Ah, well. I don't think I have enough energy to be insulted." Serena raised her coffee cup to Mackenzie's. "And I am grateful for the coffee."

Zoe burrowed deeper into her chair, but didn't open her eyes. She was curled into a fetal position, her knees to her chest. Her arms were wrapped tightly around the pillow she'd crammed between her face and the chair back. The blanket covered one thigh. Her red-gold hair covered most of the other.

"Have you been in to see Em?"

Mackenzie nodded. "I was in and out of there all night. At the moment, everything's status quo, though I'm not sure exactly what that means. There's a shift change at seven a.m. and the head of Neurocritical Care will be here to see Emma shortly after that. We need to be ready to talk to him."

They stepped out into the hallway. Serena closed the heavy door softly behind her. With her free hand she dug at the sleep in the corners of her eyes and blinked in the artificial light. Her teeth felt furry. Soon she'd have to grab her cosmetics case and head to the bathroom. For now, she leaned against the wall and sipped her coffee.

"I've been thinking," Mackenzie said.

"Good. Because I haven't had enough coffee yet to do that." Serena took another long sip and willed the caffeine into her bloodstream.

"You've got Emma's phone."

"Right."

"I was thinking about all that paperwork we signed when Zoe was a baby, right after Emma's divorce. Her agent or manager might have paperwork or at least be able to put us in touch with her attorneys."

"Right." Serena swirled the coffee in her cup. "It's possible not everything applied to Zoe." She winced. "In fact I vaguely remember telling her she might want to reconsider because if she didn't behave herself I'd be pulling the plug faster than a hound on the scent of a fox."

"Jeez." Mackenzie shot Serena a disbelieving look. "Do you ever stop and think before you speak?"

Serena downed a long swig of coffee. "I wish I could say yes, but that would be a lie. I seem to have this Pavlovian response to fear. My mouth just starts running and most of the time I'm going for laughs."

Mackenzie rolled her eyes. "Well, I have no doubt she's got paperwork on file somewhere to protect herself and Zoe in case of emergency. Adam and I did all that after we turned forty. Just in case." She didn't quite meet Serena's eye. "And it's just the two of us."

"Makes sense," Serena said, pulling Emma's phone out of her pocket, even though she had done none of those things. She was single and had never even thought about who'd make decisions if anything happened to her. How pathetic was it that she was rounding on fifty and her parents were still her only permanent connections? "We signed those papers a lifetime ago. Way before Gran died and Emma pulled away from us. I assume she's made other choices." Serena began to scroll through Emma's contacts. "We just have to figure out who knows who she named and where the paperwork is." Serena continued to scroll. After five years, she wasn't even sure she'd recognize important names in Emma's life.

"If we can't find the right people on her phone, Zoe will at least know her agent and manager. I was too freaked out yesterday to think to ask her. Do you want me to wake her up?" Mackenzie asked.

"No." Serena tapped the screen. "Here's Daniel Mills, her agent." Serena scrolled further. "And here's her manager. I think I met her once. I'll call them both right now. But it's four a.m. on the West Coast. I doubt anyone's going to answer."

While Mackenzie sipped her coffee, Serena left voice mails for Emma's agent and manager. Then she spotted a Beverly Hills law firm and left one there, too.

"God, I feel so helpless." Mackenzie leaned against the wall.

"I know."

They continued to suck down their coffees

while the hospital geared up around them. Through a window that overlooked a parking garage, they saw a steady line of cars entering while the city streets began to fill with morning traffic and pedestrians. The nearby elevator chimed with increasing frequency. Snippets of conversation reached them. Footsteps sounded down the hall.

"So what's our next move?" Serena asked. "We can't just sit here and hope for the best."

"I guess we talk to the head of the department when he gets in and ask him that. If he doesn't feel cutting edge enough, we should look for referrals and find out who is," Mackenzie said.

"Well, I want him to be good and geeky with horn-rimmed glasses and chalky white skin from staying inside all day saving people and reading medical research," Serena said. "And I'd really like him to have medical degrees from both Harvard and Yale."

"I don't think people transfer back and forth between those institutions all that regularly," Mackenzie pointed out.

"And not to be too politically incorrect, but I'd kind of like him to be Jewish. You know, with a Jewish mother who pushed him to be at the top of his medical class at Harvard and Yale." Serena pulled the lid off her coffee cup in hopes of finding a few more drops.

Mackenzie stared at Serena. "Did you just hear yourself? That's completely ridiculous.

And definitely offensive."

A male voice sounded behind them. "Could you settle for a Tiger Mom and Harvard and Columbia?"

They turned slowly, both of them wincing.

"And you are . . . ?" Mackenzie asked.

"Kai Brennan." The white-coated doctor extended his hand. He was tall and slim with glossy black hair and bright blue eyes that were not framed by glasses, horn-rimmed or otherwise. "Head of Neurocritical Care. Half Irish, half Chinese. My mother has been known to fry our Boxty in a wok on occasion."

He allowed them to squirm briefly as he looked them up and down. "So you are both Emma Michaels's sisters."

They nodded.

"I'm a huge Michaels fan. I always understood Rex and Eve had only three children. And one of them is male."

Mackenzie cleared her throat. "Yes, well, we're her half sisters, actually. Our mother . . ."

". . . had a brief affair with Rex and . . ." Even as Serena took over, she chastised herself for not insisting they rehearse or at least talk through their explanation.

"A brief and extremely secret affair," he commented drily. "Somehow I think the gossip magazines would have mentioned Georgia Goodbody's connection to the Michaels family by now. If in fact there was one."

"Well, we're *like* her sisters," Serena clarified, hoping she hadn't turned as red in the face as Mackenzie. Once they had been exactly that close.

"Unfortunately, that's not going to work legally," the doctor said. "I can't share privileged medical information or consult with unrelated or undesignated parties." He shook his head. "We need some real adult family members or a legally designated health care surrogate here pronto."

"We've put in calls to her agent and her manager and a law firm we found listed in her phone, looking for a health care directive or a living will or anything that will make sure Emma has the right representation and her wishes are followed. Believe me, no one wants to see her up and out of here more than we do. It's just that her immediate family is not only temporarily unreachable they're, well, if you're a fan I'm sure you know about Emma's 'emancipation' from them when she was a teenager."

The doctor nodded, but made no comment.

"We *are* Zoe's godmothers," Serena said. Or at least they had been. A fact she left out just as carefully as she did the "fairy" part. "Obviously, we would never leave her here alone."

The doctor considered them for several

long moments. "The first forty-eight hours after a brain injury are the most critical. Our first directive is always to protect the brain and we are doing everything medically possible to achieve this."

Mackenzie's grip on Serena's hand tightened.

"We understand," Serena said. "I've left messages but we're dealing with a three-hour time difference. We haven't been able to get anyone on the West Coast to pick up yet."

Kai Brennan nodded briskly. "Once we've determined who's legally authorized to speak for Miss Michaels, we will share information with that person or persons."

After Dr. Brennan left them Serena went to the ladies' room, where she splashed cold water on her face, brushed her teeth, and ran a comb through her hair. Out of habit, she pulled out her makeup bag and attempted to camouflage the ravages of the night before. In the cafeteria she bought another round of coffee and egg-and-cheese sandwiches, which she carried up to the family waiting room, relieved to see that they still had the space to themselves. They settled around the faux-wood table and chairs to eat. A morning talk show played on the television suspended from the wall, the images bright and jarring and largely incomprehensible with the audio turned low. But the pictures of the crowd of paparazzi that had gathered in front of the hospital where Emma Michaels was now "in a coma and fighting for her life" couldn't have been clearer. The same images from slightly different angles filled the screens on all of the channels. She aimed the remote at the television and zapped it off.

Zoe sipped at her orange juice and picked at the sandwich, her eyes on her food.

The eggs were far chewier than eggs should be, the English muffin that held them, soggy. Serena tried not to make a face as she swallowed each bite.

"Do you have any idea where your mother might have kept . . . keeps . . . her important papers and documents?" Mackenzie asked gently.

Zoe shook her head, her eyes still on her food.

"Did she ever mention what should happen if anything ever happened to her? Or if you needed help of any kind?" Serena asked.

Another shake of the head as she met Serena's gaze. Tears pooled in her eyes.

"We're going to do everything we can to help make sure your mom gets better," Serena promised. "The three of us are going to be joined at the hip until we wheel her ass out of here."

A hint of a smile tugged at Zoe's lips. "Are Rex and Eve coming?" She asked this tentatively.

"I'm sure they will once they can pick up

messages or someone from their ranch reaches them." Serena studied Zoe's face, but couldn't tell whether her grandparents' arrival would be a positive or a negative. "Our priority right now is to find out how your mother would like things handled and make sure the right adult can speak for her until she can speak for herself."

"Can't you do that?" Zoe asked, looking at both of them.

"Not without Emma's permission or written authorization," Mackenzie said gently.

A tear fell on Zoe's sandwich wrapper that now served as a plate. Another landed on the napkin beside it.

"We don't want to assume the worst," Mackenzie said. "Your mother's a strong woman and she has a lot, especially you, to come back to."

"She wouldn't even be here if it weren't for me." Zoe's tears began to fall more quickly. "I was so mad that she wouldn't let me be in *Teen Scream* that I ran out of the restaurant — like some stupid character in a crappy movie." She looked up through her tears. "She would have never been on that street if she hadn't had to come after me."

"It was an accident, Zoe. Mothers and daughters argue. I think it might even be a requirement," Serena tried to reassure her. "God knows, most of my teenage years were spent either in a shouting match with my mother — and you haven't lived until you've heard a real southern belle let loose — or not speaking to her at all. Sometimes after a skirmish, physical distance and a little breathing room are crucial."

"But she wouldn't have been hit by that van if she wasn't chasing after me," Zoe whispered. "You know she wouldn't."

"I promise you your mother wouldn't see it that way. Any one of us could be mowed down by a van on any given day." Mackenzie smiled softly. "As soon as she can speak, I'm betting she'll be the first person to tell you that."

Zoe's tears hadn't stopped, but they did slow.

Tears prickled at the back of Serena's eyelids. She felt like she might cry a damned deluge at the moment if she wasn't careful. She ordered them to cease and desist as she looked Zoe in the eye and said, "I agree with Mackenzie. First your mother will reassure you that this was not your fault. Then she'll undoubtedly give you a ton of shit for what sounds like some serious overacting."

# FIVE

It was well after noon, when Mackenzie thought she might hyperventilate if she didn't breathe some real air, that she took the elevator downstairs, practically sprinted through the lobby, and emerged onto the sidewalk, where a crowd of reporters and photographers jostled each other, Emma's name on their lips. She sidestepped the lot of them, relieved when no one noticed her. It wasn't the first time she was grateful not to be famous.

She left the crowd behind and breathed in great gulps of New York, including the gas fumes from the vehicles that clogged the surrounding streets, the scent of roasting meat from a gyro cart on the corner along with the scents of warm bread wafting from a nearby bakery. The faint scents of summer floated on the breeze from the flower stand across the street. Even the garbage smells seemed preferable to the medicinal, hermetically sealed air of the hospital. The horn honks, shouts, and tumult of the city were a reassuring antidote to the mechanical sound effects and hushed voices of the people inside.

Turning her face up into the midday sun, she headed south on Madison then cut west on Ninety-seventh toward Central Park. Stretching her legs, squaring her shoulders, drawing in deep lung-filling breaths, she speed-dialed Adam and lifted her cell phone to her ear. There'd been no answer when she'd tried him last night. No call back yet this morning. She was preparing to leave a voice mail, when he finally answered. The murmur of voices and the subtle clatter of cutlery sounded in the background.

"You're up and out early," she said by way of greeting. She drew a deep breath, needing to tell him what had happened.

"I just happen to be taking a meeting with Michael Gold at the Polo Lounge." For a moment Mackenzie thought her own panic over Emma had caused her to misunderstand. Michael Gold was at the top of the food chain at Universal Studios. The Polo Lounge was, of course, even more iconic than the production head Adam was breakfasting with. "We're in booth one," he added. "The booth that was always kept open for Charlie Chaplin." He paused to let this sink in. "There was a text waiting yesterday when I landed at LAX asking if I could make it."

Her mind cleared, processed what Adam

was saying. "Oh, my gosh. That's wonderful."
Even being seen at the same table with Michael Gold could be a serious game changer.
"I just needed to . . . we can talk later if
you're tied up."

"It's all right. Michael had to leave to take
a call — some emergency on location in
India." She heard the relish with which he
pronounced the production titan's first name,
his delight in now being entitled to use it.
"But I'll have to go when he comes back."

"Right." She could picture her husband's
face lit by his even, white-toothed smile and
engraved by the dimple. She had no doubt
he was drawing all kinds of attention in his
Hollywood-go-to-meeting clothes, much of it
female.

"It'll take a lot more acting talent than I've
got to appear only mildly interested in whatever he has to say."

"I'm so excited for you," she said because
it seemed something else should be offered.
And because it was true. All she'd ever
wanted was for him to be happy.

"So, how's the reunion going? Is everyone
behaving herself? How's the lake?" he asked
in high good spirits.

"There was only a partial reunion," she
replied, drawn back into her own far less glittering reality. "And there is no lake. I take it
you haven't been watching the news."

The mouthpiece was covered briefly, background voices became muffled. "What do you mean?"

"Emma was in an accident. We've been at Mount Sinai Hospital since yesterday afternoon."

There was a moment's hesitation and then, "Sorry, did you say you're in a hospital?"

"No. I mean yes. We spent the night at Mount Sinai. But it's Emma. Emma was hit by a van." She swallowed the lump that rose in her throat. "She's in a coma."

"Jesus." She heard movement and then the background noise faded. "What happened?"

It was a relief to pour it all out without having to censor her reactions or even the words she used.

"Adam?" She heard his name called in the background.

"Damn." Adam's curse was whispered. "I'm sorry, Mac. I . . . I have to go back in." There was a brief hesitation and then, "If you need me to come to New York I'll . . . well, I've got another meeting at the studio tomorrow. But I can check on flights right after breakfast." She could hear the disappointment in his voice, but Emma was his friend, too — or used to be. She had no doubt he would come today if she asked him to. Adam always did the right thing when push came to shove.

"Thanks for offering," she said even as she chastised herself for wishing he'd insisted on dropping everything to come to New York. There was nothing he could do here other than hold her hand. It would make no sense whatsoever to leave LA at such an important time. She turned resolutely back toward the hospital. "But Serena and I are handling things and trying to take care of Zoe. If we don't get ahold of Emma's agent or manager, you might come in handier out there."

"Okay then. Keep me posted."

She heard the relief in his voice and tried not to feel hurt by it. "I'm going to go back in and, hopefully convince them they can't live without *A Man for Many Reasons.* Or me."

Her steps slowed as she neared the hospital entrance. "I know I couldn't live without you," Mackenzie said. A life without Adam in it was something she refused to even think about. "And I told you when I read the first draft that screenplay was completely kick-ass."

"I appreciate the vote of confidence, Mac. But I don't think the studio people out here are anywhere near as discerning as you are."

"Well," she said. "I think that goes without saying. After all, who is?"

Emma:

My brain streams video I can't control. It comes in fits and starts. Bits and pieces. My triumphs. My mistakes. A twisty road paved with good intentions. I hope they count.

65

*Really, darling. I promise you there are no gatekeepers to the afterlife. It's more like getting into an "it" nightclub — you simply walk right in as if you belong.*

I see Gran. At Sardi's. Arm in arm with Elizabeth Taylor. Flirting with Richard Burton. Vibrant. Glittering.

*Quite right.* Gran's sigh of satisfaction echoes inside me. *Those really were the days.*

Like the video I come and go. In and out. Enveloping darkness. Shimmering light.

There is no time. No now. No then.

Zoe's tears mix with new voices.

"Everything's going to be okay, Em. But if it's all the same to you, this would be a really great time to go ahead and wake up." It's Mackenzie's voice. Nervous but clear. "You know, so we can head on out to the lake like we planned."

"That's right, Mom." Zoe's voice wobbles. "We're all packed and everything. We're just waiting for you."

"Now there's an understatement." Mackenzie again. "Serena has packed everything she owns as usual. Her things are spread all over the family lounge."

"It's true. You should see all the stuff she brought." Zoe's voice catches.

There's a flash of light. The words fade. Somehow it's 1986. I'm coming out the door of my apartment building on Bleecker Street, watching Serena Stockton move in. She's tall

66

and big boobed with smooth white skin and elegant features, and whatever she's saying has the cabdriver smiling despite the huge pile of luggage and boxes that he's pulling out of the cab. Everything about her is curvy and slightly oversized: the red-lipsticked mouth that seems to be constantly moving, the long dark curls she tosses over a shoulder.

She says something — using a whole lot of syllables that don't seem to have anything to do with each other. She peers at me and I'm afraid she's going to recognize me. But she pats me on the shoulder and repeats herself as if I'm a little slow and she's not the one speaking a foreign language.

"I say-a-d," — almost four syllables there — "Ah'm goin' to need some muscle. Do y'all have any frie-nds" — two syllables — "in the building? You know. Anyone who might like to help?" She motions to her possessions, which have eaten up the entire sidewalk. She sighs, long and put upon. "I guess I should have listened to Mama about the movers. Or maybe let Daddy pay so I could get a place with a doorman." There's a satisfied smile as she flashes her left hand; a diamond sparkles on her ring finger. "But my fiancé and I are absolutely determined to make our own way." She turns her charms on the driver who can't seem to take his eyes off her chest but who in the end is not willing to leave his cab to carry her stuff upstairs.

"Well, I neveh . . ." She huffs as he drives off still watching her in his rearview mirror. But in less than a minute she's stopped two guys who are walking by. I watch with amazement as they start lifting the boxes and suitcases. She rounds up a third and his friend. And the next thing she's herding them toward the door saying all kinds of complimentary things about how strong they are, how gentlemanly, how she'd had no idea they had such good-looking men in the North (two syllables). I don't think they have any idea what she's talking about but it doesn't seem to matter. She has them under some sort of spell and I can see in her eyes that she is not about to let go of them until her things are in her apartment.

"That's right, gentlemen," she calls gaily. "I believe I'm on the fifth floor and to the left." She's smiling and fanning herself with a plane ticket as if she's Scarlett O'Hara eating barbecue surrounded by admiring men in those opening scenes of *Gone with the Wind*, one of Gran's all-time favorite movies even though she was no fan of Vivien Leigh. I can see the hint of perspiration on the southern belle's upper lip, but there is not a hair out of place and her makeup is still perfect. She smiles and places her hand in mine. "I'm Serena. Serena Stockton. Formerly of Charleston, South Carolina."

"Em . . . Amelia," I say, almost forgetting

the name I've adopted and all I've done to disguise myself. "Amelia Maclaine. I'm on the fifth floor, too." I have no intention of telling anyone my real name or where I really came from.

"Well, I don't know a single person in this town, Amelia," Serena says to me. "Not till Brooks gets here, anyway." She gives me a wink. "What do you say once you get back from wherever you're headed, and I've got a few things put away, we go downstairs for pizza or out somewhere to have ourselves a drink?"

Mackenzie escorted Zoe out of Emma's room and found Serena down the hall talking with Dr. Brennan. She'd left to take a phone call, and Mackenzie sincerely hoped it had been the anticipated one from California.

"Did somebody find what we were waiting for?" Mackenzie asked cryptically.

"Yes."

"Thank God," Mackenzie said. "Talk about in the nick of time."

The doctor nodded. "How long will it take them to get here? Or shall we set up a conference call?"

"The conversation can take place pretty much anytime," Serena said.

"Oh, good." Mackenzie felt her shoulders relax slightly. "They're in New York?"

"Yes, they are." There was an odd note in

Serena's voice as she added, "The papers are being faxed to Dr. Brennan's office right now."

"Do you know the person whom Ms. Michaels named as health care POA?" the doctor asked.

"Pretty well."

"Serena," Mackenzie said. "Enough with the suspense. Just tell us what's happened and who Emma named."

"Well, it appears that Emma had an appointment with her attorneys to go in and update things after our week at the lake. But as of this moment, it's still me and you. Me first and you as backup." There was both fear and relief in her eyes. "It's going to be up to us to understand the options and make informed decisions." She whipped out Georgia Goodbody's imaginary fan and tapped the doctor lightly on the shoulder. "And the sooner the better, Dr. B. We need to get Emma well as quickly as possible. We have plans for a trip to the lake."

# Six

They left Zoe in the cafeteria staring without interest at a hamburger, a huge mound of French fries, and a Coke and joined Dr. Brennan in a small conference room just off the ICU. Pictures of Emma's brain along with graphs and charts and printouts of what looked like every breath and beat of her heart since she'd arrived were spread out before them. Mackenzie hadn't slept the night before her flight out of nervousness; last night fear for Emma and the ridiculously uncomfortable waiting room chairs had left her wide eyed. The caffeine she'd been ingesting all day surged through her bloodstream and sped up her heart, but it didn't seem to have clarified her thoughts. Serena didn't look any more rested. Not an optimal state for absorbing life-and-death situations.

"Ms. Michaels came in with multiple contusions including a small one to the lung, a bruised heart, a large laceration on her left thigh, and a deep gash on the right side of her head." He paused. "Initial scans show a two-millimeter shift from right to left and a Glasgow scale of eight. The bruising on the brain here" — he pointed to a section of what looked like a large gray cauliflower — "has caused swelling and increased intracranial pressure."

Mackenzie couldn't catch her breath as she tried not to picture Emma's brain all bruised and swollen.

"Look, Doctor, I'm an actress," Serena said. "Mackenzie is a fashion and costume designer. I've avoided maths and sciences as much as possible my entire life. You're going to have to explain this stuff in terms we have a shot at understanding. You know, I'm thinking fourth- or fifth-grade-level science, tops."

"This is not an elementary school kind of situation," Dr. Brennan replied quietly.

"We know. But you're going to have to dummy this down to a level we can understand."

Unable to speak, Mackenzie nodded her agreement. This was Emma's brain they were talking about. Emma's life.

"Okay," the doctor said. "Traumatic brain injury causes the brain to swell — just like the swelling that happens when you injure a knee or an elbow. But the brain is trapped inside the skull and as swelling increases, it can raise the pressure inside the head. If it gets high enough it can cut off the blood flow to the brain. That results in brain death."

They nodded carefully.

"Steps have already been taken to alleviate the pressure. Dr. Markham, her neurosurgeon, has inserted an external ventricular drain, or EVD, which is inserted through a hole in the skull."

Bile rose in Mackenzie's throat at the thought of a drill piercing Emma's skull. She saw Serena swallow. A hand fluttered to her throat. Mackenzie prayed she wasn't going to make some sick joke about the use of power tools. Serena remained mercifully silent.

"What happens next?" Serena asked.

"For now our best course is to continue doing everything possible to reduce the swelling and to keep the brain as inactive as possible while we monitor everything carefully."

"And what are her chances of a full recovery?" Serena asked the question Mackenzie was afraid to.

He studied their faces. "Every individual and every set of injuries responds in a different way. Many people with coma from head injuries do make a full recovery."

They sat for a few long moments trying to absorb all that Dr. Brennan had said.

"Can she hear us?" Mackenzie finally managed to ask. "Even though she doesn't react, can she hear what's going on?"

"We don't know. There are reports of patients waking after coma and mentioning things that they heard or even saw, though often in some sort of skewed way or as part of what they experienced as a nightmare."

He looked at them and added, "If you want my advice, I suggest you leave. Have a shower, some real food, and a better night's sleep than you can get in the family lounge."

"We don't want to leave Em alone," Mackenzie said. "I mean, what if something happens and we're not here?"

"We'll call you. Her vitals are good. She's relatively stable. And I promise you she's in good hands. If she worsens in any way, the nurse on duty knows to call you right after she beeps Dr. Markham and me."

The car took them to the Carlyle, where they checked Emma and Zoe out of their suite, retrieved their luggage, then drove to Serena's brownstone in the Village where the driver, unlike that long-ago cabdriver who delivered Serena to her first New York apartment, carried their luggage to the appropriate bedrooms. Emma's suitcases were tucked into the back of Serena's walk-in closet so that Zoe wouldn't have to deal with or stare at them.

They were tired and raw, the worry about Emma written on all their faces. Serena was grateful when Mackenzie turned their attention and conversation to their surroundings.

"This place is gorgeous," Mackenzie said

when they reassembled in the kitchen, which dominated the great room and opened onto a walled garden. "It's light years from that walk-up over on Bleecker that you and Emma were living in when we first met. And it's so much bigger than your last place." Although they'd spoken on occasion, there had been no get-togethers once the lake house retreats had stopped. Serena had had no reason to visit Indiana, and if Mackenzie had been in New York she'd never said so.

"Thanks." Serena had not grown up poor and Charleston was certainly no shirker in the historic home arena, but she could still hardly believe the 1901 West Village brownstone belonged to her. "It was only partially renovated when I bought it and there were times during construction that I wondered what the hell I'd been thinking. But I fell in love with the high ceilings and the windows and although I've murdered more plants than I've saved, I love the garden."

"Is that rosewood?" Mackenzie eyed the floors appreciatively.

"Yes."

"It's so spacious but manages to be cozy at the same time."

"Thanks." Her home was near the intersection of Bank and West Fourth streets, not far from the brownstone where *Sex and the City*'s Carrie Bradshaw had lived. Every time Serena walked in the front door, she was reminded of just how much Georgia Good-body had given her. "Have a seat. Anybody want a cold drink?"

They dropped onto the nearby sectional while Serena took stock of the contents of her refrigerator, not that there was much to take stock of. She brought a tray with Diet Cokes and bottled waters and small bowls with nuts and pretzels. Zoe, who'd been extremely quiet on the ride from the hospital, yawned as she reached for a bottle of water and a handful of pretzels.

"The cupboard's pretty bare since we were headed out of town. I'm going to run out for a few things," Serena said. "Any requests?"

Zoe was chewing with her eyes closed. Mac-kenzie slumped into the sofa. Serena was exhausted too, but oddly restless. She couldn't stop thinking about Emma lying there so lifeless. What if she never woke up? She couldn't sit here any more than she could sit in the hospital.

"I'm going to shower and head out to run some errands. I think you guys should catch a nap. Why don't I pick up Thai food on my way back?"

They nodded sleepily then followed her upstairs.

Thirty minutes later Serena was cabbing to the studio where *As the World Churns* was recorded. She waved hello to Catherine Stengel at the reception desk, walked past the booth where a red light glowed to indicate recording was in progress, then slipped into the control room. Lauri Strauss, a twenty-something blonde whose character, Dahlia, was far younger and dewier than Georgia Goodbody, was recording with Wes Harrison, who played Georgia's current love interest both on-screen and off. They stood at side-by-side microphones, the monitor positioned where they could both see it. Serena's eyes lit on Wes, who had pursued her for months before she'd finally slept with him. His broad shoulders strained against the fabric of his shirt. His jeans hugged a great butt and an even more impressive pair of thighs. The craggy features and whiskey-colored eyes didn't hurt, either. Despite her exhaustion and worry, she felt a small tingle of sexual awareness as she remembered their lingering farewell just two nights ago.

This evaporated when Lauri looked up at Wes as if he were God's gift to the female universe. Her heart thumped uncomfortably in her chest when Wes stared back at her as if he agreed.

"Rolling playback."

Lauri was so busy fluttering her eyelashes at Wes that she flubbed her next line. "Sorry," she giggled.

"No problem," Wes said as if her screwup was somehow endearing. Then he smiled at her in a way Serena had always thought he

77

reserved for her. And possibly, on occasion, for his wife.

"Rolling."

This time the two made it through the scene without further screwups. Serena's jaw clenched each time they smiled at or touched each other. Wes had acted so disappointed that she'd be gone a whole week. "Acted" was apparently the operative word.

She was preparing to slip out as quietly as she'd come in, when Ethan Miller entered the control room. He'd been only thirty-five eleven years ago when the series was green-lighted. Even now he could have passed for late thirties, an impression that was reinforced by his laid-back personality and clothing choices that rarely strayed from Levi's and T-shirts. His feet were typically laced into running shoes.

"Hi. I heard you were here." He was of average height and build. Even his brown hair was of average length and color — as if unwilling to declare itself. He'd been a skit writer and cast member at Second City in Chicago before joining *SNL*'s "not ready for prime time players." *As the World Churns* had grown out of several characters he'd created on his comedic journey.

When his face was in repose, he looked like the boy next door. Or the nice-enough-looking guy you sat next to in math class through high school but whose name you'd forgotten as soon as you graduated. But his unremarkable features were made of rubber and could stretch into almost any expression or look — all of them funny.

"I'm sorry about your friend," he said now.

"Thanks." Serena watched out of one eye as Lauri cracked up at something Wes said. She tensed as he laid a hand on her upper arm.

"I saw the story on the news last night," Ethan continued. "It looked like a pretty big pack of paparazzi out in front of Mount Sinai."

"Yes. Way too big." They'd had the car pick them up at the back of the hospital today and made Zoe duck down until they'd rounded the corner.

"How is she?"

"Not good. Her head was hit pretty hard. She's in intensive care."

"Is there anything I can do?" Ethan's tone left no doubt that anything she asked for would be immediately taken care of. She'd learned the first year of the show not to sit at a table with him while sipping anything that might be spewed on others. But when he wasn't trying to make you laugh, he was unfailingly polite and sincere.

"No, but I really appreciate you asking." She tried to maintain eye contact, but couldn't quite stop stealing peeks at the recording session.

"Well, if you need more than the week off just let me know," Ethan said. "We can record remotely if that would help. And I can probably cut your lines together from earlier shows if necessary."

"You're a good guy," she said, accepting a hug, surprised at the warmth and strength in the sinewy arms and lean frame. "A real mensch." She threw out one of her few Yiddish words.

"Well, that's high praise coming from a gorgeous shiksa like you," he said in an exaggerated voice that could have belonged to Jackie Mason or any other borscht belt comedian. Still in character, he bussed her lustily on the cheek then slung an arm around her shoulders as he walked her to the control room door.

Oddly comforted, she took a last peek through the plate glass window and was rewarded with a punch-in-the-gut view of Wes Harrison standing way too close to the adoring Lauri Strauss.

Ethan Miller's eyes were on her. Ethan was a mensch all right. Unlike Wes Harrison. Who was pretty much a cheater and a bastard in any accent, dialect, or language.

# SEVEN

When they drove past the front entrance of the hospital the next morning, the number of paparazzi had doubled. Like a cell that had divided and reproduced on its own. Mackenzie, who had often thought of Emma's life as glamorous and exciting, watched them jostle for position, reminded that there was a dark underbelly to fame. The cab deposited them at the back entrance, where they took a freight elevator up to the neuro ICU.

Rhonda, Emma's lead nurse, sat at the computer outside Emma's room staring at the monitor and jotting notes on a file. Rubber soles squeaked on the floor and there was a hum of low-pitched voices as white-coated doctors conferred. The patients' families wore wrinkled clothing and shell-shocked expressions. Their tired, disbelieving eyes were rimmed in dark circles like the ones Mackenzie had seen in the mirror this morning.

She'd tossed and turned for much of the previous night, but at least that tossing had taken place on a queen-sized bed rather than a molded plastic chair. Breakfast had been the Thai food none of them had been able to face the night before. They'd eaten it cold, out of the cardboard containers, their eyes glued to the small flat-screen on the kitchen wall as the morning news programs ran their versions of the Emma Michaels "tragedy," buttressed by old shots of Emma as a child star, which dissolved into shots of her entering the offices of a Los Angeles district judge as a teen, her grandmother at her side. Stories about her legal emancipation from her famous parents had pulled in a hefty audience in its day.

Serena clicked the set off in the middle of a tight two shot of Rex and Eve Michaels professing to not understand why their daughter would do such a thing. "Thank God Emma's emancipation happened before reality television," Serena said drily. "Or there might have been a show called *Making Up with the Michaelses.*"

Dr. Brennan had already been in to see Emma and left word that the night had been uneventful and there was nothing new to report. He'd stop by again in the afternoon.

They took turns sitting with Emma. Waiting at times with held breath for something, anything, to happen. Mackenzie's mind wandered as she watched Emma's chest rise rhythmically up and down. Her eyes remained closed. Her jaw slack. Her arms and hands limp at her sides.

She thought of how turbulent Emma's life had been, how much of it had played out in public and in the tabloids. Only those years when she'd lived with them and auditioned as someone else — a significant acting job in its own right — had been remotely private. When they'd discovered that Amelia Maclaine was actually Emma Michaels, Emma had been frightened that their friendship might change. But by then they'd seen the best and worst of each other. Held each other's hair out of the way while they bowed before the porcelain throne after too much partying, eaten tons of ice cream and chocolate together when men had proved disappointing, and learned when saying nothing was the best choice of all. Though some of them were better at remaining silent than others. By the time they knew that Amelia Maclaine was Emma Michaels, they were too close for an accident of birth to come between them. Or so they'd always thought.

Around one o'clock, she, Serena, and Zoe took the elevator down to the hospital cafeteria. At a quiet table in a dark corner, they picked at their food without enthusiasm.

"I had a call from Calvin," Zoe said as she picked up a French fry then put it back on her plate.

"What did your dad say?" Mackenzie asked.

83

"He just called to ask if I needed anything. He said he'd come if it seemed like that would be helpful. But I wasn't sure if he meant for me or for my mother."

"Would you like him to come, Zoe?" Mackenzie asked. "I know you said no the other day, but if it would make you feel better . . ."

"No." She looked up from her plate, her chin jutting outward.

"Are you sure?" Serena asked. "Because . . ."

"No. He asked me to give my mother a hug." Zoe's voice broke. "I don't think he understands what condition she's really in. I told him not to worry about it." She picked up the same French fry and motioned with it. "Then he asked me if I'd like to come be with him on location."

Mackenzie was careful not to comment.

Serena had no such hesitation. "He thought you'd rather be on location in New Zealand than here?"

Zoe nodded dully then looked down at her plate.

"To be fair to your father, I think it's hard to understand what's . . . going on . . . without being here," Mackenzie said, thinking about her exchange of texts with Adam just thirty minutes ago. He'd texted two brief queries about Emma and herself. Then there'd been a flood of text, most of it followed by exclamation points. *Another meeting*

84

*is scheduled at the studio! Don't want to jinx things, but this time I feel like something could really happen!!!!*

She'd kept her responses short but upbeat. A few "wows!" Two or three "greats!" each with an exclamation point of its own. It had felt so odd though, almost disloyal, to even be thinking about anything so frivolous as a movie deal when Emma was lying in the ICU like a block of wood, unmoving and unresponsive.

"I guess," Zoe said finally. "But I'm not going anywhere." She pushed her plate away. "Not until she wakes up."

Serena's mouth opened and Mackenzie braced. Serena had always prided herself on "telling it like it is," except, of course, when it came to certain personal truths she was avoiding. She shot Serena a warning look.

"I was just going to say that none of us are going anywhere until Sleeping Beauty awakens. Even if I have to find a handsome prince to lay one on her."

Mackenzie rolled her eyes at Serena, but Zoe's eyes had stopped glistening. "Well, while you're looking," Mackenzie said, "maybe you should find out if Doctor Brennan's single."

"You don't have to be single to kiss somebody awake. It's not like a fairy-tale rule or anything." Serena helped herself to one of Zoe's fries.

"That may be, but I'm pretty sure the kiss is more potent if the prince who locks lips with you isn't contractually promised to someone else."

Back at her town house late the next night, Serena kicked off her shoes and sank into the sofa with a groan. Mackenzie and Zoe joined her.

"I was really hoping for some sign, even a small one, today," Serena said, rubbing her bare feet. "Some tiny signal that Em is getting ready to wake up."

"Well, Dr. Brennan said this is a critical time while we wait for the swelling to go down. And that we have to remain vigilant for threats of infection or blood clots or other problems," Mackenzie reminded them. "Since none of those things happened, that makes it a good day."

"It didn't feel like one." Zoe's voice was quiet.

Mackenzie kept her inner Pollyanna to herself.

The doorbell rang and Serena stared briefly at the door before hauling herself up and heading over to it. She peered through the peephole then opened it to a deliveryman who handed over a large gift-wrapped box. As she set it on the coffee table and undid the bow, she wondered if it might be from Wes, who had sent her a series of increasingly lame texts that began with a slightly apologetic, "Wish I'd known you were in the control room last night." *No kidding.* And ended with a more than slightly indignant, "I can't believe you left without saying hello." As if she was the one in the wrong.

As soon as she opened the box and saw the gourmet popcorn, and boxes of Sno-Caps and Jujubes tucked into the collection of videos, she knew whom it was from. Ethan had sent all six original seasons of *I Love Lucy,* a *Dick Van Dyke Show* holiday special, an early reel of George Burns and Gracie Allen, Abbott and Costello's "Who's on First," National Lampoon's *Vacation,* and the Three Stooges' *Have Rocket, Will Travel.* A hand-labeled DVD read, *Georgia Goodbody Outtakes. Have fan, will pummel.* The card read, *Watch. Laugh. Repeat. Don't get Jujubes stuck in your teeth.*

"Very nice," Mackenzie observed.

"Is all that from your boyfriend?" Zoe asked, reaching for a box of Sno-Caps.

"No, they're from my friend Ethan. He's the producer/ creator of . . ."

"Ethan Miller?" Zoe asked. *"The* Ethan Miller who was in *Tempest in Toledo?"*

"Yes," Serena said tentatively.

"He's like the funniest person ever," Zoe exclaimed. "For an old guy, I mean."

Serena sighed. "I know. He's already forty-five. Hard to believe his sense of humor is still intact."

"Clearly Ethan Miller is one very thoughtful guy," Mackenzie said.

"Don't you wish the hot ones were nice like that?" Zoe asked. "Hot guys never have to develop a personality or a sense of humor. Because everybody's already falling all over them."

Serena looked at Zoe. "How is it you figured that out so much sooner than I did?"

Zoe shrugged. "What kind of guys did you all date? Back when you were . . . younger?" She said this last as if she couldn't quite imagine it.

"I never really had boyfriends back when I was in high school. But I fell for Adam the minute I saw him," Mackenzie said. "I'd only been in New York maybe two weeks. Your mom and Serena always got more attention in that department than me."

"I was engaged when I first got here," Serena said, taking a seat next to Zoe. "So I wasn't looking or dating."

Zoe shook a mound of Sno-Caps into her hand. "I didn't know you were married."

"I wasn't. My fiancé had been offered a job up here. But at the last minute he decided to stay in Charleston." Her jaw tightened. "To marry someone else. He went to work for her father."

There was a brief silence.

"His loss," Mackenzie said, surprised by

the hurt on Serena's face all these years later. "He was forever after known as 'The Tool.' And other less flattering names."

"It was quite the scandal back home," Serena said. "Well-bred southern boys are supposed to keep their promises."

"And my mom? What kind of guys did my mom go out with?" Zoe said, munching on a handful of white-capped chocolate.

"She always picked the strong silent types," Serena answered. "Partly I think because as long as they didn't ruin it by talking too much, you could pretend they were anything you wanted them to be."

"But she almost never went out with actors," Mackenzie added. "She once told me that there were way too many performers in her family tree — and that was before we knew she was a Michaels." She smiled at Zoe. "But what I remember most from that time was the three of us. The men, even Adam, were more like supporting players. But we were Josie and the Pussycats, Charlie's Angels — God knows we had the hair for it — the female incarnation of the Three Musketeers."

"But she married Calvin," Zoe said. "And he's an actor. I think that's the only thing they had in common."

"They had you," Serena said.

"Yeah." Zoe's tone was wistful.

"Do you remember the weeks at the lake?" Serena asked.

"Kind of. I used to wish we could live there all the time. Because in LA we were so, you know, alone. And at the lake we had Gran when I was little and you guys. It was almost like having a family."

"She always said you were the best thing that ever happened to her." Mackenzie said this quietly, her thoughts drawn back to a time she tried not to think about.

Zoe zeroed in on a teetering stack of albums on the coffee table and reached for the two on the top.

"Sorry for the mess," Serena said, straightening the remaining stack before settling in beside Zoe. "I pulled some pictures from back when we first met to bring to the lake, and I never got to put them away.

Idly, Zoe opened the first leather-covered album and began to flip through the pages. She stopped, looking up in surprise. "Was this a baby shower for me?" Zoe asked. "I mean, for my mom?"

Mackenzie's hand stole to her stomach as Serena's gaze swept over her.

"Yes." Serena hesitated. She threw another glance, this one of apology, Mackenzie's way. "Actually it was a baby shower I threw for your mom and Mackenzie here in New York. I, um, didn't have *As the World Churns* yet, so it was a bit of a low-budget endeavor."

Mackenzie remembered the shower well. How happy she'd been. How thrilled that she and Emma would have children so close in age. Children that could grow up to be best friends, too. And then the accident, the force of the air bag smashing into her. She'd never managed to carry anywhere close to term after that.

"My mom told me once that you lost your baby," Zoe said. "I didn't understand. For the longest time I was afraid she'd lose me, too."

Mackenzie inwardly flinched. Her own loss had been so fresh that the time around Zoe's birth was still blurred around the edges. It had been the only year she was unable to make herself join them at the lake.

She watched Zoe's face light up as she flipped the pages, exclaiming over the hokey decorations and the old-fashioned maternity clothes. If it came to it, she and Adam could bring Zoe home with them. Indiana, and especially Noblesville, was a far more wholesome place to raise a teenager than New York or Hollywood. She'd have a daughter to pal around with, to take shopping. And there was their theater; Zoe would love . . .

She cut off the line of thought, horrified. Emma was strong. The woman had divorced herself from her parents when she was younger than Zoe. She had a will of iron. If anyone could pull through, it was Em. Emma had always gotten everything she wanted — marriage, a career, a child. The only thing

91

Mackenzie had gotten that Emma hadn't was true love with Adam. Even if that love wasn't feeling quite as "true" at the moment.

"Here's my favorite shot of the four of us." Serena flipped the page to a shot of the three of them standing on the porch of the lake house, with Zoe, a thatch of red-gold hair and spindly legs, poking above and below the sling she'd been suspended in. Her face was pressed tight against Emma's chest.

"Your great-grandmother took this shot," Mackenzie said quietly. "We couldn't wait for our turns to hold and carry you."

"We even fought over who would get to change your poopy diapers," Serena added. "Not that any of us was particularly skilled at it."

"We felt like you belonged to all of us." Mackenzie's eyes blurred with tears as Zoe closed the album. Looking far from comforted, Zoe began to cry.

"Oh, God." Serena swiped at her eyes and stood. "We are not going to sit here crying. Emma would totally hate that." She pulled the bag of popcorn from the gift box. "Go get your pajamas on. I'm going to pop us a great big bowl of this stuff. And then it's time for a couple of episodes of *I Love Lucy.*

# EIGHT

Two days had passed with no apparent change in Emma's condition when their cab turned onto the street that fronted the hospital that morning. A white stretch limo idled at the curb and an exponentially larger mob of paparazzi littered the sidewalk. When a small gap in the wall of reporters and photographers opened up, Serena could see why. The Michaels family had arrived.

"Slow down, but don't stop," Serena directed the driver.

"Oh, my God, it's Rex, Eve, Regan, and Nash," Mackenzie said. "In the flesh."

Emma's parents and siblings might have been gods descended from Mount Olympus, and the paparazzi there to worship at their feet given the way they had amassed on the steps below them. Necks cricked back and cameras and video recorders aimed upward; they shouted questions and thrust microphones toward them. If not for the bodyguards positioned around the family, Serena had no doubt the crowd would have already surged, surrounded, and swallowed them whole.

They looked, Serena thought, like a family of superheroes. All four of them tall, long limbed, and elegant with varying shades and lengths of the trademark red-gold hair, and aquiline-nosed, square-jawed faces dominated by high cheekbones and wide-set green eyes that looked incredible in person and even more so on camera.

In theatrical terms they were the antithesis of Georgia Goodbody, pure gold versus brass; glowing lights on a Broadway marquee, not popcorn and Jujubes. They walked red carpets and won Oscars, Tonys, and Emmys. Any crowd that gathered around them, professional or otherwise, would be throwing roses and shouting "bravo," not cracking jokes.

"Impressive." Zoe couldn't take her eyes off them.

"Definitely impressive," Serena agreed. If only everything that glittered so brightly were actually gold. From what Emma had shared and even more from what she had not, Serena knew that Eve and Rex had always been a unit, faithful not necessarily to each other but to their joint ambitions and public persona. Their parenting had been aggressive in all things acting, but highly conditional in terms of approval — leaving their offspring to compete for scraps of their attention, typically won only through dramatic achievement. Emma, who'd been far smaller, younger, and seemingly softer than her siblings, had found the playing field uneven and unforgiving. Serena knew firsthand that all actors were rife with insecurity, but Emma who could *act* the movie star as well as anyone, had always been a veritable Swiss cheese of self-doubt. Serena, whose parents had been demanding but who had nonetheless showered her with love, could only imagine what kind of courage and determination it had taken to overcome having parents like Rex and Eve.

Physically, Zoe would have fit perfectly into the Michaels tableau.

"How often do you see them?" Mackenzie asked.

Zoe's gaze remained on the family members her mother had divorced. "They always send me a Christmas and birthday present. And I always write them a thank-you note. We've run into them a couple of times at awards things and parties. Once Eve and Rex came to one of my shows at school and everybody went crazy." She pulled her gaze away. "Em . . . my mom told me I could visit with them anytime I wanted. But I never really wanted to. And even though she would never tell me much about it, I figure there's a reason she divorced them. I mean, that's not something you do to parents who just irritate you the regular amount."

"Very true." Serena motioned the cab to pull around to the back entrance.

"You don't think they're going to make a scene, do you?" Zoe asked as they got out of the cab. "Or try to tell the doctors what to do?" Her voice had grown tentative. She seemed to be shrinking inward.

"I'm not sure they know how not to make a scene," Mackenzie said as they ducked into the hospital. "Especially when they're all together vying for top billing."

"But we'll do what we can to manage the visit," Serena promised. "Okay?"

Zoe nodded.

"I guess we should warn Dr. Brennan," Mackenzie said, pushing the freight elevator call button. "And make sure he and Rhonda and the rest of the staff understand what Emma's relationship is with them."

"I don't think there's anyone in the free world who doesn't know about Emma's legal emancipation," Serena said as Zoe pushed the eighth-floor button.

The doctor's first words confirmed Serena's hypothesis. "I understand we have VIPs headed up."

"You know they're not close to Emma," Mackenzie said delicately.

"I'm aware they're not her chosen health-care representatives," Dr. Brennan said.

"They're not her chosen parents, either,"

Serena said. "You're a fan, so you must know about the . . ."

". . . divorce. Yes. But this is a neurocritical ICU. I've seen a lot of family relationships change radically when someone is in the sort of condition Ms. Michaels is."

"But they can't make decisions for her," Zoe said. "She wouldn't want . . ."

"I understand," Dr. Brennan said. "I'm not planning to consult with them. But like you, they're her immediate biological family. Barring a restraining order or anything else that would legally prohibit access, they'll be allowed to see her. Even if I wanted to, I couldn't just chuck them back out onto the sidewalk."

Serena nodded. "We understand, but I'm not going to let them go in there and upset her."

"I'm not sure that's possible, given her condition," the doctor said.

"I've been reading blog posts and accounts from people who've come out of comas," Mackenzie said quietly. "And all of them say they could see and hear things no one thought they could."

They stared at each other. The doctor made no comment.

"Give me just a second." Serena slipped into Emma's cubicle and closed the door softly behind her. She was greeted by low beeps and mechanical hums as she approached the bed. "Em?" She waited briefly for a reaction that didn't come. "Eve and Rex and Regan and Nash are here." Emma's chest continued to rise and fall. There was no reaction. "Unless you give me some sort of sign that you don't want them here, they're going to come in and see you." She took Emma's hand, which was cool and slightly clammy to the touch. "Just say the word and I'll lock the door somehow. Or . . . throw my body across the threshold."

Nothing.

"Come on, Em. What do you say?" It took all she had not to raise her voice in an attempt to get through.

More nothing. Her own heart thudded dully in her chest. She felt as if she were about to allow a scalp-lusting war party to swoop in on a defenseless wagon train.

There was a sound behind her. Mackenzie materialized beside her. "What are you doing? Dr. Brennan just went to the ICU entrance to greet them and escort them in. All things considered" — she nodded to Emma's inert form — "I don't see how we could keep them from at least seeing her. Or even that we should. They are her flesh and blood."

There was a new energy out in the hall. Serena felt eyes on her back. Turning, she saw all four Michaelses standing in the hall looking through the plate glass like uncomfortable visitors at a zoo confronted with a dispirited animal or a too-mangy lion. Zoe stood stiffly to one side, a mirror image of her aunt Regan except that Zoe's face was twisted with anguish while Regan, who had cried her emerald green eyes out in *Indecent Victory* and won an Oscar for it, appeared completely dry-eyed. Rex and Nash looked ill at ease but aware, as all actors were, of the impression they were making. Rex had aged surprisingly well for a man who'd lived such an intemperate life. Strands of silver highlighted rather than diminished his red-gold hair; his jaw and cheekbones were still firm. Nash, who split his time between acting and directing, had a soulful look in his moss green eyes that would allow him to play romantic leads for decades to come. Eve was harder to read. According to Emma, her mother's brilliant green eyes were the result of tinted contacts while her slanted cheekbones and squared jawline owed more to plastic surgery than heredity. Auburn was not her natural hair color. But of the four of them she seemed the most focused on Emma rather than on herself.

"We'll be just outside if you need us." Serena gave Emma's hand a squeeze then followed Mackenzie out into the hall. "If they do anything to upset her I'll haul them out of there myself," she said to Mackenzie under her breath.

"Maybe riling her up a little wouldn't be such a bad thing," Mackenzie replied quietly as they positioned themselves on either side of Zoe where they could watch what took place. "I'd give anything to see her wake up. Even if it were just to tell them off."

Emma:
The images change. They're rougher. Briefer. I'm swept from place to place, person to person, unbound by time. My grandmother's voice isn't the only one that sounds in my head. Words. Thoughts. Feelings. All materialize without warning. Only to disappear. I'm one with these images. Yet apart. *Alone.*

I sense my family. They waver like a mirage. Pulse with energy.

I feel Nash's handsome smile. A flash of pity. All mixed up with a casting tangle he needs to unravel. Regan is beside him. Cool. Calculating. I can almost hear her thoughts. Mine is the first coma she's witnessed. She wants to know what it feels like. How she might play it. She stores my crisis away to give later to an audience. The same way she does her emotions. Like a poor man hoarding the few coins he possesses.

My father can't bear to look at me *like this.* My mother cannot look away. She takes my hand. I feel a wave of pain. Regret. Longing.

Before I can figure out which of us these

emotions belong to, there's an explosion of light and I'm at home in the huge house in the Hollywood Hills. Standing in my mother's master closet, a place I love because of all the colors and textures and the intoxicating smell of Eve, who's been gone on location for six weeks and has only just gotten home. I'm eleven, Regan and Nash already out of the house, for all intents and purposes an only child. Who works and is tutored on set all day. I have no friends, no life, no . . . anything. Even my parents are only here on occasion.

"But, sweetheart." My mother almost never calls me by name. Recently I've begun to wonder if she can't remember it. "You can't quit the show. You're under contract. And it's doing so well. You're making a fortune."

A fortune I've never seen.

"I realize playing the part of a precocious wisecracking preteen isn't exactly a stretch." She stops powdering her face in her makeup mirror in order to look directly at me. "But you are surprisingly good at it."

The word "surprisingly" pulls me up short as it's meant to. We all know I'm not as beautiful as Regan or Nash and probably never will be. I'm short and round and overly plump and I have frizzy hair and freckles that refuse to be eradicated or covered up. "You need to make the most of it while you can. Making the transition from child star to adult actress is hard enough under the best of circumstances; the teenage years can be quite brutal on even the most" — she hesitates delicately here, as if reluctant to inflict hurt — "physically fortunate and dramatically gifted." Translation: I have no chance in hell of ever working again once I become a teenager. Which is just fine with me.

"I don't care. I'm not doing the show anymore." I'd been excited when *Daddy's Girl* was offered, and I did it to show them that I'm just as talented as Regan. So they would pay attention to me. None of these things have happened. "And you can't make me. Nobody can make me."

"Don't be ridiculous, darling." Coming from my mother, the endearment rings hollow. It's not warm or infused with love like when Gran says it.

"Your father and I have already discussed this. The show is a hit. Millions of girls your age would change places with you in a heartbeat." She smiles a smile that says that she and my father would prefer one of those girls. Or preferably a clone of Regan. Who is frickin' perfect. And beautiful. And talented. And who has never wanted anything but to follow in our parents' famous footsteps.

"And when you're older" — presumably past the hellishly ugly teenage years that lie ahead of me — "why then we can look at finding you some more suitable parts."

I know what she means by this. She means

"suitable for a Michaels." The kind of roles that always come to Regan.

My mother squeezes my hand. Her lips brush my forehead. A drop of moisture hits my cheek. Wet and confusing. Eve only cries on-stage. The hums and beeps grow louder. More urgent. The door flings open. I hear footsteps. Eve drops my hand. Shrinks away.

The dark gets darker. Bigger. It smothers and swallows me.

*Gran?*

"Everybody out." The voice is calm but urgent. Not Gran's. "Her intracranial pressure's spiking out of control." The hums and beeps escalate. Sounding an alarm.

"Page Dr. Markham and Dr. Brennan! Call anesthesiology! We are going to have a code blue here!"

# NINE

The surgery to remove the blood clot in Emma's brain took two and a half hours, but felt, Serena thought, more like twenty.

They spent those hours in the waiting room off the surgical wing too frightened to eat or drink or crack even the smallest of jokes. In opposite camps the four Michaels spread out along one wall; Serena, Mackenzie, and Zoe huddled along the other.

While her husband and children texted, stared at their phones and occasionally excused themselves to take calls, Eve paced and fretted, her green eyes glittering like shards of colored glass. Occasionally that pacing brought her close enough to the non-Michaels faction to communicate her views. "You should have gotten another opinion. We could have flown in the best neurosurgeon in the country."

"Dr. Brennan assured us that Dr. Markham is one of the top five in the country," Serena replied.

"That means there are four others who could be better than him," Eve observed with a sniff.

"I'm pretty sure a blood clot isn't something you leave in someone's brain while you try to decide if your surgeon is number one or number two," Serena shot back.

"Second best is never acceptable." Regan looked up from her phone, pitching her voice so it could be heard. "There are no statuettes for second place." She cocked her head, sending a spill of silky red-gold hair down one slim shoulder and raised one perfectly arched brow. "Unless you count best supporting actor. After all, their entire purpose is to support the lead."

Nash's head snapped up. His moss green eyes shed their soulfulness. "Actually, their purpose is to enhance, deepen, and expand the plot, not prop up the lead." His square jaw jutted. He had after all won a best supporting actor Oscar not once but twice. "Best supporting actor means *best* in an entirely separate category. They're not runner-up to 'best lead actor.' They are the best at what they set out to do. It's not the same thing at all."

"Whatever gets you through the night, little brother," Regan said with a shrug.

"Nash is technically correct," said Rex, stroking his chin with one long-fingered hand. "Though I would have to agree that best actor does carry a bit more cachet than best supporting."

Regan smiled triumphantly as Nash gritted his very white, very capped teeth.

"Regan. Really." Eve's voice dripped reproach. "Must you tease your brother at a time like this?"

*Tease?* Serena thought there was way too much venom in Regan's observations to qualify as teasing, but then "warm" and "fuzzy" were not adjectives she'd ever heard applied to members of this family. She turned and moved to the window where Zoe and Mackenzie stood looking down at the crowd of paparazzi that seemed to be growing larger by the moment.

Tears slid down Zoe's cheeks. "If my mother dies it will be an even bigger story, won't it?"

"They've already got a big story whatever happens," Mackenzie said, sliding her arm around the girl's shoulders. "But there's no point in thinking that way."

"Your mother is strong. And Dr. Markham knows what he's doing," Serena added.

"But she could die." Zoe's voice broke on the word. She swiped at her eyes with the back of one hand.

"She could," Serena agreed. "But that could happen to any of us in any given moment."

Mackenzie pulled Zoe closer and shot Serena a look. "I don't think that's the kind of reassurance any of us are looking for at the moment."

"Sorry. It's all I've got." Serena folded her arms across her chest and turned her back on the plate glass window. "But I refuse to believe Em survived that accident only to die now." She tried to sound calm and certain though she was neither.

By the time Dr. Markham came to speak to them, they were all once again slumped in their respective chairs staring at the pale green walls, their hands, the floor, or nothingness.

The surgeon looked tired but not alarmed. Which, given how often he peered into people's damaged brains, didn't necessarily mean there was nothing to be alarmed about.

"The clot's been removed, and the intracranial pressure relieved," Dr. Markham said.

"How is she?" Mackenzie asked.

"She's stable neurologically, her vital signs are now normal, and she's still recovering from the effects of the anesthesia," he said carefully.

"Is she conscious?" Eve asked.

"No."

"Will she ever be?" It was Zoe who asked what they were all afraid to.

"I can't really answer that question," Dr. Markham said.

"But you must have some idea of the odds,"

Mackenzie said. "Some sense of what's likely to happen."

After a brief hesitation Dr. Markham took pity on them. "There are, of course, no guarantees. But the fact that the injury was primarily localized to the right frontal and temporal lobes is a good sign."

They waited for more. It was Rex who finally asked, "How so?"

The surgeon hesitated again. Serena wondered if he was weighing the advisability of giving hope that he might be held accountable for. "It's possible to function normally even without the front part of your temporal lobe," Dr. Markham said. "So injuries there tend to be less . . . devastating." He smiled kindly at Zoe. "If you have to have a brain injury that's a 'better' place to have it."

Serena swallowed thickly but kept her mouth tightly closed. She would not be the one to bring up the worst-case scenario that hung over all of them — Emma living but never waking up.

The doctor nodded and turned to go.

"But . . . what do we do now?" Eve asked.

"We watch and wait," Dr. Markham said.

"For?" Serena and Eve asked simultaneously.

"Any changes. Or signs of change."

The doctor left. No one spoke until he'd disappeared down the hall.

"Well, I'm relieved the surgery went well."

Regan glanced down at her watch as she spoke. "Does anyone need a ride to the airport? My car's arrived." She reached for a Prada carryall. "I was supposed to report to set outside of Paris this morning. I've already kept everyone waiting a day."

All four Michaels looked at each other.

"I do have a preproduction meeting out on the West Coast tomorrow," Nash said. "I guess I'll take a ride."

"All right. I'm going to go touch up my makeup. We can make an announcement to the press out front on our way," Regan said.

"We'll make the announcement together." Rex straightened. "As a family." None of them seemed to be considering the irony that the family Emma had divorced would be speaking on her behalf. Rex looked to Eve. "Coming, darling?"

"You go ahead. I'll join you in just a moment."

Eve Michaels moved to Zoe after the rest of her family had left. "You're welcome to come with us, Zoe. We have an apartment at the Sherry-Netherland," she said, naming an iconic Fifth Avenue co-op, "and we have plenty of room."

Eve looked and sounded completely sincere, and the hug she gave Zoe appeared genuine. But when her grandmother released her, Zoe stepped back. "Thanks. That's really nice of you." She turned to Serena and Mackenzie. "But I want to . . . I mean, I can still stay with you guys, right?"

"Of course." Their assurances were automatic and virtually simultaneous. Eve made no comment, but her face registered what looked like real disappointment before she smiled and departed.

"Can we spend the night here?" Zoe asked when they were alone.

"Absolutely," Mackenzie said. "I'd feel better being here, too. Just in case."

"All right," Serena said. "But I'm starting to get hungry. How do you feel about a corned beef on rye? I can call the deli around the corner and see if they'll deliver."

"Sounds good," Mackenzie said. "I'm going to run down to the gift shop and pick up some playing cards. So we're not staring at the walls all night."

"Yeah," Serena said. "I think I've got a couple of the DVDs Ethan sent in my bag. Which is a good thing. Those walls are way too bare. If we're here much longer I'm going to be picking out wallpaper and paint. Do you think anyone would mind if I redecorated?"

She got the laugh she'd been angling for. But as she placed their dinner order, Serena couldn't help thinking how quickly the members of the Michaels family had dispersed. That the planes they'd had to catch and the scenes they were eager to steal seemed more important to them than Emma. Who was currently playing the most serious role of her life. A role Serena hoped would soon turn into a speaking part.

Mackenzie stared at the glow of her laptop screen in the darkened room. It was still blank except for the *Married Without Children* blog post heading "When disaster strikes," a post in which she'd intended to write about the freedom to be away from home for extended periods of time when emergency struck, the strength that came from knowing that your significant other, your partner, was there for you completely in ways a parent responsible for running the family in your absence might not be. But which now seemed little more than an admission that she could be gone as long as she liked because she had no life to go back to.

*That's not true. If Adam were at home you wouldn't feel this way.* But Adam wasn't home. And he definitely wasn't "there for her." Or possibly *there* at all.

It was four a.m. Beside her Zoe was folded around her pillow, her breathing even. A few seats away Serena snored lightly, having finally conked out after the third episode of *I Love Lucy* and her second box of Jujubes. Their things were once again strewn across the table, the floor, and pretty much every chair in the family lounge. She didn't know if things were slow at the hospital or if the word was out that this lounge was uninhabitable, but she was relieved that they once again had the space to themselves.

She'd wandered the halls on and off for hours, stopping periodically to check Emma for signs of improvement, but it was hard to see beyond the bandaged head and the frightening stillness of her face and body.

A check of email showed no response from Adam. Her phone showed no return text. She stared again at the cursor and the blog post title then carefully deleted it. This was not the time to write. Not when her thoughts and emotions were in such turmoil. Not when Emma was fighting for her life. Not when Adam seemed so absent.

Closing the laptop, she picked up her cell phone and headed back into the hall then downstairs to the lobby, which was empty and only semi-lit. A janitor moved down a nearby hall, buffing the floor, his head bobbing to whatever music played on his headphones.

It was one a.m. out in California. Adam could still be up.

She hit the speed-dial key for his number and sat in the darkened hospital listening to the phone ring. Once again there was no answer. No voice mail message. No Adam.

# TEN

Emma:

Eve is here. Cool. Contained. With lightning strikes of emotion. Her scent surrounds me. Pulls at me.

*You surprised her. You surprised them both.*

It's Gran's voice in my ear. But Eve takes my hand. Flesh on flesh. And in that instant I'm fourteen and entering a wood-paneled office in Los Angeles where I have to tell District Judge Horace Mann why I want to divorce my parents.

The office is large with one bookcase-lined wall and another covered in framed photos of the judge posing with famous actors and politicians. Through a bank of windows I can see the Hollywood sign in the distance. Judge Mann looks like he was called up from central casting: silver mane of hair, Roman nose, firm jaw. He is clearly impressed by Eve and Rex. But it's Gran he can't seem to take his eyes off. As I rub my sweaty palms down the sides of my skirt, I wonder if we will end up on his wall of fame.

We're offered seats at a small conference table — Gran and me on one side, Eve and Rex on the other. The judge sits at the head. I stare down at my hands, which are folded on the table's mahogany surface, but watch my mother through my lashes. She's careful not to appear impressed or cowed by Gran, but you never really know what Eve is thinking or feeling unless she wants you to. Right now she's letting me feel her anger, which simmers even closer to the surface than usual. I've learned to look for the warning signs. But I'm pretty sure she won't unleash it in front of the judge. Or Gran.

"I do hate to see such a fine family torn apart," the judge says as he opens my file. "I'd like to see us consider ways in which we might satisfy everyone." The man is clearly an optimist, but then he's never dealt with a Michaels. Or gotten in the way of something a Michaels might want. We didn't become famous simply because we can act. We're programmed to seek success in the same way salmon are programmed to swim upstream. My desire to walk away from a highly rated television series is an aberration my parents cannot condone. A serious flaw in my character. An indication of stupidity and/ or mental illness, which they are duty bound to snuff out.

The judge looks at Rex and Eve. It's my

114

mother who speaks.

"We are, of course, hurt and stunned by Emma's wish to divorce herself from our family." She is the ice queen. Cool. Clear. "We are prepared to allow Emma to stay at the lake with her grandmother for the summer as planned. But she must be back at the beginning of September when *Daddy's Girl* goes back into production." Eve says this calmly with no sign of the molten lava I can practically hear running through her veins.

The judge turns to me. "Emma?"

I shake my head, not yet able to find my voice. My bags are already packed, but I would fly to New York with Gran today even if I had to leave with just the clothes on my back. "No."

My mother looks surprised. This is the first time we've been in the same room since the papers were filed, yet for some reason she allowed herself to believe that I'd crumble as soon as they objected. My father just looks hurt.

I keep my hands folded so that they won't shake. Because I had a meeting with Gran and her attorney yesterday, and I know what's coming. Because the thing is, even though the judge is here, I can be emancipated only if my parents agree.

"Emma," the judge says kindly. "Please tell us why you've taken this step. Emancipation is not a small thing. There are other options.

You could simply live with your grandmother for a time. Or even with one of your siblings."

I swallow and sit up straighter in my chair. I don't know if he read all the paperwork I had to file or not. So I keep my eyes on him and tell him everything I wrote. How my parents are almost never home. How my brother and sister are older and don't want to have anything to do with me. That I don't go to school, but only get tutored on the set. That I don't have any friends. That I want desperately to quit the show but my parents, who are signees on my contract, won't let me. That I never get to use any of the money I've made. I go on and on even though I'm humiliated by how pathetic I sound. How pathetic I am. The tears I shed are real, although I could have produced them if I'd had to.

Finally I run out of words. My eyes go to my mother's face. Despite the scrim of tears, I can see that her jaw is clenched. Her cheeks are flushed. Her lips are pressed into a thin line. Her eyes are like shards of glass. "I cannot bear this ingratitude," she says slowly and distinctly. "I cannot believe we are required to listen to this ludicrous litany of complaints from this outrageously ungrateful child."

Rex places a cautionary hand on hers. If Eve shrugs him off and slaps me like I can see she wants to or spews any more venom, she will make my case for me.

116

"I don't see why we need to go to extremes here, kitten." Rex looks at me as if he really doesn't understand what the fuss is about. But then I don't think I cross his mind often enough for him to have any idea of how I feel or what I think. "If you really don't want to do the show anymore, I'm sure a compromise can be negotiated. You think you don't care now, but quitting this way is a huge mistake you're too young to understand. You'll forever be tainted with a reputation for unprofessionalism. It's nothing less than professional suicide. Maybe we agree to one more season during which you can be slowly written out. Or . . ."

"This is ridiculous," Eve interrupts. "I will never agree to 'emancipate' our child. The word itself is appalling and insulting. She has no appreciation for everything we've done for her. And no understanding whatsoever of how a Michaels is expected to behave. Regan and Nash were on camera even younger than Emma and were thrilled at the opportunity."

Gran silences her with a raised eyebrow. That's all it takes for everyone, including Eve, to be reminded that Eve is not a Michaels by birth. That she may have changed her eye and hair color and even some of her features, but only became a Michaels by marrying my father and managing to hold on to him.

"I will not allow my granddaughter to live this life a moment longer," Gran says.

"It's not up to you to allow or disallow anything." Eve's voice is sharp. Something that rarely happens around my grandmother and the public at large. "*You* are not her parent. We will never agree to this. Never."

The judge's eyes flicker with surprise. I don't know what he was expecting, but this is not it. "Emma," he says somewhat tentatively. "I'm sure the contractual obligations for the television show can be dealt with. But emancipation is a very serious thing. Severing a child from her parents, forcing her to for all intents and purposes become an adult, well, it's not to be undertaken or approved lightly."

I nod to show I understand, but I can't give in. Even if I didn't have to do the show, I'd still be living virtually by myself. With parents who drop in every once in a while. I look at Gran. She nods slightly. Telling me it's time to pull out what she refers to as "the ace up our sleeve." The one we've been hoping we wouldn't have to use.

I drop my gaze. Swallow. Then make myself begin. "It's just that . . ." I look first at my father and then at the judge. "It's just that ever since Uncle John moved into the guest-house . . ." I don't have to pretend reluctance. I don't want to hurt my dad any more than Gran wants to hurt her son. But we're pretty sure that Rex's lifestyle and his current living arrangement are the one thing that my parents will not want made public.

Eve gasps. My father's green eyes darken with shock. It's 1981, not that far from the free love seventies, but most moviegoers aren't ready to accept the idea that their favorite movie star would rather kiss another man than his leading lady. Or his movie star wife.

I'm hoping I'm not actually going to have to tell the judge that when my father is in town he and his current lover, John Clemente, live and sleep together in the casita just beyond the pool on the Hollywood Hills property.

"That's enough." Eve's eyes are as harsh as her voice. And even at fourteen I know that it's more than their livelihoods she's worried about. It's one thing to let your husband choose a man, actually a string of men, over you; it's another thing for people to know it. "Go live your own life, Emma. One day you'll know what you're throwing away. I have never understood you and I never will." This is the most sincere thing my mother has ever said to me.

As always my father's silence hurts more than my mother's words. I don't understand my father any more than my mother understands me, but I've always loved him anyway. And when he was there and paying attention, I believed he loved me. *Daddy's Girl* wasn't just the name of my television show to me.

I say nothing as Gran produces the paperwork her attorney has prepared. It spells out the two most important points of our agreement: That my parents agree to my legal emancipation. That none of us will ever discuss or reveal the reasons for our "divorce."

I hold my mother's gaze. My heart is about to explode, but I make sure my determination is clear. I need her to believe that I'm ready to go out and call a press conference if they refuse. I am a Michaels. Therefore I can act.

I don't say anything while my mother and father sign the papers. And I don't say goodbye when they stand and prepare to leave. The judge remains quiet as we depart. He doesn't ask any of us, not even Gran, to pose with him for a picture.

Two hours later Gran and I are on a flight to New York. Two days later we settle into the lake house for the summer. I'd like to say I never looked back, but that would be a lie.

"He actually tried to pretend like he wasn't sleeping with her." Serena looked into her psychiatrist's brown eyes. "He's left several messages trying to make me feel guilty for my behavior." She settled back in the padded chair, crossed her arms over her chest, one knee over the other.

"You can't choose men who are unavailable and who cheat and then think they'll behave in any other way." Dr. Grant settled his glasses on the bridge of his nose.

Serena reached for a Kleenex. Her eyes were completely dry, but she dabbed at them anyway. "Ethan sent me flowers. And funny videos. And Jujubes."

"That's because Ethan actually knows you. And apparently cares about you."

"He's a good friend."

"Who'd clearly like to be more." Dr. Grant leveled a probing gaze at her.

Serena shrugged. "He's not my type."

"Do you think you don't deserve a successful, funny, sincere, and talented man?"

"I didn't say that," Serena said.

"Didn't you?"

Serena bit back a sigh. "You realize you're starting to sound more like my mother than my shrink."

Dr. Grant didn't respond. Which just went to show Dr. Grant was nothing like her mother.

"I didn't come here to talk about Ethan," Serena said. "Or my mother."

"You apparently didn't come here to talk about your friend who's in a coma, either." He watched her carefully.

Just hearing the reference to Emma made Serena's eyes moisten. Dr. Grant's features swam briefly until she finally got herself under control.

"You've been talking for the past twenty-five minutes about all kinds of things that don't seem to actually matter to you. But it's your time and money," the psychiatrist said.

Serena sighed and reached for a tissue. "It's too awful to talk about. I can hardly stand to see Em like that. And Zoe . . ." She clutched the crumpled tissue between her fingers. "Oh, God. It's so awful."

"What does her doctor say?" Dr. Grant asked quietly.

"Not enough. They removed the blood clot two days ago. I don't know if her family being there caused it or if it would have happened anyway. We don't really know anything more than we did when she went in. And I can't bear the pressure. What if I make a wrong decision? What if Emma . . . what if she dies? I don't know how to make this better for Zoe. Neither Mackenzie nor I have children, and I don't have a clue how to handle her. Or the situation. Or . . . anything."

Tears seeped from her eyes and slid down her cheeks, hot and horrible. "I've never been responsible for anyone but myself. And my parents would tell you I'm not particularly great at that." She didn't bother to blot at the tears or even try to stop them. "I've never been so frightened. Or felt so helpless."

She added another tissue to the wad in her hand but didn't use it, either. "And you know what the worst thing is?" she cried. "My onetime best friend is lying there unconscious. And I'm sitting here crying about myself." She sobbed then. All the tears she'd been so careful not to shed over the last week pouring out of her.

Dr. Grant waited her out. He sat silent until the flow slowed and she began to sniff to a stop. But his concern, his empathy, his basic human kindness were apparent on his face. So was his knowledge of her.

"Your friend is lucky to have you there and so is her daughter," he said firmly. "You are smart and competent. And if anyone can keep a doctor and/or medical staff on its toes it's you and Georgia Goodbody. I happen to know this from personal experience."

She looked at the man who had heard her cry over countless men not worth his time or her tears. Cheaters and adulterers he'd once said she chose as a means of proving that the man who'd married someone else wasn't really worth having in the first place.

"Do you feel you need to consult other doctors?" he asked.

She shook her head. "No. It's just that there've been a lot of times in my life and career that I've consoled myself with the fact that whatever I was facing 'wasn't brain surgery.' But this actually is. Emma has had brain surgery. And I don't know which potential outcome is more frightening. That she'll die without ever waking up. That she'll live, but in some vegetative state. Or that she'll wake up, but be completely incapacitated." She added another tissue to the growing wad in her hand. "From what I understand, the longer a person stays in a coma the more likely it is that the damage will be significant."

Drained, she became aware of her tear-soaked blouse, her bone-deep exhaustion. She felt a hundred and suspected she looked twice that. For once she didn't care.

"From what I can see, your friend chose well," Dr. Grant said. "It's clear that you care greatly about her and her daughter." He smiled gently. "This is an incredibly tough situation, but as long as you're listening to the doctors and carefully considering the options, you're doing the best anyone can do under these circumstances." The psychiatrist paused, waiting for what he'd said to sink in. "There is also another potential outcome you seem to have left off the list," Dr. Grant said.

Serena looked at him dully. Her own brain was numb. Unable to imagine getting up, going back to the hospital, let alone imagining another scenario.

The psychiatrist reached for and held up the trashcan, watched as she dropped the wad of unused tissues into it. "Emma could simply wake up," he said softly. "She could open her eyes and rejoin the world."

She blinked at him, noticing that even her lashes were damp.

"If you're going to expend time and energy imagining scenarios, you really need to allow for the positive. No one who's spent any time studying the brain or personal behavior would ever turn their back on the possibility of a miracle."

# ELEVEN

The lobby of Merritt Publishing was large and lavish with polished marble floors and equally elegant walls that had been fitted with niches, each of which held an artfully lit book.

Mackenzie crossed the expansive, heavily air-conditioned space and headed toward the burled wood reception desk, careful to keep her chin up, her stride purposeful, and her shoulders unhunched. The dress she wore was one of her own creations, a sleeveless knee-length wrap in abstract blocks of navy and white. She was cleared and directed to a bank of elevators. On the fifth floor a young woman waited. "Ms. Russell? I'm Cathy Hughes's assistant. Will you follow me?"

The assistant unlocked a door and as they passed through it Mackenzie wondered if the security was meant to keep aspiring writers out or the employees in. The carpeted hallway led past windowed offices on the right. A warren of cubicles filled the interior space to the left. She'd almost canceled the meeting, which had been scheduled for the day after their intended return from the lake and just hours before her flight home. But Serena had insisted that she come.

"How many people are asked to write a book?" Serena had demanded.

Mackenzie had no idea. "It just feels strange to go on a business appointment when Em is . . . well, you know." She felt more than strange. She felt guilty. That her life would not only go on but be filled with an incredible new opportunity while Emma's had shrunk to nothingness.

"We can't all sit with her at the same time anyway," Serena had reasoned. "And both Dr. Markham and Brennan have confirmed that she's stable. You should keep your appointment. Ethan asked me to come in and record this afternoon. And I thought I'd take Zoe with me — to get her out for a bit. So as long as you're back by two we're good."

"You promise you'll call me if anything . . . changes."

"Promise."

And so here she was, being shown into a large corner office with windows overlooking the bustle below on Hudson Street and introduced to Cathy Hughes, a petite, thirty-something brunette with bright blue eyes set in a heart-shaped face.

"Come. Have a seat." The editor ushered Mackenzie to a sofa. She herself sat on a brightly upholstered club chair.

Her assistant hovered in the doorway. "Would you like a cup of coffee? A Danish?"

"No, thanks. I'm fine." Mackenzie smoothed her dress over her knees and folded her hands in her lap as the assistant departed.

The editor leaned forward. "I absolutely love your blog. It's so upbeat. You know, so forthright. There are a lot of people who don't feel the need to reproduce."

"And many who can't," Mackenzie added.

"Right." The editor smiled. "Honestly, I think it's fabulous that you and your husband have not only been married for so long, but that your marriage is so successful. It's not like you're just limping along after being unable to have children."

"No. I mean yes. We wanted children. But not having them doesn't have to sound the death knell for a marriage." She felt a shimmer of unease as she considered how out of touch she and Adam had been over the last week and tried to shrug it off. Their fractured communication was not a reflection of their marriage but of their current circumstances. Being on opposite sides of the country and dealing with a three-hour time difference didn't help. But then neither did his weeklong euphoria over the possible option on his screenplay. Even in the face of Emma's situation. She smoothed her dress again.

She and Adam were not "limping along."

Their days were full, the pace of their life frenetic. Between the theater and his screen-writing, they often fell into bed at night too exhausted to talk let alone make love. This was not unusual for long-married couples whether they had children or not.

She looked up to see Cathy eyeing her shrewdly.

"Originally, I thought the book might begin with your own story, move into the standout blog posts with insights as to what had happened and what you were thinking when you wrote them, and then wrap up with advice for other couples," the editor said.

"I've always been careful not to set myself up as some sort of expert. You know, my degree is in fashion design, not psychology or social work. I just share my own experiences."

"Yes." Cathy pondered for a moment. "Which is why I've been thinking more recently that we should keep things as simple as possible." She leaned forward. Her tone turned conspiratorial. "Especially since I know you must have a lot on your mind at the moment."

"I'm sorry?"

"I was afraid you might cancel after I saw that story on *Entertainment Tonight* about Emma Michaels being in a coma over at Mount Sinai. You were identified as a close personal friend."

Mackenzie stiffened, her eyes on Cathy

Hughes's face.

"Anyway," she continued breezily. "I'm thinking that if we go with a compilation of the 'best of' blog posts, we could streamline the editorial process and publish more quickly. Which would allow us to tap into your, um, personal platform . . ." Her voice trailed off as she seemed to notice the horror Mackenzie felt, spread across her face. ". . . um, whatever happens."

Somehow Mackenzie managed to get up and out of there without telling Cathy Hughes exactly where she could shove her book idea.

Then, not yet ready to face the hospital, she wandered back toward the Village, ultimately carrying a sandwich she couldn't bring herself to eat, to a bench near the arch at Washington Square. There, as she watched New Yorkers of all shapes and sizes whirl by, she remembered just how alive the city had always made her feel. Who she'd been and all that she'd imagined in those heady years that she'd lived there.

She'd been the one to press Adam to move to Noblesville. To be near their parents and a slower, more family-friendly lifestyle, when she'd thought they'd be raising a child together. Back when she'd imagined her pregnancy was just the first of many. And not a lone bargaining chip that had won her only part of what she'd wanted.

She pulled out her cell phone, called Adam,

and was almost shocked when he answered on the second ring.

"Hi," he said. "How was the publishing thing?"

She had to remind herself that misery did not in fact improve with company. "Unclear. I'm not sure it's something I want to do."

His hand muffled the phone and she heard him say something to someone else, so she left it at that. Before she'd thought it out she said, "Why don't you come to New York?"

There was a silence she felt compelled to fill. "She was your friend, too." Mackenzie winced at the "was." As if Emma were already gone.

Another silence.

"I, um, think I'd rather wait until she wakes up," he finally said. "I mean, if I came now she wouldn't even know I was there, right?"

"We don't actually know what she does and doesn't know," Mackenzie said, determined not to beg him to come. How many times had he shied away from anything unpleasant? Her miscarriages. Problems at the theater. Their parents' frailty and the illnesses that had ultimately taken them within just a few years of each other.

"When do you think you'll be back in Noblesville?" he asked, as if the hospital might have handed out some sort of schedule — a date when Emma would wake up, when she'd be able to leave the hospital, when she might shoot her next film.

"I don't know," she countered. "When are you flying home?" As she said the word, she realized how rarely she'd heard Adam refer to the city they lived in as "home." Even though he'd grown up just a few towns away.

"I thought I'd stay on out here," he said. "I mean, there's no reason to rush back if you're not going to be there, is there?"

"No," she said, because what he said made sense. The theater was dark for the summer and she wanted to be with Emma for as long as possible after she woke up. She would not allow herself to consider the alternative. "No. I guess not."

"Good." She hated the note of relief in his voice almost as much as she hated the reasonable tone he was using to try to disguise it. "Because Matthew said I can stay in the pool house and get started on these rewrites. The sooner they're done, the sooner we can maybe strike a deal."

It was time to get off the phone before she said something she'd regret. "Okay, then." She stood and threw the uneaten sandwich in the trashcan. "Good luck with everything."

"You too," he said. "And give Em a hug from me."

Zoe Hardgrove and Ethan Miller fell in "like" at first sight. Fraught with excitement, Zoe gushed her admiration for Ethan and his work all the way to the studio. The gushing continued through Serena's introductions and an energetic handshake.

"I was so sorry to hear about your mother," Ethan said when Zoe finally let go of his hand. "I met her when she did the show. And I know she and Serena go way back."

"Yeah, they knew each other even before I was born." Zoe's tone made it clear that might have been a couple millennia ago.

"Well, I hope she'll be better soon enough for all of you to get to the lake." He said this as if Emma's recovery were a foregone conclusion. Serena could have kissed him for the way Zoe brightened.

"Do you mind if Zoe comes in with me while I record? Or would you rather she be in the control room?" Serena asked.

"Why don't we let her come in the control room and listen with me?" Ethan suggested. He paused and turned to Zoe. "Actually, I'm looking for a teenage girl to do a brief cameo on an upcoming episode. Have you ever done any acting?"

Zoe's smile widened. "I've been in a few things. I was offered the lead in *Teen Scream.*" A shadow passed over her face. "But I, um, had to pass."

"The girl is a Michaels," Serena said. "And her father's no slouch in the acting department, either." Serena felt the oddest glow of maternal pride. "And I *am* one of her fairy godmothers."

"All right," Ethan said. "I'll have someone pull the copy for you to look over, Zoe. You can take a stab at it when we're done with Georgia here."

"Cool!" Zoe's smile split her face, the first Serena had seen since the accident. *Thank you,* she mouthed to Ethan when Zoe had turned her back to step up into the control room.

"My pleasure." He gave her a wink, then took her arm to escort her into the studio and up to the microphone.

"Madame." He bowed with an exaggerated hand gesture.

"Monsieur." She curtsied and nodded regally.

"Just so you know. There's a lot of eye rolling going on in here!" The disembodied voice of Charlie Couver, the audio engineer, boomed into the studio. Zoe's giggle sounded briefly. It was one of the sweetest sounds Serena had ever heard.

As she did a voice check and watched the video cue up, Serena felt like a testament to the medicinal properties of laughter. A little silliness could go a long way.

She was still smiling almost an hour later as she and Zoe entered the reception area on the way out.

"Serena?" Catherine Stengel held up a pink message slip.

Serena walked over to the desk to retrieve the piece of paper. It took a moment to absorb the name scrawled across the top. "When did this come in?"

Catherine took the slip back and looked closely. "Yesterday afternoon." She studied Serena's face. "Are you all right?"

"Of course." Unable to look at the name again, she folded the slip of paper into a tiny square and shoved it deep into her purse. But as she and Zoe left and caught a cab back to the hospital, she couldn't shove the remembered hurt away as easily. The last time she'd heard from Brooks Anderson had been almost twenty-five years ago. And he'd been calling to tell her he'd decided to stay in Charleston. Where he planned to marry someone else.

# TWELVE

"Are you all right?" Serena asked Mackenzie.

"I was about to ask you the same thing." The last thing Mackenzie felt like doing was talking about Adam. Or her marriage.

They'd left Zoe sitting with Emma and exited the hospital in search of fresh air. In order to avoid the ever-present crowd of photographers, they'd slipped out through a little-used employee entrance that emptied onto a covered walkway that ended several blocks away. They crossed Fifth and entered Central Park, where they claimed an empty bench overlooking a section of the Conservatory Garden.

They sat in silence for a time, watching the passersby.

"So how'd the meeting at the publishing house go?" Serena asked.

Mackenzie shrugged, not eager to admit that she was afraid the editor might be more interested in her friendship with Emma than her writing talents or her audience. The truth was that although she, Serena, and Emma had had a tight and mostly harmonious friendship, it was their individual friendships with Emma that had originally brought them together. Emma was the glue that had bound them.

"Zoe was really excited about meeting Ethan Miller," Mackenzie said now in an effort to turn the conversation.

"Yeah, they formed a mutual-admiration society on the spot. It was kind of cute," Serena said.

"She said she's going to get to voice a character?" Mackenzie asked.

"Yes. He had her read a scene with me and she nailed it on the first take." Serena's smile was sad. "I almost cried thinking how proud Em would have been of her." She swallowed. "And how much I hope Emma wakes up to give her permission."

They fell into a mostly comfortable silence. A warm breeze rustled the leafy branches of the oak tree they sat beneath. Two joggers passed, their breathing heavy but even.

"Eve came to the hospital while you were gone," Mackenzie said, pulling a pack of gum from her purse and offering it to Serena.

"What's up with that?" Serena took the gum and unwrapped it.

"I don't know," Mackenzie said. "She seemed disappointed that Zoe wasn't there, though they don't seem to have a relationship of any kind. She sat with Emma for an hour or so. I have no idea what she's trying to accomplish."

Birds chirped. Bees buzzed around a nearby bed of flowers. The sounds of traffic on Fifth Avenue were there, but muted. Now if only she could relax.

"I've always just kind of automatically hated her on Emma's behalf. But I don't know. Maybe the threat of Emma's death is finally sinking in. Maybe she wants to apologize or something." Mackenzie swallowed. "You know, before it's too late." Even after they'd discovered that their friend Amelia Maclaine was actually Emma Michaels, Emma had kept the details about her relationship with her mother largely to herself. It had taken years of friendship before she'd begun to talk about her family and why she'd divorced her parents. Her grandmother, the awe-inducing Grace Michaels, whom they met shortly after Emma's true identity had been revealed, had been far less hesitant to speak out against the woman who had married her son.

"It's so peaceful here," Serena said. "I hate that the day's so beautiful and everyone's just going around enjoying it when Emma's lying there like a . . ." Her voice trailed off.

"I know," Mackenzie agreed. She felt guilty even being there with the breeze rifling her hair and the sun warm on her shoulders. "It's supposed to be reassuring that life goes on

138

no matter what. But it just feels wrong."

They sat in silence after that, lost in their own thoughts. A text dinged in. Both of them sat up. Looked down at their phones.

Zoe's text read, *It's Mom. Hurry!*

They arrived at the neuro ICU frightened and out of breath and found Zoe standing outside of Emma's room, her hand to her chest, watching Dr. Brennan through the glass with Emma.

"What is it?" Serena huffed. "What happened?"

Too frightened to speak, Mackenzie reached for Zoe's hand and gave it a squeeze almost as much to stop hers from shaking as to offer comfort.

"She moved," Zoe said.

"What?" Mackenzie found her voice.

"At first I just thought I saw something move out of the corner of my eye," Zoe said in a rush. "So then I started watching really carefully. I mean, I barely blinked for like twenty minutes. And then I saw her arm move."

"Are you sure?" Mackenzie knew what it was like to sit there staring and wishing for something positive. Some sign of . . . anything.

They stood with their shoulders touching, their noses pressed to the glass watching the doctor examine Emma, check the readouts, scribble on her chart. They were barely breathing when he finally came out to speak to them.

"What's happening?" Serena asked. "Is she waking up?"

Mackenzie could hear the same excitement she felt, and was afraid to give in to, in Serena's voice. The raw hope on Zoe's face was difficult to look at.

"There were signs of neurological lightening in the recovery room after her surgery," Dr. Brennan said. "Things are looking promising. Intracranial pressure has remained normal and her gasses look good, so we can decrease ventilation and start weaning to room air."

"Does this mean she's going to wake up soon?" Zoe asked.

"I really can't say." The doctor dropped his gaze to Emma's chart.

"We're not asking for a guaranteed wake-up time," Serena said, clearly frustrated. "But these are good signs, right?"

Dr. Brennan looked up. "Yes. There are a number of positive indicators. But a return to consciousness is typically gradual. More like a child waking up from a nap. And not at all like the movies where someone opens their eyes and jumps out of bed."

"But she is improving." Zoe's eyes were locked with Dr. Brennan's. Her hand gripped Mackenzie's painfully.

"I believe we have reason to be cautiously

optimistic," he finally said, cautiously yet optimistically. "But we're not out of the woods yet."

As he left, all three of them turned their eyes on Emma. Who was still hooked up to a sea of machines and monitors. Her eyes were tightly closed. Her body still. From the outside she didn't look any different at all. But Mackenzie prayed there was more going on than met the eye. That Emma's internal alarm clock was ringing and that soon she'd wake up and turn it off.

Afraid to leave lest they miss Emma waking up and asking what the hell was going on, they sat up all night at the hospital waiting for another sign.

During Serena's turns at Emma's side as well as those in the family lounge's molded — though not necessarily to her — plastic chairs, every moment not spent silently urging Emma to wake the hell up were filled with thoughts and memories of Brooks Anderson. She wallowed with an intensity she hadn't allowed herself since the night before his wedding to another Charleston debutante, when she'd drunk dialed him and got out only half of the names she'd intended to call him before breaking down and crying piteously instead.

He'd remained silent while she bawled. When her sobs had petered out, he'd said only, "I'm sorry. But I have to go." And she'd had no idea if he was apologizing for choosing Diana Ravenel after he'd already chosen her. Or simply for having to hang up.

News of Brooks's meteoric rise in his father-in-law's brokerage firm had arrived in regular letters on her mother's scented hand-engraved stationery and later via her mother's email account, mintjulep@aol.com. After viewing a two-page spread of Mr. and Mrs. Brooks Anderson II arriving at St. Michaels for the baptism of their second child, Serena had canceled her subscriptions to *Charleston Magazine* and the *Charleston Post and Courier*, whose society column followed them with fervent attention. By then Serena had begun dating the first in a long line of married men who were neither southern nor gentlemen.

Serena was dozing beside Emma's bed the next morning when Eve Michaels arrived. It was clear someone had already told her the news.

"Has there been further movement?" she asked by way of greeting. "Has Emma opened her eyes at all?"

Serena looked at Emma's mother through bleary, sleep-deprived eyes. Eve was immaculately dressed and made up. Her shoulder-length auburn hair appeared freshly styled.

"No."

Eve appeared to be waiting for more, but

Serena didn't have the energy or the inclination to give it to her. Mackenzie and Zoe returned from the cafeteria bearing a Starbucks coffee for Serena. She took it gratefully.

"You all look exhausted," Eve said. "I have the day free. I'd be glad to sit with Emma if you'd like to go home and get some sleep."

They all stared suspiciously at her. Part of Serena wanted nothing more than to go home and be "one" with her own bed for a few hours; the other part hated the idea of Emma waking up and finding Eve sitting next to her instead of them.

"I think I'll go powder my nose," Eve said with a sad smile. "Feel free to put it to a vote."

As soon as she'd left the room, they huddled together. "What if Emma wakes up and *she's* here instead of us?" Zoe whispered, voicing Serena's concern.

"That would be kind of a good problem, wouldn't it?" Mackenzie said. "I mean the waking up part."

"But she might think we abandoned her," Zoe said, her eyes filling with tears. No matter how many times they discussed it, the girl still felt responsible for her mother's accident. "Especially since she probably doesn't even know we're here when we're here."

"I have to believe she knows." Mackenzie, who always seemed to know the right thing to say to Zoe, squeezed her hand. "And I

143

guess I want to believe that Eve's here out of love. Or some kind of good intention."

Serena would have liked to believe in Santa Claus, the Easter Bunny, and honorable, monogamous men, but experience had taught her otherwise. "The truth is," Serena said reluctantly, "we could all do with a few hours of sleep."

After extracting assurances from Eve that she'd call or text immediately if anything changed, they took a cab back to Serena's and dragged themselves up the brownstone's steps. Stifling yawns, Zoe and Mackenzie headed upstairs while Serena puttered around the kitchen and poured herself a Scotch on the rocks. She was headed toward the stairs when the doorbell rang.

"Sign here, please." The driver handed her the FedEx envelope, collected her signature, and departed. The letter and attached documents came from Emma's attorneys in Los Angeles. Dropping into the nearest chair, she took a long sip of her drink and began to read the paperwork.

"Jesus." She took another, longer sip as she tried to absorb what she was reading. For some reason she could not fathom, Emma had named her Zoe's legal guardian. The person who would raise her daughter in the event of Emma's death or incapacitation.

The document was dated shortly after Emma's divorce from Calvin Hardgrove.

Which made absolutely no sense at all; she'd never heard of a divorce ending a father's rights or responsibilities. Surprised to find her drink gone, she carried the empty glass into the kitchen and placed it in the sink, still trying to understand Emma's motives. Because even if there was a good reason not to leave Zoe in her father's care, Mackenzie and Adam would have been a far more logical choice. Providing a stable, child-friendly two-parent home that Serena could never duplicate.

The attorney's letter had indicated that this was the latest guardianship document on file. They might never know what changes Emma would have made if she had been able to make it to her attorney's office as planned after the retreat.

Too tired to puzzle it out, she stuffed the paperwork and the problem into her carryall just as she had Brooks Anderson's phone number. Neither of these things was a "sign" of any kind. She had no intention of speaking to a man who'd tossed her aside so easily a lifetime ago. Nor did she intend to ponder why Em would have named her Zoe's guardian. She had no doubt this was a simple mistake or oversight. One that could be rectified as soon as Emma woke up.

# THIRTEEN

Two days passed and every so often, for no discernible reason and without warning, Emma moved something else. Her hand. A leg. One shoulder. Mackenzie felt a flickering of hope each time.

Zoe gasped with excitement when Emma's eyes fluttered open. But no matter how carefully they watched her afterward, she didn't open them again. A day later Mackenzie saw Emma turn her head in the direction of a sound. The restless twitching continued, but it was agonizingly sporadic. It was a bit like watching a glacier melt; you had reason to believe that one day it would be nothing but liquid, but not necessarily in your lifetime.

Still, Emma continued to improve. The ventilator had been turned down and the "weaning to room air" was well under way. The arrival of the physical therapists, who'd been moving Emma's limbs on a regular schedule since her injury, now seemed a good harbinger and not an exercise in futility.

Drs. Brennan and Markham confirmed that Emma was "lightening up" neurologically, but while the signs were encouraging, Emma remained absent.

Eve Michaels did not become warmer or fuzzier. But she didn't stop coming, either. She and Rex arrived daily at one p.m. so that Mackenzie, Serena, and Zoe could go to lunch, then left when they returned. Rex's face always looked strained while Eve's was oddly serene, though it might have been the Botox. Mackenzie didn't know whether they came out of love or for appearances, but their arrival and departure became an expected part of each day.

It was late afternoon. Zoe had gone down to the gift shop for a pack of gum. Mackenzie and Serena sat in Emma's room. Hyperalert, they kept their eyes trained on Emma, waiting for something more to happen. More movement. More awareness. More Emma.

"We just have to stay positive," Mackenzie insisted.

"I am," Serena said. "I'm positive I need something definitive to happen."

"I know." Mackenzie's eyes stung from staring so hard and the effort not to blink.

"I had this dream last night that we went on a quest. Into a fairy tale. We were searching for a prince to come and kiss Emma awake."

Serena took her eyes off Emma long enough

to shoot Mackenzie an incredulous look. "Did we find one? I mean, I have doubts that they even exist in fairy tales anymore."

"Yes, well, dreams aren't always filled with logic." Mackenzie's had been filled with bizarre images she'd rather forget.

"Hey. Maybe we should rent a prince charming for the day. You know, get one of those services to send one over. Maybe Emma's subconscious or whatever's at work at the moment would react to a little theater. Or maybe you could get Adam to do it. I mean, he definitely looked the part when he dressed up for that Halloween party. He may be the only man I've ever met who actually looks good in tights."

Mackenzie flushed. Adam had the golden locks and build of a fairy-tale prince, but he hadn't been behaving in a particularly prince-like manner. "If I thought it would help I'd put him on a white horse and let him ride into the neuro ICU," she said. "But I'm not sure kissing someone else's husband is ever a good idea. Not even in the fairy-tale world." Her tone came out more brittle than she'd intended.

"Wow," Serena said. "Where did that come from? And when did you turn into such a prude? I think you've been living in the hinterlands for too long."

Mackenzie snorted. "I don't think wives in New York or LA appreciate sharing their

148

husbands any more than the ones in the Midwest do. It isn't about geography."

"What is it about, then? This conversation, I mean." Serena's voice had risen. "Because at the moment it's not feeling about Emma at all."

Mackenzie had no answer. Or excuse. Except that her nerves were stretched so tight she could practically feel them quivering. Still, she hadn't meant to lash out like that. Serena's attraction to other women's husbands wasn't something new. And while she'd never particularly approved of it, she'd never taken it quite so personally before. "Sorry. I seem to be overreacting about a lot of things," Mackenzie said. "Your personal life, fairy tale or otherwise, really isn't my business." Besides, it wasn't like adultery was contagious or anything. She had no reason to doubt Adam's fidelity, not even with this protracted separation or how hard he'd suddenly become to reach.

She was lost in thought, reassuring herself that Adam's excitement over what was happening for him in California was no reflection on her or the state of their relationship, when the first monitor alarm went off. Her eyes swung to Emma as the door burst open and white-coated people rushed into the room.

Emma:

I hear angry voices. A bell. I'm hot. Covered in coals. The darkness begins to blur around the edges with white. The sounds fade away.

Suddenly I'm standing in the closet of my Malibu beach house. Staring stupidly at the motorized racks of clothing and the shelves of designer "fuck me" heels that are lit and showcased more lavishly than the *Mona Lisa* at the Louvre.

My closet is the Taj Mahal of storage, a decadently unnecessary example of conspicuous consumption. Yet there is not one item in this two-thousand-square-foot testament to vanity that is designed for a pregnant woman.

I stand in the epicenter of this ridiculous closet crying great big tears of panic and self-pity. I'm in the middle of shooting a movie that does not require the extra padding I'm now carrying. My makeup person has taken to tutting over the breakouts on my face and has raised more than one overplucked eyebrow at the chubbiness of my cheeks, which have never been as chiseled as the rest of my family's and now look like a squirrel unwilling to let go of a cache of acorns.

Even I don't understand how this has happened. I've been in a dry spell to end all dry spells, a sexual desert without a sign of an oasis, even if *People* magazine remains convinced I'm having an affair with my costar. Which would be funny if it weren't so

150

improbable. Calvin Hardgrove is perhaps the gayest leading man since Rock Hudson. Or my father.

I drop onto the settee and don't even care when my tears start to soak the turquoise silk upholstery. If my name were Mary I'd be tempted to claim immaculate conception. I've had sex exactly once in the last six months. And that was an accident, the result of one too many shots of tequila, that I've tried like hell to erase from my memory for all kinds of reasons.

By the time I realized I was pregnant, I was too far along to terminate, not that I think I could have. Now I'm too far along to hide my pregnancy. I come from a long line of inept mothers in both sides of my DNA. Even Gran, who saved me completely and whom I love more than anyone, admits she didn't do such a great job with her only child. I know she loves me, but I also think she sees me as her chance to make amends. Maybe I can learn from my grandmother's mistakes and get it right the first time.

I catch a glimpse of myself in the full-length mirror and can barely believe the tear-streaked, red-faced, puffy woman staring back is me. I've always been too short, too round, too far from pretty, but now I'm downright ugly. And not just on the outside.

I had sex with someone I had no right to. And now I'm having a baby that shouldn't belong to me. I am lower than pond scum.

I sit and cry for so long I feel dizzy. My sobs echo in the cavernous closet reminding me just how alone I am. I can't call the people I most want to talk to. There are secrets and then there are secrets. There are worse things than being pregnant and alone.

"Her temperature's spiking. I've got 102. Increase the Tylenol. Bring the cooling blanket."

Serena, Mackenzie, and Zoe watched helplessly as the medical people crowded around Emma.

"We've got to bring it down. I want a blood culture stat." The doctors came and went. Hematologists. Pulmonologists. Infectious disease specialists.

"She's septic. Let's start the broad spectrum antibiotic while we wait for the lab results."

Their voices remained calm and professional but there was no mistaking their urgency. Emma had moved from "lightening up" to frighteningly feverish so quickly it was hard to absorb. It didn't take a medical degree to see how rapidly she was deteriorating.

"But how could this happen?" Eve had arrived as they were ushered out of Emma's room.

"Dr. Brennan says that the spots where

tubes and lines perforate the skin are always vulnerable to infection," Mackenzie repeated what they'd been told. "They're trying to identify the source and strain of the infection now."

"Good God." Eve's whisper reflected the fear they all felt.

Unable to speak, barely able to breathe, the four of them stood outside the room, watching through the glass as the medical team worked to control the infection now threatening Emma's life.

I burn then shiver. Fire. Then ice. My body's temperature gauge is broken.

I don't know what's happening but whatever it is, it's different. The darkness is gone and I can see as well as hear. In fact, I'm floating above my body like you see in movies and hear about in near-death experiences. I look around for the tunnel of white light.

*Gran?*

*I'm here.*

Panic wells inside me. I haven't taken care of things. Haven't explained. Haven't apologized. I watch the medical staff move around my body. Touching. Adjusting. Assessing.

Mackenzie and Serena are pressed against the glass. The first friends I ever had. The only ones who loved me for me. I was wrong to do what I did. But I was also wrong to push them away.

*Am I dead?*

*No.* Gran's voice is adamant, but worried.

Zoe's beautiful face is white with fear. Her eyes glitter with tears. Her teeth clench her lips. I feel how hard she's trying not to cry.

Eve's standing next to her watching me closely. Her face registers sorrow, pain, regret. But I'm not buying it. I didn't interest her when I was alive. Why would she be interested in me now that I'm dying? *She can't have Zoe, Gran. Not now. Not ever.*

*No one can have your daughter if you stay.*

Zoe's tears stab at me. I feel their pinpricks.

*Stay? As if I have a choice. Come or go. Leave or stay.*

*You can choose.*

"We're losing her. Get me . . ."

I can't listen to the people working so feverishly on my body. I can't bear to look at Zoe. I don't want to hear Gran's voice anymore. I don't have the strength for any of this.

*You can and you do.* Gran's voice resounds in my head. *You must. You have a life waiting for you.*

A *life?* If I had the strength, I would laugh. My life doesn't feel like anything worth fighting for. The weariness seeps into me; whatever is tethering me to my body stretches tighter. If it breaks will I float away?

*Your life doesn't belong only to you. Your daughter needs you.*

I watch Zoe's tears slide down her cheeks. See Eve's arm slip around her shoulders. My daughter doesn't shrug it off.

*Now, darling.* Gran's voice is gentle but insistent. *If you're going to stay you must make it happen now.*

*But I don't know how.* Fresh panic assails me as the darkness once again descends.

The last voice I hear is my grandmother's. *Yes, darling. Yes you do.*

# FOURTEEN

In her dream Emma had apparently turned into a fish, because she was underwater and somehow breathing. She swam easily through the lake's cool depths, skimming over sandy bottoms, and slipping through its undulating plant life. When she tired of this, she began to make her way toward the crystal clear surface that sparkled with diamonds of what her small fish brain recognized as sunlight. Somehow she also knew that when she broke the surface, she'd be in the rock-edged cove near the cottage boathouse. But when she came up and opened her eyes, which were no longer walleyed but centered in her non-fish face, Zoe, Mackenzie, and Serena were peering down at her as if she were not a person or even a fish, but some fascinating specimen pinned down beneath a microscope.

"What?" Her vision was slightly blurred and her throat hurt when she tried to speak, her voice coming out in an almost unrecognizable croak. "Why . . ." She swallowed painfully and tried to focus. "Why are you look-ing at me like that?" No longer weightless, her body ached. Her eyelids seemed to weigh a couple of tons each. Her head pounded painfully.

"No. Please. Don't close your eyes!" Zoe's panicked voice halted her eyelids' descent, but it took some serious effort to open them back up. She stared up into her daughter's face, which was stretched into a mask of panic that matched her voice. Her hair stood on end. Dark circles rimmed her eyes. Her cheeks were streaked with mascara and the residue of tears. "Why do you" — she swal-lowed again, forced the words out — "look like that?"

She shifted her focus to include Serena and Mackenzie. "You all look like," — swallow — "like shit."

The three of them grinned. As if she'd complimented them. "I must have said that wrong."

They laughed. Serena and Mackenzie high-fived. Emma studied their faces and what she could see of the room, looking for some clue to where they were and why she was the only one lying down. "We need to check out im-mediately." She swallowed again. What the hell had happened to her throat? "This hotel looks worse than you do."

She was funnier than she'd thought and way funnier than she felt, because they laughed again.

"We're just so relieved," Mackenzie said, holding a glass of water to her lips.

"Thank God you're back," Serena added.

Zoe just nodded and swiped at her tears.

"Back?" She wanted to reach out to Zoe but her limbs weighed a hundred times as much as her eyelids, which still wanted to close. There were tubes running out of her. Machines all around her. "Where did I go? Why" — she swallowed again — "am I attached to this stuff?"

"We were kind of hoping you could tell us that," Mackenzie said.

Although she knew who she was and who they were and they were clearly in a hospital, she had no idea how she'd gotten there.

"You've been in a coma since the accident twelve days ago."

"Accident?" She tried to remember, tried to concentrate on something besides their faces and voices, but there was nothing there. No memories to reel in. "I was in . . . accident?"

Zoe nodded solemnly. Fresh tears ran down her cheeks.

"You don't remember?" Mackenzie asked.

"No." The croak was one of fear. How could she not know this? How could she possibly have lost twelve days and have no memory of it at all?

"What's the last thing you do remember?"

Serena asked.

She tried to think, to focus. But her thoughts moved as slowly as molasses and were just as murky. Fish dreams from the bottom of Lake George. Gran. The judge's study. Her closet. *Eve.* "Were Eve and Rex here?"

Serena nodded. "The whole Michaels clan showed up. But Eve has been here almost every day."

This made no sense. But neither did anything else.

She tried to stay tuned-in as they talked. Wanted to understand what had happened. But her eyes were so heavy. Her body so tired. The words blurred to a background hum. Her eyelids began to close.

"Mom?"

She was surprised to hear Zoe, who'd referred to her by her first name since the age of ten, call her *Mom.* But she liked it. "Hmmmm?" Emma managed, trying to hold off the threads of sleep that pulled at her.

"You're only allowed to go to sleep if you promise to wake up again."

Emma's eyelids were too heavy to open, but she had no intention of going anywhere. "Promise," she murmured, already half asleep. A moment later she was swimming again. Her fish lips turned up in a smile.

The next time Emma opened her eyes, two doctors were leaning over her. One of them was tall and slim with an attractive blend of Caucasian and Asian features, the other white haired and blue eyed with a military bearing. She didn't think she'd ever seen either of them before, but their voices were instantly familiar.

"Ms. Michaels," the younger, taller one said. "I'm Dr. Brennan. Head of Neurocritical Intensive Care here at Mount Sinai. We're very glad to have you back." His eyes crinkled at the corners when he smiled.

"And I'm Dr. Markham, your neurosurgeon," the other doctor said crisply. His blue eyes were sharp, his attention laser focused as if he were trying to see inside her head.

"Dr. Markham has been in charge," Brennan said. "He removed the blood clot that threatened earlier on and supervised the team fighting your recent infection."

"Blood clot?" Her throat was still sore, her voice rusty. "Infection?" The hits just kept on coming. She was stunned that so much could have happened to her without her knowledge. Next thing they'd tell her she'd been speaking in some long-dead language she'd never heard of, or exhibiting some other talent she shouldn't possess. "But I don't remember how I got here. I don't know what . . ." Her voice trailed off. She didn't even know what she didn't know. And wasn't sure she wanted to. Having such a huge hole in her memory made her feel dizzy and nauseated with anxiety.

"We know it's disconcerting to discover things you have no memory of," Dr. Markham said. "But it's quite common in your situation. The vast majority of coma patients who regain consciousness have large gaps that typically begin slightly before the traumatic brain injury occurred."

Her *brain* had been traumatically injured. "Why am I so tired if I've just been lying here?" she asked, unable to ask what she really wanted to know.

"You came in here pretty beat up," Dr. Brennan said. "Your brain and your body suffered severe trauma. Then the fever and infection took even more out of you. You've been through a lot even if you weren't consciously aware of it."

"And my brain? Is it . . . is it all right?"

Dr. Markham considered her carefully. "Things are looking very positive. But you're going to need plenty of time and rest to heal properly. And you're probably going to need . . ."

She sensed they weren't finished speaking, but her eyes were once again heavy. Before they'd finished talking, she'd fallen asleep. Once again her dreams were of the lake. Only this time she was on top of it, not underneath it.

When she awoke again, she was in a small but well-appointed private room and most of the tubes and machines had been removed. Rex and Eve sat nearby.

"Hello, kitten," Rex said quietly. His smile was lopsided. It was the "I know I've let you down but you know I love you" smile that used to melt her heart.

Eve said nothing, but studied her intently. Emma recognized that look, too, and wasn't at all sure she had the strength to counter whatever was coming when Eve rose and moved closer to the bed. "I, we, would like to help during the rehab phase. I wanted to take you to California, but it seems you're not yet cleared to fly and of course you'll need follow-up."

Emma's body tensed even as she blinked sleepily. Eve didn't wait for Emma to respond. "I've found the perfect place here in Manhattan. There's a long waiting list but I've managed to convince them to make room for you." She smiled triumphantly. "In fact, Zoe can stay with us and be close enough to visit you regularly."

*No!* The word resounded in Emma's head, but she must not have spoken it aloud because Eve continued. "I think it will work marvelously. We'll have an opportunity to spend time with Zoe and we can make sure you get the best possible treatment." She sounded so pleased, so certain. "It looks as if you'll be allowed to leave the hospital before week's end."

"Why?" It was all she could manage. It was the one thing she wanted to know.

"Why, what, darling?" Eve asked smoothly. "What more compelling reason could there be for mending our fences than almost losing you this way?" She stepped closer. "We're all adults now and should be able to let go of old hurts and . . . misunderstandings." Her tone had turned reasonable, almost matter-of-fact, which meant Emma needed to pay close attention to what came next. "Besides, what sort of person would I be if I didn't look after my own flesh and blood who came this close" — she held up two fingers with barely an inch between them — "to dying?" She looked to Rex for support, but her father looked slightly embarrassed. "You're in no condition to take care of yourself, let alone your daughter."

Emma studied her mother's face as she digested this. Appearances had always been more important than reality to Eve. And a far greater motivator.

There was a soft knock on the open door and Serena entered, greeting Eve and Rex as she crossed toward the bed. Her stilted tone told Emma that she'd heard at least part of

Eve's plan.

"Hi, Em." Serena took her hand and looked Emma in the eye. "You okay?"

Emma nodded, pathetically glad that Serena was here and that she didn't let go of her hand.

"I was just telling Emma that we've secured a bed for her at Edgemere, which is a five-star facility," Eve said as if it were a fait accompli. "And that Zoe can stay with us."

There was a weighty silence as Serena plumbed Emma's eyes for a reaction. The hand that held hers tightened slightly. "Is that what you want, Em?"

Emma looked directly into her friend's eyes. She shook her head slightly, trying not to appear too desperate. "No." She said this loudly enough for Eve and Rex to hear.

"Well, that's a relief," Serena said. "Because even though you 'checked out for a while,' I was pretty sure you hadn't completely taken leave of your senses." She gave Emma's hand another squeeze and shot her a conspiratorial wink, ignoring Eve's perfectly executed exclamation of shocked indignation. "Mackenzie and Zoe will be up in a few minutes. We've been working on the arrangements. It looks like we might be able to check you out of here as early as tomorrow."

"Oh, no," Eve said. "That is not acceptable. I insist on . . ."

"You have no right to insist on anything,"

Serena said in an even tone. "Emma's back." She squeezed Emma's hand again. Emma returned the pressure. "And even if she weren't, I'd never let you take her. I have written permission from Emma to make those decisions for her."

"Well!" Eve turned to look at her husband, but Rex didn't meet her eye.

Emma breathed a sigh of relief as Eve huffed out of the room. Rex came over and pressed a kiss to Emma's cheek before following Eve out the door.

"Thank God you showed up when you did," Emma said when they were alone. "There's still a part of me that's afraid Eve will sneak in, knock me out, and drag me somewhere."

"Not gonna happen, sugah," Serena said in her best Georgia Goodbody accent. "No one's about to outmaneuver or get past Mackenzie, Zoe, and me."

"But where are we going?" Emma asked.

"You promised us a week at the lake," Serena replied. "And we are all more than ready for that week to begin."

# FIFTEEN

They arrived at the hospital the next morning to find Emma dressed and seated in a wheelchair. Her face was pale, her clothes hung on her frame, but she was sitting upright. When she saw them, her lips stretched into a smile. Her eyes filled with tears.

"Don't cry." Serena leaned down and hugged Emma gently. "We're here to spring you from this place."

"I know." Emma raised a shaking hand to swipe at the tears. "I can't help it. It just keeps hitting me that I might never have seen Zoe or either of you again." She lowered her hand, her movements slow and deliberate. "I'm a mess. Last night I cried through a Viagra commercial."

There was a brief knock and Dr. Brennan appeared. Part of the nursing staff who'd seen them through the last weeks were with him. Serena felt ready to cry herself.

"Dr. Markham's in surgery. He asked me

to give you his good-byes."

"I don't know how to . . . thank you," Emma said, her eyes tearing up once again.

"Seeing you ready to leave is more than enough," the neurointensivist said. "Saying good-bye is always the best part." Dr. Brennan smiled down at Emma and accepted hugs from Serena, Mackenzie, and Zoe. "This is a field where watching someone go and knowing they don't need you anymore is a reward in its own right."

"We are all indebted to you," Serena said in her best Georgia Goodbody drawl. "You have met and exceeded all expectations. I'm quite relieved that I didn't need my 'fan' even once."

"It's been my pleasure." The doctor smiled. "Are you planning to go out the back entrance? I had a report that a couple of tabloid photographers were caught trying to lift lab coats from the hospital laundry. And it looks like they've managed to cover all the entrances and exits."

Emma sighed and ran a hand over her head, which was bald except for some patches of stubble. "I'm not ready for any close-ups. Or questions."

"You don't need to be," Serena said. "Because we have a plan." She pointed to Zoe. "Cue the *Mission Impossible* theme music."

"DA DA da-da. DA DA da-da, DA DA da-da . . ." Zoe began then dropped volume, her rendition of the tune continuing under Serena's explanation.

"Our mission," Serena intoned solemnly, "which we have already accepted, is to extract you from this hospital without exposing you to a single unwanted, and potentially unattractive, photograph or question."

"DA DA da-da." Zoe brought up the volume again as Serena paused dramatically.

"Really?" Emma looked doubtful. "How?"

Serena turned to Mackenzie. "Report?"

Mackenzie mock saluted smartly. "The private ambulance we're using for the operation is in position, engine idling, at the end of our 'secret passage.' "

Zoe increased the volume again — "DA DA da-da, DA DA dahhhh" — then lowered it to background level as Serena continued. "Ethan Miller has been recruited to provide a celebrity diversion. In truth, he volunteered to carry out this most dangerous of plans."

She cued Zoe, gave her a couple of beats, then continued. The kid was good.

"Ethan's limo is parked around the corner. When I give him the signal he will be driven to the main entrance, exit the limo, and walk directly into the waiting pack of paparazzi. He will then pause to answer questions, mug for the cameras, and let them know that he's on his way up to see Emma, thereby giving us time to make our escape."

"Very tricky," Emma said. "I'm ready to

blow this Popsicle stand." Emma's voice was still rough, her face wan, but there was no mistaking her smile. Though she'd lost almost two weeks of her life and significant bits of memory, her sense of humor seemed largely intact.

"All right, then. Let's synchronize our watches," Serena said. "Everybody ready?"

Everyone nodded. Zoe finished humming the *Mission Impossible* theme with a flourish.

"Proceed with caution," Dr. Brennan added, playing along. "And remember, should you or any of your team be captured, we will disavow any knowledge of your actions."

"Thanks, again, Doc," Serena said, putting out a hand to shake. "We're grateful, but I know we're all hoping like hell we never need you again."

"Ditto," he said clasping her hand in his. "My mother has already framed your thank-you note. She's even temporarily stopped asking when I'm going to get married."

"Thank you. Thank you all." Emma shook all of the staff's hands, her eyes once again filling with tears.

"Give yourself time to heal," Dr. Brennan said quietly. "The physiotherapy is important. I've discussed it with Serena. And she has the number to set up a follow-up visit with Dr. Markham."

"We don't plan to let her lift anything heavier than my fan," Serena assured him.

"Or possibly a glass of wine."

"For the record, I don't recommend alcohol," Dr. Brennan said. "Booze clouds the mind. Even a glass or two reduces a person's ability to make recent memories. And Emma already has gaps that may not come back."

He noted their dismayed expressions. "I'm not in favor of drinking during a patient's recovery, but I also know there are a lot of patients who ignore this advice." He shrugged. "I'd be careful, but I doubt if a single glass of wine would hurt much."

"Understood." Serena shot him a wink.

The nurse pushed Emma through the door and toward the elevator. They formed a protective ring, shielding Emma from view, and headed for the employee exit and walkway. As they left the hospital, Serena sent the text to Ethan. Ten minutes later Emma was settled in the private ambulance, they'd taken their seats around her, and the driver was pulling into traffic.

Serena's only regret was that they wouldn't be able to watch Ethan Miller's performance.

Emma dozed for most of the four-and-a-half-hour drive up to Lake George, ensconced in a bed that sported four-hundred-thread-count linens. The mahogany-paneled "bedroom" also came with a flat-screen TV with Wi-Fi and digital surround sound as well as a sofa and chairs. If not for the unnecessary medical equipment and the boulder-sized, heavily accented nurse that Serena insisted she hadn't requested and who'd been banished to the front where she was currently riding shotgun, they might have been traveling in the stateroom of a small yacht or five-star motorhome.

Mackenzie had been put in charge of music, and the playlist included Celine Dion, Sarah McLachlan, and Natasha Bedingfield, whose voices played softly from the Bose speakers, a soothing background soundtrack as they talked quietly among themselves.

As they traveled north on the New York State Thruway toward Albany, the landscape became greener and lusher, the terrain hillier. Mackenzie thought of all the trips they'd made to the lake together, how their spirits had risen with each mile. At first the lake house had been the place where they could shed their newly acquired sophistication and simply "be." Later, when they'd scattered geographically, it had become the place in which they renewed their friendship, effortlessly picking up where they'd left off, strengthening the bond none of them imagined could ever break. And yet five years ago Emma had severed that bond without a word of apology or explanation.

"God, I almost can't believe this is happening," Serena said quietly. "Not after the last two weeks. And how close we came to losing her."

"I know," Mackenzie whispered, her eyes on Emma. "I kept telling myself she'd wake up, but . . ." Mackenzie couldn't bring herself to admit aloud that she hadn't really believed it would happen.

Emma roused as the ambulance slowed for the Lake George Village exit then turned north on Route 9N. The two-lane road, which hugged the western edge of the spring-fed lake, was appropriately named Lake Shore Drive, and had once been known as Millionaires' Row. It wound and rolled gently beneath a leafy canopy of green on its way to the town of Bolton Landing. To their right, small, sometimes unpaved roads wended down toward the water, bisecting and break-ing up the marinas, restaurants, and inns that dotted the landscape and affording the oc-casional glimpse at the bright blue waters of the lake itself.

Zoe pulled the curtains wider so that Emma could see the sights as they passed.

"Erlowest," Emma said softly, noting the entrance to one of the remaining original lakeside mansions, which had been restored and was now an upscale B and B. "Read about new chef. Maybe dinner."

"I think that's a great idea," Mackenzie said, pleased to see Emma's eyes remaining open. "And when you're feeling up to it we definitely need to get to the Sagamore," she said, naming the sprawling historic hotel that sat on its own island across a small bridge from Bolton Landing. "Maybe we could do a spa day there. Or just sit out and have lunch overlooking the lake."

"I'm in," Serena said as the vehicle slowed to a crawl. "Although I think I could be perfectly happy stretched out in a hammock or on a chaise on the boathouse deck." A long line of cars heading south passed on their left. "Wow, look at all this traffic."

"It's . . . end of June, right?" Emma asked sleepily. "Season. It'll be packed for the Fourth." She spoke slowly and with effort, but Mackenzie detected a note of happiness rather than complaint. "Did you call Martha?"

"I had a text from her a half hour ago saying the house has been aired out, the refrigerator is stocked, and everything's good to go," Mackenzie said. "And she said she left something in the oven."

"I hope it's a cottage pie," Zoe said. "Or her famous mac and cheese." Zoe had barely let go of her mother's hand since leaving the hospital. "Or both."

Mackenzie just hoped it would be something that tempted Emma to eat.

"Oh, God you're making me hungry," Serena said. "Just so you know, I don't intend to count a single calorie while we're here. I think we're all ready for some home cooking after all that hospital food and takeout."

"And we definitely need to put some meat back on Emma's bones," Mackenzie added. When Emma was stronger, well, then they'd make her explain what had caused her to jettison them.

"Ironic," Emma said. "Only had to lose consciousness to lose weight."

She had, in fact, lost fifteen pounds over the last two weeks, a situation Mackenzie was determined to rectify.

"Yeah, well next time do us a favor and try Weight Watchers first," Serena said.

"Funny." Emma's smile was tired. "Wish I had the energy to laugh."

They exchanged glances, all of them aware of how large an effort was required for Emma to put a sentence together.

"Good to know. You owe me a belly laugh when you're feeling better, then," Serena quipped. "Although I'd settle for a chuckle. Or maybe you could text or email me an LOL!"

The smile that flickered on Emma's lips ended in a yawn. Her eyes fluttered shut. The jagged stitches that showed through the patches of red-gold stubble that dotted her scalp underscored her frailty.

"When we get to the cottage, I'm carrying a drink out to the lake with me. Maybe even two," Serena said.

"I'm going for a swim," Zoe exclaimed. "And then I'm going to lie on the floating dock. Forever."

Emma just smiled sleepily, only opening her eyes when the ambulance slowed at the low stone wall then turned onto a narrow, unmarked asphalt road. They wound through the densely wooded area toward the lake. Several smaller roads branched off to the right and left as they continued through the trees and scrub, finally coming to a stop in a clearing dotted with trees. Slivers of lake sparkled between their tall trunks. The whine of a boat engine reached them, and Mackenzie saw the frothy white wake it had left behind.

Emma's sigh was a contented one as the vehicle turned onto the driveway and followed it up the rise. The sprawling clapboard house sat atop the grassy hill and commanded a stunning view of the yard that sloped down to the private beach and the protected cove it bounded. Steps made of river rock led down to the beach, where a matching clapboard boathouse with a large railed rooftop deck overlooked an L-shaped dock. The beach and cove were horseshoe shaped and private, shielded on either side by stands of trees and shrubbery. A floating platform bobbed on the water, an easy swim from the beach and boathouse. At the edge of the cove lay the narrow triangle of land called Hemlock Point. Beside it a small army of buoys marked the rocky shoals where an island had once been. Beyond that the lake opened up, stretching out of sight to the north and south and reaching some three miles eastward to the opposite shore.

Emma sighed in pleasure, accepting the nurse's help up the stone front steps to the large covered porch with its uninterrupted view. There she sank gratefully into a cushioned wicker chair.

"Do you want to wait here while we get things stowed inside?" Serena asked.

"Thanks." Emma nodded. Her face looked haggard and the look in her eyes made Mackenzie think of the photos she'd seen of wounded soldiers who'd recently come back from places and horrors they might never fully forget or completely remember.

"Where do you want us?" Serena asked after she and Zoe had deposited Emma's things in the master bedroom.

"Where you've always stayed," she said as if there had been no five-year gap since their last visit. "Unless you want to . . . change?"

They looked at each other then shook their heads. There were three more bedrooms and two baths upstairs, one a Jack and Jill that stretched between the two guest rooms that had been Serena's and Mackenzie's. Zoe had what was once Emma's room.

"Those rooms . . ." Emma swallowed.

"Always yours. Still the same."

Mackenzie noticed that the first floor was also reassuringly the same. Original plank floors throughout the downstairs, a light golden anchor to the whitewashed walls that surrounded them. While the exterior footprint of the five-thousand-square-foot cottage had never been changed, its interior had been carefully updated over the years so that it maintained its period charm with none of the inconvenience.

Stack stone fireplaces anchored the northern and southern ends of the house. A central foyer opened to a huge U-shaped eat-in kitchen and dining room with a farm table that seated twelve running perpendicular to the fireplace. A screened porch off the kitchen was a preferred summer dining spot.

On the northern end lay a massive great room with walls of floor-to-ceiling bookshelves that framed the fireplace while a cushioned window seat stretched beneath a bank of windows that overlooked the lake. A former sunroom on the western end of the house had been turned into a den with a flat-screen TV and an impressive sound system. French sliders allowed the room to be closed off or opened to the rest of the space. A small hallway led to what had once been servants' quarters and was now a guest suite.

They stowed their things and came downstairs to wave off the ambulance. But the nurse, a large, almost mountainous woman with a head of spiky bleached-blond hair, refused to leave.

"I am Nadia. I am paid for month by mother of patient," she said in an accent straight out of *Rocky and Bullwinkle.* "I'm not take money for job I don't perform." She crossed large, muscular arms across her massive chest. "Miz Mickhels need help. Take time build strength. Who help her to bathroom in middle of night? Who dress and undress her? Carry where she needs go? Make sure she get nutrients for put back on weight?" She stared at Mackenzie and Serena out of eyes that were a blue so dark they looked black.

Mackenzie glanced at Serena, relieved she wasn't the only one who squirmed.

"We assumed we'd take care of her," Serena said.

"So. You stay here the twenty-four/seven for next month?" Nadia's crisp white uniform pulled tight against her rock-hard bosom. Like her body, the planes and angles of her face appeared carved from granite, but her pale skin was surprisingly unlined. She might have been anywhere from forty to sixty, and her dark eyes crackled with intelligence and determination. When she'd introduced herself, she'd scoffed at Serena's joke about the only other Nadia they'd ever heard of. "I am not the Comaneech," she said dismissively.

"She too tiny, too delicate." It was clear Nadia considered these lamentable defects. "I am Kochenkov. Am not gymnast. Am weight lifter. A champion. I lift you both with one arm and not break sweat."

Mackenzie and Serena took a small step back. "You think it'll be a whole month before she can be on her own?" Mackenzie had already been away two full weeks when she'd planned on one. Serena's show was not on hiatus. Could either of them stay that long? Would Emma even want them to? And who was going to tell her it was Eve who'd retained this weight lifter turned RN?

"Six to eight weeks most realistic," the nurse said. "But stronger in four." Nadia placed ham-sized fists on her hips. "Miz Mickhels should be in rehab facility. It big thing recovering from coma and blood clot and sepsis. You two can be responsible for her?" One excruciatingly thin eyebrow went up.

Mackenzie and Serena winced in unison.

"I stay. I be bad cop. You good ones. I bully her when needing it." Her look said this would not be a problem. "You and the daughter give emotional support. She going to need it."

Nadia looked like a woman who knew when she'd won a match and didn't waste breath confirming her victory. "I put things in room down here. Then I make Miz Mickhels's room ready. I sleep on sofa in dressing room so I be there when she needs me."

# Sixteen

The floorboards groaned and the mountain named Nadia was standing over her bed when Emma opened her eyes.

The woman had only smiled when Emma attempted to inform her that she didn't want some stranger watching her sleep in her own bed, not after all the nights of observation in the hospital, but had given up for lack of energy and a fuzzy brain. At which point the nurse had pretty much carried her up the stairs in her arms, put her gently but firmly into her pajamas, and tucked her into her bed while Serena, Mackenzie, and Zoe made themselves scarce.

When she'd awoken in the middle of the night needing to pee, Nadia had been there to help her, silent and efficient.

"Good morning," the nurse said now. "You get up now?" At Emma's nod, the massive blonde swept open the draperies, letting daylight into the room, then returned to Emma's side.

Mist clung to the lake and softened the early morning sky to a wispy gray. The sun was already on the rise as Nadia helped Emma out of the master bedroom's French doors. Barefoot and leaning heavily on the nurse, Emma stepped out onto the dew-covered deck, her bare feet growing damp as they slowly crossed to the railing.

It had been a relief to go to sleep in her own bed in the place that had always provided such comfort, and yet that sleep had been fitful, filled with yet another jumble of dreams she didn't understand. Gran had been there urging her on to something she couldn't quite make out. Eve had been there, too, her smile enigmatic, her eyes hinting at something that was also unclear. Did any of it mean anything? Or was it all just random bits of imagined memory? Electrical impulses of long-ago impressions?

No matter where she tried to turn her thoughts, the blank of the last weeks loomed dark and cavernous, an empty void she wanted to sidestep and yet couldn't stop attempting to peer into. Its nothingness frightened her and so did the spottiness of her memory and the fuzziness of her thoughts. A fuzziness she prayed would ultimately pass.

Across the still waters of the lake, the first rays of sun rose above the mountains, announcing the day's arrival. She watched the red-rimmed yellow ball send shimmers of light dancing across the water's smooth surface as the lake came to life.

How many sunrises had she seen from this house? How many times had Gran told her each signified not only a new day, but also a new opportunity to be whoever she wanted to be? She felt a peace here she'd felt nowhere else. If the jumble of thoughts and emotions that filled her could coalesce anywhere, it would be here.

Just beyond the boathouse a family of ducks floated nonchalantly, occasionally bobbing their heads beneath the water to scoop up an interesting morsel. A platoon of gulls skimmed low over the surface scouting for breakfast. A dog's bark echoed in the quiet while an orchestra of insects tuned up for the day's performance. The breeze was gentle on her bare arms, the temperature mild. She thought of Gran, to whom this master suite, this private deck, and this home had once belonged. God, she wished she were here in all her no-nonsense, take-no-prisoners glory.

*I'm always with you. And I'm quite relieved we've left that hospital behind.*

The words that sounded in her head offered comfort, but at the moment Emma wanted her grandmother in the flesh. Wanted her elegant arms wrapped tight around her. Wanted to bury her head in her grandmother's shoulder and inhale the mingled rose and jasmine of her Joy perfume.

*Shoulders back, chin up, darling. You worry too much.*

She leaned against the railing as Nadia wiped down the nearby wrought-iron dining set, then helped her into a chair.

Behind her the bedroom door creaked open, footsteps treaded on the wood floor. China clattered as something was set down.

"Em? I thought I heard you moving around. You didn't really eat last night, so I brought coffee and some of Martha's cinnamon buns." Mackenzie came out onto the porch in shorts that revealed the long legs that Emma had always admired and an ancient New York Is for Lovers T-shirt. Her straight dark hair had been pulled up in a high ponytail and secured with a scrunchy. "God, it's gorgeous out," she said. "Would you like to have coffee out here?"

Emma nodded.

Mackenzie placed the breakfast tray with its coffeepot, mugs, cream and sugar, and plate of iced cinnamon buns on the table.

"I straighten bed." Nadia nodded, practically clicking her heels together and departing.

Mackenzie poured Emma a cup of coffee and pushed the plate of warm buns toward her. "Oops." She patted her pockets. "Forgot my phone. I'll be right back."

"Thanks." Emma reached for the mug, shocked that she needed both hands to lift it to her lips and keep it there. She wanted to believe the mug was exceptionally heavy, but was forced to admit that she was just exceptionally weak.

Birds chirped on a nearby branch as she savored the first sips of coffee then carefully set down the mug in order to pinch off a bite of her cinnamon bun. It was warm, the melted icing sweet and gooey. She chewed slowly, glad that Serena and Mackenzie were here, grateful that they'd been with her and especially Zoe at the hospital, but she could not separate what, if anything, she actually remembered, from what surely must have been dreams.

She felt a tug of anxiety as something flitted through her mind. Something she was meant to do or say. Something important that was supposed to happen here at the lake. She tried to focus, tried to call it back, but it was gone.

Serena wandered out in her nightgown over which she'd thrown a short white terrycloth robe. Her feet were also bare; her toenails had been painted a bright blue.

"Nice polish," Emma said.

"Thanks." Without asking, Serena turned the extra mug upright and poured herself a cup of coffee, which she loaded up with cream and sugar. She took a long sip. "Ahhhh, I love this place. Is there still a boat in the boathouse?"

"We're down to a canoe, a Jet Ski, and a paddleboard," Emma replied, pleased that the memory came easily.

"And do we have a car?"

"The Jeep should be in the garage. Martha's son Jason drives it every once in a while to make sure it's still running. And we have a small motor scooter."

Mackenzie returned, her eyes trained on the cell phone in her hand.

"Expecting a call?" Serena asked.

"I've been waiting to hear from Adam. But the three-hour time difference is a killer."

"What time is it?" Emma asked, realizing she had no idea.

"Almost ten," Mackenzie said, glancing at the cell phone again. "I seriously doubt I'll hear from him until after seven his time."

"In my experience a watched phone rings about as fast as a watched pot boils," Serena said.

Mackenzie's head snapped up. "Maybe that depends on whether you're married to the pot you're waiting to hear from." Mackenzie noted the cup of coffee in Serena's hand. "Nice," she said. "I guess I'm going down for another mug. Do we need anything else?" She aimed the question at Emma, who shook her head.

Emma and Serena sipped their coffees in a companionable silence. Emma eyed the cinnamon bun but didn't have the appetite or strength to reach for it. Mackenzie returned with another half pot of coffee and a third mug then pulled another chair over to the table. She set her cell phone on the table within easy reach. "Have I mentioned how much I love this place?"

Serena raised her mug of coffee to Mackenzie and Emma. "I will definitely drink to that."

Mackenzie eyed the cinnamon buns as she sipped at her coffee.

"If anyone can afford to have a cinnamon bun, it's you." Serena reached over and deposited one on Mackenzie's plate. "Seriously. You don't look like you've gained an ounce in the last five years. And it totally pisses me off."

"Me too," Emma said. "The tall and slim just get taller and slimmer. The round just get rounder."

"Ha!" Mackenzie said but she reached for the pastry and took a large bite. Her eyes closed as she began to chew. She moaned in a paroxysm of ecstasy. "Oh. My. God. That's soooo good."

"Sweet Jesus," Serena bit out. "Give me one of those things." She snatched up a bun and brought it to her lips. "At the moment I don't care how round I get. I told you I wasn't counting calories this trip and I don't see any attractive men hiding in the bushes. Plus my only on-camera opportunities are handled by a caricature of me." The bun disappeared in a matter of bites.

They drank coffee and chatted idly while the sun continued to rise and the number of boats out on the lake multiplied. Zoe still hadn't appeared when they heard a car approach and pull into the drive.

Serena glanced down at her pajamas. "Are we expecting company?"

"Not that I know of." Mackenzie looked to Emma.

"Nope," Emma said. "Unless it's Martha. Or Jason checking on the Jeep."

Serena got up and leaned out over the balcony railing as a car door slammed shut. "Whoever it is is kind of short and blond. And he's got equipment of some kind with him."

"Well, whatever he's selling I'll get rid of him," Mackenzie said, glancing down at her phone again then scooping it off the table. "Seeing as I'm the only one actually clothed."

"Thanks." Emma couldn't stop the yawn that followed. "I hate to say it, but I think I . . ."

Nadia was there before Emma had even made it to the edge of her chair. "You need nap." She helped Emma to her feet. Waited for what felt like an eternity while she straightened.

Mackenzie stuffed the phone into her shorts pocket and headed downstairs, taking the breakfast tray with her as Emma moved slowly inside. Serena tagged behind Nadia. As if Emma might not be able to make it even with a former Soviet weight lifter supporting her.

She didn't protest as Serena bid her good night and Nadia helped her back into bed. Emma yawned, unable to believe she could be this tired, this soon, but she could already feel tendrils of sleep wrapping around her, ready to pull her under. There was a brief stab of fear that she might once again fail to wake up, but she pushed it aside. They wouldn't have let her out of the hospital if there were a chance that could happen. Emma settled onto her side and pulled the pillow closer. The morning coffee hadn't exactly roused or infused her with new energy, but she felt better, calmer, after the time with Mackenzie and Serena. Except for that thing, that thought, that disappeared each time she tried to grab it.

*It's all right, darling,* Gran's voice said in her head as she began to doze. *See how much better you feel? Sometimes a coffee klatch is the answer.*

Emma burrowed into the pillow. But her last thought as she slipped back into sleep was, *Doesn't that depend on the question?*

Mackenzie snuck another peek at her silent cell phone before answering the front door to a stockily built man in his early thirties. Despite the heavy equipment bag looped over one muscled shoulder, he managed to hand her a business card. "Bob Fortson," he said, his craggy face breaking into a smile. "I'm here for Ms. Michaels's first physical therapy session."

"I'm sorry?" Mackenzie considered the man in front of her. He had a tanned face with a slight smattering of freckles, sun-streaked hair, and a friendly smile. His handshake was firm but not bone shattering.

"Where would you like me to set up?"

Mackenzie looked into his eyes and saw no subterfuge in them, but she had no idea how he'd gotten there.

"I think there's been some mistake," she said, preparing to close the door.

"I was hired by Eve Michaels. Services paid in advance. The PT and OT were prescribed by a Dr. Markham. Two times a day, no more than thirty minutes per session."

"Everything okay?" Dressed in shorts and an *As the World Churns* T-shirt, Serena came down the stairs to join Mackenzie at the door.

Bob Fortson's mouth dropped open briefly. "Georgia?" he said awestruck. "Emma Michaels and Georgia Goodbody in one place?"

Mackenzie sighed. This, of course, would make her the chopped liver.

"You don't any camera gear tucked away there anywhere do you?" Serena asked the young man.

"Oh, no, ma'am."

Mackenzie smiled at Serena's sigh. She might be chopped liver, but Serena had just been "ma'am-ed."

"But I am a huge fan!"

Serena turned to Mackenzie and raised an eyebrow.

"He says he's a physical therapist prescribed by Dr. Markham and paid for by Eve." Mackenzie wasn't sure what should happen next. "I was going to call Glens Falls Hospital to follow up on the list of referrals in the morning."

"But Eve beat us to it," Serena said. "First the nurse, now the PT. How weird is that?"

"Extremely," Mackenzie said. In all the years they'd been friends with Emma, she'd only spoken about her mother when pressed, and what she'd shared had been almost always negative. It was hard to imagine Eve Michaels with an altruistic agenda. Or even one that put someone else first. "She's asleep right now," Mackenzie said to the young man. "And regardless of who's paying, we'll need to see your ID and references." There was still that small possibility that they'd let him inside and the only equipment that would come out would be a camera. She looked to Serena for confirmation.

"Agreed."

"You want I come interrogate him?" Nadia

stood on the stairs. "Make sure he who he say he is?"

The physical therapist blanched slightly at the disembodied voice.

"No, thanks, I think we've got it, Nadia," Mackenzie called up to the nurse. "But, I think Emma needs at least one transition day before she gets started."

"And let's see that ID and references now," Serena added. "Otherwise we'll have to turn you over to our resident former KGB agent."

Bob Fortson's eyes got big. "Sure. No problem." He pulled out his wallet and showed them his hospital ID. "There's more information and references on the website." He handed Serena a business card and pointed to the URL. "We have an occupational therapist on staff, too."

Mackenzie looked up to gauge Nadia's reaction. The nurse shook her head slightly. "Nyet."

"I'm pretty sure Emma already has an occupation," Serena said drily.

Bob chuckled. "Wow. You're as funny in person as you are in cartoon."

Mackenzie wondered if he was about to pull out a pen and paper and ask for an autograph. Serena was apparently thinking the same thing. "There's just one thing, Bob," she said. "Emma needs privacy and quiet in which to recuperate and regain her strength. And it looks like you're going to be a part of that recovery."

He smiled happily, apparently not yet hearing the steel beneath Serena's honeyed drawl. "But if you tell a single person that Emma is here, or share anything you see or hear while you're in this house no matter how small or seemingly unimportant, I'll personally make sure that you regret it."

"Y-ye-yes, ma'am," the physical therapist stammered as he backed away from the door. "But there's no chance of that. I take the HIPAA promise of privacy very seriously. My lips are sealed. Mum is the word." He'd reached his fingers to his lips and started a zipping motion when Mackenzie closed the door.

"Well done," she said to Serena with unfeigned admiration. "I've never seen anyone scare another person so sweetly."

# Seventeen

Serena tried not to worry about the fact that Emma slept much of their first full day at the lake and a good part of their second. When Em was awake Nadia brought her out onto the upper balcony for fresh air and so that she could feel a part of what was happening.

Zoe did as she'd promised and spent most of the daylight hours in her bathing suit either in the lake or sunning on the swim platform. Serena and Mackenzie stayed within hailing distance of the house so they could join Emma when she wanted company, but they, too, wore little more than bathing suits, oversized T-shirts, and flip-flops. No one unpacked a blow dryer, curling iron, or makeup bag. Only Nadia remained fully clothed, starched, and shod.

In those first days they began a routine that revolved around morning coffee, afternoon drinks and snacks, and dinner on Emma's balcony. It was agreed, if unspoken, that as long as she was too tired to come to them, they would come to her. And that no one was going to bring up Eve's "gifts" unless Emma specifically asked where her nurse and physical therapist had come from. Together they began to work their way through the homemade offerings that Martha had stuffed into the refrigerator and freezer. They sat around the wrought-iron table eating, talking, and staring out over the lake while Nadia proved herself adept at seeming to disappear while remaining within earshot, a surprising accomplishment for someone built like a tank and with the personality of a steamroller. Unless, of course, their jokes about a possible past in the KGB weren't jokes at all.

That afternoon, they consumed a platter of homemade chocolate chip cookies and rum balls washed down with an assortment of beverages: white wine for Serena and Mackenzie, milk for Zoe, and tea for Emma, whose appetite had not yet returned but whose legendary sweet tooth had begun to make itself known.

"These taste way better than those weird energy drinks Nadia keeps trying to pour down me," Emma said as she nibbled on a cookie.

"Are you ready for physical therapy tomorrow?" Mackenzie asked after glancing at her phone.

"Maybe it'll help me wake up." Emma yawned. "I feel like a total slug. I haven't even made it to the lake yet."

"We'll get you there," Serena promised, but she wished she knew how long it would be until that was possible. "Even if we have to put you on our backs and carry you into the water."

Zoe nodded emphatically and popped half a cookie into her mouth. Her haunted look had begun to fade, though Serena saw how often the girl's eyes sought out her mother as if to reassure herself that she was all right. How carefully she studied Emma's facial expressions and movements.

"We could put you in the bottom of a canoe and float you out into the lake like a Viking warrior," Mackenzie said.

"As long as nobody tries to set me on fire," Emma said.

There was laughter, all of them glad to see any sign of the "old" Emma.

They talked desultorily, wandering from topic to topic, trying to keep things interesting enough to hold on to Emma's attention. The sound of the ringing phone was jarring in the quiet. Mackenzie sat up and grabbed the cell phone she'd been eyeing for the last two days. It took several more rings before it became clear that the phone that was ringing was Serena's.

Mackenzie put hers down abruptly. Serena, seeing the studio's phone number, got up and moved to the other edge of the porch to answer hers.

"Serena? It's Catherine."

"Hi." Serena stared out over the railing to the lake where something, maybe a turtle's head, had just broken the surface. "What's up?"

"Ethan wants to know if you can come in to record. He offered to send his car for you."

Serena watched the rings in the water that marked the turtle's progress. She'd already been largely unavailable for the last two weeks and now she was looking at at least another couple of weeks up here. Ethan had been great about the time off and everything else. The least she could do was be there when he needed her.

She looked over her shoulder to where Nadia Kochenkov was helping Emma up and escorting her back to her bedroom. Emma was in good hands and Mackenzie might be clinging to a phone that never rang, but she didn't seem in any hurry to leave.

"Of course," she said into the phone. "I can do that. Can it wait a week? I'd just like to get things settled for Emma."

They worked out the details and Serena was about to hang up, when Catherine said, "By the way, I've been meaning to let you know that guy who left his number keeps calling."

"What guy?" Serena glanced over her shoulder once more and lowered her voice.

"The one with the sexy southern accent like

yours," Catherine teased.

"This is the first time I've ever heard a New Yorker call a southern accent sexy," Serena said, aware that she was stalling. "Stupid, hillbilly, redneck, maybe, but never sexy." Her heart was skittering in her chest in a ridiculously juvenile way. She ordered it to stop.

"What can I say?" Catherine replied. "I'm a sucker for anything that didn't originate in Long Island or New Jersey."

Serena drew in a calming breath, determined not to overreact. Emma's situation had almost pushed thoughts of Brooks Anderson out of her mind. *Almost.* She had decided there was no reason to call him. After all, she'd been the injured party. He'd been the one who'd never shown up in New York, who'd married Diana Ravenel, gone to work for her father, had a family. Serena didn't owe him one single thing. Ever. And that included a return phone call.

"I meant to call him back. But in all the excitement over Emma I must have lost his number." Serena had no idea why she was lying. She knew exactly where the number was and had, in fact, looked at it so many times she could have dialed it from memory.

"Oh, gosh, I'm so relieved to hear that," Catherine said in a rush. "I was afraid you were going to tell me you didn't want to speak to him. Because, well, I know it's completely against the rules, but he was so sweet and so . . . I didn't mean to do it, but when he said he was going to be in New York and really wanted to make arrangements to see you, I . . . I went ahead and gave him your cell phone number."

Serena gasped before she could stop herself. Mackenzie and Zoe turned to look at her.

Serena found her voice. "You're joking, right?"

"I'm so sorry," Catherine said. "I know better, really I do." Her voice had sunk to a frightened whisper. "He's just such a . . ."

*Sweet talker,* Serena thought but did not say. How could she chastise Catherine when she knew just how potent the man's charm could be?

"I'm so, so, sorry!" Serena could practically hear the young receptionist wringing her hands. This was, after all, a firing offense.

"No, it's okay," Serena insisted as Catherine apologized again. Which made two big fat lies in one phone call. "Really, don't worry about it." She continued to look out over the lake, but it did nothing to soothe her. "It's fine. Tell Ethan I'll see him next Tuesday."

As Serena ended the call and tucked her phone into a pocket, she told herself this was nothing to worry about. Her cell phone hadn't rung. It was unlikely he'd ever use the number. They hadn't seen or spoken to each other in twenty years. Why should that change now? And if for some unknown reason he did decide to call her . . . maybe she should put him in her contact list so that he'd show up in her caller ID. Wasn't that why it had been invented? Forewarned was forearmed. There was no reason why she should feel like she had to answer any call.

The past was the past. Dead and buried. Done if not forgotten. She had no interest whatsoever in anything Brooks Anderson might have to say to her today or at any time in the future.

Despite how fanatically she watched it, Mackenzie's phone didn't ring until late the next morning, not too long after Bob Fortson had arrived and carried all his gear up to Emma's balcony.

She'd watched him set up before heading out to what had always been her favorite spot, stretched out in the hammock strung between two tall pines at the southern edge of the cove. The shade was sweet. The breeze off the lake that skimmed over her bare skin kept the hammock swaying gently.

She'd given up reading the novel now splayed across her stomach and had tuned out Emma's squawks of protest that occasionally reached her, finally falling asleep. It took several rings to wake up fully. Another to find the face of the phone and register the time and the person calling. It was Adam and it was noon. Which made it nine a.m. in LA.

She almost fell out of the hammock as she tried to sit up too quickly. Her book landed in a pile of dirt. Her phone landed right beside it. Frantic fumbling followed.

"Mac? Are you there?" Adam's voice was low pitched and unhurried. When she answered, his apology for taking two full days to return her call didn't sound at all apologetic. "So how's everything going?" he asked when she didn't ask him first.

"Okay," she said. "Emma's sleeping a lot of the time, but apparently that's to be expected. She started physical therapy this morning." Mackenzie paused, thinking she'd tell him how beautiful the lake was at this moment, how Emma's nurse was a former Soviet weight lifter who could bench-press all three of them without breaking a sweat, how desperately she'd wanted to believe that the blue heron she'd seen standing on the lawn early this morning was a good omen.

"That's great," he said the moment she paused to take a breath. "Em's tough. I knew she'd fight her way back." He said this as if there'd been no doubt, as if the most traumatic thing Mackenzie had ever witnessed or lived through had been a sporting event whose outcome had never been in question.

A silence fell and she knew he was ready to change the subject, ready for her to ask about him. She realized with some surprise that she didn't really want to hear what he'd been up

201

to. What she really wanted to know was why he'd been so out of touch, why it had taken him two full days to return her call, though she supposed those were really both the same question.

But what would be accomplished by a long-distance argument? "So, how are things going there?"

"Great. Couldn't be better." Adam launched into a detailed explanation of where things were with the script, who'd said what about it and why, and then recited the list of actors that Matthew, Adam's agent, thought might play the leads if the studio he thought might be interested in the screenplay signed on.

For the first time she could remember, she just wasn't interested. She had spent two weeks with a friend who was fighting her way out of a coma. She'd barely slept or eaten. Even now she worried that Emma might not fully recover. Yet she'd barely gotten two minutes of her husband's attention two days after she'd needed it.

She watched a sailboat prepare to come about, saw the captain push hard on the tiller. On cue the life-jacketed family ducked and shifted as the sail swung to the opposite side. As the sail filled with air and moved off in a new direction, she realized with startling clarity that despite having almost lost Emma, despite all that she'd been through, this conversation with Adam was no different than a million others they'd had in that it revolved almost entirely around what Adam thought, what Adam felt, and what Adam wanted.

How had she never noticed before? Had she really been that busy? Or had she simply not wanted to see?

Without her usual prompts and murmurs of praise and encouragement, his monologue finally ended. "So how long do you plan to stay at the lake?" he asked.

The sailboat receded and her eyes resettled on the opposite shore. It was July. There was no reason to rush home with the theater closed until after Labor Day. There were no longer elderly parents nor were there young children back in Noblesville waiting for her to come home. No husband, either. "I don't know," she said. "I thought I'd stay until Emma was stronger."

"Then that's what you should do," he said agreeably with a disturbing note of relief. He didn't suggest that he'd like her to come out to LA. "Maybe when I've got the screenplay the way I want it and the deal is signed, I'll come out there."

"Sure," she said. "That would be great. I'm sure Emma would like that."

"Okay, then," he said, clearly ready to sign off. "Give Em a hug from me, okay?"

"Okay."

"And take care of yourself."

"Will do," Mackenzie said. But Adam was already gone. Gone to live the life he was so clearly enjoying. The one he would have chosen if she hadn't gotten pregnant. If he hadn't felt compelled to marry her. If she hadn't begged him to move back to Indiana to raise the children they never had.

Several days later Emma sat on the cushioned chaise watching Bob Fortson pack up his instruments of torture.

"I'll see you tomorrow, same time, same channel."

"Right." They'd just completed her fourth session of physical therapy and she was so tired she could barely move her lips. She twisted them into what she hoped would pass for a smile.

"You do good job. Try hard." Nadia hung a towel around Emma's neck as if she were a fighter coming out of a boxing ring or a tennis player leaving center court after an especially difficult match, when in fact she'd spent only thirty grueling minutes doing strength-building exercises. "Drink thees." The nurse handed her a glass filled with a thick lime-green-colored liquid. The nurse's energy concoctions came in a rainbow of colors, none of them particularly tasty, each with a pungent aroma. Emma was too tired to argue. She'd take any form of energy she could get.

It was a gorgeous midsummer day filled with clear blue sky, puffy white clouds, and a comfortable seventy-five degrees. The doors and windows were all thrown open to catch the breeze that came off the water. Everyone else was on or near the lake enjoying themselves. She was determined to get down to the lake under her own steam, but was appalled at how far away the achievement of that goal seemed. At the moment she couldn't even make it inside, let alone downstairs, without assistance.

She sucked the drink down dutifully and had finally reached the bottom of the glass when a phone rang nearby. She realized with some surprise that the ringtone was hers, a melody she hadn't heard since, well, she couldn't actually remember the last time she'd heard it. Serena, who had turned the phone over to her just yesterday, had told her it had only survived her accident because it had been in the purse that flew out of her hands and landed in a nearby flowerbed. A detail that she didn't remember, couldn't picture, and might well have happened to someone else.

The phone was still ringing when Nadia brought it out to her. "Is Mrs. Mickhels."

"No."

The nurse tried to exchange the phone for the empty glass.

Emma refused to take it. "I don't want to speak to her." She left off the "ever," but thought her tone implied it.

"But she your mother."

"Not really."

The phone continued to ring, for some reason failing to go to voice mail. Not that she'd want to hear a voice mail from Eve any more than she wanted to speak to her.

"You talk." Nadia tried again to hand the phone to Emma, who kept her hands at her sides. "Is boss. Make paycheck."

Emma could have happily continued to pretend that she had no idea where the nurse had come from, that she had magically appeared like some larger, more muscular Mary Poppins. She did not want to be beholden to Eve.

"Then you talk to her." Emma assumed that would end the conversation, but Nadia Kochenkov raised the phone to her ear.

"Kochenkov here." A salute and maybe a parade ground should have accompanied that voice. *"Da."*

The nurse snuck a look at her. *"Da.* Is better." Another question. "Nyet."

Nadia looked at Emma again. "You talk." It was not a question. "Tell mother you happy with me." She didn't bother to cover the mouthpiece when she issued this command, but the eyes that typically brooked no argument had turned beseeching.

Emma sighed and put out her hand. "Hello?"

"Oh. Hello, dar . . ." Eve halted abruptly. ". . . Emma."

There was a silence that Emma had no intention of filling.

"I just wanted to check and see how you're doing."

"I'm okay." Emma fought back the Pavlovian panic that seemed tied to even the thought of Eve.

"That's good. I'm very glad to hear it."

Emma stared out over the railing to where Zoe lay in her favorite spot on the swimming platform. Serena and Mackenzie sat in two Adirondack chairs on the beach, their feet in the water. They had what looked like glasses of iced tea in their hands and were talking.

"Are you satisfied with the care you're receiving? Because I'm sure I could find someone else if . . ."

"It's fine. She's . . . fine." At first Emma had just been too tired to argue about the nurse's presence. Then she'd been too tired to argue *with* her. Now it was hard to imagine how she would have even gotten out of bed without her. "Thank you."

Nadia's smile was large, revealing one missing tooth near the back and two gold crowns. Eve, who had far better teeth, sounded both surprised and pleased. And oddly not in control of the conversation. "Oh, I'm so . . .

207

that's good."

Silence fell between them once again.

"Is there anything else that might be helpful?" Eve asked. "Anything at all that you want or need?"

"Nyet," Emma said, shooting Nadia a look. She was exhausted and more than ready for this conversation to be over.

"Oh, of course," Eve said. "You must be tired. But you will let me know if there's anything, anything at all that I can do. Or . . ."

Emma hung up before Eve had finished. Wearily, she handed the phone to Nadia Kochenkov. "Don't ever do that again," she said as the nurse hefted her up out of the chaise. "And if I ever hear that you've been reporting back to Eve, you'll be out of here. Understand?"

*"Da,"* the nurse said. But Emma could tell that the woman didn't understand at all. Nadia Kochenkov might have left Mother Russia, but that didn't mean she'd divorced her.

# EIGHTEEN

Each day dissolved into the next, marked by small signs of improvement that Mackenzie and the rest of Emma's cheering section celebrated as major victories. Emma fell asleep before the fireworks on the Fourth of July but her arrival downstairs for breakfast a few mornings later, after only minimal leaning on Nadia's broad shoulder, was commemorated with stacks of Mackenzie's soon-to-be-famous chocolate chip pancakes, which she served to Emma and the others on the screened porch overlooking the lake.

"Just making it down here this morning makes me feel like I've won an Olympic medal," Emma announced as she raised a forkful of pancake in victory before popping it into her mouth. Mackenzie made the call and the next day when Bob Fortson arrived, he set up his equipment on the front porch instead of the bedroom balcony. Then he hung a gold-colored plastic medallion strung on a red, white, and blue ribbon around

Emma's neck and made her stand on the practice step, arms raised triumphantly, while they all hummed a horribly off-key rendition of "The Star-Spangled Banner."

There were benchmarks as small as Emma's first trip to the bathroom alone, an accomplishment she clearly relished and which won her an entire half hour of privacy there interrupted only by Nadia's gentle (for her) knock. "Just checking you not on floor in pool of blood."

When Emma managed to dress herself, she received one-third of a white wine spritzer, which she savored with two of Martha's fudge brownies, a reward Emma admitted she would go to great lengths for. And about which Nadia observed, "Next time put brownie crumbs on stair steps. Get down faster."

On the tenth day, physical therapy moved from the front porch to the yard and Emma sweated through it in an ancient one-piece bathing suit and a battered baseball cap over the thickening red-gold stubble that now covered her head. Her efforts were focused on what she announced as her ultimate goal: getting to the beach and into the lake, which Bob Fortson agreed would be a great place to build strength.

They gathered in Emma's bedroom at night to watch television. There Emma claimed to feel like Rocky Balboa training for his first big fight — a movie Serena chose the first night — only minus the raw egg and the sweat clothes. *Rocky* was followed by *Chariots of Fire, Braveheart, Seabiscuit,* and *Miracle,* films Emma said she appreciated but mostly slept through. Mackenzie was cueing up *The Rookie* the night Emma called a halt. "Enough. I promise I'm fully motivated. I need some escape here." At which point Serena pulled out Ethan's gift basket so that they could binge-watch *I Love Lucy* and *Dick Van Dyke* episodes. Emma didn't necessarily stay awake all the way through these programs either but, Mackenzie noticed as they tiptoed quietly out of the master bedroom, at least they put Emma to sleep smiling.

But even as Emma improved, Zoe's worry never seemed to lessen. "Would you like another cookie?" Mackenzie asked her one afternoon when Emma had gone up to rest.

"Yes, please," Zoe replied.

"Do you want to come to the grocery with me?" Serena asked.

"No, thank you," Zoe replied. "After Mom gets up, I'm going to sit with her."

Mackenzie and Serena exchanged glances.

"Colleen McAfee called," Mackenzie said, putting the cookies on a plate. "She wanted to know if you'd like to go to the club with them tomorrow." The Lake George Club, which the Michaelses had been members of since the original Valburn had been built, was maybe a half mile away.

"No, I'm good here, thanks." This had been Zoe's response to every invitation and opportunity to leave the cottage no matter for how short a time. Even an invitation to go out on the Jet Ski with Jason had been politely turned down.

When Emma was with them Zoe positioned herself inches away from her. When they ate, Zoe watched each forkful that went into Emma's mouth as if figuring out calories and nutrients and checking them off on a list.

"Am I the only one who's finding this behavior of Zoe's alarming?" Serena asked when Zoe had gone upstairs to see if Emma needed anything. "She's practically super-glued to Emma's side and she's scarily polite."

"Her mother almost died," Mackenzie said. "Did you expect her to be out partying all night and engaging in shouting matches with Emma?"

"I'm just saying it seems like a little acting out would be more normal. She's become like some Stepford child. And have you noticed she hasn't gone farther than the cove? Not once. Not to the store. Not for a walk. Not even for an ice cream cone. And you know that club has to be filled with teenage boys right now."

They were lingering on the porch one

afternoon after lunch the day Zoe turned down an invitation to go out on a local friend's family boat to see the Thursday night fireworks.

"I don't want to go. I want to be here," Zoe said to Emma. "With you."

"Nothing's going to happen to me, Zoe," Emma said softly. "Really. I'm getting stronger every day. Even Nadia thinks so. Tell her, Nadia."

"Is true. Not exactly ready for Soviet team, but better."

"Tomorrow I'm going in the water even if I have to crawl the last few yards on my belly to get there," Emma said. "I'm serious, Zoe. I want you to go out and have some fun. You deserve it."

But after Nadia helped Emma upstairs to rest that afternoon, Serena and Mackenzie found Zoe pacing the beach. They led her to a trio of Adirondack chairs and motioned her into the middle chair, trapping her between them in a fairy godmother sandwich.

"Zoe, you're going to have to let go a bit. You heard your mother. She wants you to leave occasionally, have a good time," Serena said. "I think she'd even welcome a little bratty teenage behavior."

"I can't do it."

"I know you can see how much she's improved," Mackenzie said soothingly. "She's never going to be left here alone."

Zoe shook her head. "Every time I look at her I see her lying there on the street. In that coma in the hospital. Fighting off that infection. All of it's my fault."

"No. It's not," Serena replied. "It was an accident, Zoe. One she doesn't even remember."

"But one day she's going to." Zoe stared out at the lake as she talked. "I see her concentrating sometimes, trying to remember things. Like she knows there's stuff there and she's trying to get it back. I know you've seen it, too."

Mackenzie nodded. Every once in a while Emma would startle when she walked into a room, then stare at Mackenzie intently as if something were hovering there and if she only held still long enough, it would come to her.

"Dr. Markham seems certain she'll never remember the day of the accident or even most of what happened in the hospital." Mackenzie reached a hand out and placed it on the back of Zoe's neck.

"Dr. Markham deals with head trauma all the time," Serena added. "The more-distant past is all there, but even the things happening now get kind of jumbled for her."

"But what if he's wrong?" Zoe whispered. Her arms wrapped around her bare midriff, and her eyes stayed on the distant shore of the lake. "What if one day she looks at me and it all comes back to her? What if she remembers our fight about that stupid movie and all the nasty things I said to her? What if she remembers chasing after me? What if she remembers that van that hit her?"

Tears streamed unchecked down Zoe's cheeks. Mackenzie ached for her. "Aw, Zoe, honey. You need to let go of this. Your mother loves you more than anything. She wouldn't want you to feel this way even if she remembered every single detail." Mackenzie might have been denied the daughter she'd dreamed of having, but she knew this with absolute certainty.

"I can't go out and have fun like nothing happened. I can't do it. I don't want to."

They sat in silence for a time as gulls wheeled overhead and boats crisscrossed each other's wakes out in the lake.

"Interesting," Serena said. "I don't remember Emma or your grandmother ever mentioning any Catholic or Jewish ancestors, so I'm not sure where all this guilt is coming from."

Zoe turned to look at Serena. So did Mackenzie.

"But I'm wondering, is there a certain amount of penance you're planning to do? Or is this a lifetime commitment of misery?"

Zoe blinked.

"Are you thinking two weeks? A month? Until your twenty-first birthday?"

Mackenzie raised an eyebrow, impressed

with Serena's calm logic.

"You might want to give this some thought," Serena said. "The timing of it, I mean. Because if you're not going to be available to come in and record your part on *As the World Churns* next week, I'm going to have to let Ethan know so that he has time to find someone else."

"Oh." Zoe's face registered her surprise. Her eyes were still wet, but the tears had stopped falling.

"I figured we'd stay over in the city. Maybe go see *Once* on Broadway. A good friend of mine has the second lead." Mackenzie could see that Zoe was trying not to react. She herself was trying not to smile. "We'd come back the next day."

Serena shot Mackenzie a wink over Zoe's head. The woman might not know anything about parenting, but she seemed to understand how to make an offer that was too good to refuse.

"We're going to go check on Em," Serena said. "But I'll give you an hour to think about the New York trip. If you just don't feel like you can do it, let me know. And I'll call Ethan."

They left Zoe sitting in the Adirondack chair staring out over the lake. They were careful not to look back as they made their way up the yard and the porch steps. "Wow, I have to say that was really impressive," Mackenzie said.

"It was, wasn't it?" Serena said. "Who knew watching *The Godfather* so many times would come in so handy? If I weren't afraid she'd turn around and catch me, I'd be patting myself on the back."

On the porch, they turned for a quick look. Zoe was hunched over seemingly staring at her feet. "Do you want to lay odds on what she decides?" Serena asked.

Mackenzie shook her head. "I don't want to take a chance on jinxing anything. And I guess it's safe to assume that whatever she decides, no one will be finding a horse head when they wake up tomorrow morning?"

Emma lay prone on the L-shaped dock, the brim of her baseball cap pulled low, one hand shielding her eyes from the late morning sun. The fingers of her other hand trailed in the water. "This is one of those 'be careful what you wish for' moments. Why did I think I wanted to do water exercises?"

"Good question." Mackenzie lay head-to-head, their bodies stretched out in opposite directions on the thin stretch of dock.

"What kind of masochist am I?"

"I don't know," Mackenzie said. "How many kinds are there?"

Emma smiled. "I thought it would hurt less in the water."

"Doesn't it?"

"Kind of. But I still feel like I just ran a marathon. I'm so tired of being tired all the time."

She could hear Bob on the beach packing up the floaties and other equipment he'd brought with him for the water workout. Nadia sat under a tree nearby talking softly, for her, in Russian on her cell phone. From the lake came occasional shouts and the whir of engines.

"I'm glad Zoe went with Serena," Emma said. "I was afraid she was going to sit here all summer worrying."

"Yeah."

They fell silent. Emma heard the low hum of an engine, felt the vibration of a boat stirring the water as it approached. She was too tired and too comfortable to move.

"Ahoy there, matey!" A male voice called out.

Before Emma could get her eyes all the way open and her arm out of the water, Mackenzie had sprung to her feet. Other feet pounded toward them on the dock, causing it to shake. Before the boat had reached them, Bob and Nadia had moved to either side of Emma.

"No, it's . . ." Emma began.

"Stop right there," the physical therapist shouted to the driver of the boat, who'd cut speed but made no attempt to stop.

Nadia helped Emma up then tried to put

her behind her broad back, but the deck was way too narrow. "Nyet! Halt! Don't closer!"

The driver idled the engine then turned it off completely. The boat floated in on its momentum, horizontally aligned to the dock, an impressive parallel parking job relying only on wind, current, and experience. Emma reached out to grab the side of the boat.

"No, don't!" Bob lost his footing and fell into the water with a loud splash. Nadia windmilled her massive arms. Just when it looked as if she'd regained her balance, she fell to the side, pulling Mackenzie in with her.

"Some bodyguards you've got there." The voice was wry with amusement. "Kind of reminded me of a Three Stooges movie I saw one time."

Emma caught and tied a line to the cleat on the dock. "How have you been?"

"That's what I came here to ask you," Jake Richards, longtime neighbor and first crush, said as he stepped onto the dock.

# NINETEEN

Serena and Zoe had just relaxed into the backseat of the limo that Ethan Miller had sent for them, when Serena's cell phone rang. A glance confirmed that it was the call she'd both anticipated and dreaded, the one she'd convinced herself was not going to happen. The one that had been placed from a Charleston, South Carolina, number that she'd recently memorized, and that happened to belong to one Brooks Anderson II.

"Aren't you going to answer that?" Zoe asked, looking up from her own cell phone.

Despite the anticipatory dread, Serena had not completely decided the answer to Zoe's question. She knew she should just drop the call. Except that there was a tiny part of her that wanted to at least hear his voice and what he had to say, so maybe she should let him leave a message? Her thumb began to move, but it seemed to have a mind of its own. Instead of hitting the drop button it accepted the call.

"Hello?"

She glanced at Zoe. If she'd been alone, Serena would already be speaking with some foreign accent. Pretending to be someone else so she could hang up the phone.

"Serena?" The voice was rich and full and confident.

She hadn't heard it for more than two decades except in her memory. Yet it was exactly as she'd remembered it, maybe better. Warm and husky with the long, drawn-out vowels and prep school delivery of home.

"Serena? Are you there?"

Her hands felt clammy. Her heart beat too fast. Her breathing turned shallow but there was no way in hell she'd let him know that. Just as she did before stepping on a stage, she drew a deep calming breath, tuned out everything else, and imagined her mind cleansed of all the excess debris, like a desk that's cleared, so that only the essential remained. "Who's calling?" Serena asked impatiently.

"It's Brooks."

She said nothing.

"Brooks Anderson."

He had placed the call. He had some purpose she did not want to speculate about for getting in touch. It was, in essence, his dime. She would not make it easier.

"I . . ." He paused and she half expected an apology, which she could either reject or pretend to accept before ending the call, getting herself off the line. Out of harm's way. "I'm calling because I've accepted an assignment in New York. I arrived yesterday and I'm going to be here for the next six weeks."

Her thoughts skittered to a stop. Restarted. He'd called before he flew up and had continued to call after he arrived. She could not imagine why. Did not want to imagine why.

"Ironic, I know." His tone turned self-deprecating. But he didn't add any of the things she realized she was hoping to hear. That he'd made a huge mistake not coming twenty-odd years ago. That he'd married the wrong woman. Lived the wrong life. All he said was, "I'd really love to take you out to dinner to catch up. It would be great to see you."

Serena exhaled the breath she'd been holding. Now was the moment to tell him she had no interest in anything but an apology. Except asking for an apology would indicate that she still thought about him, that he still mattered. Did she want him to know that his choice, his rejection of her, had altered the course of her life every bit as much as it had his? That it had left her feeling, not really worth marrying, not truly desirable, just not enough, no matter how many times she'd denied it to everyone but James Grant, MD, PhD? No way in hell.

"Why? What would be the point?"

She sensed the surprise in his silence and smiled grimly.

"I don't know that I'm interested in a walk down memory lane," she said in an intentionally casual tone. "Plus I'm staying up at a friend's place on Lake George. I'll only be in and out of town for work on occasion."

"Yes," he said. "I read about Emma Michaels's accident and release from the hospital. I'm glad she's okay. I remember you mentioning her the last time we spoke." So he remembered that last call, the night she'd drunk dialed him and cried so pitifully.

"I understand if you don't want to see me, Serena. It's been a lot of years. But I'm here for the next six weeks. I'm happy to meet at your convenience when you're in town. Or I can come to where you are. I know it's not the Lowcountry, but I hear the Adirondacks are quite spectacular. My time is my own."

What the hell did that mean? Was he divorced? Separated? Or simply an adulterer? No, her mother would have told her if he were any of those things.

She felt Zoe's eyes on her and realized she hadn't said anything for some time. Neither had Brooks Anderson. She stared out the window watching the scenery flash by. Now was the moment she'd been waiting for and didn't think would ever come. Her opportunity to cut him off at the knees, to tell him that the next time she'd see him would be in

223

hell, or better yet, when hell had frozen over. She could close the loop right now. She could have her say and then finally move on.

But before she could open her mouth, she was waffling, wondering. Wouldn't it be better to do this in person so that she could see his face when she told him what an asshole he'd been? What he'd missed out on?

She averted her head so that Zoe wouldn't see how hard this was for her. Despite everything she was ridiculously tempted to see Brooks one last time. Thank God Zoe's presence helped her resist that temptation.

Mackenzie lay in what she'd come to think of as "her" hammock, her laptop propped on her stomach, watching Emma do her water exercises. Smiling over Emma's protests and attempts to get Nadia into the water and working out alongside her, Mackenzie checked her email. There was no word from Adam just as there'd been no phone calls or messages since their last conversation. She'd just spent thirty minutes trying to come up with a blog post that would address what a separation could do to a couple and ideas for how a determined twosome might overcome the obstacle of distance, but she had not been able to write the first word.

She stared out over the lake at the distant mountains, a sight that normally soothed and helped put things in perspective. But she was too hurt and irritated by Adam's lack of communication, his excitement about things that didn't seem to include her, to figure out how to bridge the gap that had opened up between them. It occurred to her that she was tired of having to work so hard at their relationship. Especially when Adam seemed to think everything was fine.

Her fingers dropped from the keyboard. She checked the screen to make sure she hadn't actually typed that.

As childish as it might be, she resolved that this time she was not going to be the one to call.

She skimmed down the rest of her inbox, which was full of what could only be labeled junk, pausing at an email from Cathy Hughes at Merritt Publishing. The communication was short and upbeat indicating that the editor understood from media reports that Mackenzie was in Lake George with Emma Michaels. Was Mackenzie ready to proceed with the book? And if so, did she have an agent they should contact?

The answer to these questions were "not sure" and "no." Since the day she'd practically fled the publishing house, she'd done her best not to think about it.

At the sound of a vehicle approaching the drive, Mackenzie checked over her shoulder. It was the UPS truck. She closed the laptop, grateful for a legitimate excuse to stop working, and slid out of the hammock to go sign for the delivery.

It was an envelope addressed to Emma. The sender was Eve Michaels.

Barely a day went by without some sort of message or gift from Eve and Rex or sometimes just Eve.

Mackenzie stowed her laptop in her bedroom and left the envelope on the foyer table.

"It was so great!" Zoe's smile was broad when she and Serena got back to the lake house late the following afternoon. "Ethan said I did a really great job. He said that my performance 'blew him away'! Can you believe it?"

They'd had dinner out on the screen porch not too long after Serena and Zoe returned from New York, a large meal of chicken and steak kabobs and corn on the cob cooked on the grill and served with yellow rice. There were ice cream sandwiches for dessert.

Zoe chattered with excitement through most of the meal and afterward, when they went out to the Adirondack chairs lined up on the small beach to watch the sky pinken then gray and the stars begin to come out.

"The script was so well written," Zoe enthused. She had played Georgia Goodbody's current boyfriend's long-lost daughter. Whom he had never mentioned and who turns up on Georgia's doorstep. "Ethan says that I have a real future in front of me."

Emma watched her daughter's face as she shared the nuances of Ethan's direction, the jokes he played on cast members, the fun atmosphere in the studio and the set. She felt a flicker of unease. "You have plenty of time ahead of you for that. There's no need to rush into the business." A fragment of memory niggled. She stopped and tried to grab on to it. "I know we've talked about that before."

Zoe looked anxiously at Emma, and fell silent.

"We both had a great time," Serena said. "And Zoe did a fabulous job. Everyone thought so. If Ethan were to bring back her character on occasion, I can't see how that would be a bad thing."

Emma shot Serena a look. It was on the tip of her tongue to point out that Serena didn't have a daughter and wasn't in the business as a child, but she could never say that in front of Mackenzie, who would have given anything to have a daughter like Zoe.

"You should have seen the way Ethan looked at Serena whenever she wasn't look-ing," Zoe said, raising her eyebrows dramati-cally. "If he weren't so old I'd be crushing on him myself."

"He's just a friend," Serena said. "We've worked together a long time and we have a good rapport, that's all."

"The guy thinks you're hot." Zoe giggled.

"And he's like a comedic genius. You should totally be going out with him."

Emma watched the exchange with interest. The lighting wasn't great, but she would have laid money that Serena was blushing. Which was not something you saw every day.

"I think Zoe's right," Mackenzie said. "The man sent you *I Love Lucy* and Jujubes. That makes him a keeper in my book."

"You should never underestimate a man who can make you laugh," Emma agreed. "Clearly he knows you better than most."

"A little knowledge can be a dangerous thing," Serena quipped.

They laughed. Emma felt her spirits rise.

There were holes in her memory and she had the stamina of a ninety-year-old; she wasn't going to be training for or running a marathon anytime soon. But her hair was starting to grow back and she could handle the stairs on her own, brush her teeth, put on her clothes. And the women around her continued to celebrate each and every improvement no matter how minor.

"I heard that you've already had a gentleman caller," Serena said, giving Emma a look that said turnabout was fair play. "Not bad for someone who can barely touch her toes."

"I didn't realize that toe touching was a requirement," Emma replied.

"Touché." Serena conceded the point.

"You would have thought the poor man was

a terrorist the way my 'bodyguards' sprang to action and attempted to protect me," Emma said drily.

"It's kind of hard to protect someone when you're floundering in the water," Mackenzie said. "Emma's visitor likened us to the Three Stooges. It's a good thing he was an old friend and not a stalker." Mackenzie smiled. "I'm just glad there's no video of it."

"Is true. I have getting soft," Nadia said sadly when she brought out a shawl, which she placed on Emma's shoulders. "Losing edge here in lap of luxury."

Emma smiled as she remembered Jake Richards's visit. "I've known Jake since I started coming here as a toddler. His family's been here since the French and Indian War, I think. They were among the founding families of Bolton Landing and the club."

"He was definitely cute, Em," Mackenzie said. "In that 'don't need to impress anybody, salt of the earth' way. Is he married?"

"He was. But I think I heard he'd gotten divorced."

"Aha!" Serena said.

"Not aha!" Emma replied firmly. "Just an old family friend who stopped by to see how I'm doing. Believe me, he's not someone looking to get caught up in the whole Hollywood thing."

She caught Serena's considering look and hoped to hell she wasn't blushing like Serena had. "It was nice to see an old friend who asked after my health and invited us out on his boat. End of story."

"Can we go?" Zoe asked.

"I not send you on boat without help," Nadia said.

"Then I guess you can come and protect me from . . . overly aggressive mosquitoes?"

The air grew cooler and after a time they headed inside for the night. In the foyer, Mackenzie picked up a large envelope that had been lying on the table and handed it to her. "This came this afternoon."

Emma yawned. "It doesn't say urgent anywhere on it, but you can go ahead and open it if you want."

Mackenzie did. "It's a gift certificate," she said, pulling out a single sheet of vellum paper and scanning it. "It's for a spa day at the Sagamore for all four of us."

Emma was tired and not in the mood for Eve's games. "I'm not sure why she keeps flinging gifts at me. But I wish she'd stop."

"There's no place where you have to sign that you'll be her BFF or formally forgive her," Serena said. "And this gift is for all of us. My nails are in an embarrassing condition and my pores are the size of a small country. You are so not going to return this."

"It's too late," Emma said. "I can't be bought."

"Me either," Serena said. "But I think I can

be rented."

"Can we go?" Zoe looked at her mother. "The Sagamore is so awesome!"

Emma looked at her daughter and something teased at the back of her mind. She went still for a moment trying to focus enough to identify it. Just when she thought she had a piece of it, it fluttered out of reach. A flush of panic rose inside her, but she beat it back. "Okay," she said reaching out a hand to caress her daughter's cheek. "A spa day it is!"

# TWENTY

"If I were any more relaxed I'd be asleep." Serena sighed happily and took a sip from the glass of chardonnay.

"Me too," Mackenzie agreed. "How about you, Em?"

They had spent the morning in the Sagamore's newly renovated salon and spa, being manicured, pedicured, exfoliated, massaged, buffed, and waxed. Now they sat at a prime table in the open-air restaurant that perched on the edge of the lake. The ends of the brightly patterned scarf Emma had tied over the duck fuzz that now covered her head fluttered in the breeze.

"I'm looking to sleep less not more," Emma said. "But I have to say that hot stone massage pushed me right over the edge into fabulous."

"I bet Nadia gives a mean deep tissue massage," Mackenzie said.

"I think 'mean' is the operative word. My tissues don't want anyone going that deep.

Ever," Serena said. "You should have seen her face when Emma insisted she take the day off." `

"She works hard," Emma replied. "She deserves it."

"I don't think relaxation is something former Soviet weight lifters with possible ties to the KGB know a lot about. Country invading? Dictator toppling? Yes. Downtime? Not so much." Serena laughed.

"Well, I hope she's having as nice a day as we are," Emma said. "I feel refreshed and restored. Just like the Sagamore." She turned to consider the sprawling Victorian edifice that had burned and been rebuilt more than once.

"To getting better!" Serena raised her glass. Everyone joined in the toast.

"And to friends who . . ." Emma swallowed and readjusted the scarf on her head. ". . . friends who stepped up for me and Zoe in a way that I will never, ever, allow myself to forget. I really don't know how to thank you."

They clinked and drank again, but even as her own eyes grew damp, Serena wanted to know why Emma had let go of them without explanation five years ago and why she'd invited them back to the lake as if she'd never discarded them. She glanced at Mackenzie's face and imagined she saw the same questions there. They'd been too worried, too focused on Emma's recovery and being there for Zoe, to ask the questions and demand the answers they would have if the accident had never happened.

"I'm guessing Adam is already begging you to come home," Emma said.

"No. No begging." Mackenzie drained her glass. "Adam's actually out in LA. Universal's interested in his latest screenplay and he's got his nose to the grindstone trying to get it ready."

"Wow," Zoe said. "That's so cool."

Mackenzie nodded, but her smile didn't quite reach her eyes. "It looks like this could be it."

"How long has he been there?" Emma asked.

"We flew out the same day," Mackenzie said. "He's been asking about you. You know, checking in to see how you're doing."

"I'll have to thank him for managing without you for so long," Emma said. "I know you both have things to get back to, but I hope you'll stay as long as you can. At least long enough to help celebrate Zoe's Sweet Sixteen. I did promise you a lake vacation, which up until now hasn't been particularly vacation-like."

"Well, today's been stellar," Serena said. "And I wouldn't miss Zoe's big day. In the meantime since Eve's paying, who's up for something sweet?"

They finished their meal with a variety of

decadent desserts that they ate off each other's plates. Feigned sneak attacks left them with crumbs in their laps and smiles on their faces.

Afterward they parked on Lake Shore Drive and strolled along the sidewalk window-shopping in Bolton Landing, ultimately following Emma into a small antiques store. Inside, the air was cool and slightly musty. Every available inch of floor and wall was covered with memorabilia, antique tools, boating or fishing gear.

Zoe took one look at the boy who came out to greet them, and went quiet. Serena didn't blame her. He was well over six feet with an athletic build, slightly shaggy blond hair, and friendly brown eyes. "Hi, Miss Michaels. Zoe. Good to see you. Dad said you were in town."

Emma introduced Ryan Richards to Serena and Mackenzie.

"Aren't you about to start college?" Emma asked.

"Yes, ma'am," he said politely. "I'll be a freshman in the fall."

"Ryan comes from a long line of Harvard men," Emma said.

"That's assuming they don't realize they made a mistake when he gets there." An older, more polished version of the boy came out of the back room. "Jake Richards," he said, shaking hands with Mackenzie and Serena, then hugging Zoe and Emma. His brown eyes crinkled in good humor.

"These motors are great," Serena said, nodding toward several small boat motors displayed on wooden stands. "From the twenties?"

"Yep." Jake placed a large, capable hand on the top of a motor. "Designers like them for restaurant décor, and collectors have started driving the prices up."

"So you don't miss corporate law now that you're here year-round?" Emma asked.

"Nope." Jake shrugged, leaned comfortably back against the counter. "I'm exactly as busy as I want to be. I talk to people who stop in. Help out at the historical society. Go to the club. Get out on the lake every chance I get."

"And the winters?" Emma asked.

"I've come to love them. It's quiet and I've got a small warehouse where I work on things."

"You should see the boat Dad restored," Ryan said.

"You restored a whole boat?" Emma asked with interest.

"Oh, yeah. She's a beaut. A 1929 Chris Craft Cadet Triple Cockpit. I thought we'd take her out whenever you ladies are ready."

"I'm ready," Serena said.

"Me too," Mackenzie added.

Zoe nodded, stealing a glance at Ryan from beneath her lashes.

"What do you say, Em?" Jake asked. His

tone was casual, but his brown eyes were intent. It would be hard to say no to those eyes.

"I've got physical therapy tomorrow," Emma said. "But if you have room for all of us plus one former weight lifting Russian nurse, we could make it the day after?"

"Sounds good," Jake said. "Ryan and I will pick you up at your dock at ten. We'll get out on the lake, cruise around a bit, and maybe have a picnic out on one of the islands. Just like in the old days."

Serena bit back a smile as identical blushes spread across Emma's and Zoe's cheeks.

They were gathered in Emma's room that night making a show of tucking her into bed in Nadia's absence, when Mackenzie's phone rang.

"I really don't need anyone to tuck me in," Emma protested, though her predinner nap had hardly put a dent in her exhaustion. As she spoke, Mackenzie pulled the phone out of her pajama pocket. "I only let Nadia do it because I haven't been able to figure out how to stop her."

"Where do you think she can be?" Mackenzie asked.

"I don't know, but she drove off on that scooter like a woman on a mission," Serena said. "There isn't exactly a ton of nightlife in either Lake George Village or Bolton Landing. So I'm sure she'll be back soon."

Mackenzie frowned down at her phone, and then answered it with a hesitant, "Hello?"

With a quick look at Emma, she stepped away from the bed. "Yes, yes, it's Mackenzie. . . . Fine, thank you. . . . Yes, it was great. Thank you so much for . . . everything. We had a lovely time. . . . Yes, I know Emma enjoyed it too. . . . She's in bed just now. I don't think . . ." Mackenzie's shoulders hunched. "Um, yes. . . . Yes. . . . Um, no. Really, it's not . . ."

She turned around with a sigh, and held her phone out to Emma. "Eve, um, wants to talk with you."

"No. Tell her I'm asleep already. Tell her I . . ."

Mackenzie winced, mouthed an apology, and handed her the phone. Everyone else stopped what they were doing to listen.

"Emma?" Eve's voice sounded in Emma's ear, too close and too eager. "I . . . I just wanted to make sure you enjoyed the spa."

Emma sighed. "Yes. Thank you. Everyone had a nice time." She made to hand the phone back to Mackenzie but Eve was already talking.

"I've left a card on account at the spa. So anytime you want to go, don't hesitate. And I was thinking maybe you and Zoe would like to go to lunch one day. If I were to come up we could . . ."

Tired and irritated, Emma cut her off. "You're going to fly from California for lunch in 'the *boonies*'?" She emphasized the term Eve had always applied to the lake house, Bolton Landing, Lake George, and the entire 6.1 million acres that comprised the Adirondack Park.

"I'm not in California. I'm in New York," Eve said tautly. "And I'd love to come up to take you and Zoe for lunch. Or . . . perhaps you and she could come down to celebrate her birthday with dinner and a show. Or maybe a shopping spree . . ." Eve named all the things she had done rarely with Emma and then only grudgingly.

"No."

"No, what?" Eve asked in the too-reasonable manner she'd adopted.

"No, I don't want to go to lunch. No, I don't want you to come here," Emma said. "No, don't keep calling and guilting people into putting me on the line with you." Emma drew another breath, but she couldn't stop the words rushing from her lips. Not that she made any great effort to do so. "No, I don't want your credit card on account at the Sagamore or anywhere else. No more gifts. No more anything. No means no. Nothing. Nyet."

"But . . ."

Emma disconnected the call and handed the phone back to Mackenzie.

239

They were all still staring at her.

"What's going on?" Serena asked.

"Eve is still in New York. She claims she wants to come up and have lunch or something."

"Because?" Mackenzie asked.

"How the hell would I know?" Emma replied. "I've never understood anything she's done or more to the point didn't do. But I have no doubt she has some ulterior motive."

Zoe had been watching the conversation as one might a tennis match. "Do you think maybe she just wants to try to make up for everything?"

"That would be nice, Zoe, but highly unlikely," Emma said more quietly.

"I'm sorry for giving you the phone," Mackenzie said. "It just felt wrong to have enjoyed her gift and then tell her to go screw herself."

"It's not wrong," Emma said, attempting to at least approximate calm even if she didn't feel it. "As soon as she sees a chink in anyone's armor she goes in for the kill. It's not wrong. It's self-preservation."

In Emma's dreams that night Eve hovered above her like a dark cloud. Large and menacing she obliterated the light of a summer moon that was trying to shine down on some odd forest/closet combination whose floor appeared to be covered with what was

240

either lush grass or really old green shag carpet.

The cloud glowered above the girl, who cowered on the forest/closet floor, imploring her to behave like a Michaels. But this time the cowering red-haired girl wasn't Emma. It was Zoe.

"No!" Emma fought to reach her daughter's side, determined to shield her from the cloud that even now was changing shape. But Zoe remained just out of reach.

*Whoever the set decorator is in this dream should be fired.* Gran's voice sounded in her head, wry and comforting. *There's a reason green shag didn't survive the seventies.*

*Not funny.* Emma watched in horror as Zoe straightened, took a step toward Eve. But Zoe didn't beg permission *not* to act as Emma once had. She was demanding the right to be onstage. She wanted to perform.

*This is not your movie, darling. It's Zoe's,* Gran's voice whispered.

*But she's too young to know what she wants.*

*You knew.* Gran's voice was warm. *I wouldn't have done what I did if I'd had any doubt.*

*But she has no idea what the business can do to a person.* Fingers of fear trailed along Emma's spine. The fear was not for herself.

*No. But Zoe has something you did not.* She could feel Gran's smile.

*What's that?*

*A mother who will be there to help her navigate. One who will have her best interests at heart.*

Zoe and the closet faded. Emma didn't wake, but she could still feel her grandmother's presence even as the images changed. In the new dream Emma was nine or ten. Her parents were home for a visit. Eve and Rex had even tucked her into bed. But something woke her, some sound.

Quietly she padded into the kitchen of the Hollywood Hills house to get a drink of water. She'd set the empty glass on the counter, when something moved out near the pool house. Emma went to the window and peered out. It was Eve barefoot and wearing a lacy white peignoir that floated around her like a cloud. Emma pressed her nose to the glass, unable to look away as her mother backed away from the pool house window, sagged into the nearest chaise, and dropped her head into her hands. Her shoulders shook as she cried.

*Your father was never meant for marriage or fatherhood.* Gran's voice was soft, filled with regret. *And your mother knew it; she believed if she looked the other way it would cease to exist.*

*I married a man just like my father. Only I told myself it was for more noble reasons. But I was just afraid.* Emma wished Gran were here now and not just in her head and her dreams, but the nightmare images had faded. *What does Eve want from me? Why won't she leave me alone?*

*I'm not sure.* Gran's voice sounded less certain.

*But I thought you were supposed to know all and see all.*

Gran's face wavered before her. An amused smile on her lips. *You're thinking of those Johnny Carson episodes I let you watch. When Johnny played Carnac the Magnificent.* Emma felt as much as heard her grandmother's sigh. *The afterlife doesn't work like that. Sometimes there's too much static. Sometimes a person has so many motives it's hard to tell which ones matter.*

# TWENTY-ONE

The day dawned clear and bright with a pale blue sky, pulled-cotton clouds, and a bright yellow ball of sun vaulting up into it. A faint breeze teased at the tree branches and shrubs but barely raised a ripple on the calm waters of the lake. It was a day that belonged on a postcard with the words "Wish You Were Here" scrawled across the bottom. A postcard Mackenzie would definitely not be sending to her husband.

They stood on the dock in their bathing suits and cover-ups, clutching beach bags and towels. A picnic basket and a cooler filled with food and drinks sat at Nadia's feet. "I carry, no problem," she'd said when Mackenzie had finished packing it with an array of goodies Martha had left for them.

The nurse had been smiling since she'd returned from her day off the day before last, but had so far offered no clue as to where she'd been or what she'd done. Her smile was pure Mona Lisa — if the Mona Lisa could have bench-pressed six hundred pounds and had short spiky blond hair. And if da Vinci had thought to paint her in a pair of cutoffs that exposed tree trunk thighs and a halter bathing suit top that left her muscular shoulders and arms bare. A tattoo in the shape of the Soviet Union with Cupid's arrow through it had been inked on her back just behind her right shoulder.

Having the blessing and curse of the Michaels red-gold hair and white skin, Emma and Zoe slathered sunscreen all over each other then donned sunglasses and baseball caps — Emma's covered the uneven new growth that was a stark reminder of what she'd been through and how vulnerable she still was.

Mackenzie, who'd made it through one of the coldest Indiana winters on record, took the lotion bottle when they were done and applied it liberally. Her beach bag had a long-sleeved T-shirt and a towel. Serena, who'd grown up in a southern family that prized smooth creamy complexions on its women, did the same. Only Nadia, whose bare limbs were, according to Serena, "as white as a field of new cotton," didn't bother with sunscreen.

"Want color. Was told it good with my hair and eyes."

The Richardses arrived in *The Mohican,* a gleaming mahogany twenty-two footer with pinstriped decks, and a flag that flew from

245

the stern. It reeked of 1920s glamour, and Mackenzie wouldn't have been surprised to see Jay Gatsby behind the wheel, although Jake Richards didn't look too bad there, either.

"She's gorgeous," Emma said over the rumble of the engine as Jake handed her into the front seat then reached a hand out to Zoe.

"Why, thank you, ma'am," Jake said gallantly. "I could say the same for all of you."

Nadia handed the cooler and picnic basket to Ryan, who stowed it on the rear seat and then offered a hand to help the rest of them aboard.

Mackenzie, Serena, and Ryan sat in the bench seat behind Jake, Emma, and Zoe while Nadia happily claimed the seat behind the engine deck, which she shared with their picnic basket and cooler.

The engine's rumble turned throatier as Jake put the throttle in gear then pushed off from the dock to motor out of the cove. Once in open water he gave it gas. The rumble rose to a roar and the bow rose as *The Mohican* gained speed.

Cool air buffeted them as the boat planed off and began to skim over the lake's sun-dappled surface. Jake drove with one hand, his other arm slung across Emma's seat back. Zoe's ponytail poked through her cap and flew out behind her. When he thought no one was looking, Ryan reached up and gave it a tug. When she turned he feigned ignorance. But as soon as she turned around he tugged it again. Their laughter, along with Emma's and Jake's, floated lightly above the sound of the engine. It was a glorious day to be alive, and Mackenzie could feel Emma treasuring each moment of it.

Everyone they passed noticed *The Mohican.* A friendly lot, the boaters pointed and waved and called out as the classic wooden boat swept by.

Mackenzie rested her elbow on the side and tried to take in everything at once: the tree-covered islands that flashed by, the white frothy wakes they cut across, the birds winging their way through the summer sky. Her mind wandered to Adam and she pulled it back. She had tried to stop counting the days that had passed without a call from him (five) but found herself ticking them off like a castaway on a desert island beach. Yesterday there'd been a quick text — *headed to meeting, how r u?* — which had caused her to waste an entire thirty minutes debating whether to respond. Finally she'd settled on an even briefer "fine," which she did not even bother to punctuate. He'd asked a question; she'd answered. Done.

*The Mohican* turned north and began to hug the eastern shore. Jake had informed them that since it had been years since they'd been out on the lake together, even Emma and Zoe were going to be treated like tourists. He pointed out the sights along the way and as they passed what he identified as Fourteen Mile Island and Shelving Rock, he cut speed. "We're entering the Narrows here," he called back to them, and sure enough the lake shrank to about a mile across with the Black Mountain range to their right and Tongue Mountain to their left. Deftly, Jake began weaving through a cluster of small, tree-covered islands strewn across the lake like dice. "There are a lot of shoals and shallows through here so we'll have to take it slow, but to my mind it's the prettiest section."

Jake knew what he was talking about. They'd been on the lake many times over the years while visiting with Emma but while Mackenzie saw things she recognized, she'd forgotten just how beautiful the lake and its surrounds were. How visceral an impact such natural grandeur could instill. As they entered the aptly named Paradise Bay, they fell silent. The jagged shoreline was shrouded in trees whose branches skimmed the water and cloaked the rock face that rose to tower above it. Encircled by lush green mountainside, the bay was secluded and magical. Boats of all sizes floated on the deep blue water. "There's no anchoring or rafting to other boats here," Jake said as he idled the engine. "It's crowded this time of year. And with the tour boats always coming through, the locals typically stay away. But it's a hard spot to resist.

"In the early nineteenth century the rich folk who populated the mansions on Millionaires' Row used to bring guests here in steam-driven yachts for afternoon tea and sometimes for dinner," Jake said.

"Ah, yes, as opposed to you poor peasants who've owned acres and acres of land here since the seventeen hundreds," Emma teased back. "Jake has little respect for us upstarts who didn't arrive until the eighteen hundreds." It was wonderful to see the easy smile on her lips and the saucy tilt of her head.

They floated companionably, cradled in the sleek wooden boat that creaked comfortably beneath them. The breeze was soft, the temperature somewhere in the seventies. Occasionally a puffy cloud passed in front of the sun.

"Can we go over to Calves Pen and do some cliff jumping for a while?" Ryan asked his father.

Nadia, who had stretched out on the deck with a contented sigh and whose large expanses of white skin could undoubtedly be spotted from outer space, roused for this. "Miz Mickhels not jumping off cliffs. Not even over dead body."

Emma smiled impishly. "And here the only thing that's kept me going is the possibility of flinging myself from a cliff again sometime soon."

There was a ripple of laughter.

"I know that's what I live for," Serena said. "Not." She'd turned in her seat and brought her knees up to her chest. Her dark hair had been mostly tucked up under her hat, but wisps of it fluttered around her face. "I think the yacht tea parties sound way more attractive. I can just picture the white glove service and silver tea set with Paradise in the background."

"Your mother was a stellar cliff jumper back in the day," Jake informed Zoe. "Though I don't think she ever managed to keep her eyes open on the way down."

"Ha, that shows how much attention you were paying," Emma retorted.

Jake made no reply, but from the look on his face, Mackenzie suspected that Jake had been paying plenty of attention.

"I could take you one day if you want," Ryan said to Zoe. "I've got a twelve-foot runabout. And I don't head up to school until after Labor Day." The girl smiled up at him, and Mackenzie had the feeling Zoe's reluctance to leave her mother's side might have met its match. Emma and Zoe slathered on sunscreen and pulled their baseball caps lower on their heads. Serena shrugged into a long-sleeved T-shirt and straightened her straw hat. Mackenzie did the same.

"Nadia?" Emma offered the nurse the bottle of sunscreen, but the woman shook her head slowly; her normally vigilant eyes looked ready to close. "I know it's clouded over a bit, but the sun is strong and it's reflecting off the lake."

"Is okay," Nadia replied. "My skin strong. Like me."

"Anybody else ready for lunch?" Jake asked when his son's rumbling stomach made itself heard.

It seemed all of them were and so they motored through the bay to nearby Hazel Island, which Jake had finagled a last-minute permit for. There Jake eased the boat up to a temporary dock. Despite both Richardses' offers of help, Nadia hefted the cooler smoothly to her chest then up to one impressive shoulder. The path they followed was strewn with pine needles and led to a picnic site comprising a large wooden table, a grill, a fire pit, and a breathtaking view down the Narrows. They munched on thick tuna and ham sandwiches, gobbled down cut fruit and potato salad, then dawdled over Martha's duly famous chocolate chip cookies.

Jake, Ryan, and Zoe waded out into the water. Nadia followed behind them.

"So what are we thinking for Zoe's birthday?" Mackenzie asked when they were out of earshot.

"Eve's idea of dinner and a show in the city

would be a good one except I don't think any of us have the energy. I'm even thinking about doing my next recording session by phone patch from up here," Serena said.

"As I'm pretty sure I mentioned last night, I'm not up for anything Eve suggests," Emma said.

"Yeah, we got that," Serena replied. "But Zoe brought up an interesting point. I mean, has Eve ever worked this hard to connect with you before?"

They both watched Emma's face. Mackenzie was surprised to see Emma seemingly considering the question.

"No." Emma's admission was reluctant.

"Maybe you almost dying forced her to see things differently," Mackenzie said. "I know it's made me think about a lot of things in a way I never have."

Serena nodded. "It's pretty hard not to."

Emma looked out over the water. "Well, I guess anything's possible, but I definitely wouldn't count on it."

Zoe's laughter reached them, followed by the sounds of serious splashing. There was a victorious shout in Russian.

"All right, so we're going to be celebrating locally. Why don't we just chill and cook out. And maybe let Zoe pick a film?" Mackenzie suggested.

"It doesn't sound very exciting for such a milestone birthday," Emma said.

"All things considered, I don't think she's expecting an extravaganza," Mackenzie said. "I have no doubt your daughter would be the first to say that having you back among the living is present enough."

"I know what'll make it more exciting," Serena said with a nod toward the four who were headed back to the boat. "Invite Ryan and Jake. And we'll pile on some extra presents. Maybe even start the day with birthday cake for breakfast like we used to do back in the day."

A short time later they climbed back into *The Mohican* for the ride back to the lake house, where they arrived pleasantly tired, happily windblown, and satisfyingly sun kissed.

As it turned out, some of them had been kissed harder than others. Emma looked the healthiest Serena had seen her, with a touch of color in her cheeks and a couple of new freckles across the bridge of her nose, while Zoe's glow was a combination of sun, youth, and a budding crush on a good-looking boy. Mackenzie, like Serena, had fared pretty well. Only Nadia moved carefully, her arms held away from her body like the Tin Man in need of an oilcan, her face a shade of red that hurt to look at.

The woman who could bench-press the lot of them took each front step at a turtle's pace, expending a great deal of effort not to bend her knees, brush her legs together, or allow her arms to touch her sides. They gathered on the porch above her unsure what to do.

"Are you okay?" Serena asked though it was obvious she wasn't.

"Nyet." Nadia said this quietly, careful not to shake her head or even move her lips more than necessary. "I too hot. Too . . . red."

"But you could land a job as a stop sign if you ever get tired of nursing." Serena winced as the words tumbled out. "Sorry."

"Don't make laugh," Nadia said. "It hurt." She continued to speak with as little movement as possible, but the shock in her voice matched what showed in her eyes. "I burnt. Turn red like lobster."

"Okay," Emma said. "Before we go any further I think we should go ahead and take 'I told you so' off the table."

The rest of them nodded. Nadia made it up one more step.

"Do we have any oatmeal?" Mackenzie asked.

"Not need breakfast. Need cool down." Another step was conquered.

"Good thinking, Mac. An oatmeal bath is definitely the way to go," Emma said.

"I'll check the pantry." Zoe turned and went inside.

"Okay, I'm sorry but I'm feeling this horrible urge to put on Alicia Keys's 'Girl on Fire,' " Serena said.

"Don't you dare. I don't even want to hear you humming it." Mackenzie reached out a hand to the struggling nurse.

"No. Don't touch." Nadia made it up the final step and stood swaying slightly on the porch, her arms outstretched, her legs straight and apart. Like some large starfish cast up on a beach.

"Got it." Zoe appeared in the open doorway, a canister of Quaker Oats in one hand.

"Start a cool bath," Emma told her daughter. "We'll sprinkle a cup or two in it."

They hovered around Nadia all the way to the guest room and into the attached bath.

"You need to get undressed," Mackenzie said.

"Feel like baby," Nadia whispered. "Afraid to move."

"We've got this," Emma said to the woman who despite her size and tough manner had tended her so carefully. "Zoe, Martha has an aloe plant growing up in the master bath. Can you bring it and that bottle of Aveeno moisturizer down?" She moved toward the nurse. "Serena, Mackenzie, and I are going to get these clothes off and get Nadia into the tub."

By the time Zoe got back with the things Emma had requested, Serena, Emma, and Mackenzie were a sodden mess and the bathroom floor resembled the deck of a sinking ship, but Nadia was in the tub and Emma was pressing the wet washcloth gently to her face.

"Now we know just how many puny American women it takes to get a Russian weight lifter into a bathtub," Serena said, eyeing the disaster area that the bathroom had become. "I think some of us need a new exercise program."

"All I know is I'm ready for a shower and a nap," Emma said with a tired smile as Serena's cell phone vibrated in her pocket. "But it feels good to take care of someone else for a change."

They left Nadia soaking to go upstairs and get cleaned up. Emma leaned heavily on Zoe. Serena felt the vibration that signaled a message being left, but it wasn't until she'd showered and pulled on a light robe that she checked her messages.

Brooks Anderson had called not once but twice. More to the point, Brooks Anderson was driving up to Lake George. He'd made a reservation for dinner tomorrow night at the Inn at Erlowest, the restored mansion down the road. "I hear they have an incredible chef and the place is right on the lake not too far from you."

There was a brief silence before the voice that sent unwelcome shivers of memory up her spine continued, "I made a reservation for eight p.m. I hope you can make it." And then the words that she'd yearned to hear for so long: "There are so many things I need to say to you."

# TWENTY-TWO

"Are you sure you don't mind if I take the Jeep?" Serena stood in the doorway of the den, where the others were settling in to watch a movie. She felt conspicuous in the tight, short black dress with the plunging neckline that she'd chosen, especially given the fact that everyone else was still wearing the shorts and T-shirts they'd pulled on that morning. They were also makeup free, while she had spent a full hour and a half applying makeup and twisting her hair into an intentionally messy knot that brushed one shoulder. A girl needed her armor and a couple of weapons at her disposal if she was going to confront her past. It wasn't every day you got the chance to make the person who'd dumped you see exactly what he'd lost.

"You want scooter?" Nadia, who apparently saw no conflict with a minidress and the necessity to swing a leg over a motorcycle seat, was slathered in aloe lotion, her face a tight cherry red, her arms and legs still splayed starfish-like. Although she'd protested mightily that she was there to "take care Miz Mickhels" and not the other way around, she'd succumbed when Emma promised not to tell Eve and then presented the nurse with the first of the Xanax Mackenzie used for flying. That with the special salve that Martha had whipped up had served to make her more comfortable.

"You missing Three Stooges in *So Long Mr. Chumps,*" the nurse said. "And popping corn, too."

"I take it your 'friend' " — Mackenzie made air quotation marks for emphasis — "is male." As if Serena might, for some inconceivable reason, have gone to this trouble to impress another woman.

If Zoe hadn't been there, Serena had no doubt Mackenzie would have added and air quoted the word "married" to her observation. Which might have something to do with the fact that Mackenzie now barely mentioned the husband she'd always seemed to worship. "My feet hurt from just looking at those heels."

Serena shrugged. "I'm willing to dress for a gourmet meal. And I'm not planning to walk one step farther than in the door and to the table."

"I've heard the new chef at Erlowest is first rate," Emma said. "We're open to doggie bags."

"If it's as good as all that we'll all go there together," Serena said. "You seem stronger and your hair's starting to look less like a baby chick's. Maybe we should go out and celebrate." In fact, watching Emma take charge of Nadia's sunburn had been an impressive sign of improvement. "Or maybe you should let Jake Richards take you."

Emma laughed but sidestepped the comment about Jake. "I do feel better, but not enough to go anywhere that would require as much prep time as you've put in. It was time well spent though. You do look mah-veh-lous." Emma had always done a fair Ricardo Montalban impression.

"Why thank you eveh so much." Opting for Georgia Goodbody, Serena batted her lashes and mimed her fan. "Y'all know how compliments do go straight to my head."

Mackenzie and Emma rolled their eyes. "You are quite welcome, Katie Scarlett." Emma did a pretty fair southern accent when she had a mind to. And had watched *Gone with the Wind* on more than one occasion in deference to Serena's southern roots.

"Don't wait up." Serena gave them a finger wave and tucked her evening bag beneath her arm. Outside, she climbed carefully into the Jeep, her trepidation giving way to an embarrassingly giddy sense of excitement. It was the moment she'd imagined since Brooks Anderson II had up and married someone else, her own personal shoot-out at the OK Corral. The moment when she would force him to confront the mistake he'd made. At which point she would succinctly and articulately call him all the names he so richly deserved before making an unforgettably dramatic exit. Serena smiled at the scene as it played out in her head.

It was only a matter of minutes south on Highway 9 before the sign for Erlowest appeared. She turned left and followed the narrow road that curved down toward the lake. "Goodness," she breathed at her first sight of the huge turn-of-the-century stone castle that sat high on a hill overlooking the water. Careful not to teeter, she walked across the parking lot, stopping briefly to take in the stone patio with its outdoor fireplace, around which guests sat enjoying the flickering flames and the expansive view of Lake George.

Inside, everything spoke of the home's luxurious history. Through a pedimented and framed doorway to the left lay two small formal dining rooms with white-cloth-covered tables, intricate woodwork, and period wallpapers and furnishings. Just beyond it an elegant staircase angled upward. A stained glass window bearing a coat of arms gleamed above the landing.

She stepped up to the small welcome desk that had been set in a corner of the living room.

"Mr. Anderson is waiting for you in the lounge, Miss Stockton." The young woman escorted her past the stairs and through a short hallway to a small wood-paneled room. It was a masculine space with a wooden bar at one end and a sitting area and fireplace at the other. A small wooden door led onto the stone patio.

Brooks Anderson was seated near the fireplace and stood as she entered. He was still tall and broad shouldered with the build of a former athlete who had most definitely not gone to fat. The years had not diminished his appearance; in fact, just the opposite. His brown eyes lit with the warm smile that she'd never forgotten. His nose was still patrician, his cheekbones strong, his chin firm. His dark hair was still thick and only lightly threaded with gray. A tan that came from hours on a golf course and no doubt a family beach house on Fripp or Kiawah or some other expensive Lowcountry island tinged his skin. He was living the life they'd both grown up in. And which he'd chosen over her.

His lips, which she also remembered too well, said, "I wasn't sure you'd come."

He came forward and took one of her hands in his, and at that simple touch she was overwhelmed by memories. Only they weren't the angry final ones she'd been reliving for so long. Their families had always known each other but what she remembered now was the moment he'd really seen her for the first time. It had been the summer before his senior year at Carolina, when she was still in high school. Both of their families had been delighted when they'd started dating. They'd become less so when she accepted a scholarship to NYU's drama school. But Brooks had claimed to admire her sense of adventure and, with his newly acquired MBA, had agreed to accept a job at Morgan Stanley in Manhattan, where they'd live while she studied acting and he began to build his career. The rest, as they said, was history.

"Me either."

They stared into each other's eyes and she felt a shiver of . . . She wasn't sure whether it was anticipation or apprehension. She'd come prepared to unleash her anger, to make him regret what he had done. But she hadn't expected the feelings that were flooding through her now, hadn't thought his touch could ignite anything except more anger.

"Would you like a drink?"

"Sure." She took back her hand and followed him over to the bar, where the bartender poured her a glass of prosecco. She needed to be careful. In control. Make him regret what he'd done and get out. "The inn is beautiful," she said, falling back on the manners and small talk that had been drilled into her from childhood. Underneath it all her heart was beating too wildly. "I understand the chef is new and well thought of." She took a sip of her drink.

"Yes, I was given a grand tour when I checked in." He said this with a smile that creased the corners of the eyes that were considering her so carefully. "There are apparently ten fully restored suites, thirteen fireplaces, two formal dining rooms, several living rooms, and this lounge, all of it built by and for a bachelor." His Charlestonian accent flowed over her, smooth and familiar.

"There's no accounting for the things some men will do," she said more flippantly than she felt.

"Too true." He looked her right in the eye.

"Mr. Anderson?"

He placed a hand on the small of Serena's back as they followed the young woman to the dining room where they were seated at a table for two beneath a leaded stained glass window. Crystal and silver glinted in the candlelight. The wallpaper was a deep red, the chairs a warm mahogany, and the carved coffered ceiling, moldings, and architectural details turned the formal room surprisingly intimate. Far more intimate than she intended for this meal to get.

They'd barely been seated when a bottle of champagne arrived in a silver bucket. After a look to Serena for approval, Brooks nodded and the cork was removed, first glasses poured.

"It's a good thing I'm staying less than a mile from here." She reminded herself to be careful how much she drank, but she could feel a heady excitement bubbling up inside her in the same way the champagne bubbled in their glasses. Brooks's intent gaze confirmed that her efforts on her hair and makeup had paid off.

"The suite they've given me takes up a good quarter of the second floor," he said. "If you don't feel comfortable making the drive, I have plenty of room."

Serena smiled but made no comment. She would walk every step in these murderous overpriced heels before she'd end up in what was probably a curtained tester bed.

They clinked their glasses. "To old friends," she said.

"And new beginnings," he added before they drank.

*What the hell did that mean?* She dropped her eyes to the menu and focused on the handwritten descriptions. "Everything looks delicious," she said.

"Yes, everything does," he murmured. She didn't have to look up to know he was looking at her and not the menu.

"What do you think sounds better for a starter, Hudson Valley foie gras or bison tartare?" she asked, though she couldn't have cared less. She lifted her eyes and sipped the champagne, studying him as he studied her.

"I say we each order one so we can taste them both," he said.

She nodded and smiled again, though she had no intention of allowing either one of them to slip so much as a morsel into the other's mouth. But it seemed the balloon of her long-held anger had sprung a slow leak now that they were sitting across the table from each other. She felt as if she'd gone on-stage certain of her lines, only to have the other actor veer wildly off script.

But she was a professional actress, and a script or scene could only be hijacked if she allowed it. "So," she said. "Tell me what you're doing in New York."

She listened as he talked about the deal his client was putting together with a large New York hedge fund and the role he would play in seeing that it got done. "I couldn't help thinking about our plans, yours and mine. How I would be a titan of finance and you would be a famous actress." He raised his glass of champagne to her. "I've done well by Charleston standards. But you" — he shook his head and smiled — "you've achieved exactly what you set out to. Just as I knew you would."

She didn't drink, she couldn't. And she damned sure wasn't going to point out that she was famous for playing a cartoon of herself, as she usually did. The truth was the way he was looking at her, his obvious admi-

266

ration and attraction, were balms to her soul.

Somehow they made it through the starters (no spit was swapped) and she managed to choose an entrée and even a dessert as she pressed him for more details of the project and how long he'd be in New York.

He asked about *As the World Churns,* whether she still loved New York, what part of it she lived in, and how Emma was feeling. Somehow, neither of them mentioned his wife or his children, whom she happened to know were now in college. Nor did he ask if she'd ever been married or currently had a boyfriend.

She'd barely picked at the delicious food that had been served and cleared with elegant efficiency, but at least she'd managed not to drink enough to allow herself to end up in his suite — something she'd begun to imagine in embarrassing detail somewhere in the middle of the main course she hadn't eaten. It was past time to bring this conversation to a head, to say the things she'd come here to say and then make her exit. She did not want to like him or forgive him. And she most definitely didn't want to be attracted to him.

She set down her fork. Pushed away the untouched warm bourbon and banana bread pudding. "Why are we here right now?" she asked.

"You mean other than to eat dinner?"

"Yes. To be more specific, why, after you

broke our engagement over twenty years ago in order to marry someone else, are you now here a half a mile from where I'm staying feeding me a five-course meal and hinting that you have room for me in your suite."

"Well, I thought it was more than a hint." He gave her the smile that had once melted her from the inside out.

She sat up. Folded her hands in her lap. "There is no way you actually thought you could show up, buy me a dinner, and take me to bed."

"I wasn't counting on it, no." He gave her a rueful smile that was almost as devastating as the fiery melting one. "But it is almost criminal to sleep in that suite alone." He did the crinkly-eye thing. "Did I mention there's a two-person hot tub next to the fireplace and overlooking the lake?"

"That's it." She moved to scrape back her chair prepared to stand, deliver the devastating monologue that she'd been composing in her head for the last two decades, and leave him in a pool of regret.

His hand encircled her wrist. The touch sent sparks shooting inside her that she wanted to believe were sparks of anger.

"I'm sorry," he said. "Don't go. I guess I'm nervous and I — I — just wanted to lighten the mood."

She stayed put, but she could feel her muscles tighten in their eagerness to flee. She tried to remember the first name she'd wanted to call him.

"The sole purpose of tonight was supposed to be a sincere apology for my behavior all those years ago. At which point I'd sit quietly while you told me off for being such an . . . imbecile."

Imbecile had definitely been on her list, but nowhere near the top.

"So you were just going to apologize for being *stupid*?" His apology had thrown off her timing. As had his manner. But the time had come. He made no move to stop her.

"You broke my heart. You went back on everything you promised. Everything we'd dreamed about. One minute you loved me, the next you loved someone else. You've left me all these years wondering what I did wrong." She was whispering where she'd planned to shout. Exposing herself in ways she hadn't meant to. She had planned to call him all kinds of ugly things, not reveal her own vulnerability.

"You were far more than stupid. You were cruel and — and — cruel." She tried to call up all the names she'd been hoarding, but every one of them had fled in the face of the emotions that she'd believed she had exorcised but which now churned inside her. "Shit." She closed her eyes, opened them.

His eyes had lost their sparkle, but not their warmth.

"Why are you here and what do you want from me?" she asked finally.

"I don't know exactly. Except that it seems that my marriage is over. With the kids gone we're, well, there's nothing really holding me there." He looked into her eyes in a way she'd only dreamed about, and said words she'd never expected to hear. "And I've always wanted to know what my life would have been like if I'd spent it married to you."

# TWENTY-THREE

Emma sat propped up, her back against her bed pillows. Zoe lay beside her, a onetime regular occurrence that had disappeared when Zoe became a teenager and had only now resurfaced. Her long legs were bare beneath the oversized *As the World Churns* T-shirt Ethan Miller had given her after her recording session, and which she'd slept in every night since. In the morning sunlight with her long red-gold hair splayed across her slim shoulders, she looked so much like her aunt Regan it almost took Emma's breath away. Except that Regan had never smiled anywhere near as sunnily as Zoe was now. Nor did Emma have one single memory of herself, Nash, or Regan, ever the favorite, in any bed anywhere near this close to their mother. Unable to let go of this train of thought, she closed her eyes for a moment trying hard to remember if she'd ever witnessed a single informal or spontaneous gesture between Rex and Eve and barely came up with a handful.

"Is Ryan coming to my birthday?" Zoe asked. Emma noticed she made no mention of Ryan's father and suspected they could all probably sit this one out as long as Ryan Richards was there. But both Richards men had accepted and Jake had insisted on bringing his specially marinated baby back ribs to cook on the grill. "I know it's a cliché," he'd said. "But I cooked every meal on the grill the first year after my divorce. So if Zoe's not up for ribs, we can have pretty much anything she can come up with. I even have a recipe for barbecue birthday cake, though it doesn't look all that impressive."

"You know Jake offered to grill you a birthday cake," Emma said, smiling over the memory.

"Uh, pass."

"Can't say that I blame you." The ancient memories seemed so much easier to retrieve, and Emma thought back to the birthday cakes of her childhood. They'd always been served at restaurants and not necessarily on her actual birthday but rather when Rex, Eve, Regan, and Nash could fit it into their schedules. Affection wasn't the only thing reserved for the cameras. Birthday celebrations had been public affairs as well, played out with lots of happy emoting, candle blowing, and professionally wrapped gifts that Eve's latest assistant had purchased.

Gran hadn't exactly been a cook, either, but the celebrations she threw for Emma after she'd come to live with her had been joyous and sincere. Milestones had been formally celebrated. Her Sweet Sixteen took place in Bemelmans Bar, downstairs from Gran's apartment at the Carlyle, where she and her school friends had eaten cake surrounded by the large murals of Madeline in Central Park created by Ludwig Bemelmans, creator of the *Madeline* children's book series.

Her twenty-first birthday to which she'd invited Serena, Mackenzie, and Adam Russell, had been held in the Café Carlyle, where Woody Allen and his jazz band often performed and Gran's famous friends stopped by to sing "Happy Birthday" to her and share a slice of cake.

But the majority of Emma's birthdays were celebrated in private at the lake house — just her and Gran. When Gran was still performing, she'd had time off to observe Emma's birthday written into her contracts.

"Okay," Emma said. "Scratch the grilled birthday cake." She pretended to ponder. "I could bake you a cake with my own two hands."

"Oh, no, I . . ." Zoe sat up straighter. "I don't think you're strong enough for that yet. Please don't feel like you have to go to all that trouble."

Emma bit back a smile. She'd attempted a

homemade birthday cake exactly twice. Both had been hugely unattractive and largely inedible. "It's all right. I wouldn't eat one of my cakes, either. Besides, I've had enough of hospitals. And I wouldn't want to put anybody else in one."

Zoe laughed.

"I'm thinking we should ask Martha to bake one to your specifications," Emma said.

"Good plan."

"So what kind of cake would you like?" she asked Zoe now.

"How about chocolate?"

"That goes without saying."

"And chocolate raspberry filling and topped with chocolate fudge icing."

Emma smiled. "When I was pregnant with you I managed to cut out coffee, but I craved chocolate so much I considered it the fifth food group. I feel terribly guilty about that sweet tooth you got from me."

"I might forgive you. But only if we get to eat my cake for breakfast like you and Mackenzie and Serena used to when you lived in New York."

"Done. There's nothing more decadent than chocolate cake for breakfast, but I think sixteen is old enough that I won't feel like a completely crappy mother for giving you that much chocolate first thing in the morning." Emma ruffled Zoe's hair and when Zoe reached up to stop her, she got a good couple of tickles in on her belly.

Mackenzie followed the sound of Zoe's laughter into Emma's bedroom. She walked in without knocking but stopped in the doorway at her first sight of Emma and Zoe tickling and laughing with huge identical grins on their faces. She felt a physical stab of envy at this demonstration of the mother-daughter bond she would never experience.

Emma looked up, a smile lighting her face even as Mackenzie's smile faltered. It was the most animated she'd seen Emma since she'd been released from the hospital. Mackenzie hated that her first thought was to crush that smile rather than applaud it.

Zoe looked up and spotted her. "Guess what, Mac? We're going to have birthday cake for breakfast. And it's going to be totally chocolate."

"That's great." Mackenzie forced a smile to her lips. Then she stepped forward.

She knew the minute Emma recognized the expression on her face for what it was, because Emma got out of bed, walked over to grab Mackenzie's hand, and pulled her toward the bed. "Here," she said. "Slide over, Zoe. We're giving Mackenzie a Michaels sandwich whether she wants one or not."

They pushed tight to either side of her, laughing eerily similar laughs. Mackenzie felt their warm skin press against hers, felt them intentionally include her in their warmth. She breathed deeply, their scents so similar and yet so different, then willed herself to let go, to let herself join in their laughter, not to hold her hurts and disappointments against them. It wasn't Emma's fault she'd miscarried while Emma had carried Zoe full term. And it sure as hell wasn't Emma's fault that she and Adam hadn't been able to have a child.

"Frankly," she said when she'd regained her equilibrium, "I think we should call this a reverse *ham* sandwich, since the actresses are on the outside and my poor little white bread self is smooshed in the middle."

This got the laugh she was hoping for. By the time Nadia had come in to see what was going on, Mackenzie had joined in.

"So," she said to Zoe. "How would you like an 'original' creation for your birthday? We've got almost ten days to design and sew it."

"You can do that?"

"We can," Mackenzie said. "Because I'm not going to be doing this alone. It'll be a lot more fun if we do this together."

Zoe appeared stunned. "Seriously?"

"You're really in luck now," Emma said. "Mackenzie's one of the most talented designers I've ever known."

"I think that might be a slight exaggeration," Mackenzie protested, but she felt a warm glow at the praise and the certainty with which it was delivered. She couldn't remember the last time she'd thought of herself in terms of talent.

"Gosh, I don't even know what to ask for." But Zoe was already looking at her phone screen, typing in fashion sites.

"You can take a day or two to think about it," Mackenzie said. "Then we can go into town and pick up some fashion magazines to look over if you want to."

"That would be cool!"

Mackenzie was puzzled by Zoe's excitement. The girl had grown up in Hollywood. She and Emma probably could and did buy designer clothing all the time. Yet Zoe threw her arms around Mackenzie and hugged her with all of her might. "This is going to be so awesome. Can we go pick up those magazines this afternoon?"

Mackenzie nodded, smiled, and once again pushed away the envy. This at least was something she could give Zoe that Emma could not.

The rain started late that afternoon and didn't let up. After dinner when the table was cleared, Serena watched Zoe and Mackenzie begin to pore over a collection of glossy magazines that included *Vogue, Elle, In Style,* and *Seventeen.* They'd found and set up a small corkboard on an easel they'd unearthed, and Mackenzie had started pinning pictures of things Zoe had torn out of the magazines.

"I don't know which of these I like better," Zoe said, pointing to photos of everything from capris to gauzy mid-length skirts.

"Remember, we don't have to choose anything in its entirety. We can take elements you really like and then design an article of clothing, or an outfit, that will make those elements work together."

Emma was sitting on the window seat staring out through the sheet of rain as it fell from the dark sky. A novel lay open in her lap. Serena sat at the kitchen counter watching Nadia build a smoothie for Emma's dessert.

Zoe had decided she wanted something that she could wear for the birthday cookout. Something casual but special and attention getting. She didn't come out and say that its sole purpose was to make sure Ryan Richards couldn't take his eyes off her, but then she didn't have to. Mackenzie had appeared surprised that Zoe didn't want something more elaborate to wear to some dressy awards ceremony or party, but Serena understood completely. Because at this particular moment she would have traded her entire wardrobe and any wardrobe she might own in the future, for one thing that would ensnare and entrance Brooks Anderson. *Brooks.* The man she'd just barely managed to resist after their dinner at Erlowest. And whom she'd spent the whole next day thinking about, a day in which she'd seriously considered tying herself to the hammock, the dock, and even briefly, to Nadia, in order to prevent herself from returning to the historic inn in order to try out the double Jacuzzi and the tester bed. *Brooks.* Whom she'd ultimately agreed to see in Manhattan.

"So, can someone drop me at the car rental agency tomorrow morning?" she asked casually. "I need to go into the city."

She waited for the third degree or at least a few pointed questions, but Mackenzie and Zoe were immersed in clipping pages and sticking things up on the board, then arranging and rearranging them. Emma continued to stare out the window. Serena had prepared answers to a wide array of potential questions including why, after she'd said she didn't feel like going into the city and would probably record from here, she was now going into the city. But no one asked that question. No one asked anything.

"I thought I'd go in tomorrow so I can take care of some things in the afternoon," she explained as if someone had questioned her. "I have shopping to do and a, um, a doctor's appointment," she expounded, although she'd already canceled her standing appointments with Dr. Grant. "I'll spend the night and record the following morning and, you know, then I'll head back."

She could tell that she was blathering and yet no one called her on it.

"I take you." Nadia looked up from the smoothie she was blending for Emma, whom the nurse insisted still needed "blowing up." "Have date for day off."

This got everyone's immediate attention.

Nadia took the lid off the blender and began to pour a truly horrendous orange concoction into a large glass. "Why you surprise? Kochenkov women are known for beat men off with stick."

No one spoke. But no one looked away, either.

"I take you. But I not comink back until next morning."

No one commented on Nadia's announcement or her obvious intention to spend the night with . . . someone. Serena didn't say anything, either. But then she was far less certain about anything than Nadia Kochenkov seemed to be. Including her reasons for agreeing to see Brooks Anderson again.

# TWENTY-FOUR

Serena sat on a favorite shaded bench in Washington Square not far from its famous arch. The day was hot and muggy, the sky a dull gray that promised rain. Idly she watched camera-toting tourists stop to take photographs of the arch and the nearby fountain from every conceivable angle. As far as she knew this place didn't have a bad one.

The drive in had passed in a blur of scenery but Serena's thoughts had been thoroughly occupied with how best to handle the time she'd agreed to spend today with Brooks. She'd always thought of herself as an orderly person, far more so than most actresses she knew, but today her brain had pretty much abdicated, leaving her emotions and, yes, the fantasies she'd held so tightly in check all these years, free to run amok.

She'd debated whether to meet him near his hotel in Midtown? Get tickets to a show? Make reservations somewhere impressive for dinner? More than once she'd wondered whether she should be meeting him at all. He'd said he was in her hands, but she'd been determined not to turn into putty in his. Whatever she did or planned, falling into bed was not the goal. Which of course led to the question, what was?

In the end she'd decided to meet him on her turf, where she could show as much or as little of herself as she chose. After coming across so woefully vulnerable at dinner the other night, she intended to demonstrate her strengths not her weaknesses. What better way than to give him a tour of the life she'd created without him?

She studied him as he approached. Taking in the polished Ferragamos, the sharply creased gray dress pants, and the obviously custom-made white lawn shirt, she was reminded of just how easily he'd always carried off designer clothing. If he'd worn a jacket or a tie earlier, he'd shed them. His sleeves were rolled up to reveal lightly muscled forearms. The vee of his open collar revealed a tempting patch of taut, tanned skin that she had used to love to bury her face in. He took a seat next to her on the bench. Dropping both arms to the seat back, one of them skimming her shoulders, he crossed one knee over the other. "Nice spot."

"It's always been one of my favorites."

She used to picture them strolling down the shaded walkways, hands entwined. Or over on a blanket having an impromptu picnic or lingering over a kiss. "The NYU campus is all around us. Washington Square is almost like a commons of sorts." She watched him take in their surroundings. "Of course, the campus has grown a lot since I studied here. A lot of people aren't happy about that."

"What about you?" he asked, turning his eyes on her. "Are you happy?"

"I'm an alum. So I guess I'm mostly okay with . . ."

"You know that's not what I meant."

"I do." She studied his face and wondered if he'd been hoping for a "yes" or a "no," before reminding herself that she didn't care.

"Okay," he said when he realized she wasn't planning to answer.

For a few minutes they watched kids play in the fountain and the people strolling by them in silence. A few looked her way as if they thought they recognized her, but she was careful not to look back and was relieved that none of them approached her.

"If you're up for walking, I thought I'd show you around," Serena finally said, ready now to give him a tour of her world, her life, starting with when she'd arrived until now. To show him what he'd missed.

He stood when she did and motioned with his palm. "Lead the way."

They strolled through the park and then

she showed him some of the NYU buildings that surrounded it. They crossed MacDougal Street, passed through Father Demo Square, with its tiered wrought-iron fountain dedicated to the former pastor of Our Lady of Pompeii, which sat nearby, its Italianate bell tower thrusting into the gray cloud-filled sky. The breeze was warm and smelled of rain.

"I am completely turned around," Brooks admitted as they left the square and began to walk down a busy shop-filled street.

"That's not uncommon here. The further west we head the more chaotic the street layout becomes. This is Bleecker. We can take it all the way to my town house, but we won't exactly be walking in a straight line."

Shops and restaurants lined both sides of Bleecker and she pointed out those that had been here for as long as she could remember and others that were new. Above them rose apartment buildings and condos. Just past a glass-fronted doorway, Serena stopped in front of a window whose neon sign proclaimed it John's Pizzeria. Another sign announced that this was the original location and that it had been here since 1929. Large white letters on an awning screamed NO SLICES.

Brooks smiled. "I'm trying to imagine a restaurant on Broad or King Street in Charleston announcing what a customer can't have."

"Unlikely in the extreme." Serena laughed. "But the 'whole pizza only' thing isn't uncommon at old coal oven pizzerias like John's. There's some story about it having to do with Al Capone's one-time control of pizza cheese."

"Interesting," Brooks replied.

"Actually, this building is the first official stop on the Serena Stockton memory tour."

"Because?" Brooks prompted.

"Because this is where I lived when I first moved up here." It was, of course, where they would have lived together had he come up as planned. Serena pointed upward. "That's my former living room window. Fifth floor, far left." She waited for his eyes to find it. The window was small and still dirt caked, though it was likely newer dirt. "The even tinier window off the fire escape was my bedroom." Where she'd dreamed about and cried over the man standing next to her. She hesitated as the anger she'd nursed over the years wavered once again. Serena took a slight step away from him. "Emma, well, we knew her as Amelia back then, she lived in that apartment." Serena pointed to another window farther to their right. "I met her right here on the sidewalk the day I moved in." She smiled at the memory. "Mackenzie lived a few blocks down Jones Street." She motioned across Bleecker to the next intersection. "In this really cute daylight basement apartment.

Adam, her husband, waited tables here to help pay for school."

She opened the door and led him inside the restaurant so that he could see the place that had served as their unofficial headquarters and clubhouse. The place where they'd lingered in both good times and in bad.

It was well after lunchtime and not yet time for dinner, and the restaurant was nearly empty. Serena breathed in the tomato-y smell of memories and pizzas past. She watched Brooks take in the scuffed checkerboard linoleum floor, the ancient wood booths with the hat racks attached to their sides, the dark red tin ceiling with its exposed ductwork and fans, the murals of what she'd always assumed was the Amalfi Coast or Italian Riviera, the old concert posters. The kitchen was in the back, mostly hidden by a tall takeout counter. A waiter poked his head out and asked if they needed anything. "No, thanks. Just showing my friend here my favorite pizza place."

Brooks ran a hand over the side of the nearest booth. "Did they hand out switchblades when you came in the door?" His eyes skimmed over the walls, the tables, the coatracks. Every nonmoving surface had been carved, inked, or painted with the names of patrons and sometimes their thoughts or favorite phrases.

"No." She smiled. "But it was a point of

honor to leave your name here somewhere."

"Where's yours?" he asked, a smile tipping up the corner of his lips.

"Oh, back by the ladies' room," she said, sorry now that she'd opened up this line of conversation. Because on one especially bad day she'd carved his name and enclosed it in a heart with hers. On an even worse day she'd added what were supposed to be teardrops that spelled out the word *ASSHOLE.* "I'm not even sure I could find it."

She shifted uncomfortably at the collision of her old and current life, but it was too soon and too late to call a halt. "You okay to keep walking?"

"I think I can keep up," he said. "Lead on."

In the brief time they'd been inside, the sky had grown darker. Thunder rumbled. The breeze had picked up sending her hair whipping around her face. Serena stepped up their pace, continuing west on Bleecker and angling across Seventh Avenue into the heart of what she thought of as "her" neighborhood, a place whose architecture and history differed from the city of her birth but whose beauty she felt just as keenly.

Here the blocks were leafy and tree lined. Ivy-covered brownstones and Federal-style townhomes sat side by side, most of them renovated, many of them combined so that they took up a good part of their block. Front steps were bracketed by wrought-iron banisters that were works of art in their own right. Flower boxes clung to stone sills beneath tall lentil-topped windows. Decorative pots overflowing with bold-colored plants and greenery anchored front stoops and accented massive wooden doors of differing shapes and colors that were topped and framed in stone and wood details.

They passed Grove and Christopher streets and were crossing West Eleventh when the first raindrops fell.

She had planned a leisurely stroll between Bank and Charles streets to look at the shops before heading to Cafe Cluny for drinks and dinner, thereby giving her time to decide whether she wanted to merely point out her own home or invite him inside. But the rain grew stronger and in less than a block they were both drenched.

"Where to?" Brooks grabbed her hand and they broke into a run. Without even debating it she led him to her town house and raced with him up the steps.

"Crap!" She bent toward him and yanked open her purse, intent on locating her house key. Brooks hunched over her in a vain attempt to shield her from the now driving rain as she pawed through the bag, her head practically buried in his chest. "Got it!" She raised the key and looked up at him in victory. Before she could register what was happening, he'd leaned down. Then he was kissing her while the rain pounded down on them, soaking them to the skin.

"God, I've been wanting to do that since I saw you sitting on that bench," he breathed against her lips while her heart pounded in her chest and every nerve ending in her body sprang to life.

She pulled away, shocked at how much she wanted to kiss him back. Her heart pounded in her chest. Her breath was labored, as if they'd run much farther than they had. This was not what she wanted. Not at all what she had planned. She hadn't avoided his suite at Erlowest just to fall into bed with him here. But what was she supposed to do now — send him out to get a cab? Turn around and drag him through a thunderstorm to the nearest café, where they'd sit soaked and dripping because she was afraid to let him in her home in case she couldn't resist him? Was she that big a coward? What had happened to the steel-willed self-control that had kept her on the outside looking in at every relationship she'd had since him?

She turned and fit the key into the lock then pushed open the door. They rushed into the foyer, dripping water, spraying droplets all around them. He pulled the door closed and then before she could reason her way through anything, he was reaching for her, pulling her to him, crushing his lips down on hers.

Her first thought wasn't how to stop him. Or even if she should. This was Brooks. *Her* Brooks. The man for whom all the others had been merely stand-ins. Even as she thought these things she was already kissing him back.

Rain and wind beat against the windows. Thunder pounded at the door. Desire pooled within her as stark and elemental as the storm that raged outside. Her shaking fingers went to the buttons of his shirt. His snaked up beneath hers. Their clothes came off in a sopping pool of rainwater. Naked, he stepped over them, palmed her breasts, and brushed his thumbs across her nipples.

He groaned as a spark lit deep inside her. All those years imagining this. Remembering him. All of it paled in comparison to what pulsed and rippled through her now.

She tried one last time to pull up the reasons not to do this, but they were flimsy and insubstantial compared to his naked body against hers, the strength of his hands as he lifted her, the feel of her bare legs wrapping around his waist.

And then there was no room for anything but the heat of his body fusing into hers.

# TWENTY-FIVE

"What do you think?" Mackenzie turned the sketchpad so that Zoe could see it. The sundress was deceptively simple and had a halter top, fitted bodice, and short skater-style skirt that would flatter Zoe's tall hour-glass shape and show off her long legs. "This would work in virtually any color or pattern, although I'm kind of seeing it in a soft cream or even a pale pink."

"I like it," Zoe said. "A lot. But what's that?" She reached for a much rougher pencil drawing that Mackenzie had done on a scrap of paper. It was closer to a doodle than a design. It showed a wrap skirt in two differ-ent lengths and a crop top that could be paired with either. "And what are those panels on the skirts?"

"The wrap skirt is pretty basic," Mackenzie said. "It's the fabrics that would make this really stand out."

"What kind of fabrics?" Zoe asked.

"I think it could be fabulous in jersey or

even T-shirt material. Actually, I was thinking it might be neat to slice up brightly colored T-shirts into different shapes and sizes arranged in a mostly vertical pattern." Mackenzie pulled a photo of a jacket that had been done in bright turquoise with blocks of charcoal and black. "These just jumped out at me, but any color combination could work. In fact, it could be really cool to use T-shirts that you already own that mean something to you."

"Kind of like a memory skirt?"

"Yes," Mackenzie replied, pleased at Zoe's enthusiasm. "Exactly like a memory skirt."

"Could we use some of the lettering from the T-shirts, too?" Zoe asked.

"You're a genius!" Mackenzie looked down at the sketch and the photo. "I was only thinking about the stretchy comfortable fabric and the bold blocks of color. But using a couple of the logos or headlines would really make it unique and individual to you."

Zoe's smile was blinding. "I'm going to pick a few right now. I might even sacrifice the T-shirt Ethan gave me."

"We can always buy fabric to fill in and accent what you choose. And maybe we should use a Lake George tee to commemorate our time here and what this house means to you and your mom."

Emma had been sitting at the window seat but she'd obviously been listening. "There are a couple of oldie but goodies in my bottom dresser drawer that I'm glad to contribute," Emma called out as Zoe headed for the stairs.

Emma got up and walked over to the table. "I love it. I wish I had the height to carry off something like that long skirt and crop top," she said, studying the sketch over Mackenzie's shoulder.

"And I always wished I were shorter and more rounded like you," Mackenzie admitted. "Serena and Zoe managed to split the difference and ended up tall but not giraffe-like." Mackenzie smiled. "Zoe's great, Em," she said. "It's . . . fun working with her on this." Her smile began to falter. Doing anything with Zoe was a bit like balancing on a double-edged sword.

"Well, she's obviously having a blast. And it's nice to see you smiling like that," Emma said.

"Like what?"

"I don't know, like you're enjoying yourself." Emma hesitated. "You have looked kind of torn."

"I did have a friend in a coma, you know," Mackenzie said, stacking the magazines closest to her. "And she had a daughter we were worried about." Now that the imminent danger had receded, now that Emma was no longer in jeopardy, the old hurts and jealousies had begun to ambush her, sometimes when she least expected them.

And the thing was, she and Adam could have become parents. While both their parents were alive Mackenzie had tried to talk Adam into adoption as a possible road to parenthood. He'd refused this out of fear of ending up with a child with a genetic heritage that they'd have no knowledge of.

"Biological children get sick and fall prey to disease, too. Or end up in accidents," she'd pointed out. "A child doesn't have to be of your blood to be *yours*."

But Adam had refused to be swayed. Finally Mackenzie understood what he wouldn't say: That he didn't really want children, had never really wanted them. That although he'd married her when she became pregnant, her dreams of parenthood weren't his. That after their forced marriage, everything had seemed like a trap to him.

"You're so talented," Emma said, reaching for the sketch. "Why did you give up fashion design?"

"I hardly remember making that choice," Mackenzie said. "It just sort of happened."

First she'd made costumes to be a part of Adam, Emma, and Serena's theatrical world. Then when they'd moved back to Indiana and she'd convinced Adam to buy the theater, she'd begun designing sets and costumes, doing both for as little money and as quickly as possible for their shoestring productions.

And why was that? She watched Emma compare the two sketches, even as she realized that she'd always felt so guilty for making Adam work on such a small scale that she'd done everything in her power to try to make him happy. In truth, she'd always felt she needed to make the compromises and concessions. It had been her penance for dragging Adam away from New York and his dreams of making it on a national stage.

And now that Adam had his shot at something bigger? Now that his dreams had a chance of coming true? What would happen now?

"I need a glass of wine." Mackenzie jumped up and moved into the kitchen. "Can I fix you a spritzer or something?"

They could hear Zoe tromping around upstairs. Dresser drawers opening and closing. "It's quiet here without Nadia and Serena," Emma observed, taking a seat on a barstool. "But since cat ees away," she said in a dead-on imitation of the absent nurse. "I take full glass."

Mackenzie grinned, her mood lightening. "She is one formidable weight lifting nurse. I confess I can't help wondering who she's spending the night with."

"Well, whoever it is I don't think there's any question who's in charge," Emma replied.

They giggled.

"Do you think she bosses people around in

295

bed the way she bosses her patients?" Mackenzie asked, stifling another giggle.

"Take clothes off. Before count of three!" Emma definitely had the accent and the bluster down. Their giggles dissolved into laughter. "Nyet! Not there!"

"Oh, God. Now I can't stop picturing it. I need something to block the images."

"Here, maybe this will help." Emma poured another half glass of wine. Both of them took a sip. "All right, then, what do you think Serena's up to?"

Mackenzie shot her a look. "Are you serious? You really are off your game."

"Meaning?" Emma asked after another sip.

"Well, think about it. First she goes to this fancy dinner at Erlowest with a 'friend.' Whom she doesn't identify and doesn't even consider introducing to us. Barely two days later she's racing into the city just after saying she's too lazy to go in and will probably record from up here." Mackenzie shrugged. "That has screwing around with some married guy all over it."

"Oh, I don't know. Do you really think so?" Emma asked.

*"Da."* Mackenzie raised her wineglass. "This toast may only go with vodka but, *'Nostrovia!'* "

*"Nostrovia."* Emma took a long sip. "Ahhh," she said with pleasure. "It tastes way better full strength. But don't tell Nadia. I know

296

she wants me to build back up slowly."

"Are you going to let her go now that you're starting to feel better?"

"I'm not sure I can do that," Emma said.

"Why not?"

"First of all, I don't know if she actually has anywhere to go." Emma got up and pulled a jar of peanuts from the pantry. "And second of all, well, if Eve wants to keep paying her salary I'm inclined to let her."

"You are?"

"Yes," Emma replied. "Because I don't know what Eve really wants, and if I let go of Nadia it's possible her next offering will be a lot less palatable."

"How Machiavellian of you." Mackenzie shook out a handful of peanuts. "I like Nadia. She kind of grows on you."

*"Da."* Emma smiled.

"I was kind of hoping Serena would finally get over being dumped by that Brooks Anderson shmuck and fall for someone actually available," Mackenzie said. "Someone nice and sweet and funny like Ethan Miller."

Zoe, who'd pounded back down the stairs, her arms filled with T-shirts in a vibrant rainbow of colors, heard Mackenzie's last comment. "Ethan's the coolest ever. He's perfect for Serena. And I really think he has a major thing for her."

"It's not like we can control who we fall in love with or even who we're attracted to,"

Emma said as Zoe spread the T-shirts out for them to peruse.

"No, but I believe we can control what we do about it," Mackenzie said. "Don't you?"

"I guess." Emma took another sip of her wine and watched as Zoe and Mackenzie went through the T-shirts, offering a comment or two of her own.

Mackenzie sent Zoe back upstairs to find the good pair of scissors, straight pins, and a measuring tape, all of which Emma said had to be upstairs though she wasn't sure exactly where.

"I read some of your recent blog posts the other day," Emma said. "They were good."

"But?"

"No buts," Emma insisted. "They were really good. I don't think I realized how well you could write, and I guess I always thought of you only as a fashion designer. I forget sometimes that there are creative people who have more than one talent."

"How about you?" Mackenzie asked. "Do you secretly paint or take backstage photos of rock bands?"

"No. I can act, that's about it," Emma said. "Though my family might not agree with that." She took a sip of wine. "And I think I'm pretty talented at consuming chocolate."

"Ah, well, then," Mackenzie teased. "That makes you set for life."

A shadow passed over Emma's face even as

they shared a smile that reminded Mackenzie just how close they had once been. A closeness that was never quite as pure after Zoe was born and Mackenzie had been left childless. She had never envied Emma's career as Serena sometimes had, but she had and still did envy Emma her daughter. "You're pretty good at parenting, too." The words were out before Mackenzie realized she was going to say them. "You've done a great job with Zoe."

"Do you really think so?" Emma's question was out in less than a heartbeat, her expression hopeful, yet disbelieving. Like someone who'd just stepped forward to accept a beauty pageant crown but was afraid she might have misheard the name that had been called.

"I do. And I don't know how you can doubt it," Mackenzie said, already regretting raising the topic she'd always avoided.

"You mean other than because I'm desperately afraid of being a parent like mine? Or because it's only the two of us and Zoe's father will never really be a part of her life? Because it turns out it's not all that easy to act for a living and still maintain anything that resembles 'normal'? Or maybe because other than Gran who was way more *Hello, Dolly* than *Happy Days,* I have no real example of healthy parenting to follow?" Emma's outburst came to a halt and a look of surprise flashed across her features as Zoe's footsteps pounded back down the stairs.

Her expression changed yet again as Zoe reached the table and began to lay the things she'd retrieved out next to the array of T-shirts, which she began to rearrange.

Mackenzie and Emma stood.

"You look . . ." Mackenzie wasn't sure how Emma looked. But the expression on Emma's face was one of shock and possibly, recognition. But recognition of what? ". . . are you all right?"

"Yes."

"Em?" Mackenzie turned as casually as she could so that her back would be to Zoe.

"No, it's okay I'm going to . . ." Emma swallowed. "I, um, I'm going to go look through the DVDs and pick out a movie for us to watch. When you're done."

Mackenzie stepped closer to Emma so that Zoe wouldn't hear. "You'd tell me if there was something wrong, wouldn't you?" she whispered to Emma. "I mean if you felt something happening in your brain. Something we'd need to get to a hospital or call Nadia back for?"

"I would," Emma said. "Yes. Yes. Of course I would."

But Emma's mouth had gone dry and it was hard to even find the words of reassurance or the strength to turn and walk away as the memory that had been eluding her slammed into her.

"I'm fine," she lied, falling back a step. Because Emma had just remembered the thing that had been niggling. The thing that had been teasing at her memory just out of reach. The thing her traumatized brain had hidden away.

She watched Zoe and Mackenzie huddle over the T-shirts and Mackenzie's sketchbook. Saw them debate which shirts to use, where the blocks of color should be placed, how large and what shape to make them, and she remembered.

She had invited Serena and Mackenzie to the lake this summer, finally prepared to confess the secret she'd spent more than a decade trying to hide and the last five years trying to bury. More importantly she had chosen this summer for a *reason*. A reason that her recent accident and coma only made more urgent. But which also made the idea of asking them to forgive the unforgiveable even more impossible.

# TWENTY-SIX

Serena pretty much floated to the studio that morning, her smile too large, her heart too full, her feet way too far off the ground. She stunned Catherine by presenting her with the two beignets she'd picked up in Grand Central; her stomach had been fluttering too hard to even consider eating them. She startled Wes, whose last name she seemed to have momentarily forgotten in the middle of a PDA in the hallway with his new squeeze Lauri Strauss, whose name she hadn't, and sent them a cheery wave.

"Isn't it an absolutely gorgeous day?" Serena beamed at Ethan as he stepped out of his office.

"It is." Ethan cocked his head to study her face, unruly brown hair falling over one twinkling eye. "And so are you. I don't think I've ever seen you look more beautiful." He said this quite gallantly.

"Thank you ever so much, darling," she answered in regal leading-lady style. And then rather than allow him to kiss her hand as a regal leading lady might, she threw her arms around him and hugged him because she wanted, actually needed, to share her happiness. At the moment she was just a great big hunk a hunk of burnin' love.

"Did you have something done?" The younger actress's eyes had narrowed.

Serena just arched one brow mysteriously. She was far too full of good will to cheapen what had happened with Brooks by revealing that the only thing she'd had "done" was herself. But she wasn't necessarily so full as to completely ignore Lauri's comment. "No, I haven't," she said sweetly. "But if you'd like to step up from whatever bargain basement plastic surgeon gave you those unfortunately oversized breasts, I'm sure we can find you someone who can make more of those few assets you do have." She waited for the girl to register the insult then added, "Maybe Wes would like to contribute to the cause."

Lauri huffed off. Wes made no comment.

"Clearly you're in fine Georgia Goodbody form," Ethan said, struggling to contain a grin. "Are you ready to record?"

"I am." Serena practically pirouetted.

"Wes?" Ethan asked.

"Um, yeah. Sure." Wes followed her into the studio and set his script on his stand. Serena did the same at hers. As the engineer set their levels, she contemplated the actor and wondered how she could have imagined herself interested in such an appallingly uninteresting man. She skimmed the script and scribbled notes and accent points as the playback was cued up. She felt like someone who'd finally finished slogging through a swamp and reached dry land. Everything was crisper, cleaner. *Clearer.*

She hadn't meant to sleep with Brooks. At least not until she'd been certain of his sincerity, but the thunderstorm had made that decision for her. And she was glad. Knowing that Brooks had been thinking about her all these years. That he'd regretted what he'd given up and been eager to know the woman he'd been missing had made the act so much sweeter. She felt a satisfied smile lift her lips and made no attempt to hide it. Making love with Brooks Anderson, having the real thing after all those imitations, was like consuming a gallon of Häagen-Dazs after single-serving cups of fat-free yogurt.

She and Georgia were on fire. Serena nailed each take on the first attempt and then watched Wes try to keep up with her. She enjoyed herself immensely as she delivered the put-downs Ethan and his writing staff had provided her with, an appreciation she had lost track of somewhere along the way.

"When was the last time I told you how completely talented I think you are and how grateful I am to be playing Georgia Good-

body?" she asked Ethan after he'd complimented her on her performance and escorted
her out to the lobby.

He blinked.

"Please tell me the answer isn't never."

"Okay, it's not exactly never."

"But not often enough," she apologized.
She'd lost sight of her good fortune when it
had finally sunk in that playing a cartoon
character was what she was likely to be most
remembered for. "I hope you also realize how
much I appreciate the diversion you created
when we snuck Emma out of the hospital,
the gifts you've sent, and the flexibility you've
given me so that I could be at the lake with
her. You are quite simply phenomenal."

His smile of surprise turned quickly to
pleasure. His brown eyes shone with a
warmth that she realized she'd come to take
for granted. He so often gave, but never asked
anything in return. Their shoulders rubbed
slightly as they moved toward the door.

"I've been working on a plotline for Zoe,"
Ethan said. "Maybe we could work in her
scenes with you while she and Emma are still
on the East Coast."

"Oh, God, she'll be over the moon. She's
already half in love with you and this will seal
the deal," Serena said.

"Good." He gave her a wink. "I can use all
the adoration I can get."

"But we'll have to get around Emma. She's

not exactly a fan of child stardom."

"I can certainly understand that," Ethan replied. "Let's see what we can work out that will put her at ease."

"You are one of the most understanding men I've ever met."

Ethan's eyes lit with more than pleasure. He was looking at her in a way she'd never let herself notice before.

"I hope I was clear about how much I appreciate the opportunity you've given me. I've been way too focused on what I didn't have rather than what I do."

"It's an easy thing to do," Ethan said, shoving his hands into his jeans pockets. He shifted his weight on his sneakered feet and she could feel him weighing his next words. "I'd be interested in hearing what's opened your eyes. Can I take you to lunch before you head back up to the lake?"

Before he'd finished issuing the invitation, the door opened and Brooks stepped in. Serena felt her lips tip into a smile as she noted how great he looked in the Armani suit, crisp white shirt, and newly polished dress shoes. A slim black leather briefcase dangled from one manicured hand. The smile he directed at her caused her heart to lurch.

"Ethan, I want you to meet Brooks Anderson. Brooks, Ethan Miller, my brilliant director and good friend." She watched as the two shook hands and exchanged pleasant noncommittal smiles.

"Brooks had already invited me to lunch," she said, unable to cut back the smile she felt stretching across her face. "He's up on business from Charleston. Our families have known each other forever."

Ethan's face had gone carefully blank. His eyes dropped to Brooks's left hand. She happened to know Brooks's ring finger carried an unmistakable white circle from the years spent wearing a wedding band.

"You're welcome to join us," Brooks said to Ethan as the handshake ended. Serena startled slightly in surprise.

"No, thanks." Ethan's smile remained but his eyes were more shuttered than she'd ever seen them. "I wouldn't want to intrude. I'm sure you have a lot of catching up to do."

"Okay," she said, pecking Ethan on the cheek, careful not to meet his eyes or show her relief that he wouldn't be joining them when her time with Brooks was so limited. "I'll take a rain check then." And then she walked out through the door that Brooks held open for her, her feet never touching the sidewalk.

"Where to?" Brooks asked as he first hugged her then slung an arm around her shoulders. "I didn't have time for breakfast. Some hussy kept me up all night and then I had to get back to this side of town this morning for a meeting. I'm famished."

"Me too," she said, a happy shiver running up her spine. "Does your hotel have a restaurant?"

"I'm pretty sure the Four Seasons must have a coffee shop or something," he teased as he leaned down to brush a kiss to her ear.

This time the shiver ran deeper.

"And I think it just might have room service, too."

Nadia returned from her day off oddly subdued. Arriving just as Bob Fortson was packing up, she did not wave at Zoe out on the swim platform and barely nodded to the physical therapist she would normally have slapped on the back and grilled for details on Emma's progress. She approached the steps slowly, moving carefully. Each step was first assessed and then taken as if great effort were required.

"Mornink." Her voice was a shadow of its normal heartiness. Her eyes were concealed behind dark sunglasses. Her entire body drooped.

"Good morning." Emma watched the nurse with interest. Emma had slept badly, her dreams filled with her refound knowledge and a dream in which she'd argued with Gran about what should and shouldn't be said to the people you considered your closest friends. "What happened?"

The nurse raised her head but did not

remove her sunglasses. "I am become weak-link. Too soft. Ashamed behavior."

Mackenzie came out onto the porch with a pitcher of lemonade and took in the nurse's long face. "Morning," she said to Nadia as she refilled Emma's glass. "You look like you could use . . . something."

"Sit down," Emma said to the nurse, who surprised her again by doing as instructed.

Mackenzie came back with a tall glass of water and two aspirin. They waited as the nurse downed them. She was almost relieved that Serena had stayed in the city an extra day. In her head she could hear Georgia Goodbody's voice pointing out that Nadia Kochenkov looked like she'd been "rode hard and put up wet."

"What happened?" Mackenzie asked.

Nadia downed most of the glass of water before setting it aside. She squared her formidable shoulders but her normal bluster was missing. "Always I see man I like, I take. I strong woman. Is good be strong."

Emma and Mackenzie nodded, though Emma didn't think Mackenzie had any more idea where this conversation was headed than she did.

"I arm-wrestle. I win. I do drink contest. I used drink vodka in my mother milk, so I win." Nadia's voice had dropped. "Always, I win."

"But you didn't win this time?" Emma asked.

Nadia shook her head sadly. "Nyet."

"So you came up against someone who can drink more or arm-wrestle better," Mackenzie said with a shrug. "It's not the end of the world."

"Is to me. I not meet man who can beat me."

"I think we're missing something here," Emma said as she and Mackenzie studied the nurse.

"Clearly," Mackenzie agreed.

Nadia sighed. "I meet Edmund like arrange. At bar. I stronger. Better drinker. But I lose to him in arm wrestle *and* number of vodka we consume."

"And Edmund didn't like that?" Emma ventured.

Nadia closed her eyes as if in pain. "Oh, no. He like it. Like Nadia. Make love to me all night long. And I not even give one single direction." Nadia's lips twisted. "Even though I think he maybe do better. You know. Find right spot sooner."

Emma noticed that hers wasn't the only jaw that had dropped. But Nadia's earnest delivery made laughter out of the question.

"So what's the problem?" Emma finally asked. "It can take time to learn what a partner likes in bed." She tried to eliminate the mental image that had just formed of

Nadia directing some man twice her size and/or weight on how he might improve his performance. She, who had experienced long bouts of unintentional celibacy since divorcing Calvin Hardgrove, was the last person who should be offering sexual or dating advice to Nadia Kochenkov. She was careful not to look in Mackenzie's direction even as she wondered how one said "G-spot" in Russian.

"I cheat. Because . . ." The nurse looked completely miserable now. "Because I lose on purpose."

Emma felt a muscle twitch in her cheek, but managed to stifle her laughter. "You're not the first woman to try to boost a man's ego."

"It's true." Mackenzie was biting her lip. "Big, muscular, macho men don't easily recover from losing tests of strength to women."

"But Edmund not like that," Nadia protested. "Not big macho guy." She looked up at them now, her own face awash in disbelief. "Edmund different from all men before."

"What does he do?" Mackenzie asked.

Emma knew they were both picturing the same things. An oversized manly man who worked on the docks. Or as a bouncer. Or maybe even a biker who'd come for one of Lake George's Americades and never left.

"Edmund has good job. And good brain,"

Nadia said. "Edmund head librarian over in Glens Falls." She looked down for a moment, her broad face clouding over. "I think he too smart think he beat me fair square. But first time, this man. Nadia not sure."

# TWENTY-SEVEN

The sun had already set when Serena got back to the lake house late that evening. She found Emma, Mackenzie, and Zoe at the dining room table, which was littered with sewing paraphernalia, scraps of fabric, as well as torn magazine pages and sketches. A sewing machine had been set up on one end. A full-length mirror had been propped against the wall.

Zoe stood with her arms held out from her sides while Mackenzie pinned a cropped jersey top in a gorgeous aqua shade that landed just above her belly button.

"Oh, my gosh," Serena said. "That color is great on you."

"Isn't it awesome?" Zoe said. "Look!" She turned so that Serena could see the word *Landing* that angled across one shoulder. "And the skirt's almost all pinned together."

Serena moved closer to examine the skirt, which was composed of varying shapes of solid colors fit into a sophisticated patchwork.

The words that crissed and crossed in strategic spots clearly applied to Zoe. *World Churns. Lake George. Applause.*

"I'm thinking about making some gemstone flip-flops to wear with it," Zoe said.

"That's a great idea," Mackenzie said. She had Zoe spin slowly, then had her stop so that she faced Serena. "Okay, Serena. We need your opinion."

"I have no shortage of those."

"All right, then." Mackenzie adjusted the top slightly. "Boatneck or off the shoulder?"

"Off the shoulder," Serena answered. "Gosh, think of all those years we spent hiding our bra straps. Why didn't someone dye them bright colors and tell us they were worth seeing sooner?"

Emma laughed.

"Notched vee in the center, or off-center slash like this?" Mackenzie demonstrated.

"Center vee."

"Ha! That's what I said too!" Zoe smiled at herself in the mirror. With Mackenzie's help, she pulled the top carefully back over her head, attempting to avoid the straight pins. Clad only in short shorts and her bathing suit top it was hard to miss Zoe's young, taut skin. For once Serena didn't envy anyone their youth or firmness. Brooks seemed enamored with her and her body just the way it was. As he'd proved repeatedly that afternoon.

Serena flushed with remembered pleasure and imagined the surprise on Emma and Mackenzie's faces when she told them about Brooks and how he'd simply sailed back into her life gorgeous, repentant, and available, though he hadn't clarified exactly what that meant. For now she hugged her secret close, not yet ready to question or share it.

Emma and Mackenzie eyed her as Zoe disappeared upstairs to change.

"Good God, I've never seen a smile quite that satisfied. You look like a cat that's just lapped up every available drop of cream," Emma observed. "Somebody has most definitely gotten laid."

"Meooooow." Serena drew the word out and arched in a feline way. Then she licked the inside of one curved hand as if it were a paw. She wanted to purr as she flashed back to the feel of Brooks's hands skimming leisurely over her bare skin.

"I'm feeling very sorry for some poor wife right now." Mackenzie was no longer smiling.

"What makes you so sure I've been with someone's husband?" Serena asked, stung.

"Isn't that who you're always with? When have you *not* been?" Mackenzie's tone had taken on a scolding edge.

Serena bristled. "Does writing a blog about not having children make you some kind of marriage expert?" she snapped. "Because between the two weeks at the hospital and almost three weeks here plus another until Zoe's birthday, that's six weeks away from your husband and your *perfect* marriage," she pointed out. "How do you think women like me end up with other women's husbands?"

"Ladies," Emma began, her tone distinctly uncomfortable. But for the first time since they'd ended up at the hospital, Serena and Mackenzie were focused only on each other.

"Oh, really." Mackenzie's disapproving eyes were fixed on Serena. "So you're not a predator looking for weakness then? We're just not attractive enough to hold on to our men."

"If the shoe fits . . ."

"That's enough." Emma cut them off, an odd look on her face, her tone making it clear she wanted nothing more than to change the topic. "I'm grateful that you've *both* been able to be here so much longer than you'd planned. I just . . . I don't think we need to be attacking each other."

"Sorry. But I didn't start the attack, I'm only trying to finish it. And whatever Mackenzie thinks, I'm not looking under rocks anymore. I'm done with the men who climb out from underneath them."

Mackenzie shot her a look. "You expect me to believe that?"

"You can believe whatever you want," Serena bit out. "Exactly what kind of proof were you looking for?" She imagined producing

Brooks Anderson as exhibit A. But she was not about to fling him into this fray.

"Not that anyone should be forced to prove such a thing to her friends," Emma said to Mackenzie, but there was something in her eyes Serena couldn't quite identify. "On the bright side I must really be getting better, because this is the first time you've let loose around me." She gave them both a look. "I can't tell you how thrilled I am." Her tone was dry, her expression deliberately deadpan.

Neither Serena nor Mackenzie gave her the laugh she was going for.

The silence was broken when Zoe pounded back downstairs to shriek. "Oh. My. God. You'll never guess what happened!" She came to a halt in front of them, oblivious in that way that only teenagers who are certain the world revolves around them can be, to the tension that still hung in the air. "Ryan invited me out to a party after my birthday cookout! It's going to be at the club and everybody's going to come by boat! I can go, right?" she said to Emma. "Because I told him I could." She turned to Mackenzie before her mother could answer. "Please tell me my outfit will be ready in time!"

"Absolutely." Mackenzie smiled at Zoe.

Zoe's cell phone rang again and she didn't even look at the screen before answering. The excitement on her face made it clear she expected it to be Ryan again. "Hello?"

Zoe's tone changed, the excitement dissipating. "Oh. Yes. Hello. Thank you." Her eyes went to Emma. "Yes, she's here." Zoe covered the mouthpiece. "It's Eve. She says she has a birthday present for me and wants to deliver it in person." She looked pleadingly at her mother. "I don't know what I'm supposed to say to her."

Emma's lips tightened. "No problem," she said, though it clearly was. She stuck out her hand. Zoe placed the phone in her palm.

Mackenzie took the crop top and began to point out something to Zoe. Serena retreated upstairs as Emma turned and moved into the kitchen.

Stopping in front of the kitchen window, Emma watched the running lights of a slow-moving boat just east of Hemlock Point. "I asked you not to use other people to call me," she said to Eve.

"I wouldn't have to if you answered your phone."

"I don't answer because I don't want to talk to anyone right now," Emma replied. *Especially not you.* "That's what voice mail is for."

A silence fell. Emma made no move to fill it.

"I'd like to come up to deliver Zoe's present," Eve finally said. "I can come anytime that's convenient."

"So she said," Emma replied, unable to

think of any time that seeing Eve would be good or convenient. The breeze had picked up and the sway of the branches down near the beach drew her eye. "If you have a gift for Zoe, I'd prefer you send it."

"It's not really that sort of gift. It's a bit more complicated than that. And may require some explanation and, possibly, discussion."

"Then I suggest you choose a different gift."

Eve made no comment.

"We're keeping the celebration small. Zoe's going out afterward. It's her first date." The information was out before she could stop herself.

"Oh, I'd love to be there for that." Eve sounded almost like any grandmother might. Wistful even.

The comment hit Emma like a blow. "Really? That's odd. You were never there for any first of mine that I can think of," Emma said. Except of course for her first role and then for her audition for *Daddy's Girl.* Eve had been all over those.

The silence was weightier this time. Moonlight danced across the slightly choppy surface of the lake.

"Why don't you just tell me what this is really about?" Emma said.

"It's not about anything," Eve insisted. But with Eve it was always about something else. In Emma's experience that something was almost always Eve.

"I really have to go," Emma said finally. She'd already turned and begun to move her thumb to disconnect when Eve said, "Well, the thing is, I am at a bit of a loose end."

"A loose end."

"Yes. Regan and Nash are off on location. And . . ." Eve's voice trailed off.

"Perhaps you should have gone back to California with Rex," Emma said. "Or maybe it's time for one of your spa vacations." Emma was more than ready to hang up. "I don't know. And honestly I can't really say that I care."

"Rex isn't in California." Eve's words came out in a rush.

"No?" Her mother had never bothered to share her or Rex's plans before. Emma breathed an impatient sigh. "Then go meet him wherever he is."

"He's gone to France," Eve said. "On an extended . . . vacation."

"Alone?" Her father had never been particularly into solitude. Or anything else that might invite or result in introspection.

"No," Eve said. "He's taken a house in Cannes. With Gerald. And I'm fairly certain I'm not invited."

This was something new. Her father had always had relationships, some of them of a long duration. But he'd publicly been dashingly heterosexual, careful to maintain his devoted husband/father/leading man image.

"I'm sorry for everything I missed or ignored. All of it," Eve said now without preamble. "I thought I had plenty of time to make it up to you one day. But, then there you were in that horrible coma. And . . ." This was the point in the scene where an actress would have lit a cigarette or performed some other bit of "business" to heighten the drama. The camera would move in on a close-up of said actress's distressed face. "Haven't you ever wished you'd done things differently?" It was an award-winning delivery from a highly skilled actress. But it was the question, not the delivery that left Emma feeling nauseated. If she'd chosen a different path there would be no Zoe.

She closed her eyes and held tight to the phone as she thought about why she'd invited Mackenzie and Serena here.

"Haven't you ever done something you've wished you could take back or change or at least try to make right?" Eve asked quietly.

"You know what," Emma said more shrilly than intended. "Sometimes after you make your bed, you have no choice but to lie in it."

# TWENTY-EIGHT

*Thou shalt not covet thy best friend's daughter. Thou shalt not covet thy . . .* The modified commandment echoed loudly in Mackenzie's mind as she sat at the sewing machine finishing off the hem of Zoe's new patchwork skirt. Zoe worked nearby, her lip clenched firmly between her teeth, her head nodding to the beat of the music that played from her iPhone through a small but powerful speaker, as she contemplated how best to attach the large gem-colored stones to the straps of the white flip-flops she'd chosen. She'd bought three additional pairs so that she could make gifts for her mother and fairy godmothers once she'd finished the "prototype."

"What do you think?" Zoe showed her the tentative arrangement of stones. "I thought I'd try to build a small pyramid of them here at the center of the vee and then decrease the height and width gradually along the straps."

"I like it," Mackenzie said, impressed with Zoe's concentration and her innate confidence. "I think they'll work perfectly with the outfit. You've got a good eye."

Zoe had been smiling since they'd sat down to work; the smile grew wider at the praise.

"Who's that singing?" Mackenzie asked, tuning in to the haunting young female voice. "She's really good."

"That's Lorde — her real name is Ella Marija Lani Yelich-O'Connor. She's from New Zealand." She noted Mackenzie's blank look. "She's BFFs with Taylor Swift." An oddly familiar look of exasperation passed over Zoe's features. "You have heard of Taylor Swift, right?"

"Absolutely."

Zoe bopped her head and reexamined the pile of gems spread out before her with a critical eye. "Do you know Selena Gomez?"

"Is she the one who dates Justin Bieber?" That at least was a name you'd have to be living under a rock to miss.

"Not anymore," Zoe said. "Listen to this." Her thumbs moved so quickly over her phone they were a blur. "It's called 'Come and Get It.' "

Zoe gave her a tutorial as they worked. It turned out there was a whole slew of young recording artists Mackenzie had barely heard of and given no thought to. She leafed through the *Teen Vogue* Zoe had bought for inspiration. It set Mackenzie's mind racing down paths she'd never set foot on. There was so much youth and energy in the music and fashion worlds. And she'd missed all of it.

The last time Mackenzie had spent time with Zoe, she'd been ten, a child. Now she was her own person, a teenager on the cusp of womanhood. And Emma had been a part of the whole journey. One day, God willing, she'd send her off to college, throw her a wedding, hold her daughter's children in her arms. While Mackenzie might attend some of those events, she would do so as a secondary character in someone else's story.

*Thou shalt not covet thy best friend's daughter.* She sounded out each word in her head, but like the real commandments this one was easier to say than to stick to. She would definitely not be using it as a blog post title anytime soon.

The song changed. Miley Cyrus's "Wrecking Ball" came on, hard driving and plaintive. Her thoughts turned to Adam and their life in Noblesville. Her sewing room at one end of the house, his study on the other. Her life reduced to helping bring Adam's visions to life.

She'd had visions of her own once. Visions that had been interrupted by an unplanned pregnancy just as his had. Unlike Adam she'd embraced the interruption, but she'd let go of all of her dreams when life had taken a turn. She'd never really replaced them.

Having a child, a teenager in their lives, would have taken them outside themselves, given them a joined purpose other than the theater, kept them younger, more current. She caught herself bobbing her head along with the music but froze at the thought that followed.

Did this jealousy, this covetousness, nullify everything she'd been writing? Did it make a mockery of the readers who'd rallied behind her? Did it make her a fraud?

By the time they broke for dinner Mackenzie was certain that if there'd been lightning bolts thrown for commandment flouting, she would already have been struck.

She straightened the materials as she always did before quitting, helped Zoe do the same, then volunteered to set the porch table where they'd taken to eating their evening meal.

She was outside, her eyes on the lake, when her phone rang. This hadn't happened in so long that she almost didn't recognize the ringtone.

"Hey, Mac." Adam's voice bore no sign of their recent awkwardness or lack of communication over the past weeks. It was, in fact, jubilant. "You won't believe what just happened."

She pressed the phone tighter to her ear. Barefoot, she moved over the grass and toward the beach, where the sand that cushioned her toes was cool and damp.

"Universal loved the revised screenplay," he said before she could ask. "Matt and I met with them yesterday. We've reached a basic agreement. I've got a deal!"

"Oh, my God," she said. Tears pricked the back of her eyelids and the lake blurred before her. "Really?"

"Really."

Her mind was awash with thoughts and emotions that rushed by too quickly to cling to. The first was pure joy for him. "Oh, my God," she said. "You did it. You sold your screenplay. It's going to be a movie."

"Well, it has a very good chance of becoming a movie. Plus they're paying a nice chunk of change for the right to develop it. And with Mitch Silverman on board to direct, well." He laughed happily. "The odds are good. And in my favor."

"So, what happens next?" she asked, trying to take it all in, trying to squash the fear that had suddenly reared its head. Fear for herself. Fear of change. Adam had been writing a screenplay since she'd met him. Despite all the cheerleading over the years, she realized now she'd never really envisioned this happening.

"That's still being discussed. But I thought that while everything's being finalized I'd come out to see you all." He hesitated slightly. "You know, to check on Emma. And so that we can explore our options."

"Our options?" The word hung heavy between them. It was a business word, one used in negotiation. *Not in a marriage.* Mackenzie turned to pace the small beach, trying to dispel her nervousness.

"Yeah, you know," Adam replied. "What we're going to do about the theater. Whether we want to keep the house or sell it." He sounded so happy, so excited, while she felt as if she'd been kicked in the stomach without warning. The items they needed to discuss tripped off his lips while his tone made it clear he'd already reached his own decisions.

Mackenzie felt suddenly like she imagined Emma might have as the van bore down on her. She felt her life changing and splintering in that very instant. There would be only "before the call" and "after." Whatever happened next, there would be no going back to how things had been.

"I'm not sure whether I'll be coming through LaGuardia or flying into Albany." The mouthpiece was covered and Adam's voice muffled as he spoke to someone else. She heard his laughter and even muffled it was sharp and joyous. "Listen, Mac," he said a few moments later. "I've got to go. I'll let you know when I have my flights set so you know when to expect me."

Two seconds later she was staring out at the lake, no longer connected to Adam. Or, she thought, to much of anyone at all.

327

■ ■ ■ ■

"Okay, that's it." Zoe had just carried her plate into the kitchen and gone to pick out the evening's movie when Serena stood up from the table and waved her cloth napkin in front of Mackenzie's face. Mackenzie barely blinked. "I think we've got someone else who's slipped into a coma," Serena said. "What are the odds?"

Mackenzie's eyelids blinked rapidly. She sat up and focused on Serena. "You did not just say that."

"Yes, I believe I did."

"Then you should definitely apologize to Emma."

"No apology needed." In truth Emma was greatly relieved that they'd finally stopped treating her like she was made of porcelain and might shatter at any moment. She was also glad that someone was ready to address Mackenzie's distracted silence, which they'd all been tiptoeing around since the meal began. "But we would like to know what's wrong."

"Wrong?" Mackenzie asked.

"Um, yeah," Serena replied. "As in, you and your head are somewhere else entirely and we'd like to know where."

"LA," Mackenzie said slowly. She looked down at the table, brushed a stray crumb out of the way. "Adam called." She looked up. "He sold his screenplay to Universal. Mitch Silverman's going to direct."

"Wow," Emma said, shocked.

"No shit?" Serena said.

All three of them began to talk at once. It was Serena who asked what Emma had been thinking. "So why do you look so unhappy?"

"Unhappy?" Mackenzie asked as a lone tear slid down one cheek, across her chin, and plopped onto the table. "I'm not unhappy."

Serena rolled her eyes.

"You look like man who find out the dacha he just bought is not in Ozero but in Siberia," Nadia, who had just carried in a purple-hued smoothie that Emma did not want, said. "Very big disappointing."

Mackenzie smiled, but the tears continued to fall. "He's coming to talk about our options. I think he wants to sell everything and move to LA."

"And you don't want to do that?" Emma asked, although the answer seemed obvious. Mackenzie's was not the face of a woman who couldn't wait to pick up and start a new life.

"I don't know. I feel like he's already made the decisions." Mackenzie looked down. "I'm not sure if he'll care what I think. Or even whether I come with him or not."

"That's crazy," Serena said. "You guys have been married for, what, seventeen years? And together for a frickin' lifetime before that. He's damned lucky to have you."

"I don't know. He seems to be doing just fine without me."

"Aw, sweetie." Emma got up and came to put her arms around Mackenzie. "If you hadn't gotten stuck trying to take care of me, you'd have already been out there and part of the celebration."

Serena came over to join them. They swayed together with their arms around each other.

"Remind me of Kosmarokov Brothers Family Circus I see one time in Moscow," Nadia observed. "You ever try double back flip off other one's thigh?"

The three of them stopped swaying to look at the nurse.

Nadia shrugged her large shoulders. "Sorry. Try for comedy relief. Maybe timing off?"

Emma blew a stray hair out of her eye as their group hug disbanded. She pushed the beet-colored drink back toward Nadia. "Thanks. I'll drink this later." She tried not to wince at the thought. "Mackenzie and Serena and I need something with a different kind of kick right now. We're going to go out and watch the sunset."

They poured themselves hefty glasses of wine and headed out to the beach, each of them claiming an Adirondack chair. They sipped silently for a while as the sun sank lower behind them and the sky began to leach of color.

"If it helps, we can talk about it." Emma's offer sounded lame even to her own ears. "I mean, we have known Adam almost as long as we've known you." Though their relationship with him couldn't have been more different. Mackenzie shook her head and drank more deeply.

An uncomfortable silence fell.

"Speaking of longtime friendships, I'll tell you what I'd like to talk about," Serena said after draining her glass. "I'd like to know why after five years of near silence, why you decided to invite us now."

The night was quiet, the breeze stiff enough to discourage the mosquitoes that would otherwise be feasting on them.

"That might require more alcohol," Emma said.

"Not a problem." Serena picked up an open bottle from the sand near her feet and topped off Emma's and Mackenzie's glasses. She raised her glass. They clinked then drank.

Emma sat silent for a few long moments not sure how or where to begin. Coward that she was, she began with the part that was most understandable. "Earlier this year I was told I had breast cancer."

She heard their indrawn breaths. Felt their eyes turn to her. Once again she tasted the fear she'd felt the day the doctor first uttered the C-word. "But they were wrong. And it, it turned out to be a mistake."

"Jesus," Serena breathed.

Mackenzie swallowed, set her glass down.

"Yeah. But while I was getting ready for what I thought was going to be a lumpectomy followed by a course of radiation, I realized that I . . . that the only people I wanted to tell or have with me were you two."

She took a long sip of wine, waited for it to make its way down her throat. "And then it hit me that I'd given up the right to call and ask you to come and hold my hand. But it wasn't only me I'd left stranded without people who really cared about them. And if the worst happened and I was gone, then . . ." It was her turn to swallow. "Then Zoe would need her fairy godmothers."

"Good lord," Serena said. "The threat of cancer, an accident, *and* a coma. This has not been your year."

"Oh, Em. How awful." Mackenzie's tears were not for herself this time. "I'm glad you called us. And I'm glad we were here with you and Zoe when you needed us."

"Me, too," Serena said. "Although I hope the next time you invite us back to the lake, things will be a little less eventful."

"I'll drink to that." Emma raised her glass even as she braced. She was not ready to explain her reasons for distancing herself in the first place. She couldn't. Not yet. Not until after Zoe's birthday. Not until . . . Oh,

God, she was beyond pathetic. It wasn't as if there would ever be a "good time" to lose the friends she'd just regained.

Emma was actually trying to think of how she might create a diversion, when Zoe's voice rang out behind them. She stood on the edge of the porch and yelled, "The popcorn's ready! And I've got two movie contenders picked out." She held up a cell phone in one hand. "And Serena's cell phone rang three times. It was the same Charleston phone number and I was afraid it might be an emergency so I thought she might want to check and see if it was something important."

# TWENTY-NINE

"I could definitely get used to this place." Serena sighed and slid back in the oversized Jacuzzi, tilting her head so that her neck rested against the edge as Brooks brought his lips down on hers.

"And I could get used to you." He lifted her onto his lap, her back up against his chest. His arms snaked around her, his touch joining the warm jets of water on her bare skin. His large hands splayed across her abdomen and she let her head fall back on his shoulder. His teeth grazed her earlobe and then he bent to trail his lips down her neck.

This time they'd skipped the drink in the bar, the multi-course meal in the formal dining room and even a cozy spot in front of the roaring fire on the patio overlooking the lake. Brooks had simply had a bottle of champagne and a gorgeous cheese and fruit tray sent up to the Montcalm suite, which was every bit as elegant and romantic as he'd promised. Two guest robes lay on the turned-down king-sized bed, which was in fact elegantly draped and bracketed by antique nightstands. A settee sat at the foot of the bed and commanded a view over a private balcony, the patio and grounds and the lake itself. The door had barely closed behind the server before Brooks had turned on the water taps and poured the first glass of champagne. Before they'd consumed the second glass, they were naked.

"God, you feel good." His hands slid over her. His lips skimmed up her bare shoulder to nibble at her earlobe. Outside, the night sky had turned an inky black. She could see the Morse code of fireflies flickering between the trees and across the lawn. Stars winked dense and bright. But the most beautiful thing there were Brooks's gray eyes and the way they darkened as she turned in his lap, slipped her arms up around his neck, wrapped her legs around him. She stared up into those eyes that looked at her with a tenderness that cut right through her. Their lips joined and he kissed her almost reverently. As if he'd found some unexpected treasure and couldn't believe his good fortune.

This was what she'd dreamed of; this was what she'd been afraid to ever hope for.

"Are you hungry?" he murmured against her lips. Because I don't know how long the dining room is . . ."

"Only for you."

"Good," he said as he stood, lifting her easily and stepping out of the tub with her in his arms. "Because I think I'm ready for the main course." And then so gently it made her want to weep, he dried her with an oversized Turkish towel, laid her on the bed, and proceeded to consume her.

Serena awoke the next morning to pinpricks of sunlight stealing in through the gaps in the heavy drapes.

"There you are," he said. He was dressed in a pair of gym shorts. He carried two cups of freshly brewed coffee. "Take a look at this." He pulled the drapery back from the eastern wall of windows. Bright shards of sunlight crowned the lush green mountainside that rimmed the lake and sent a bright white arrow across the deep blue water.

"I've seen more than my fair share of sunrises across the Atlantic, but this has an intimacy, an intense beauty I wasn't expecting at all."

"I know what you mean," Serena said, cupping the coffee with both hands. "I remember when we first started coming up to the lake house, when Emma's grandmother was still alive. I think I got up every single morning to watch the sun come up. It was so hopeful, you know?" She winced at the admission of how desperate she'd been for anything positive after she'd lost him. "Of course I was younger then, and getting up after a night of drinking was a whole lot easier."

He smiled. "It seems like an eternity ago, doesn't it? The college party days? I still remember that first fraternity party you came up for. I thought I was going to have to knock out a couple of the brothers for the way they couldn't stop looking at you."

A shaft of sadness pierced her happiness as she remembered his jealousy and how important, how secure it had made her feel. But she'd misinterpreted a lot of things about this man. She hadn't been irreplaceable at all. Was she crazy to think she might be now? Was she just setting herself up to be hurt again?

"I see my own boys at Carolina and . . ." His voice trailed off.

"How old are they?" she asked.

"Cole is twenty-one. He's a finance major and he'll be going for an MBA. Brett is nineteen. I don't think he's committed to much besides drinking and Gamecock football." He smiled, his pride evident despite the rueful tone. "But they're both good boys."

She had no idea what to say to that. Not after she'd spent the last decades trying to pretend that Brooks's wife and children didn't exist. "Are y'all close?"

"Always have been," he said, his eyes trained out the window. "Diana used to refer to the boys and me as the Three Musketeers." He stumbled briefly on his wife's name. "Sorry," he said when Serena flinched. "But they're pretty upset about what's happening with their mom and me."

She wanted to ask exactly what it was that was happening, but couldn't quite form the words. Already she could feel his other life intruding into what they'd begun to carve out for themselves, whatever that was. She'd always kept the lives of the married men she'd seen separate from what she shared with them. She'd never wanted to be that woman who listened to or commiserated about a man's marital troubles; their time with her was meant to be something enjoyable for both of them, not a therapy session. And so she did now what she'd always done, what she'd learned to do because of Brooks Anderson the second. She changed the subject.

When their stomachs' growls became too loud to ignore, they breakfasted on eggs and bacon cooked to order down in the formal dining room then went back upstairs, shed the clothes they'd pulled on, and hung the Do Not Disturb sign on the door once again.

A number of texts and emails dinged into both of their phones but it was several hours before Serena, pleasantly numb and ready for a shower, reached for hers. Propped against a pile of pillows they checked their messages.

"Do you have anywhere you need to be tonight?" Serena asked, scrolling through a text that had come from Emma.

"Nope," he said drowsily. "I'm all yours if you'll have me."

She stilled at his words and thought how desperately she'd once wanted to hear them. How different her life would have been if he had remained hers and if they'd built the life they'd once envisioned.

"Good answer." She pushed the thought aside and stretched luxuriously, her thigh pressed against his. She would not ask him his "intentions" or ask for details of his separation. This was not the time to question. This was a time to be enjoyed as thoroughly as possible. "Because we've been invited to join Emma and her friend Jake along with Mackenzie. We're going to go out on the boat for drinks and dinner."

"Perfect." He set his coffee and phone on the nightstand then turned onto his side, propping his head in one hand. "I'll finally get to meet the infamous Emma and Mackenzie." He traced a finger up her inner thigh, which drew a small gasp from her. "What do they think about us reconnecting?"

"Oh, I'm sure they'll be good with it once they meet you. You know, once the shock and horror wear off."

"You haven't told them?" He moved closer and trailed his finger upward.

"No." She turned on her side and wiggled closer, reaching out for that part of him she'd already claimed. The truth was she might not have told them even now if there'd been an easy way to avoid it. She wasn't at all sure she was ready to let the women who had watched her deconstruct when she'd lost him know just how quickly she'd allowed him back into her life.

"Not yet." She held on as he slid onto his back and settled her on top of him. "But I'm sure it will be fine. As long as you're prepared for the Inquisition."

Mackenzie sat on the side porch, her legs crossed on the nearest chair, her sketchpad in her lap, trying to envision exactly what Nadia might have meant when she'd asked her to design her "sometink girlie."

Serena had not yet come back from meeting her current "friend," who had apparently once again made the trip up from the city, no doubt to evade the wife Serena insisted he didn't have. Through the porch screen she could see Zoe and Emma lying side by side on the swim platform, which bobbed gently on the occasional wake from a passing boat. Periodically they sat up, slathered lotion on each other, then flipped over like self-basting turkeys who'd placed themselves in the oven and turned it on, but were determined not to get brown. Emma had seemed oddly distracted lately, as if something troubled her, but each time Mackenzie had questioned her she'd shrugged it off and made some joke about her brain not yet being up to speed.

It was a spectacular July afternoon filled with blue skies, towering white clouds, and an armada of boats gliding past Hemlock Point. The hum of insects and the thrum of boat motors floated on the warm breeze. Her breathing slowed. Her eyes fluttered shut. Her chin had come to rest on her chest, when the sound of a door slamming inside the house pierced her consciousness. Nadia was off today and Martha was not expected. Heavy footsteps sounded somewhere in the dining room, headed toward the kitchen.

"Mac?" She'd been expecting Serena but the voice was not southern or female. Mackenzie sat up straight, pulled her legs off the nearby chair. "Adam?"

He must have followed her voice. Lord knew she was too surprised to do much more than register his. The sketchpad dropped from her hands as she attempted to stand.

"I'm out on the porch," she called as she bent to pick it up. She couldn't seem to decide whether to stay seated or stand. Which left her in an odd sort of crouch.

She struggled to banish the nerves that had turned her mouth dry and her hands clumsy. This was Adam. Her husband. She stood, but her legs had turned rubbery and her thoughts weren't thoughts so much as worries. That they'd been apart too long, communicated too little. That maybe he'd enjoyed himself too much without her.

He stepped out onto the porch with an added cockiness. His dark blond hair appeared freshly cut and styled. It swept back off his forehead and fell to one side. Feathery layers touched his shoulders. The neatly trimmed mustache that framed his lips and the narrow beard that hugged the line of his jaw were new. He looked even more sophisticated than she remembered in the low-slung jeans and the plain white tee that showed off his abs. Dropping an overnight bag on the nearest chair, he leaned forward and opened his arms.

She walked into them.

He kissed her on the cheek. She kissed him back, but everything felt off. If only she'd had warning, she could have prepared herself.

"I thought you were going to let me know when to expect you," she said. It was not what she'd meant to lead with, but they were the first words that presented themselves.

"I caught a ride up from the city at the last minute and I wasn't really sure what time I'd get here."

It was an answer but it wasn't.

"So I thought I'd surprise you. Is everything okay?" he asked, his brown eyes narrowing slightly.

"Yes. Of course." But she took a step back. "You just surprised me, that's all."

He continued to study her, clearly waiting for something. It was too late now to make that first kiss more enthusiastic. Or squeal her congratulations at her first sight of him, but she felt small and petty. This was Adam. Whom she'd loved since the first moment she saw him and who had somehow managed to achieve his most cherished goal. Was she going to nurse her hurts and grievances now that he'd finally come? Or was she going to celebrate his success and share his happiness with him?

She threw her arms around him, kissed him hard on the lips, and said, "You must be so excited." She breathed in his familiar scent, felt the familiar tightening of his arms around her.

He smiled full out then. "Oh, I am. I'd almost given up, you know? I have to pinch myself every once in a while just to prove this is all really happening." He laughed delightedly.

"But it is happening," she said. "You did it!" She tucked her arm through his then led him toward the kitchen, eager to get back on more solid footing. "Come on. Let's open a bottle of wine to toast your success and you can tell me all about it. Then we'll go out and take a swim with Emma and Zoe. Oh, and tonight we're going out for drinks and dinner on Jake Richards's boat. And we can all celebrate together."

She let him select the bottle then rummaged through the cabinet for two wineglasses as he pulled the cork. She saw his shoulders relax with the first sips of wine, watched his white-toothed smile begin to flash as she gave him her undivided attention. His sentences came out in a torrent and each began with "I" or ended with "me." A trait she'd never noticed in him before.

*He's earned it,* she told herself as he talked nonstop. But it was hard not to notice that it took little more than an occasional smile or nod to keep the flood waters of her husband's self-satisfaction rising.

# THIRTY

Early that evening the sky had turned an inhospitable pewter gray and the wind had begun to pick up. Zoe stood on the dock watching Jake and Ryan approach in *The Mohican*. Emma stood beside her as the boat rounded the buoys that marked the rocky remains of Rush Island. "Don't you think he's cute?"

"Who?" Emma teased, though there was no question at all as to which Richards her daughter was looking at or referring to.

Zoe turned and rolled her eyes, which Emma chose to consider a testament of sorts to her improved medical status and a step closer to normalcy. Who would have thought that that teenage gesture of dismissal would have proved such a morale booster? "Jake's not bad for an older guy," Zoe finally conceded after an assessing look at Emma in which she undoubtedly factored in her mother's date-worthiness. "I mean, he probably looked a lot like Ryan when he was younger, right? And he does have a sense of humor. But he's not as funny as Ethan Miller."

"True," Emma conceded. "But it's not exactly fair to compare him to a professional." She glanced back at the house to see if Serena's "friend" had arrived. Serena had come back that afternoon glowing in a way that only came from great sex, not that Emma would have any recent experience with that, and a secretive smile on her face that Mackenzie insisted meant he was married. But would a married man show up for a group outing with people he didn't know? Emma sighed and reminded herself that whom Serena dated was her own business and the least of Emma's concerns.

"Ryan's so different from the guys at home," Zoe said, her eyes trained on the boy as the boat drew closer. "He's way more grown up and interesting. Everybody back in LA spends all their time trying to impress everybody else."

Footsteps reverberated on the dock behind them. As if summoned by Zoe's West Coast reference, Adam Russell joined them on the dock, his arm slung casually across Mackenzie's shoulders as if she were an additional appendage. He looked, as he almost always did, as if he'd stepped off a *GQ* cover. In this case, in billowy white linen pants and a black Polo shirt that would go perfectly with Jake's classic boat.

346

Adam stopped next to Zoe, who was built with the same kind of tall ranginess as Mackenzie and Adam, and who with a little reddish gold mixed into their blond hair, could easily have been cast as Zoe's parents. Even Nash and Regan could have played her daughter's parents more convincingly than Emma. "I really can't get over how you've shot up," Adam said giving Zoe's long ponytail a tug. "Is she really going to be sixteen, Em?"

Mackenzie flinched but Adam didn't seem to notice. Could he really have forgotten that Mackenzie and she had been pregnant at the same time? An occurrence that had put so many irreversible things into motion. His unexpected presence was a complication she hadn't planned on when she'd invited Mackenzie and Serena to the lake. "I can't even remember the last time I saw her."

Emma stepped between Adam and Zoe. She remembered the last time in graphic detail. "She was five and we were all in New York at the same time. We had drinks at Bemelmans with Gran. You'd just finished that script based on a group of people eerily similar to us who met while they were studying drama at NYU and lived near each other in the Village."

"I guess it was a tad derivative," Adam said.

"A tad?" Mackenzie said. "There were lines of dialogue that were word for word from our real life."

"True," Adam conceded good-naturedly. "But I remember I'd written in parts for all of you."

"Mackenzie was the only one who didn't want one," Emma said.

"I'd take a part in a heartbeat," Zoe said.

Emma closed her eyes. Wondering when others would notice the things she couldn't help seeing. When she opened them *The Mohican* was beginning its approach to the dock. Thunder rumbled in the distance. The previously smooth surface of the lake had turned choppy with the wind.

"Now, that's a boat," Adam observed as Jake cut speed and drew closer. "I've seen some classic wooden boats on Lake Michigan but I've never seen one prettier than this."

Jake threw the boat into reverse and docked smoothly. "You know boats?" he asked as he cut the engine.

"Not really. But I love to ride in them. Boats are a little like lake and beach houses. As much as we might like to own them, sometimes it's even better having friends who do."

Emma introduced Adam to the Richardses as she moved forward to take the bowline from Jake. Ryan shot Zoe a smile as he stepped off the stern. The boat rose and fell slightly on the now choppy water.

"The forecast was iffy before we left," Jake

said. "But I figured we could make it up to the Algonquin and eat out on the docks. Only the weather's moving in a lot quicker than projected." Jake pitched his voice above the sound of the water slapping against the sides of the boat. "I'm thinking maybe we should tuck her in the boathouse and sit tight for a while, see how quickly it passes through."

"Good idea," Emma said. "Zoe and Adam can stay and help. Mackenzie and I'll go forage for snacks and drinks while you get her settled. We'll see you inside."

"You need help?" Nadia narrowed her gaze at Emma as she and Mackenzie entered the house. "You look funny."

"I'm fine." Emma swept a hand over her head surprised as always by the feel of what was now a little longer than a crew cut. At the moment that crew cut was slick and damp. "We just had a change of plans due to the weather."

"You call if need me," the nurse insisted. "I go in room. Read important book Edmund recommend me." She held up the tome in all its weightiness. "Is *War and Peace* by famous comrade Leo Tolstoy. Edmund say it real page burner."

"Are you sure you're feeling okay?" Mackenzie asked Emma after Nadia's bedroom door had closed behind her and they had begun to take stock of the kitchen.

"I'm good."

"I don't know," Mackenzie said. "Something seems . . . off to me."

"I'm fine." Despite what Emma thought was a perfectly executed "cease and desist" tone, Mackenzie did not cease or desist.

"I don't know; you seem to be somewhere else. Like you're seeing something no one else is. And the first time you saw Adam you looked . . . so shocked."

Emma tried not to react, but apparently she wasn't completely in command of her facial expressions, either.

"There," Mackenzie said. "Like that."

"I don't know what you're talking about." Emma stuck her head in the refrigerator and took her time perusing the potential offerings. She found a container of Martha's homemade spinach dip, an assortment of cheeses, slices of prosciutto, and most of a salami. She began to pull them from the refrigerator. "You seemed a little surprised to see Adam, too," she said as she laid her finds on the counter then went into the pantry in search of a box of crackers. "But you haven't seemed all that excited to see him."

"I'm extremely happy and excited for Adam," Mackenzie insisted.

Emma remained silent as she retrieved two bottles of red and two bottles of white from the wine refrigerator. She wondered if Mackenzie had even noticed how evasive her answer had sounded. "That's not what I said."

"It's just that I haven't seen him for a month, which has never happened before. At least not since we got married." Mackenzie never alluded to the months before their wedding when Adam had broken things off and hitchhiked out to California. "And . . . I don't know. I'm not sure I'm as ready for as many major life changes as he seems to be."

"Amen, sister." Emma was still trying to determine whether she'd thought the words or spoken them aloud, when the front door swung open letting in the sounds of laughter and footsteps along with the unmistakable sounds of a lashing rain. That was the thing about change. Even when you were the one shaking things up, you had no real control over how things would turn out or even how others would react. When she'd invited Mackenzie and Serena to the lake with the purpose of setting things to rights and making provisions for Zoe, it had never occurred to her that the women whose lives she might be turning upside down would have spent the last month suspending their own lives in order to take care of her and Zoe. And she most definitely hadn't imagined that anyone else, especially Adam, would be there when and if the shit finally hit the fan.

Serena came inside shaking her head to dispel

the raindrops, her hand clenching Brooks's. Adam's arm was around her waist as he called out, "Hey, look who I found!"

They tromped into the kitchen in what could only be called a mob, everyone talking at once. Until Emma finally said, "All right everybody. Hang on. Let's let Serena introduce us to her friend."

Serena froze in the silence that fell, suddenly unsure whether springing Brooks this way was such a good idea after all. She hadn't envisioned this kind of pandemonium or, apparently, even stopped to think it through any further than wanting to share her current state of happiness. "Well, um, okay," she said. Adam's arm left her waist. Brooks gave her hand a quick squeeze and turned a friendly smile on the others. He seemed genuinely unperturbed. "So, this is, my, um . . ." Serena swallowed, keenly aware that every eye was on her. She wasn't sure if it was rain or sweat dripping down her forehead and trickling between her breasts. "As I was saying . . ." Another swallow, this one more desperate than the last.

"It's nice to meet you, Emma," Brooks finally said, flashing his pearly whites. "You too, Mackenzie. I've been looking forward to meeting all of you. Adam." He shook all of their hands while Serena watched in silence, suddenly unable to remember her own name, let alone his. She had never actually envi-

sioned this ever happening. "I'm Brooks Anderson."

For a moment a silence fell.

"I'm Serena's friend from Charleston," he
clarified. As if there were another Brooks
Anderson from some other city that Serena
had once planned to marry.

"Nice to meet you." Jake Richards stepped
forward, introduced himself, and shook
Brooks's hand, shooting a look at Emma as
he did. Ryan did the same. Serena realized
the name must have finally registered when
Adam swung around to get a closer look.

"Well, hell," Adam said. "I'm not sure
whether to say hello or punch your lights
out." He turned to Mackenzie. "This is kind
of like Little Red Riding Hood bringing the
Big Bad Wolf to the party." He shook his
head.

"Are you referring to me as Little Red Riding Hood?" Serena finally found her voice if
not her equilibrium.

"What do you say, Mac?" Adam asked her.

Mackenzie shook her head. Serena had the
distinct impression that if Zoe and Ryan
hadn't been present she would now be demanding to know whether Brooks had
brought his wife with him, too.

"You all help yourself to whatever you can
find." Emma gestured vaguely at the things
lying all over the counter. "And, um, feel free
to talk amongst yourselves." She exchanged a

look with Mackenzie, then the two of them headed toward Serena.

Brooks might or might not be the Big Bad Wolf, but he was not stupid. He stepped out of their way as they took hold of Serena, wheeled her around, and led her toward the stairs.

"You've been sleeping with Brooks Anderson. The man who dumped you to marry someone else. The man you cried over for a good four years and who caused you to develop a married man habit that has not made you happy," Mackenzie said. "And now you're sleeping with him, a married man?"

They'd escorted her to Emma's bedroom without a word then shut the door behind them. If there'd been a bare light bulb and a length of hose available, Serena had no doubt they'd be using them on her right now.

"Is there a question in there somewhere?" Serena asked even as she wondered why she was surprised by their reaction. She'd been pressed into a club chair next to the fireplace. Emma sat on the edge of her bed. Mackenzie was pacing back and forth like an attorney grilling a hostile witness.

"Why are you seeing him?" Mackenzie asked.

"And this is your business because?" Serena asked.

"Because we care about you," Emma said.

"Then be happy for me," Serena said.

354

"Most people don't get a second chance with someone they loved."

"You were in love," Emma said. "He chose to marry someone else. Someone he's lived with for twenty-plus years and with whom he's had children." She said this gently, but the words still stung. Emma had apparently fallen into the role of "good cop," but she was a cop nonetheless.

"And a life," Mackenzie said.

"I've had a life." Serena stood, angry now. They had no right to talk to her this way. Or to snatch away her pleasure so meanly.

"Of course you have," Emma said. "And you've been very successful."

"Professionally," Mackenzie cut in. "But your personal life has been spent trying to prove that no man is worth marrying. And that all married men cheat."

"Are any men worth marrying?" She glared directly at Mackenzie. "Are there married men who don't cheat?"

"This is not about us or our choices," Emma said.

"Isn't it?" Serena asked. "Your marriage barely lasted a year after Zoe was born. And you." She turned again to Mackenzie. "You dragged a man who only ever wanted to be a success in New York theater or Hollywood films to frickin' Noblesville, Indiana, to run a community theater. And as far as I know this is the first glimpse of him you've had in a month."

She could see that her jabs had hurt, that her aim was true. But she could also see that if they didn't stop this now, there would be no turning back.

"His marriage is over," Serena said. Though she was pitifully short on details because she'd been afraid to press. If they hadn't just attacked her, she might have even admitted to the uncertainty that she hadn't been completely able to banish. Too good to be true was almost always too good to be true. "And that's all I'm going to say on the subject."

Emma's tone softened. "We were there when he first hurt you so badly, Serena. And we've spent the decades since thinking up names vile enough to call him. We don't want you ever to be hurt like that again."

Jaw tight, Mackenzie nodded her agreement.

If the house hadn't been full of people, they would have undoubtedly gone to their own rooms and, well, Serena didn't know exactly what she would have done in hers other than pack. They stared uneasily at each other. They'd spent the last month being there for each other. Emma's hair was starting to come in, but at the moment she looked like a really weird cross between GI Jane and a duckling. Two weeks ago she'd barely had the energy to walk or talk. They had almost lost her completely.

The house was filled with guests that they'd invited. Guests they were not about to hurl out into a thunderstorm because they'd exploded at each other.

"I'm not spending the night being pissed off at you, Emma," Serena said. "I really don't want to. Not after all we've been through."

"What about me?" Makenzie asked, her tone lighter but her jaw still tight.

"*You* haven't been in a coma and almost died," Serena said. "But you have had to live in a very small town in Indiana through a lot of mind-numbing winters." She did not add, *with a man who now seemed primarily pre-occupied with himself,* though it was tempting. "So, I say we get back to the people who are probably wondering what the hell is going on up here."

Emma nodded her head and stood. Stiffly, they moved toward the door.

"But this doesn't mean you're ever again allowed to tell me whom I should or should not see," Serena said as she reached for the doorknob. "I've got a psychiatrist I pay a lot of money to to do that."

# THIRTY-ONE

They managed to squash back their anger in front of the others, but moved carefully around each other, as if venturing too close might spark the explosion they had narrowly avoided.

"Come on over here, Mac," Adam said as she passed the spot near the stairs where he and Jake had been engaged in conversation. The light citrus scent of his cologne teased her nose as he reached out to her. His pull had always been magnetic, as if she were a planet and he the sun she'd been designed to revolve around. "I was just telling Jake here how sorry I am not to get out on his boat. I was lucky enough to be invited on Michael Gold's boat last weekend after we signed the deal."

"Michael Gold is the production head at Universal," Mackenzie said, noting Jake's blank look.

"He's definitely the man," Adam went on. "And his boat is more of a yacht with a captain and all that. I have to tell you the Pacific Ocean from the deck of a boat — that is a sight to behold.

"We'll have to make sure Jake here gets however many tickets he wants for the New York premiere of *A Man for Many Reasons,*" Adam concluded. As if this not-to-be-missed event were imminent and not what would likely be several years down the road if at all. Mackenzie watched Adam's face as he spoke. He'd always had charisma, could draw attention simply walking into a room. But this intentional attention seeking was a different thing altogether.

Jake smiled and nodded. "Wouldn't miss it. The plot sounds fascinating." He turned to include Mackenzie. "You must be very excited that Adam's screenplay is getting made," he said.

"Oh, I am."

"Personally, I think my wife is totally shocked that I finally sold something to Hollywood." Adam smiled when he said this and even added a self-deprecating, "Hell, I'd be lying if I said I wasn't a little surprised myself." But she could tell from the look he turned on her that he'd found her level of enthusiasm lacking.

"I've been surprised by a lot of things lately," she murmured. "But I have never doubted Adam's talent or drive."

"She's had me in Noblesville directing little

children and retirees with the occasional middle-aged drama queen thrown in." Adam's tone remained teasing, but the things he said about her felt anything but. He had apparently forgotten that Mackenzie had always been his biggest fan and personal cheering section. Even when there had been little to cheer about.

An awkward silence fell. Jake extended his hand to Adam. "It's good to meet you. The rain seems to be over. Ryan and I will be heading out." He gave Mackenzie a friendly hug. "We'll see you Friday at Zoe's cookout."

Brooks Anderson came over to say goodbye, too. Serena was tucked under his arm and looked happy to be there. She looked less happy when Mackenzie leaned in to hug her. "Sorry," Mackenzie said quickly before Serena could draw away. "Apparently you're not the only one who thinks I'm a wet blanket." Was that really what she'd become? Smothering everybody's good time? Keeping her husband from living the life he really wanted?

Even Emma seemed to be keeping her distance, and Mackenzie had caught her looking oddly at both her and Adam.

"Brooks, my man!" Adam offered a hearty handshake, any dilemma he'd felt earlier over whether to punch or embrace him clearly resolved. "If you ever come out to LA you just let me know. I've met lots of people through Mike Gold at Universal. He's very well connected in financial circles, not just in the movie business. Maybe we could take a lunch."

It was Serena who finally stopped him. She did this by putting her arms around him and giving him a hug. "Good to see you, Adam. We're going to run now in case the rain picks up again. Brooks has to head back to the city tomorrow. I'll see you all in the morning."

When they'd left and Emma and Zoe had walked the Richardses out to the boat, Mackenzie began to straighten up the kitchen. Adam leaned against the counter and watched her, taking his time with his drink.

She puttered, keeping her hands busy, even as she tried to keep her thoughts from traveling down paths from which there might be no return. She snuck a look at her husband as he took a long pull on his drink.

"You could have knocked me over when Serena introduced us to Brooks," Adam said. "He seems like a nice enough guy, but I never would have figured Serena would ever forgive him or get over what happened."

"Me either," Mackenzie admitted. "Not after all those years spent referring to him as 'The Tool' and worse."

So many things seemed to be out of kilter: Emma's accident, the coma, even her slow but steady recovery. Serena involved with the man who'd scarred her so badly. Adam finally achieving his closest-held dream. The words she and Emma and Serena had hurled at each other earlier. It was as if the earth had tilted slightly on its axis turning the unimaginable into reality. It seemed to be working in everyone's favor but hers.

"I hate that you think I'm not excited for you," Mackenzie said, surprising not only Adam but also herself. "Did you mean what you said to Jake?" She stopped short of asking him why he'd been so unavailable all month. There were some things she really didn't want to know.

"Nah," he said. "I think I may have had one too many of these." He handed over his empty highball glass. "And I guess I was a little surprised that you didn't look happier to see me when I got here."

This, she reminded herself, was Adam. The too-charming man she'd loved since she'd first spotted him. The sometimes-unpredictable man she'd nonetheless spun her whole life around. The man who had unaccountably chosen her when he could have had almost any woman he wanted.

"Listen," he said. "We can sit down tomorrow and figure out our next steps. For now . . ." He gave her the sexy, impish smile that had always melted her. "Well, I haven't seen my wife for an awfully long time." He leaned down and brushed his lips across hers, turned her into his arms. "And I can't think of a better way to celebrate than to make love to her."

By the time he'd finished kissing her, Mackenzie's worries had been pushed under the rug of her desire for him. That desire was a sharp keening thing that had always both shocked and delighted her. It went hand in hand with the never-spoken-of "love at first sight" that she'd discovered for herself at that first party in the ratty apartment in the Village so many years ago.

Her hand was warm in his. Her legs trembled on the way up the stairs. Her skin tingled to his touch. By the time he'd undressed her and pushed her down onto the bed, she'd ceased to think at all.

The rain had stopped. The dark sky had cleared and the moon shone bright and full. Its beams arrowed onto the lake's surface and disappeared into the still-wet trees.

"Thanks for coming." Emma and Zoe stood in the boathouse, its doors flung open.

Jake started the engine and let it warm up while Ryan untied the lines. "Thanks for having us. I can come early on Friday to get the ribs cooking."

"Sounds good," Emma said. "I have my follow-up at Mount Sinai this week. I'm not sure who all's going into the city but Zoe and I will be back on Thursday. Martha's going to do the grocery shopping. I told her you'd let her know if you needed anything special to go along with the ribs."

"Will do."

Emma and Zoe stood on the dock and watched *The Mohican* back out of the boathouse. With a last wave Jake and Ryan headed out and rounded the shoals off Hemlock Point. The boat accelerated as it hit open water.

"Have a good time?" she asked Zoe.

"Yeah. I like it here. Ryan's, you know, cool."

"He is," Emma agreed. "It's okay to have a good time without worrying too much what it might mean or develop into. That's part of what being sixteen's all about."

Zoe smiled. "And I'm really glad Serena and Mackenzie are here, too. How come we haven't seen them in so long?"

"Oh, you know, people get busy. Everybody's running at such a hectic pace. Sometimes we just kind of let things slide."

"Really?"

"Yes." The lie stuck slightly in Emma's throat. But she wasn't ready for Zoe to hear what she had to share with Mackenzie and Serena. Nor did she need to know that Emma was making arrangements for her in the event of Emma's death — not given their too-recent brush with it. Emma had given herself until after Zoe's birthday celebration on Friday before she would come clean to Mackenzie and Serena. Something she still wasn't quite sure how to handle. She stumbled slightly on a nail that wasn't quite flush with a board. Zoe reached out a hand to steady her. Once she'd squared things with them, she'd find a way to explain to Zoe.

"Thanks." Emma laced her arm through Zoe's.

"You're feeling okay, right?" Zoe asked as they neared the end of the dock. "I mean, you'd tell me if you weren't?"

"I do. And I would." She'd heard the tremor in Zoe's voice. All the more reason to get things settled.

They walked through the wet grass toward the front porch, where the light twinkled like a beacon. Upstairs, Emma noticed that Mackenzie's bedroom door was closed. She kissed Zoe good night, her thoughts once again turning to all that lay ahead.

Nadia was waiting for her in her bedroom, the bed turned down, the drapes pulled closed. "Come," she said. "I tuck you in." The nurse's gruffness no longer hid the warmth at the woman's center. Her large solid presence radiated comfort. Nadia yawned. "Head hurt from so many words. That Tolstoy need editing."

Emma's dreams could have used some editing, too. They were long and drawn out. Each image overflowed with foreboding. In one she lay in a small wooden boat that was taking on water. Heavy winds howled overhead. Waves smacked against the hull and spilled inside. She cowered in the boat, drenched and weeping.

*Really, darling. These drowning metaphors are exhausting.*

*Gran.*

*You are lucky to be alive. You do not need to explain. Just change the paperwork and be done.*

The boat began to sink taking her with it.

*But the truth. It's important.*

*In my experience,* Gran's voice said, *the truth is highly overrated.*

The boat settled on the bottom. Emma did not turn into a fish. She did not sprout gills. As she opened her mouth to protest, her lungs slowly began to fill with water.

# THIRTY-TWO

Mist clung to the lake and softened the early morning sky to a pale wispy gray. Hemlock Point was only partially visible and the mountains that rose on the distant eastern bank were completely shrouded from view. It was quiet, almost mystical.

Mackenzie had woken in the predawn lying next to but not touching Adam. He slept like a man with nothing on his conscience — or possibly, no conscience at all — on his back, a contented smile on his face, his arms flung wide as if ready to embrace the world. Mackenzie had woken curled in a fetal position, her head pressed against his side. In sleep as in life they had declared themselves. It didn't take Freud to figure out where they were coming from.

The mist was not yet ready to lift when she carried a cup of coffee out to an Adirondack chair on the small sliver of beach. She swiped off the dew and settled into it, a blanket around her shoulders, the cup clasped in her hands.

She sipped the warm comforting brew and waited for the first glimmers of sunlight to pierce the grayness. It was hard to tell where the sky left off and the lake began.

She pulled her knees up as she listened to the sounds of the new day coming alive. A small splash, a quack from an unseen duck. A sound of oars in the bay though she couldn't imagine rowing blind in this mist. The sounds were muted and hushed like the shrouded sky.

Resting her chin on her knees, she closed her eyes and let her thoughts wander. She felt slightly sore and pleasantly satisfied, something she hadn't expected. She'd been certain she could never focus given all that had worried her, but the opposite had been true. Now she needed to get her thoughts in order, to marshal her energy. She felt the urge to prepare a defense but had no idea what she would be expected to defend against.

She knew he was awake when she heard his voice out on the dining porch. Heard his laughter at something Nadia said. The porch screen creaked open. The mist made it difficult to tell the time, but she'd expected him to sleep in. He was, after all, on California time.

"Good morning." He came and dropped down into the chair beside hers, unconcerned with its dampness. "Man, I was out like a light," he said. "Thanks for putting me to sleep with a smile on my face."

"Ditto," she said, attempting to match his tone and wishing she could find another smile.

They watched the lake in silence, the bay slowly separating itself from the sky, as the shards of sunlight began to burn through the mist. The outline of the dock on the western edge of Hemlock Point became more distinct. The line of buoys surrounding the rocky remains of Rush Island appeared.

"It's beautiful here," he said.

"Yes it is." She kept her eyes on the bay cataloguing each discernable detail as it emerged from the mist.

"California's beautiful, too." He turned to her.

"I know." She waited for what would come. Braced but not necessarily ready.

"I've waited my entire adult life, and possibly most of my childhood, for this opportunity," Adam said carefully, looking her directly in the eye. "I want to be there through production. And I want to reap the rewards that follow. If this film is well made and successful, even moderately successful, all those doors that have shut in my face for so long will finally open."

She nodded, forced herself to not look away. Unlike her, Adam had never given up.

Somehow he'd always managed to believe in himself. It was one of the things that had first attracted her.

"Someone's interested in the theater, or at least the building," he said. "I think we should list the house. I want to move to California. Permanently." There it was. The vast unknown made known, which made it unavoidable.

"And what about what I want?" she asked.

"The last twenty years have been about what you want, Mac." He said this as if she had arbitrarily bullied him into things against his will. Was that really what she'd done?

"We didn't only move to Noblesville because I *wanted* to," she retorted, stung. "Neither of us were making it in New York. We couldn't afford to live there. We could have never raised a child there."

"A child we never had." It was a simple truth, delivered without heat but it still burned.

"Have you really been so miserable?" she asked.

He gazed out over the lake as if the answer might be there. She braced once again.

"With you? No," he finally said. "With my life?" He shook his head. "I can't believe you'd have to ask that. You knew who I was when you married me, knew exactly what I wanted. You acted as if you supported that." His jaw hardened. "I'm not going to turn my back on this chance at the life I always wanted. Don't you think it's my turn?"

Her head snapped up. Did he expect her to throw her arms around him, tell him how wonderful he was, and ask how quickly she should pack? As if all these years had been a wasteland he'd had to slog through. "And if I don't want to go to California?"

"Then maybe you should think about why you're still clinging to the place you grew up in and the small, safe life we've lived there," he said. "The woman I fell in love with ran away from that kind of life. She even learned to trust in love at first sight. I'm not sure what's happened to that woman. I haven't seen her for a while.

"But I'm going, Mackenzie. I love you. I'd prefer that you come with me. I hope you will. But I'm going even if I have to go alone."

Mackenzie sat staring at the lake long after Adam had gone inside, her thoughts shrouded in a mist that seemed reluctant to burn away.

The torture at Bob Fortson's hands was over for the day. Emma was floating on a raft, one hand trailing in the water, a cap pulled down low to shade her face, when her cell phone rang.

"I get." Nadia, who had avoided the sun like a vampire since that day on Jake's boat, was seated in an Adirondack chair she'd dragged beneath the stand of trees. She'd eyed the nearby hammock only briefly, having discovered early on how hard it could be to fight one's way out of it.

Emma's eyes drifted shut as the nurse answered the phone. The day was warm, the breeze gentle. The whine of a boat motor carried across the water.

"Nyet. No. Not available."

Emma smiled sleepily. There was no longer much need for Nadia's nursing skills, but she'd proven adept at screening calls, and with her boulder-sized body with its muscled arms and legs, she could run interference as well as any bodyguard. And whether or not she meant to be she was highly entertaining, provoking smiles as she reenacted scenes between Tolstoy's Pierre and Natasha, or extolled the many virtues of the librarian they had yet to meet.

"Sorry," Nadia was saying now. "I tell you. Emma nyet available."

Emma smiled at the determination in Nadia's voice. And yet when she opened one eye to see what was going on, Nadia still had the phone to her ear and appeared to be listening unhappily.

"Who is it?" Emma paddled closer, her eyes now on the nurse.

"Is Eve." Nadia put a hand over the mouthpiece. "I tell her no. She threaten fire me." Her face contorted. "I think tell her go ahead.

But words get stuck. Is not money. I just . . . I not ready leave you."

Emma waved an insect away and reached for the phone. Nadia placed it in her hand and mouthed a final apology.

"What is it?" Emma asked.

"I just called to check on you."

"Thank you," Emma said politely. "I'm fine. Now if you'll excuse me . . ."

"Wait."

"Please," Emma said holding on to her temper. "Just tell me what you really want."

"All right." Eve's voice was tight. "I understand you're coming into the city and I'd like to take Zoe to lunch so I can give her her birthday present."

Emma closed her eyes. Her free hand trailed through the water in what she hoped would prove a soothing motion. "I thought we agreed you were going to choose something you could send to her."

"No. You told me I wasn't welcome and that I should find another way to deliver her gift. We're both going to be in the same city at the same time. And it's too late to mail anything anyway."

Emma flashed back to the birthday celebrations she'd looked forward to as a child, which had always turned into photo ops and acting out her role in her famously happy family. "I'm not sending Zoe alone."

"Then join us." The trap snapped shut.

"Bring whomever you'd like. I'm certain I can get a private room or a quiet unobtrusive table somewhere."

Experience told Emma this was highly unlikely, but Eve was Zoe's grandmother. Wanting to see Zoe, wish her a happy birthday, and give her a gift wasn't exactly a hanging offense.

"All right," Emma said. "But no photographers. No media. And no acting." This last was even more unlikely, but she tacked it on anyway.

"Darling. I understand perfectly," Eve said. But she sounded frighteningly satisfied. As if she'd offered an apple and seen it accepted and was now just waiting for the right person to bite into it. "I'll send you a text to let you know what I've arranged."

Even as Emma tossed her phone back to Nadia, Serena stared stupidly down at hers. It was receiving a signal. It had not been dropped on pavement or fallen into the lake, or any other wet place. No matter where she stood, there appeared to be plenty of bars and a decisive dial tone. And yet her phone had not rung for almost thirty-six hours. Not, to be precise, since she'd kissed Brooks goodbye and watched his rental car drive off for the return trip to Manhattan Sunday morning.

*He's busy. He just hasn't had time to call,* she

374

told herself. But he'd been busy since he'd arrived in New York, sometimes rushing from one meeting to the next, but he'd always made time to at least call. Or text. Or even send some random picture captioned with some wry, witty observation.

A small knot of dread tightened in her stomach. *Too good to be true was too good to be true.*

*No.* If he hadn't had time to call her that didn't mean she couldn't call him. Women called men all the time. Before she could talk herself out of it, she hit redial for his cell phone and waited, barely breathing as it rang. She began to breathe again as the ringing stopped and Brooks's voice came on the line. "Hi."

*Oh, thank God.* "Brooks," she began in a relieved rush. "You won't believe what I . . ."

"This is Brooks Anderson. Please leave your name and number at the tone and I'll get back to you."

She waited through the tone, her heart thudding in her chest, her face flushing with embarrassment. She did not leave a message. *Get a grip,* she instructed herself. She'd try him again before they left for the city if she hadn't already heard from him.

A small desperate part of her wanted to call her mother in Charleston and ask if she'd heard anything about the Andersons or his marriage. Except that would be even more humiliating than the sinking sensation she was currently feeling, that she had somehow been "had." Right now she was the only one who knew anything might be amiss. And that was the way she planned to keep it.

# THIRTY-THREE

In the end, everyone but Nadia came into the city. The size of their party made keeping Serena's misery to herself both easier and more difficult. Adam came in to see friends and meet with his theater agent. Mackenzie came to hold Emma's hand at her doctor's appointment and afterward at Zoe's birthday lunch with Eve — a celebration whose guest list had expanded to include all of them.

They'd taken their time settling into "Chez Serena" then strolled down their shared memory lane to John's Pizzeria for dinner, during which Adam reminisced about his table-waiting days and Emma, Mackenzie, and Serena gave Zoe a guided tour of the first years of their friendship. Serena joined in and even laughed at the right spots as they told stories on each other, but every ring of a cell phone or ding of an incoming text sent adrenaline spiking through her bloodstream; each time it wasn't Brooks, she crashed a bit harder. Trying to keep her thoughts off herself, she watched Adam and Zoe, who sat next to each other, noting the mobility of their smiles and their improbably similar laughter. Mackenzie watched them, too, and although she joined in and even shared some stories of her own, Serena noticed that she occasionally fell silent as if turning over things in her mind that she couldn't quite let go of. It took a worried woman to recognize one.

Serena chided herself for feeling so bereft when she was surrounded by the people she'd always cared about the most, and yet she kept seeing Brooks's face when she'd showed him John's. When she went to the ladies' room, she actually stood in front of the heart that contained both their names. When tears threatened, she ran her fingers over the word "ASSHOLE" she'd carved in tear-shaped letters. Resolute, she called his number. This time she left a message. "Hey," she said brightly at the beep. "It's me. I'm at John's with the gang for pizza. Everybody says hi. We're staying at my place. Zoe and I are recording at the studio in the morning and then we're all having lunch at Le Cirque before we head back to the lake." She hesitated, her eyes drawn again to the heart that held both their names. Had she really just given him every possible place where he might find her? "I hope you're okay. I'd really like to see or at least hear from you."

The next morning Serena stood in front of the microphone at the studio with Wes Harrison on one side of her and Zoe on the other. All three of them watched the playback of the scene between Georgia Goodbody, her boyfriend, and her boyfriend's long-lost and heretofore unknown daughter, that they were set to rerecord.

There'd been no sign of Lauri, though it was unlikely that Serena would even have had the energy to insult her after a sleepless night spent willing her silent phone to ring. Wes barely registered. In truth, although she tried to stay tuned into Zoe, Serena's mind kept straying to Brooks. Who still had not called, emailed, or texted.

"I'm sorry?" she said, coming out of her reverie only after realizing that Ethan had just asked for something.

"I said, can you make that line a little saucier?" It was the third time Ethan's voice had sounded in her earphones asking her for more or less of something, which was three times more than he'd ever needed to ask her for anything before.

Serena flushed. "Sorry. I'm ready."

She pushed her worry aside long enough to complete the line as requested, then flubbed the one that followed. *Jesus.*

"Do you need to take a break?" Ethan's voice sounded again, not angry or aggrieved as it should have been. "Would you like

Catherine to bring in something to drink?"

"No. Thanks," Serena said brightly. "I'm really sorry. If I don't get this next bit on the first take, I'll hand over Georgia's fan and let you hit me with it."

"I'm in."

"Not you, Wes," Serena snapped.

Zoe laughed as Serena rolled her eyes at the man beside her. Serena wished she were having as good a time as Zoe. But then the girl was about to turn sixteen — a number Serena could no longer personally remember — and she was beyond excited to be here. Serena's job was to help her shine in this session, not throw everyone off.

"Rolling playback!"

The session finally ended without further mishap but Serena filed out of the studio badly shaken. She'd never allowed her personal life to intrude on her professional one. Even when a relationship had come to an end, she hadn't let her disappointment show in her work. But then none of those endings had really mattered. And, of course, she'd almost always been the one to walk away. She'd made sure to choose men who weren't really available and whom she didn't care too deeply about. That had been her modus operandi from the moment Brooks Anderson had walked out of her life. Right up until the moment he'd walked back in.

She and Zoe lingered briefly in the reception area. Serena kept one eye on the door secretly hoping that Brooks would walk through it as he had the last time she'd been in to record.

"Are you expecting someone?" Ethan asked.

"No." Serena pulled her eyes from the door. "We're going to Le Cirque for lunch. Eve Michaels is throwing a small birthday luncheon for Zoe."

"Sounds like fun." Ethan shot Zoe a wink. "Happy Birthday. Be sure to tell your mother we're ready to add you to the cast anytime she's ready to sign off on the paperwork."

"Maybe you could come for lunch and talk to her about it," Zoe said. "I bet she wouldn't say no to you."

Ethan snorted. "I don't know that I'm that persuasive. And I wouldn't want to intrude on your grandmother's plans."

"But she told me I could invite anybody I wanted to," Zoe insisted. "And you won't be the only guy, 'cause Mackenzie's husband Adam's coming."

"Oh, I don't know."

Serena shoved her silent phone deep into her pocket. "Oh, stop being so modest. You'll add a much-needed sense of humor to the proceedings. I promise you Emma will be glad to see you."

Le Cirque was not a celebrity-free zone; well-known faces came and went on a regular basis, and despite the occasional gawking they were typically left alone. But the party that filed into the table tucked into a semi-private alcove and that included three Michaelses, Georgia Goodbody, and Ethan Miller was pretty hard to ignore. Emma imagined Adam was even now consoling himself with the fact that even the most successful screenwriters often went unrecognized, but Emma sensed that his well-formed nose was somewhat out of joint.

Eve seated them as any grand dame might, automatically flirting with Adam and Ethan in the process. Emma moved to sit between Adam and Zoe, but Eve insisted she sit on Zoe's other side, then studied them with an appraising gaze Emma did not understand.

Mackenzie sat opposite her husband, her eyes pinned to his face whenever she thought no one was looking. Adam leaned over to say something to Zoe, and Emma quickly looked away.

After the cork on the first bottle of champagne had been popped and the glasses filled, Serena set down the phone that had apparently been surgically attached to her hand and said, "Before the festivities begin I'm sure I'm not the only one who'd like a report from Emma."

"That's right."

"How'd it go?"

"What did the doctor say?"

Emma stood. "I am happy to report that while my mind may have some holes and gaps and there are apparently some memories that are never coming back, my brain seems to be intact and relatively untraumatized." Emma smiled. "Which isn't bad for someone living with the group that's been inhabiting the lake house." She raised a glass of the champagne that had just been poured. "Thank you to everyone and especially to Mackenzie, Serena, and Zoe for sticking by my side through everything." She then tipped her head toward Eve. "And to Eve, for the gifts that I was unable to refuse. And for hosting Zoe's lunch today." Eve flushed as they raised their glasses and drank, but whether it was from pleasure or something else, Emma didn't know.

"And while I'm standing I'd like to propose a toast to my daughter, Zoe, who will spend the rest of this week milking, er, celebrating, the unbelievable fact that she is turning sixteen." Her eyes grew damp and she blinked rapidly in an effort to hold back the tears. "I am incredibly grateful to be alive to be a part of it."

They clapped and drank to that as well. Appetizers arrived and Emma began to relax. Until she noticed Serena studying Adam with a narrowed gaze that caused a prickle of unease. Serena's attention moved to her phone again. She frowned as she contemplated it.

"I'm sorry we didn't think to invite Brooks," Emma said.

"It's all right," Serena replied. "He's tied up anyway. I'm not even sure I'll see him this trip."

Ethan's attention, which had been focused on Serena, shifted to Emma. He leaned toward her and lowered his voice. "You know, I'd love to have Zoe join the cast on occasion." At the mention of her name on Ethan's lips, Zoe stopped pretending she wasn't listening. "The part was originally intended as just the one shot, but we all loved what Zoe did, and it could be a great way for her to stick a toe in the business without a major commitment." Emma could feel her daughter thrumming with excitement that she tried to conceal. "And of course we'd love for you to join her for a cameo anytime."

Zoe looked at Emma, her eyes and tone pleading. "Please say yes. I love the part. And Serena would be there even if you couldn't be."

"You're quite the salesman. Does anyone ever say no to you?" Emma asked Ethan wryly.

His eyes flicked briefly to Serena. "Unfortunately, yes."

"Please let me do this," Zoe begged. "If you say yes I promise I'll never ask for anything ever again."

"I think I've heard that before," Emma said.

"This time I'll give it to you in writing," Zoe said. "We can have it notarized."

"And I'll be glad to have Zoe's offer sent over to your agent for review," Ethan added. His tone was matter-of-fact. Nice guy that he was he nodded, smiled, and turned, withdrawing himself from the conversation.

"Oh, God, you can't possibly say no." Zoe was anything but matter-of-fact. "You know it's the chance of a lifetime."

"Stop, right now. I appreciate Ethan's confidence in your talent, really I do. It matches mine. But you'll have plenty of chances. And this is not the time or place for this conversation."

"But you'd already starred in a television series when you were my age."

"Yes," Emma said, lowering her voice in an attempt not to be overheard even though she sensed Eve listening. "Which is why I think I know a little bit more about the downside to this than you do."

Through what appeared to be a superhuman act of will, Zoe closed her mouth. Her eyes, however, both begged and implored. Eve's eyes flickered briefly with what looked oddly like apology before she turned them on Ethan Miller.

"I'll give it real thought," Emma finally said. "But we're not going to discuss it now."

With effort Zoe let go and Emma sipped on the champagne and took a small taste of the elegantly simple tartare and caviar.

Eve's laughter rang out, shocking in its unfamiliarity. It seemed that even her mother who had no discernible sense of humor and whose disdain for comedic "shenanigans" was legendary, couldn't resist Ethan Miller's quick wit. Adam and Mackenzie also laughed heartily. Only Serena, whom it was clear was Ethan's true audience, didn't fully respond to the comedian's humor, which snuck up on you when you least expected it then rendered you helpless with laughter.

Eve laughed and told stories of her own, drawing her audience in and holding them easily. Her eyes had never gleamed quite so brightly. Nor had she ever flashed so many dazzling white teeth in Emma's presence. Was it possible her mother was mellowing?

Their main courses were devoured and cleared. Eve rose and left the table to confer with the maître d'. Shortly after she came back and sat down, a parade of waiters appeared. One pushed a cart that held a large multitiered cake, each tier a brightly wrapped present, the whole stack tied with a huge fondant bow.

Zoe gasped with pleasure and pretended to be their conductor as they sang "Happy Birthday," proving quite enthusiastically that not all actors could carry a tune. At Eve's prompting, Zoe stood and moved to Eve's side. With everyone's encouragement she closed her eyes, made a wish, then blew out the oversized polka-dotted number sixteen candles.

Emma didn't know where the photographers had come from. But suddenly there was a small ring of them at the open end of the alcove where the best shots of everyone at the table and particularly of Eve and Zoe and the megacake could be framed. Eve had her arm around Zoe and was helping her slice the first piece of cake, but her smile was aimed at the cameras. Just as it always had been when Emma was little. It was a smile that was overdone for real life but would look fabulous and completely natural in photos. Eve was the only one who didn't appear at all surprised to see the pack of paparazzi.

Emma's heart sped up as she realized just how carefully the table's location, their seating, and in fact every element of the party had been orchestrated. Eve planted a large kiss on Zoe's cheek, leaving her lips in place while turning her eyes once again to the photographers. The headwaiter handed Eve a long rectangular box tied in an oversized fuchsia ribbon that matched the cake's fondant bow. Eve placed it in front of Zoe as the photographers moved around the table snapping photos as if shooting fish in a barrel. A two shot of Zoe and Adam. A three of Ethan, Serena, and Zoe. Emma sat frozen at her seat as Zoe lifted the top off the dress box. She gasped again as she pulled a silver metallic strapless gown rimmed with what looked like Tiffany jewels out of the box and held it up in front of her. It was far too adult and sexy for a sixteen-year-old but it was beautiful — most likely Chanel or Valentino. Zoe's eyes glittered with excitement.

"This gown is for you to wear to your first Academy Awards ceremony. I know you're going to need it." Eve's face was lit with happiness and if Emma hadn't seen her fake the emotion so many times before, she might have thought it was also infused with love. Eve paused dramatically and waited until all the cameras were aimed and settled on her and Zoe. "Because your real gift is a part in my new Scorsese film. In which you will play the granddaughter I've saved from a violent home and sworn to raise as my own."

Zoe wasn't acting when she turned, threw her arms around Eve, and placed a kiss on her grandmother's cheek. Flashes went off all around the room. Somehow a video crew had arrived and begun shooting, all of it choreographed by Eve, who appeared to be valiantly smiling through what might have been real tears.

"Oh, thank you. Thank you! This is the best gift ever!" Zoe was crying now, too. But Emma's eyes were dry and tight with anger.

"I want these cameras out of here as soon as I make my statement," she said, motioning not at the photographers but at the maître' d' whom she saw beaming with happiness nearby. No doubt due to the size of the tip Eve had given him to arrange the photo op and because all of the headlines and articles that accompanied them would mention where Zoe Michaels's birthday celebration had taken place and probably every morsel that they'd eaten.

She rose and turned to face the cameras, pitching her voice so that it could be heard. "I wouldn't bother reporting on the possibility of Eve making a film with my daughter directed by Martin Scorsese or anyone else. Because that is something that will only happen over my dead body."

# THIRTY-FOUR

Ethan Miller helped facilitate their escape from Le Cirque just as he had from Mount Sinai by virtually throwing himself in front of the paparazzi. He wrapped an arm around Eve's shoulder and pulled her close as everyone else fled. "Boy, you really know how to clear a table," he said. Mugging for the cameras, he held up one of Eve's hands and pretended to examine it closely. "And you didn't even get your hands dirty." Eve carefully withdrew her hand but held on to her smile. "Well, not physically anyway."

Serena blew him a kiss as she exited the restaurant. He sent her a wink. She hoped there'd be enough video of Ethan outwitting Eve to present to Emma somewhere down the road, but any tentative truce Eve had forged with Emma had been violated and therefore nullified.

The drive passed in an oddly agitated state of silence heavy with all the things that were thought but not being said. Zoe didn't yell, beg, or plead with her mother to allow her to do the Scorsese film or even *As the World Churns,* but there were far more dramatic sighs and hair tosses than was comfortable in the sardine-like dimensions of the overfilled rental car.

Emma didn't rant about her mother, either, though any one of them would have been willing to add an "Amen, sister" to whatever she might have said. Nor did she try to explain herself further to Zoe. Once they'd left the city behind she simply closed her eyes and appeared to sleep for the entire drive back to the lake.

Mackenzie sat in the front seat next to Adam drumming her fingers on her leg as Adam drove and tried to talk her through the steps they'd need to take to make the move out to LA. How the sale of the house in Noblesville would impact what they'd be able to afford in the far more expensive California, how they'd get the cars out there. He continued to talk despite Mackenzie's somewhat lackluster responses, but whether he was trying to desensitize her to the move or simply trying to dissipate some of the tension in the car was unclear.

Serena passed the trip alternately staring out the window and down at her damned phone while berating herself for her stupidity and for her wishful thinking. If it hadn't been for the plans for Zoe's birthday and cookout she would have hugged everyone good-bye outside Le Cirque and gone back to her place, where she would have gladly climbed into bed and never come out again.

They reached the lake house shortly after seven p.m. Nadia took one look at them, said, "Holy Tamoley," and retreated to the kitchen, where she pulled out food Martha had delivered. She then set about fussing over Emma, who appeared far more wilted than any of them felt good about. "You come with me," the nurse tutted as she directed Emma to a seat.

Without enthusiasm the rest of them settled around the table and helped themselves to cold meats and cheeses. Mackenzie warmed up a container of homemade macaroni and cheese and passed it around.

"Here, Em." Adam put a large spoonful of the cheesy concoction on Emma's plate. "Try some of this. It's really good."

Emma stared at the mac and cheese, clearly not the least bit tempted.

"If you not eat, I make double big smoothie," Nadia said.

Emma managed a few bites. Zoe did the same. Only Adam consumed his food with any real enthusiasm.

As soon as Nadia took Emma upstairs the rest of them retreated to their own rooms. Serena carried a glass and an open bottle of red wine upstairs. In her room she poured herself a generous glass and drank it down as she checked her phone for what might have been the hundredth time.

She eyed the bottle for a long moment, considered cutting out the glass altogether. Midreach she pulled back her hand. The last thing she needed was to become uninhibited enough to drunk dial Brooks. Having one's worst fears realized while sober was bad enough; having them come to fruition while all your defenses were down seemed downright suicidal.

And so she paced her room for much of the night eyeing the silent cell phone and the beckoning bottle even as she willed Brooks to call with some simple explanation that she could find a way to accept.

In the morning she watched the sunrise from an Adirondack chair on the beach, too numb and bleary-eyed to appreciate it. By seven fifteen a.m., a time when Brooks would presumably still be in his hotel room, she had had enough. This time she called the front desk at the Four Seasons and waited while the operator put her through.

The phone rang four or five times. Serena was still trying to gather her thoughts when the ringing stopped.

"Yes?" The word was clipped. The voice impatient. But the voice wasn't Brooks

Anderson's. The voice belonged to someone else, someone who was pissed off at being interrupted. Someone who was female.

Serena couldn't speak. Nor could she decide what to do. Should she slam down the phone like some teenager? Did hotel room phones have caller ID? She dislodged her heart from her throat and said, "I'd like to speak to Brooks Anderson please."

"Is that right?" What the voice lost in impatience it made up for in imperiousness. "I'm afraid he's in the shower at the moment." The woman paused to let that sink in. "But if I should decide to let him know he has a phone call, who exactly would I tell him is calling?"

The air left Serena's lungs. There was no mistaking the Charlestonian accent or the inherent note of privilege wrapped up inside it. Serena searched for her backbone. "You first," she said even though she didn't want to hear it.

"This is Diana. *Anderson,*" she emphasized the last name. "Brooks's wife. But then I bet you already knew that." Diana paused dramatically. "How have you been, Serena?"

Serena remained silent as her mind raced. The knot in her stomach pulled tighter as the woman laughed softly.

"No comment?" Diana Ravenel Anderson spoke haughtily as only a woman with the upper hand could. "Well, I have one. I don't

394

know what Brooks has told you, but this is not the first time this has happened. Boys will be boys and all that. Who knows? Perhaps you're lucky he chose me instead of you."

Serena couldn't seem to catch her breath. Her heart pounded so hard she imagined she could hear it. Was she old enough to drop dead of a heart attack? Diana Anderson would undoubtedly appreciate that. And Brooks? Would he care? He'd seemed so sincere. So finished with his marriage. Which only proved the man was a far better actor than she was. All these years of dating other women's husbands and the first time she'd believed she wasn't was the first time she'd been called on it.

"This kind of sucks for you, doesn't it?" The words were crude but the tone remained haughty.

Once again Serena didn't answer. But she couldn't quite hang up, either.

"On the bright side, you got to be the memory of his first love." She continued in the same soft, relentlessly matter-of-fact tone. "I guess I don't need to tell you that it's always the one who got away that can seem the most . . . tempting."

Mackenzie was out of bed and looking for something that might help her blow off steam before Adam had even thought about stirring. He'd stopped trying to convince her overtly but couldn't — or wouldn't — stop sharing his excitement about all the changes that lay ahead. It was clear he could hardly wait to leave here and get back to LA. Something he planned to do by Monday.

Mackenzie opened the laundry room door and set about sorting and organizing the baskets of dirty laundry that Martha had been unable to get to. As she worked and sipped coffee, she tried to make sense of the emotions bombarding her, anger at being expected to make so many life-altering changes so quickly and fear of what would happen once her decisions had been reached. She had not gone looking for a whole other life. She did not want or need to cast off the old and embrace the new. She wanted to go home to Noblesville where she could give this the thought it deserved. But what if she did this while Adam went about his new life in LA and he finally realized, if he hadn't already, that she was no more exciting than the place he couldn't wait to put behind him?

As she started the first load of wash, her agitation grew. She'd sacrificed her dreams just as he had. Why was she the only one who'd thought the cost worthwhile? What about the book she'd been asked to write? The blog that had begun to feel so fraudulent. Searching for a distraction she moved through the house straightening things that were not crooked, plumping cushions, restacking magazines as she began to think about how much every one of her roles — at the theater, in her blog, in almost every facet of her life — revolved around Adam. If she was not Adam Russell's wife, who was she?

She saw Serena outside on the phone, but was far too agitated to consider making conversation. The next time she glimpsed her she was still in the exact same position in the Adirondack staring out at the lake. The same was true a half hour later. Mackenzie wiped the kitchen counters, rinsed dishes, realigned the dining room chairs. Serena continued to sit as still as a statue.

Her inner turmoil spurring her outside, Mackenzie strode out onto the porch and down to the lake. "Serena?"

There was no answer or movement. Mackenzie walked closer, knelt down next to the arm of Serena's chair. Still Serena didn't turn or move. Tears slid down her cheeks, skimmed down her chin, and fell unheeded on the hands clenched in Serena's lap.

"What happened?" Mackenzie placed a hand on Serena's arm. "What's wrong?"

Serena sniffed but didn't speak.

"Okay, you're starting to scare me now." Mackenzie moved into the chair next to Serena and slid an arm around her shoulders. "Tell me what's going on."

"I haven't heard from Brooks since he left on Sunday. No calls, no messages. Nothing."

Mackenzie winced and waited. Had she noticed this? She'd been far too freaked out by her own situation to pay attention after her initial shock when Serena had introduced him.

"This morning I couldn't take it anymore so I called his hotel room." Now she looked up. Her face ravaged by tears and unhappiness. "And his wife answered the phone."

"Oh, God." Mackenzie's stomach turned over. "I thought he was divorced."

"Me too. Or at least seriously separated."

Mackenzie had no idea what to say. Serena had been dating married men for decades. If this was the first time this had happened, she was lucky. What had she expected?

"Aren't you going to say, 'I told you so'?"

"I'm tempted," Mackenzie admitted. "But I'm thinking that sort of goes without saying." She thought about her marriage, the blog she wrote about it. How could she have been so judgmental of Serena when her own life seemed just as fraudulent?

"Yeah." Serena snorted softly. The tears had slowed but they hadn't stopped. She reached out her tongue and licked one out of the way. "I can't believe this. It was like this incredible miracle having him back. After all those years of feeling second best and unwanted, he told me he'd always wondered what being married to me would have been like." She closed her eyes. Shook her head. "It was too good to be true."

They sat for a few minutes staring out at the lake as the day kicked into gear.

"Can I get you something? Coffee? A cold drink? A cyanide pill?"

Serena sniffed but one corner of her mouth lifted in an attempted smile. "I'd rather the pill go to Brooks Anderson. And maybe one for his wife while we're at it."

"Now, that's the Serena I know and love." Or at least a small part of her. "Why waste time on inner reflection when you can direct your aggression outward?"

"Exactly," Serena said, attempting and failing at her usual dark humor. "Only I don't think I should have this phone in my hand right now. I might do something I'd really regret."

"Like?" Mackenzie prompted, hoping to get Serena riled enough to stop feeling so sorry for herself.

"I don't know. I can't seem to jump-start enough brain cells to give that the thought it deserves." She sighed a Grand Canyon–sized sigh that didn't have even an ounce of Georgia Goodbody in it. "Will you stash it in my room for me?"

"Sure."

"Thanks."

Mackenzie left Serena once again staring out over the lake, unable to come to terms with the teary silent version of her friend, which was a far more frightening thing than an angry verbal one. She slipped Serena's phone in her pocket, took the clothes out of the dryer and folded them. As she placed Serena's clothes on her bedroom dresser, Serena's open purse went flying.

"Crap!" Crouching, she picked up two lipsticks and a pack of gum, retrieved Serena's wallet from under the dresser then reached for the papers that had spilled from a manila envelope. She'd begun tucking them back into the envelope when she noticed that they were on Emma's law firm's letterhead. Her throat tightened and her chest actually hurt as she read the legalese that named Serena Stockton as Zoe Hardgrove's legal guardian in the event of Emma Michaels's incapacitation or death.

Serena? Zoe's legal guardian? Mackenzie's fingers turned clumsy as she attempted to shove the papers back the way they'd been. Her vision blurred and the pages trembled in her hands. She sat on the bed, staring at the words in disbelief, trying to make sense of them. Serena possessed not an ounce of maternal instinct; she was not a nurturer. Her personal life was not remotely stable. Mackenzie had always assumed that if Zoe were left parentless, she would step in. That she and Adam would become Zoe's parents.

Had she made a mistake in not making her willingness clear enough? She read the paperwork again, but could find no mention of Calvin Hardgrove. Why didn't the papers say that if something happened to Emma and Zoe's father, Serena would be legal guardian?

Mackenzie stood and all but slapped the purse back on the dresser. She had always wanted a child and Emma knew it. She was born to be a mother. Furthermore, she was married and monogamous. *She* and her husband were a hundred times more qualified to raise a child than Serena ever would or could be. The injustice of it sliced through her. Any sympathy Mackenzie had felt for Serena's heartache evaporated in that moment. If bad behavior was so rewarded, why had Mackenzie always lived by the rules, been so worried about always doing the "right" thing? She could not for the life of her understand why Emma would have chosen Serena over her and Adam without so much as a conversation. Why Emma would think Serena deserved to raise her child while Mackenzie did not.

Fighting back tears, she flung the remaining clean clothes onto Serena's bed and raced for her own room, more relieved than she'd ever admit that Adam wasn't there.

# THIRTY-FIVE

Mackenzie's mood had not improved during the night, which had been long and sleepless. Nor had her stress level over the choices she was being forced to make lessened. Adam snored happily beside her, occasionally murmuring words that almost certainly belonged in an Oscar acceptance speech. Feeling guilty for begrudging him his happy dreams, she gritted her teeth and stared up at the ceiling until early morning light finally pierced the bedroom curtains and she heard movement downstairs.

"No really, I couldn't have done it without my . . ."

Mackenzie grasped Adam's shoulder and shook hard.

"What?" he asked groggily. "What is it?" One of his eyes opened warily.

"Time to get up." She let go of his shoulder. "It's time for Zoe's birthday cake and presents."

He yawned, stretched contentedly, sat up

slowly. With his tousled hair and his face covered in familiar morning stubble, he was once again the man she'd woken up next to for twenty years. Would he still be this man if they ended up together in Los Angeles? Or would he wake up each morning pressed and polished with that sharp-eyed excitement he'd acquired in LA?

He pulled on shorts and a T-shirt, followed her downstairs, and added his "Happy Birthday, Zoe!" to hers as she set Zoe's present in front of her. She watched him hug Emma and drop a kiss on Zoe's head. Before she could stop herself she was imagining what *their* daughter would have looked like. Given both their heights she would have been tall and rangy like Zoe; she might even have had Zoe's wide-set eyes, which were not dissimilar to Adam's. Only their daughter would have had blond hair and brown eyes like them.

Mackenzie pulled her bathrobe tight and moved to the coffeemaker as the familiar ache spread in her chest. If she hadn't lost their baby, their daughter would have been here right now, only a month or so older than Zoe, and maybe one of Zoe's closest friends as she had been Emma's. They might have celebrated both birthdays together.

She took her time with the coffee, her mind thick from lack of sleep, her fingers fumbling with the creamer and the sugar. The birthday cake sat on the counter, the candles ready to be lit, but she could no longer imagine eating it.

"Mornink," Nadia said. "We waiting for Serena. You hear her upstairs?"

"No." She'd barely glanced at the closed bedroom door other than to be glad she hadn't had to speak to her yet.

As she set Adam's coffee in front of him and settled in a vacant seat, Mackenzie noticed Emma's eyes trained on her daughter and Adam. The ache in Mackenzie's chest intensified. Emma not only had the daughter she didn't, she'd chosen to entrust that daughter to Serena — a woman who tromped through life saying whatever happened to be on her mind, and taking pretty much anything she wanted regardless of whom it belonged to. Yesterday Serena had gotten dumped on, but would she learn anything from it? Unlikely. By tomorrow she'd have her eye on someone else's husband. Mackenzie's jaw tightened in anger even as she fought back tears.

"Are you all right?" Emma asked. The concern (or was it pity?) in Emma's eyes hit Mackenzie like a slap in the face. How could Emma be so sensitive to Mackenzie's feelings and still have chosen Serena instead of her and Adam?

Zoe stole a glance toward the stairs, undoubtedly looking for Serena. Who in addition to her other sins, apparently couldn't be bothered to show up on time.

"I'll get her." Mackenzie stomped up the stairs and pounded on Serena's door.

When she got no answer, Mackenzie pounded harder.

"What?" Serena opened the door. Her face was haggard, her eyes red.

"Everybody's waiting for you." Mackenzie steeled herself against Serena's ravaged face.

"Sorry. I was just wrapping Zoe's present."

"Is there some reason you waited until now?"

Serena's head shot up at her tone. "I only fell asleep around six and then I couldn't get up when my alarm went off."

"Zoe's waiting." She would not be sucked into Serena's drama. She had more than enough drama of her own. "Do you need help?" she asked, though she could not hear even a note of helpfulness in her voice.

"Wouldn't want to keep you from your cake," Serena bit out.

"Yeah, well not everybody can have their cake and eat it, too," she snapped back, apropos of nothing except the anger and hurt bubbling inside her.

"I don't think we have time for you to deliver a frickin' lecture."

"Then just hurry up!" Mackenzie stood in the doorway. Glowering.

Serena swore under her breath, but belted

a robe over her pajamas and grabbed the present.

"Seriously?" Mackenzie looked at the package, which might have been wrapped by a five-year-old. How could a woman who couldn't even wrap a gift raise a child?

"Get over it. There's a reason stores offer gift wrapping. And I'm one of them. Not everyone aspires to domesticity."

Mackenzie snorted. "You have an excuse or an explanation for everything, don't you?"

"What the hell does that mean?" Serena's eyes hardened. "What's gotten into you?"

Mackenzie knew this was not the time or the place, but that didn't seem to matter. "Let's try this one. How do you explain Emma naming you Zoe's legal guardian?"

"What?" Serena asked. "What are you talking about?"

"Don't even try to deny it. I accidentally saw the paperwork from Emma's attorneys when I brought your phone and laundry in for you."

"Accidentally?" Serena asked. As if Mackenzie had gotten some wild hair to come in and pilfer through Serena's things.

"Yes," Mackenzie shot back. "Why don't you tell me how that happened."

"I have no earthly idea," Serena said. "The paperwork arrived when Emma was in the hospital. I was as shocked as you apparently are."

"And you don't think it's strange that it doesn't read 'if something happened to Emma *and* Calvin'?" Mackenzie demanded.

"I promise you I barely thought about it."

"But you didn't say anything to me," Mackenzie insisted, hating the whiny tone in her voice.

"I didn't think there was anything to say. I was too busy praying Emma would regain consciousness and make the issue moot — which she did." Serena shook her head. "You do remember that part, right?"

"And you don't think it's bizarre that she chose you rather than me and Adam?"

"Yes, actually I do. But I'm not the one who made that decision."

"But it's obvious we're the better choices."

Serena blinked. Crossed her arms over her chest. "Are you shitting me? You mean because your marriage is so solid that you haven't even seen Adam for a month? Or because you blog regularly about how great it is to *not* have children? Or maybe because you've been hiding out in Bumfuck, Indiana, and are afraid of moving to a real city where Adam finally has a real opportunity to do what he's always wanted to do?" She flung the words at Mackenzie, smiling grimly when they hit their mark.

"At least I'm not out screwing other people's husbands!" Mackenzie shot back.

Serena snorted. "I'm shocked it took you a

whole day to get to the 'I told you so.' "

"Okay, then I told you so! I told you so!" Mackenzie practically shouted. "Everybody told you so!"

They glared at each other, neither of them moving.

"I'm just going to point out that I'm not the one who made this decision," Serena said. "Maybe you should take your little hissy fit and rain it down on Emma. Assuming you don't have a problem dumping on someone who's still adjusting to being alive!"

Both of them were vibrating with anger, which in a troubling way felt a lot better than the hurt and panic that had kept her up all night. Mackenzie was aghast at just how much she had left just waiting to spill over.

"Hel-lo?" Zoe's voice reached them from downstairs. "Are you guys ready for cake?"

Both of them blanched. Neither of them moved.

"We'll be down in a minute," Mackenzie called down the stairs when she finally found her voice. Turning back to Serena she added, "This is Zoe's big day. It would be a real shame to ruin it."

"No shit, Sherlock," Serena retorted. "I can control myself if you can."

They arrived downstairs with smiles plastered on their faces. But their emotional baggage accompanied them like uninvited guests that refused to leave.

As far as Emma could tell, Adam and Zoe were the only two people in the room who were unaware that Serena and Mackenzie had had a go at each other. Adam still seemed to be half asleep while Zoe was completely and joyously focused on the exciting here and now of her cake, her presents, and her upcoming first date with Ryan.

After Eve's sneak attack, Emma had renewed her resolve to make Zoe's Sweet Sixteen something they could all treasure, just as she'd treasured the more intimate celebrations with Gran. Tomorrow she'd say what had to be said and attempt to put things to rights no matter the cost. But today was to be savored and enjoyed.

Emma carried the chocolate birthday cake to the table and set it in front of Zoe while the assembled "cast" sang "Happy Birthday" for the second time that week. This cake didn't scream "look at me" like the package-shaped extravaganza delivered at Le Cirque had. It was a round three-layer orgy of chocolate with *Happy Birthday, Zoe* scrawled in bright pink icing. Sixteen neon-colored candles arranged in the shape of a heart blazed brightly.

"If we're going to perform this song this often, we're going to have to spend a little time figuring out how to sing it on key," Serena said when they'd finished singing. "Maybe we need to call a small choral practice before the cookout tonight. Or see if there are any voice coaches currently vacationing at the lake." Her tone was wry even though her eyes were red and her face more haggard than Emma had ever seen it.

"*You* could just sing softer," Mackenzie suggested. Her tone was not the least bit wry or teasing.

"Is that right?" Serena smiled a saccharine smile. "And who made you the new celebrity coach on *The Voice*?"

"All righty, then," Adam said, seeming to notice the tension for the first time. For a creative person Adam Russell had an amazing tendency to ignore the obvious.

"Well, I don't care what key you sing in as long as there's cake after," Zoe said happily. "I've never had three celebrations before. I think I'm going to like being sixteen."

As they waited for Zoe to make her wish, Serena and Mackenzie looked everywhere but at each other. Neither of them appeared to have slept. As Zoe drew in a deep breath and began to blow out her candles, Emma made a wish of her own that somehow turned into more of a prayer. *Please God, let everyone forgive me once I finally confess. And please don't let Zoe's wish include being allowed to take the part Eve dangled in front of her.* She held her own breath until the last candle sputtered out.

"Yes!" Zoe's fist pumped in victory. The rest of them applauded.

"Girl have good lungs. And determination," Nadia observed. "She make good weight lifter."

"I could get behind that," Emma said, thinking she'd much rather see Zoe lifting weights with Nadia than acting with Eve. "Presents or cake first?" she asked her daughter, instructing herself to relax. Hoping Serena and Mackenzie would do the same.

"I vote someone starts cutting the cake while I open the presents," Zoe said.

"I like the way this girl thinks," Serena said.

"Me too," Mackenzie added with a toss of her head and a more conciliatory tone.

Emma shot them both a look of gratitude.

"Here, I'll cut it." Mackenzie pulled the cake closer. The first slice went to Zoe, who took a large bite and groaned dramatically. "OMG. This is so good. I might be able to wait the three seconds it's gonna take to finish it before I open presents." She did exactly that while everyone else began to dig in. Emma, who'd had little appetite since they'd fled Le Cirque, downed her first bite mostly to join in. A moment later she, too, was closing her eyes and groaning with pleasure.

"This chocolate cake was definitely worth

411

getting up for," Adam announced.

"And I'm not?" Zoe asked, pretending shock.

Emma looked up as Serena snapped a photo of Adam and Zoe wearing appallingly similar expressions.

Serena, who'd set down her phone and was once again eating cake, noticed Emma's questioning glance. "I'm not much of a photographer, but, well, I know we're pretty much at the end of our stay. And I thought I'd put together one of those photo books of Zoe's birthday celebration for all of us to remember."

"Cool!" Zoe said with an enthusiasm Emma didn't feel. "I bet there'd be fewer wars if more people ate chocolate cake for breakfast," her daughter observed as she finished her last bite.

"No doubt." Emma smiled. "Maybe we should start a movement. See if we can get an armada full of them shipped to the Middle East or something."

"I'm in," Serena said. "I just need one more sliver to get properly motivated."

Emma waited for Zoe to lick the last bits of chocolate off her fingers then retrieved a black velvet box from the pile of presents and placed it in front of Zoe. "This is from me. And Gran." Her voice was hushed as she waited for Zoe to pull off the ribbon and open the box. "Gran gave these to me when I turned sixteen. Now it's your turn to wear them."

Zoe's eye pooled with tears as Emma fastened the string of perfectly matched pearls around her neck. She looked at Emma. "I expect you to be here when it's time for me to give these to my daughter."

Emma pulled Zoe into a hug even as her eyes filled with tears. "You just try to keep me away."

"Oh, my God. Stop it." Serena's voice broke the weighty silence. "You're wrecking my sugar high with all those tears."

Emma nodded numbly as she let go of Zoe, but it took considerable effort to shut off the waterworks. She couldn't even look at Mackenzie.

"I agree with Serena," Adam said. "I feel like we've stumbled into some Nicholas Sparks movie. Crying over birthday cake is way too maudlin."

"Well, I think the pearls look especially lovely with Zoe's pajamas," Serena quipped as she picked up her phone again and framed a shot of Emma and Zoe. "You all squish closer so I can get all four of you." She waved Adam and Mackenzie into position next to Emma and Zoe.

"Nadia, will you get a shot of all of us?" Mackenzie asked. "I think we need at least one with Serena in her pajamas without makeup — just in case she finds herself tempted to post anything of us to Facebook."

"I want one with Nadia in it, too!" Zoe said.

Adam, who had the longest arms, volunteered to take the "selfie" of all of them. Then he took one of Emma, Serena, Mackenzie, and Zoe. "For posterity," he said.

Emma offered up a small prayer that tomorrow's confession didn't prevent them from ever wanting to be in a room with her again let alone close enough to fit in a photo.

"Here, open mine," Mackenzie said, pushing a gaily wrapped box toward Zoe.

"But you already gave me my outfit that we designed together."

"This is just a little something extra," Mackenzie said.

Zoe opened the box and shrieked with happiness. "You made the sundress, too!"

Mackenzie's smile was brittle, but bright. "And if you'd like we could probably turn the gown Eve gave you into something a little more age appropriate."

Emma braced for Zoe to reject the offer in favor of keeping it for her acceptance speech, but Zoe threw her arms around Mackenzie and then around Adam while Serena continued to snap photos. "This is all so great. Thank you!"

Next she opened a gift bag from Nadia. It contained a DVD of *Doctor Zhivago*. "We watch one night. Omar Sharif pretty hot for bridge player. I show you where Nadia from."

"My turn." Serena put down her camera and pushed the last, appallingly wrapped, gift closer to Zoe. They watched her unwrap the oddly shaped package.

"Oh, how perfect." Emma smiled.

"I may not know how to gift wrap." Serena shot Mackenzie a look. "But I understand the importance of a theme." She lifted her phone to get a shot of Zoe holding up her new tote bag. It was designed by Kate Spade and had big black letters that proclaimed, EAT CAKE FOR BREAKFAST. There was a matching iPhone cover inside along with an *As the World Churns* T-shirt to replace the one that had been sacrificed to Zoe's new outfit. The last item was an exact duplicate of Georgia Goodbody's fan.

"The fan's from Ethan," Serena said. "But I can teach you how to bat your eyes behind it and look mysterious. If done properly this can turn a man into your slave." She sighed as she flipped it open to demonstrate. "But you have to remember to use it when it matters most."

Emma watched her old friend work the fan and bat her eyelashes, though it was obvious her heart wasn't in it. In just twenty-four hours Emma wouldn't have anything left to hide behind. Not even a fan.

# THIRTY-SIX

"Come and get 'em!" Jake Richards held up a metal triangle and dinged it loudly. "The ribs are officially ready for consumption."

The day had been mild and as the sun began to slip in the sky, the breeze was just strong enough to keep the mosquitoes at bay. The deep pungent scent of barbecuing meat wafted on that breeze. Paper lanterns swayed gently on the tree branches and twinkled above the picnic table that had been covered in a brightly checked tablecloth. Large earthenware bowls of Martha's homemade coleslaw and potato salad anchored the cloth. Bottles of red and white wine sat open and ready; beer had been tucked in the cooler. Nadia had contributed and chilled several bottles of Stolichnaya "wotka," which she referred to as the "Neketar of the Gods" and offered around for a birthday toast. Cookies, brownies, and birthday cupcakes as well as what remained of that morning's birthday cake had been plated for dessert.

Emma lined up behind Zoe, who glowed with excitement. Her hair had been drawn into a messy knot at the nape of her neck. Her makeup was subtle, a soft blush on her cheekbones, her lips stained a warm red. Her emerald green eyes framed in sooty lashes sparkled with happiness. The crop top and patchwork skirt skimmed her curves without clinging and exposed her long graceful limbs as well as a small, tasteful rectangle of skin just above her waist. Mackenzie stood behind Emma.

Ryan, who'd been helping his father, placed a small rack of ribs on Zoe's plate.

"Hang on!" Serena stepped up and raised her phone. "Let me get a shot of that."

Zoe blushed prettily as Ryan moved closer for the shot.

"Perfect!" Serena shifted slightly to snap a photo of the line as Zoe and Ryan carried their plates to the beach.

"Here you go." Jake put a small rack of ribs on Emma's plate and shot her a wink, which Serena duly documented. "There's hot and mild sauce over on the table," he added. "As I recall you're a hot and spicy girl."

Emma laughed. "You do say the sweetest things." She batted her lashes much as Serena had demonstrated that morning and channeled a little Georgia Goodbody of her own. Tonight was for enjoying. Tomorrow, well, tomorrow would come soon enough.

"Well done," Serena said after capturing the shot. "Thank God you've remembered how to flirt. I'm thinking that's a sign that someone's feeling better."

Jake handed Serena a plate of ribs then filled one for Mackenzie. While the two didn't exactly throw their arms around each other and announce a formal truce, they weren't aiming poison darts at each other, either. The three of them made their way to the table.

Zoe's laughter carried to them from the beach. Emma looked and saw her daughter leaning toward Ryan and looking up at his smiling face.

"She looks so adorable in that outfit," Emma said to Mackenzie as they neared the table. "And I know what a great time she had working on it with you."

"It was fun. She's very talented." Mackenzie dropped her eyes and Emma could see how eager she was to change the subject. Did she think of the child she never had every time she looked at Zoe? If anyone should have been a mother, it was Mackenzie. But life rarely turned out the way it "should" as she knew firsthand. And it was rarely fair.

"May I say that I think both of those Richards men are very hot?" Serena asked.

"You may," Emma replied, more than happy to keep things light. "Though I'd feel a little more comfortable if Zoe's first date was with someone slightly less attractive and polished than Ryan. A little social awkwardness can go a long way."

"So you'd rather your daughter go out with a character actor than a leading man?" Serena asked.

"Absolutely," Emma replied.

"I agree with Em," Mackenzie said. "Even at our ages, an Ethan Miller, say, is a better and safer choice than a Brooks Anderson."

Emma noticed that this time it was Serena who dropped her eyes. The plot thickened. "Speaking of Brooks, why didn't you invite him?" Emma asked.

"When you nap too much you miss the occasional mini-drama." Serena sighed contemplating the plate of ribs before finally meeting Emma's eye. "He's done a bit of a vanishing act. And the last time I tried to reach him his wife answered the phone."

"But I thought his marriage was over," Emma said.

"Yeah, me too." Serena frowned. "But as Mackenzie has pointed out, even when I think I'm not dating married men, I'm dating married men."

Emma considered both women. Was it Mackenzie's observations about Brooks that had set them off that morning? Whatever had happened she was not going to disturb the fragile peace between them.

They fell silent as they helped themselves to coleslaw and potato salad. Adam and Jake chatted next to the grill, pausing to accept a shot glass of Stoli from Nadia. The three raised and clinked their glasses. *"Nostrovia!"* Adam laughed and slammed the shot glass down triumphantly.

"Maybe you should check with Brooks and not just take her word for it," Emma said to Serena.

"His wife was in his hotel room, Em. She said he was in the shower and couldn't come to the phone." Serena shivered at the memory. "Even if she was lying, they're not exactly uninvolved in each other's lives."

Serena composed her features, but Emma could see how much effort it took to hide the hurt. She wondered how Serena's disappointment would come into play when Emma dropped her bombshell tomorrow. Whose side would Serena come down on when the shit hit the fan?

Emma pushed these worries aside as they started on their food. It took exactly one bite to discover that Jake had not exaggerated his grilling expertise. Martha's sides were a perfect addition.

A cell phone rang. Nadia walked away from the group to answer it.

Emma finished a rib then licked the sauce from her fingers. "So how are you feeling about California?" she asked Mackenzie.

Mackenzie set down her fork, dabbed at her mouth with her napkin. "I don't know. I mean, I think I'm almost over the shock of it." Her eyes strayed to her husband, who was laughing and regaling Jake with some story that had him chortling. "He looks so happy. And I'm really glad for him." She hesitated. "But I'm just not sure I can pick up and leave our . . . whole life . . . anywhere near as quickly or easily as Adam apparently can."

Adam slapped Jake on the shoulder and tilted another shot of vodka to his lips. Adam had always known how to move on, had always kept his eye on the prize. It was, Emma thought, quintessentially Adam that he didn't seem to realize how easily mistakes could come back to haunt you.

"This summer has been a prime example of how quickly things can change," Serena said. "One minute you're dating the man you thought you'd never see again. The next his wife is in his hotel room telling you to take a hike." She blew a bang off her forehead. "Then there's the even more critical 'one minute you're eating lunch in an expensive restaurant and the next you're in a coma,' " Serena said. "Life really can turn on a dime."

Emma considered the two women she'd once felt so close to. After Gran they'd been the nearest thing to family she'd ever had. Her fear of losing them had caused her to lie; maintaining the lie had pushed them out of her life anyway. "This summer has been a great big reminder to me of what matters most," Emma said. "And a lesson that having people you love and who love you is more important than anything else." She looked Serena and Mackenzie in the eye, felt tears well in her own. She'd made such a mess of everything. "I just." She swallowed, made herself continue. "I just want you to know that whatever happens, I love you both. You are the sisters I never had."

"Okay, now you're freaking me out," Serena said. "You haven't heard something from Mount Sinai or either of your doctors?"

"No." Emma found a smile. "My brain feels . . . good." Her heart, on the other hand, hurt like hell.

Jake and Adam came to join them at the table. "We're going to head out in a bit," Jake said. "Don't even ask me why I agreed to chaperone this party."

"Those young girls have to have somebody to crush on," Emma teased, once again pushing her sense of foreboding aside. "But don't tell any of their mothers how great you are with a grill. I think we should keep that our little secret."

"My lips are sealed." Jake smiled. "Unless of course you'd like to 'use them.' "

Serena took a picture of Jake placing a fish-faced kiss on Emma's cheek. Then a shot of Adam and Mackenzie, who sat side by side but seemed not to be touching. Zoe and Ryan came up and joined them at the picnic table and she took a picture of them, too.

Nadia delivered the dessert platter to the table then lit a sparkler she'd placed in the fanciest cupcake. Their third, final, and most wince-worthy version of "Happy Birthday" followed as the sun slid further down the sky.

"I told you we should have practiced this afternoon," Serena said as she framed and shot more pictures.

Smiling more happily than Emma had ever seen her, Zoe opened the Richardses' gift. It was an antique frame that held a double photo; one of Emma and Jake lounging on the floating dock as children, the second of Ryan and Zoe digging in the sand of the lake house beach as toddlers.

It was a beautiful reminder of their ties to these people and this place. Emma clutched it to her chest, waving good-bye as Ryan, Jake, and Zoe climbed into Ryan's runabout and motored out of the cove.

After they'd cleared the table and put the leftovers away, Nadia departed on the scooter for a date with her librarian. Too tired to continue pretending that the loss of Brooks Anderson was no more than a blip on her emotional radar screen, Serena retreated to her room. Propped up in bed, she booted up her laptop and pulled up all the birthday photos she'd taken.

For a time she lost herself in moving them

around the screen, positioning them next to each other, in an effort to weed out the unflattering shots that no one would want saved for posterity. She then agonized over the shots in which some looked far better than others and set aside the funniest to insert periodically to give the photo book some semblance of pace and flow.

The stress on Mackenzie's face next to the happiness on Adam's was telling. So were her own tight-lipped smiles, which she knew were in stark contrast to those that would have existed during her brief time with Brooks if only she'd thought to get so much as a photograph to document it. She noticed that Emma's eyes and attention had been focused on Mackenzie and Adam far more often than Serena had realized.

Serena dragged and zoomed, unable to miss the pronounced hurt on Mackenzie's face as she looked at Zoe. But it was the photos of Mackenzie, Adam, and Zoe that made the breath catch in her throat. One photo that she barely remembered taking was of Adam and Zoe with their heads bent together as Zoe blew out the candles on the chocolate cake. It was that photo that made her stop breathing altogether for a long, uncomfortable moment as she tried to absorb what she was seeing.

Footsteps sounded on the stairs accompanied by a cheery whistle. Adam poked his head in her open doorway, his handsome face as content as she'd ever seen it. He held up what remained of the bottle of Stoli. "Do you want a good night shot of 'wotka'?" he asked.

Serena peered at the pictures on her computer screen, then back up at Adam's handsome face.

"What is it?" he asked, brushing the lock of hair off his forehead. His wide-set brown eyes intent. "Are you okay?"

Serena looked from him to the screen, then back at his face, desperately wanting to reject what she was seeing. The knowledge slammed into her like a fist, knocking the breath from her, impossible to ignore. The more closely she studied the photos and Adam, the more perfectly the mental puzzle pieces she hadn't realized she'd been moving around, fit together. The picture they formed was an ugly one.

# THIRTY-SEVEN

"How could you?" They were the first words that came out of Serena's mouth. The only thing she could think of to say.

"How could I what?" Adam stepped into the room, the bottle and small shot glasses in his hands.

His face swam in front of her; far too content, too pleased with himself for someone who had apparently done what he'd done.

"How could you do that to Mackenzie?"

He set the bottle and shot glasses down but didn't look at all alarmed or even particularly troubled. "What are you talking about?"

Keeping her eyes on his face, Serena turned her laptop so that he could see the images of him, Zoe, and Mackenzie. "This."

He glanced at the photos then poured two shots. Placing one in her hand, he clinked his against hers, still unperturbed. Either Adam Russell was a far better actor than she'd ever given him credit for, or he was completely lacking in conscience. Her palm grew sweaty around the small glass. After he'd downed his shot, he looked at the photos more closely. "What is it I'm supposed to see here?"

"Zoe's resemblance to you. Are you her father?" The words were out and unretractable before she could stop them.

His head jerked up. He took a step back. But his expression was one of shock not admission. "What in the hell are you talking about? Of course not."

She peered at him more closely. Looked down at the photos then back up at him. "She has your forehead, Adam. And the set of your eyes. Even her chin looks like yours. She's built like you." And it would explain a lot.

"Don't be ridiculous," Adam said. "Calvin Hardgrove is Zoe's father. Every once in a while someone tells me I look like him." He shook his head. "He and all of the Michaelses are built like me, well, except for Emma."

It sounded completely logical. And he seemed to believe what he was saying. "Right," she said. "Only Calvin Hardgrove doesn't share custody. And legally, according to the documents I received while Emma was in the hospital, Zoe wouldn't live with him in the event of Emma's incapacitation or death. Why would Emma cut out Zoe's real father? And if she did, why wouldn't he fight it?"

"How would we know why they decided whatever they decided? And if Emma hasn't told you why, she probably has a reason. I don't know where you're going with this, Serena, but I'm thinking you don't need that other shot." He leaned against the dresser, crossed his arms over his chest. "But if you're saying she'd be living with us it makes sense. I mean, Mac would be a great mom. I can see why Emma would choose her."

Serena studied his face, considered his body language. Either he really didn't know what she was talking about or she wasn't being clear enough. "No," she said. "Not you and Mackenzie. Emma chose me." The glass grew slippery in her hand and she set it down. "Which Mackenzie is not at all happy about. So, I've been wondering, why would Emma leave Zoe to me when Mackenzie would be a far better choice? When Mackenzie always wanted a child, but couldn't have one? When the two of you could provide the kind of solid, two-parent home Emma always wanted and didn't have?"

He shrugged. "I have no earthly idea. And I don't think it's any of our business, either." He said this without stumbling, as if she were talking crazy and he was just trying to reason with her. But something flickered in his eyes.

For a moment Serena wished she'd downed the shot. Wished that her mind were less sharp, her thoughts less clear. But everything inside her said it was too late to turn back. "Did you ever sleep with Emma?" she asked because the only way any of this made sense was if her first instinct had been correct.

He laughed, but it was nowhere near as confident as before. The carefree attitude was rapidly evaporating. "You definitely don't need this shot." He picked it up. "You've clearly had way more than enough already." He set the shot glass in the empty one and picked up the bottle as if to leave.

"Seriously, Adam. Just answer the question. Did you and Emma ever have sex?"

"Of course not. I . . ." He faltered, went still. Almost reflexively he downed the shot of vodka. Swallowed it. She thought that was all he was going to say, when he continued. "Once."

She waited him out, her eyes never leaving his face.

"Back when Mackenzie and I had broken up for good."

"You had rebound sex with Emma? Seriously?"

"It was forever ago." He closed his eyes as if recalling a painful memory.

"Like just under seventeen years ago?"

She read the shock on his face, as if he'd actually managed to forget it until this moment, which apparently in his playbook was as good as having never done it.

"This is frickin' unbelievable," Serena said.

"It's not like it was intentional," he snapped.

"No? How unintentional was it?" she asked.

His jaw tensed. He closed his eyes once more. When he opened them he said, "I was staying at her place while I was in town talking to agents. We were both going through a rough patch." He held up the bottle. "We drank too much. Tequila as I recall, not vodka." He paused. Swallowed. "I . . . I don't know which one of us was more freaked when we woke up together the next morning. But it was a mistake and we both knew it. It didn't mean anything. And we never mentioned it again."

Serena studied his face. He seemed to be telling the truth. As he knew it. "Then what happened?"

"Nothing," he insisted. "Nothing happened."

She watched him. Waited.

He drew a deep breath. "A few weeks later Mackenzie told me she was pregnant. We got married. That was it."

"And Emma?" she asked, although she already knew the answer.

"Emma was already shooting that movie with Calvin. She got pregnant. They got married and had Zoe. End of story."

Except it wasn't. The story had been edited. The backstory tweaked. The characters sent off in different and unanticipated directions to mislead and confuse.

Serena looked at the photos on the screen then once again at Adam, who was looking less belligerent and more uncomfortable. Now that she knew what she was looking for, the resemblance was even more obvious. The way he tilted his head. The way his smile started as a hint before it got bigger. She'd seen these things in Zoe and not understood why they seemed so familiar. Was that why Emma had distanced herself from them? Because she was afraid one of them would notice?

"This is totally crazy," Adam said. "You're jumping to all kinds of conclusions. Conclusions that could seriously fuck up a whole lot of lives. If I was the father, don't you think Emma would have left Zoe in my hands? Or at least told me?" He shook his head as if he might dislodge their conversation, make it cease to exist. "Given everything that's going on, this is the last thing in the world Mackenzie needs to hear."

"Is that right?" Mackenzie was standing in the doorway staring at Adam as if she'd never seen him before.

Serena had no doubt her own face shone with guilt just as Adam's did. As if they were the ones who'd been caught in bed together. Mackenzie looked as if she were more than ready to kill the messenger.

Emma heard the commotion even before her door flew open. One look at Mackenzie's face told her that the very thing she'd been brac-

431

ing for and dreading was in fact now happening whether she was ready for it or not.

Neither Adam nor Serena looked as if they wanted to be there any more than she did. It was Mackenzie who'd flung open the bedroom door and practically pushed them through it. Mackenzie, whom Emma had never seen truly angry before, looked as if she might explode.

"How in God's name could you have done this?" Mackenzie demanded.

"Okay, don't take this the wrong way." Emma could feel her thoughts swirling, words and sentences ducking and weaving. Could even feel the holes and gaps that might never be filled, and wished desperately that she could shove her guilt into one of those dark caverns and be rid of it. "But you're going to have to be more specific than that." She pulled her robe tighter around her and got up from the chair, though she didn't move one step closer.

"So you've done other things besides sleep with my husband and give birth to his baby without ever telling me?" Mackenzie asked.

"Or me," Adam said as if still trying to absorb this.

Mackenzie turned long enough to give him a withering look. "She didn't tell you that she slept with you?"

"You know that's not what I meant. But that was a simple . . . mistake. It happened exactly once and . . ."

"That would be one time too many," Mackenzie said.

"Yes. But you and I weren't seeing each other anymore. And it . . . it just sort of happened. Only that once. It never happened again."

He looked to Emma for corroboration. She nodded. "I know that doesn't excuse it, but that part is true. It meant absolutely nothing to either of us except for how shitty we felt afterward."

"And the fact that he made you pregnant," Mackenzie bit out. "He gave you Zoe."

"But I didn't know that," Adam said. "She never even told me."

Mackenzie closed her eyes briefly as if she couldn't bear to look at him. "That makes me even sicker to my stomach. That you had sex with my best friend. That it meant nothing. That you could do that and then marry me."

"I married you because you were pregnant."

Even Emma winced at how badly Adam was mucking this up.

"And because I loved you," he added softly, seeming to recover his senses. "I've always loved you."

"Right." Mackenzie drew herself up.

"If I'd known I would have . . ." Adam began.

"You would have what?" Mackenzie asked.

"I don't know," Adam admitted. "But Emma should have told me."

"And me," Mackenzie said, her eyes, which were filled with hurt and anger, turning to Emma.

"I know. And I'm so sorry," Emma said. "I didn't think there was a reason to hurt you by telling you that we'd ended up in bed together. You'd broken up for what you swore was the last time, and Adam and I turned to each other exactly once. For about ten seconds."

Serena shot Adam a look but for once she didn't take the opportunity to offer a wisecrack about Adam's sexual stamina or anything else.

"It meant less than nothing," Emma continued, unable to keep the pleading tone out of her voice. She hadn't allowed herself to imagine this conversation, but she had imagined herself somehow forgiven. She saw no sign of forgiveness in Mackenzie's face. Or Adam's for that matter.

"By the time I realized I was pregnant, you were back together, getting married, and you were going to have the baby you always wanted. Would that have been a better time to tell you? Just how would that conversation have gone?"

Mackenzie didn't answer. Her jaw remained set; her hands were still fisted at her hips. Her long blond hair hung down beneath her

434

squared shoulders. She looked like an Amazon warrior princess. Emma had always been short, but she'd never felt this small.

"Please try to understand. I was afraid of losing your friendship. I . . . deserved to lose your friendship, but I . . . you were pregnant and Adam loved you. I thought we'd both have children, who'd be best friends with each other." She willed back the tears. "That was why I married Calvin. So that no one would ever know. And that was why I left Zoe to Serena, so you would never be forced to know after I was gone and couldn't explain."

"Friends tell the truth even when it's painful," Mackenzie said.

Serena nodded but stayed mercifully out of the conversation.

"I couldn't do it. I was so afraid of losing your friendship that I . . ." Emma swallowed. "I was sitting here working up the nerve to tell you tomorrow. It's why I invited you both here. I never told Serena, either. I was going to confess that Zoe was Adam's daughter. Then once you'd had a chance to absorb it and hopefully come to terms with how it happened, I was going to change my will and all the paperwork so that Zoe would be yours, Mackenzie. And Adam's, too."

"And you were planning to let me know this at some point, too, right?" Adam asked curtly.

"Of course. I just wanted the chance to

435

apologize and explain to Mackenzie first."

"And what about me?"

Emma's knees trembled at the sound of Zoe's voice. The blood began to whoosh through her veins at the sight of Zoe stepping out from behind Serena and Adam. Her heart began to pound as Zoe came forward pausing only briefly beside Adam, where Emma was forced to look at both of their angry faces, their expressions far too similar to ever deny again.

"When exactly were you planning to explain all of this to me?" Zoe cried. "On my twenty-first birthday? Right before I walked down the aisle and we had to decide who would escort me? Or never?"

"Zoe, honey!" Emma stepped forward, but Zoe had already turned and begun striding out of the bedroom. She sprinted across the upstairs hall. Before Emma could get close enough to stop her, she'd stomped into her bedroom and slammed the door behind her. The last sound Emma registered was the lock clicking into place.

# THIRTY-EIGHT

Unable to lie in bed staring blindly at the ceiling a moment longer, Mackenzie paced the confines of her bedroom as the hurt and anger rose like a tide within her. She clung to the anger as best she could, a life raft bobbing on a sea of hurt that threatened to pull her under. She held on to their betrayal, replaying Emma's big lie that made a mockery not only of Mackenzie's marriage, but of the friendship that had meant so much to her. She nursed her fury at Serena, who should have kept her damned suspicions to herself and her big Georgia Goodbody mouth shut.

*Adam's daughter* was in the next room. The child whose very existence had fueled her envy of Emma, the girl she'd come to love and sworn to protect was not her godchild but her husband's daughter. *Adam and Emma's daughter.* She had no idea who she was angriest with, whose actions had hurt the most. As if it were some awful contest in which there could only be one winner. Adam had slept with Emma.

She turned and paced to the opposite wall then back to the window. What would have happened if Emma had said something all those years ago? What would Adam have done if he'd discovered he'd impregnated two women, best friends at that? Now there was a screenplay with Oscar potential.

Thoughts pierced her at every step, sharp as arrows dipped in poison. Would this have hurt less if she and Adam had had a child? Would the betrayal have seemed smaller? She couldn't imagine it would have softened the blow. Because despite the technicality of their breakup, Emma should never have slept with him. Hysterical laughter bubbled at how quickly her subconscious had gone to work trying to pin this whole thing on Emma. Because how else could she forgive Adam, who had not banged on the door to beg forgiveness or to offer comfort?

Hot tears scalded her cheeks, the struggle to banish them useless as wishes. Her insides were wrung so tight she could barely breathe even after all these hours.

A lifetime later, Mackenzie stood at her bedroom window, staring nearly unseeing as the sun began its climb over Pilot Knob, when a knock sounded on the door.

"Open up, Mac." Adam's voice reached her through the solid wood. "It's me."

438

Tired of this room and her own garbled thoughts, she opened the door. His clothes were rumpled, his hair disheveled. One cheek carried the imprint of the family room sofa's tweed fabric. The fact that he had obviously slept while she'd spent the night aflame in hurt and anger stoked those flames higher.

She stepped back to let him enter, but could no more have touched him than she would have touched a coiled rattler. Nor could she stop her mind from forming images of him and Emma locked in an embrace. Emma. Who had never been a head taller than everyone in her class, who'd never been forced to design her own clothes to camouflage a too-tall, too-boardlike body. Had Adam preferred her? Would he have ended up with Emma if Mackenzie hadn't been pregnant?

"I'm sorry," he said. "I know it sounds so . . . insufficient. And it's such a cliché. But I never meant to hurt you." He ran a hand through his hair, sending it in even more directions. She'd never seen him this unkempt or at such a loss for words. His face seemed altered and it wasn't just because she was seeing it through the blur of tears and haze of anger.

"Maybe you should have thought of that before you slept with my best friend. Isn't that the biggest cliché of all?"

"Yeah." Adam sank down on the bed,

dropped his head in his hands. "I am sorry, Mac. I wish to hell it had never happened. But she should have told me." He turned weary eyes to hers. "I've never felt the way you do about children; I barely know Zoe. I've spent more time with her this week than I have her whole life." His voice broke. "I would never have turned my back on my own flesh and blood."

Flesh and blood. His flesh and blood. The words hit her anew. Zoe was Adam's flesh and blood, she carried his DNA, not hers. Not *theirs.* She could try all she wanted not to picture him with Emma, but trying to block the image didn't make the truth any less true. She thought about Emma's words, her explanation for her actions. No matter how you looked at it, having sex and making a baby took two participants.

"She had no right to keep this from me," Adam said. "How do you think I feel?"

He reached for her hand, but she didn't reach back. Anger thrummed through her veins.

"I don't actually give a shit how you feel right now," Mackenzie said. "For the first time in my life, I don't give a good Goddamn how you feel."

He stiffened. His eyes clouded with emotions she had no desire to identify. "We're going to have to talk about this, Mac. We're going to have to figure this out."

440

Questions swirled in her mind, but she was far too raw and too tired to discuss them with anyone, let alone come up with answers. "Not now we're not," she said. "I don't have to *do* anything."

"I think we should head back to the city," Adam said. "To get some distance and a little perspective."

"We?" She had to hold her hands tight to her sides not to reach out and slap him. "What makes you think there's still a 'we'? I'll decide if we're a 'we' or not!"

"Got it." Adam stood and started stuffing things into his bag. In five minutes he was packed. "Are you coming or staying?"

She didn't want to go anywhere with him. But she didn't want to stay here even more. "Get out. I'll come down when I'm ready."

Mackenzie packed then showered and dressed trying to imagine what on earth would come next. She walked past Emma's open door, which she ignored, slid a note under Zoe's, which was closed. There'd been no sign of Serena, for which she was grateful.

Adam carried their bags out to the rental car while Nadia hugged her good-bye. "Maybe you stay. Work things better," the nurse said, her eyes downcast.

"Not right now." There was no room on her life raft for the oversized emotions that swamped her. Desperate to stay afloat, she attempted to throw those feelings overboard along with her vows to hold tight to her friendship with Emma and Serena and to be there for Zoe.

As she walked out the door and across the front porch, she knew only that if she stayed a moment longer, she, her life raft, and her marriage could break apart on the rocks of reality and go under.

Serena stood near the family room window seat and watched Adam and Mackenzie drive off. Her bags were packed, and if she could have taken their silent condemnation for all those hours she might have asked for a ride. Instead she'd asked Nadia to take her to the rental car office. She turned now to see the former weight lifter coming down the stairs carrying Serena's considerable collection of luggage as if it weighed nothing. If the nursing thing didn't work out, the woman would make a first-class bellhop.

"I'll be out in a minute," Serena said, taking the stairs two at a time and walking through Emma's open bedroom door without pausing to knock. She found Emma staring out the window, her back illuminated against a sky in the process of turning from sunny to cloudy as if intent on matching their moods.

Emma turned, her face as tear streaked and angry as Serena's had been when she'd spied it in the mirror that morning. "I was planning to tell everyone today," Emma said. "I can't imagine why you felt the need to hurl all those accusations around."

"And you've convinced yourself that that would have gone better somehow? That you would have sat everyone down and explained everything and no one would have been upset with you?"

She watched Emma closely. "I mean, you could have called the cancer card. And maybe the coma one, too. But I don't think anybody was going to give you a pass on this one, Em. Because you had no right to keep this secret and you know it."

Emma didn't respond or even move. It didn't matter. Serena had spent the entire night stewing at the injustice of it all, and she didn't plan to leave until she'd had her say.

"I wish to hell you had made the announcement. Because then everybody wouldn't be pissed off at me. I'm just the shmuck who noticed the resemblance," Serena said. "I didn't actually do anything to you, Mackenzie, Zoe, or Adam."

Emma just stood there and listened. Serena couldn't have stopped herself if she'd wanted to.

"Despite my dating track record, I'm not actually the one who slept with one of my best friend's boyfriends then kept it, and my pregnancy by him, a secret for seventeen years." She paused, allowing this to sink in. "Come to think of it, I'm not the one who invited my friend, whose husband fathered my child, to be my child's fairy godmother, either. Even though she'd lost her own child and I knew it must be killing her every time she played with mine."

It was a direct hit, one that drew tears. Still Emma didn't speak or attempt to defend herself.

"How could you call me a best friend and never share something this important? Who knows? Maybe I could have helped. At the very least, I wouldn't have tipped your hand if I'd known there was a hand to tip." She shoved away the impossibility of the choice Emma had been forced to make. She did not want to put herself in Emma's shoes, did not want to think about what would have happened if Emma had told Adam she was pregnant and he'd married Emma instead of Mackenzie. "When you pushed Mackenzie away so she wouldn't discover your secret, you pushed me away, too. You were my best friends and you just shoved me right out of both of your lives."

Serena drew a deep and somewhat shaky breath. She'd spent much of her adult life on her own, but she'd never felt quite so alone as she had when she'd lost Emma and Mackenzie. "Then you named me Zoe's guardian as, what, a smokescreen? So Adam and Mackenzie would never know?" She took another step into the room. Emma's eyes followed her. "Did you ever stop and think for even one second what all of this might do to us?"

"Of course I did," Emma said. "I thought about it all the time. I couldn't stop thinking about it."

"Sometimes there's no good way to tell a thing. But that doesn't mean you don't have an obligation to tell it." Serena shook her head. "From what I can see, you're lucky Zoe doesn't have a Gran to swoop in and take her away from you."

"That's enough," Emma said, but her voice carried no weight.

"You can try and tell yourself this is my fault for spilling the secret a few hours ahead of time all you want. But if you're lucky enough to get your daughter to listen to you, I wouldn't waste any time trying to justify anything. I'd use it to apologize. Because you owe everybody, especially your daughter, a big-ass apology. And then you better pray like hell that she's willing to accept it."

Emma watched Serena turn and stalk out of the room. From her spot at the window she watched her climb into the passenger seat of the Jeep. As Nadia backed the vehicle down the drive Serena's words echoed in Emma's head, ugly and harsh. And worst of all, true.

Her heart felt tight, as she forced herself to examine her actions and motives. First she'd told herself she was keeping silent about

Adam's paternity to protect Mackenzie and then Zoe. But what if she'd only been protecting herself? Making sure she and her reputation weren't open for attack? Trying not to lose a friendship she'd given up the right to? And what about her daughter's rights? At what point should she have told Zoe the truth?

She crossed the hall and knocked on Zoe's door.

"Zoe?" She swallowed. "Zoe, honey. Please open the door. I need to talk to you. I . . . I want to explain."

There was no answer. Emma knocked again.

Only Zoe wouldn't open the door or even respond.

Emma sank down the wall next to Zoe's door and pulled her knees up to her chest. With her chin tucked against them she gave in and cried.

She was still crying in her room that night as she fell into what could only be called a troubled sleep in which she was chasing after something elusive just out of reach, ahead in the fog.

*You know how I feel about* Gone with the Wind *references, darling. I wish you'd stick with those fish dreams. They're so much more interesting and nowhere near so melodramatic.*

*Gran. Thank God. Where have you been?*

*I've been hoping you'd buck up and take care*

*of things. It's not like you to be such a wuss.*

Even in her dream, Emma flinched.

*I used to give you twenty-four hours to get over things and not a minute more. You can't give Zoe too long to stew. That won't do either of you any good.*

*But it's so much worse than I was expecting. Zoe won't speak to me. Serena and Mackenzie have fled. And Adam . . . honestly he was the last person I ever considered in this. Because I knew he never wanted to be a father. I don't know what I was thinking.*

*There, there.* Her grandmother's voice gentled. *There are no easy answers. You've been outed, which was your ultimate goal. Now you have to do whatever it takes to reassure Zoe — all she really wants is to know that you love her and will be there for her.*

*And the others?*

*That's a little dicier. But groveling coupled with a well-thought-out grand gesture can sometimes be effective.*

Emma was gifted with a flash of her grand-mother's smile.

*That's what your grandfather was doing when I got pregnant with your father.*

Emma woke hours later to a ringing telephone. When she finally answered, it was her father. In her half-dream state she imagined he'd been summoned by her grandmother's

447

revelation of the circumstances that had led to his conception.

"Hello, kitten. How are you?" Hearing his pet name for her launched a fresh flood of tears. She sat up in bed. "Daddy." The word slipped out. Rex Michaels was vain and too self absorbed for fatherhood, but as a child Emma had loved him madly and wanted nothing more than to please him. He'd had much of his mother's joie de vivre with none of the sense of responsibility, but his neglect had been more benign than Eve's. She commanded the tears to stop. "Where are you calling from?"

"I'm in Cannes. We just arrived yesterday morning."

"We?" Emma swung her legs over the side of the bed.

"Yes, Gerald and I have taken a house here for the rest of the summer."

"Oh, right." Emma walked to the window seat and settled into a corner of it so that she could see out over the cove. Shafts of midday sun peered from behind the clouds as if struggling to come back out.

"I know I'm a little late given the flight and the time difference, but I wondered if I might wish Zoe a happy birthday. And congratulate you on producing such a marvelous child. She was quite fierce and protective of you when you were in the hospital, you know. She's very like you."

"I'm afraid she's not here right now," Emma lied. "But I'll be glad to tell her you called when I, um, see her."

"That would be nice, darling. I'll find something suitable here and send it to her when I have the chance."

"As long as it's not a part in a film like Eve offered," Emma replied.

"The Scorsese thing?" Rex's voice was tinged with amusement.

"Yes," she replied. "And there's nothing funny about it. Zoe is not doing a feature film anytime soon and especially not with Eve. She called in the paparazzi personally at the birthday lunch she set up at Le Cirque to announce it. It was a complete ambush."

Rex sighed. "Yes, well. You know Eve. She's always been a master strategist and not one to admit defeat. Far more cunning than me, as I discovered the first time she stopped letting me win at chess shortly after we were married." There was an oddly fond chuckle at the memory.

"I guess a leopard never changes its spots," Emma said.

"No, but in this case I believe she's attempting to cover them up." Rex hesitated briefly before continuing. "I've finally left her, you see. We're getting divorced. After all these years your old father is officially coming out of the closet."

Emma tried to picture her parents as

completely separate entities. Despite the time they'd spent apart and their disparate interests, and, she'd discovered later, sex lives, she had never envisioned one without the other.

"And I suppose lots of press about her and her granddaughter appearing in a motion picture together might counter some of the harsher publicity. She did lay it on a bit thick with all those stories about maintaining the romance in our marriage, and how we defied the horrible Hollywood marital odds," Rex said drily.

"Are you worried about the public reaction?" Emma asked. Rex had spent his entire adulthood pretending to be something he wasn't both on- and off-screen. "Don't you wish real life could be controlled like a screenplay?"

"Not anymore, kitten," her father said. "I find I prefer real life. It's messy and filled with all kinds of mistakes and heartaches. But I can't tell you what a relief it is to finally be allowed to be who I really am." His tone turned even more reflective, a rare thing for a man who was used to providing sound bites rather than deep thoughts. "I should have come out long ago. But I told myself I was protecting everyone, from your grandmother to Eve to you children, when in fact I simply couldn't face the condemnation and possible loss in income and stature." He snorted in a surprisingly inelegant way. "Telling the truth is incredibly important. You just can't always control how it will be received."

Emma stood and moved from the window surprised not only by her father's revelations but also by how relevant they were to her own sad state of affairs. The truth had set her father free while hers had left her isolated and alone. "Well, congratulations, Rex. I hope you and Gerald will be very happy."

"Thank you, dear. I'll let you know how things go. But I will tell you that in my experience happiness isn't something that just occurs. Sometimes, to borrow Jack London's comment about inspiration, 'you have to go after it with a club.' "

# THIRTY-NINE

Serena was ashamed of herself before she placed the call. And even more so once she'd made it. She'd never called in sick or failed to show up for any acting job no matter how small, but today she was far too busy wallowing in hurt and disappointment to face the studio, Wes Harrison, Lauri Strauss, or even Ethan Miller.

"You have a bunch of messages from Brooks Anderson," Catherine had said just as Serena had begun to hang up. "Do you want me to give you the number or read you any of them?"

"No!" she'd snapped, forgetting to croak as if she'd lost her voice.

Feeling even more pathetic and alone than she had when she'd returned from the lake two days ago, she slogged back to her bedroom and climbed back beneath the covers. There she once again chastised herself for letting her guard down so completely that she'd fallen for Brooks Anderson's lethal line of bullshit. Not to mention being so sucked in by Emma's invitation to the lake house and the intensity of Emma's struggle to regain consciousness.

Turning on her side, she drew the pillow to her stomach, wrapped her arms around it, and wallowed some more, only dragging herself out of bed when it was time for her appointment with Dr. Grant who had — thank you, God — a last-minute cancellation.

Only now that she was sitting across from him with a wad of crumpled tissues in one hand, the good doctor was proving to be anything but sympathetic.

"You did not just tell me to pull up my big girl panties and get on with it."

"Actually," he conceded, unperturbed, "I believe I did."

"Well, that's not good," she said. "And as someone who is paying you three-hundred-plus dollars per forty-five minutes, I demand that you stop reading women's fiction and watching reruns of *Sex and the City* immediately. You may be getting too in touch with your feminine side."

He smiled broadly. "Point taken. I'm only trying to say that this is not the end of the world you're making it out to be."

"No?" She helped herself to another tissue. "Because that's exactly what it feels like."

"In fact, I think you've made great strides

this summer."

"You do?"

"Look, you've claimed to be fine without Brooks Anderson for twenty years, but that wasn't really true, was it?"

"Well, no," she admitted.

"And you've insisted for the last five years that you didn't really miss Emma or Mackenzie." He speared her eyes with his. "Which wasn't exactly true, either."

She nodded. She had only realized how lonely she'd been without them when she'd seen Emma lying unconscious in that hospital room. She'd thought she'd left that kind of loneliness behind her when she and Mackenzie had helped each other and Zoe through it. "I thought . . . I thought we were back. But Emma had her own agenda. And everyone's pissed at me when all I did was point out something that Emma was planning to admit to anyway."

Dr. Grant's face blurred in front of her. "Friendships and relationships can be complicated. The only way to avoid that is not to engage. Or to choose only safe relationships where nothing is really expected." He eyed her pointedly but his voice was kind. "You've been forced to confront and reassess the things that have been missing from your life."

"I should have known that Brooks appearing like that out of nowhere after all this time was just too good to be true." She dumped the soaked tissues in the garbage can and plucked new ones from the box.

"Maybe," he said. "But how many people do you think could have walked away from finding out for sure?"

She remained silent, deploying her tissues to mop up the new flood of tears.

"The answer would be not very many, Serena. And to be fair, you don't actually know what happened."

Serena thought of the messages Brooks had left for her at the studio. How real his emotions had seemed when they were together. But there was no getting around Diana's malicious glee on the phone that day.

"Finding out what happened could help you finally find some closure. If he's prepared to explain it at some point, you might want to listen."

Serena couldn't imagine it. But then her heart felt so heavy right now, she wasn't sure how her chest could contain it.

"And as for your friends. I'm not saying it was fair, but it sounds like you mostly got caught in the crossfire. You're going to have to ask yourself whether you want these women in your life. And if the answer is yes, you'll have to figure out what you're prepared to do to help make that happen."

"It all sounds good, Dr. G. but" — Serena shook her head — "honestly, I don't know that I'm ready for any of it." All she really wanted to do was go home and crawl back into bed. Her only wish was that she lived closer.

"I understand." His tone made it clear that he did. "But you're strong, Serena. And you're smart. And I have no doubt you're a good friend."

"Should I be worried that you didn't mention attractive, talented, and interesting?" she asked, searching for but not quite finding her sense of humor.

"No, those are givens."

"Why, thank you." She briefly considered batting her eyelashes at him à la Georgia, but she didn't have the energy or the heart for it.

"It seems to me the time is ripe for you to think about who and what you want in your life. You may be surprised at the answers. Change is never easy, but it can be rewarding."

Serena took the subway back to the Village from Dr. Grant's office, then made a lame attempt to cheer herself up with stops at Abingdon Market, where she bought a bouquet of sunflowers, with their bright yellow faces bobbing on thick green stalks. At the ice cream cart outside of Cafe Cluny, she bought a pint of mint chocolate chip then treated herself to the latest *Vogue* and *Glamour* at Casa Magazines. Mothers pushed strollers down the sidewalks. A group of tourists followed a tour guide, who was busy pointing out Carrie Bradshaw's brownstone from *Sex and the City.* A smile tugged at Serena's lips as she thought about Dr. Grant and his "big girl panties" comment. Passing beneath the leafy canopy that shaded West Fourth, she began to really consider what he'd said. She'd always believed in choice and determination. Perhaps the time had finally come to stop playing the victim.

By the time she turned onto Bank Street she'd begun to shake off some of her malaise. Wallowing was not her style. She wasn't even particularly good at it. Instead of lying in bed when she got home maybe she'd sit out in the garden for a while. A glass of wine would be nice. Tomorrow she'd call the studio to reschedule the recording. Whether she'd ever be ready to stitch up the tear Brooks Anderson had ripped open in her life, she didn't know. For now she'd do what she'd always done. Plant one foot in front of the other.

Readjusting the flowers and her packages, she looked up and saw movement ahead. Her heart did a strange sort of tattoo and her steps faltered when she saw the man sitting on her front steps.

In another part of Manhattan, Mackenzie sat at a table in the window of a small sushi restaurant several blocks off Broadway with Adam and two of his oldest friends. Most of the meal had been filled with reminiscences about the "good old theater days," which Liam and Dan were still living. The three of them entered into the eternal debate between live performance and film and the actor's and director's roles in both. Mackenzie smiled and nodded when it seemed appropriate, but mentally she'd checked out shortly after they'd arrived.

"I've got this," Adam insisted when the bill came. "And I expect you two to come see us the next time you're in LA," he added as Dan and Liam rose to depart. He said this as if there was no question in his mind that he and Mackenzie would soon be settled out on the West Coast. But Mackenzie was still trying to come to terms with pretty much everything. Since they'd fled the lake house, Adam hadn't mentioned Zoe or the fact that she was his daughter even once. Which seemed especially unbelievable to Mackenzie, who hadn't stopped thinking about it for more than an isolated couple of minutes now and then.

She managed to smile and accept hugs from Dan and Liam before sitting back down with Adam, who had ordered more tea. He was flying out later that afternoon and she could tell that part of him had left already. He was excited about "their" new life and, of course, his movie deal. "I'm sure we can stay in Matthew's pool house for a few weeks after you come out. You know, to give you time to look around for something you like."

She looked at him. Took in his hopeful expression. He seemed to believe that if he just set the scene properly, everything, including her, would fall into place. "And you know I was thinking that we don't really have to sell the house in Noblesville right away. I mean, if the theater sale goes as quickly as I think it might, we'll have enough pad to take our time. So that you can have a little more time to go through things and . . . come out when you feel ready."

A week ago all of this would have made her feel better and decreased the pressure she was feeling, as he clearly now intended. She might have found a way to overlook how he seemed to be ignoring that housing cost four times as much out in LA, that it could be years before the film was actually shot and edited; let go of her anger that he spoke as if her acquiescence was a foregone conclusion. She would have given a lot for those to be their only issues.

"Are you just going to pretend that you aren't a father now?" she asked after the tea was poured. "That you are not Zoe's father?"

Adam's shoulders drooped. He ran a hand through his hair. "I told you I had no idea. And I've apologized repeatedly. I wish that night had never happened. But it meant absolutely nothing."

"Zoe's not nothing," she said, cutting him

off when he tried to continue. "There's a part of me — a very small part to be sure — that understands how you and Emma could have . . . happened. I even grasp the 'technicality' that we weren't seeing each other at the time. But we can't really pretend it never happened." She pushed her teacup out of the way. "Because Zoe is your daughter and all of us, especially Zoe, know it now."

He stared back at her. For a few long moments he said nothing. "So you think that now that I know something I should have been told seventeen years ago, I should just 'jump to' and start acting like her father?" He exhaled sharply. "For someone who's been demanding time to adjust to and think over a simple move from one city to another, I'd think you might understand that this . . . whole thing . . ." He gestured vaguely. "Would take some time to absorb." His chin jutted stubbornly. She saw a confusion in his brown eyes that belied his argumentative tone. For Adam the best defense had often been a strong offense. Typically it had worked for him. She'd almost always been the one to back down.

"It's not something either of us are going to be able to walk away from. Not even if we wanted to." Mackenzie thought about Zoe's shocked face, the tears that had already been flowing before the girl turned and fled to her bedroom. Even if Mackenzie managed to erase the mental image of Adam and Emma in bed together, there would still be Zoe. Who'd never asked for any of this. And who deserved to be loved by all of them. "I left her a note saying that she would always be welcome in our home. And I meant it. Even if I'm not sure whether she'll see me as a 'fairy godmother' or more of an evil stepmother." She looked her husband in the eye. "But you need to be on board for your role as her father."

Adam looked down into his tea, swirling the cup before him. "I can get you a ticket out with me this afternoon," he said. "Come to LA with me now. A change of scenery will be good for us. And we'll find some way to sort this all out."

That was how they'd always done things. He did and she supported him. But she wasn't ready yet to simply say yes and follow him wherever he wanted to go. "I'm not ready to do that. I . . . I don't even know anymore what I want to happen next."

He sighed, looking more defeated than she'd seen him since he first agreed to leave New York for Noblesville. It was a look she'd tried to forget and had hoped to never see again. He reached for her hand and she felt the warmth of his surrounding hers. He looked her in the eye and held her hand as if it were a priceless possession; another thing that hadn't happened in recent memory.

"I love you, Mackenzie," he said quietly. "I feel like I've loved you forever." His eyes were clear and earnest. "I can't imagine my life, even in a place I want desperately to be, would be worth much without you."

His eyes plumbed hers searching for the reaction she was unable to give him. "In case you have any doubt, I want you to understand one thing. I would have married you even if you hadn't gotten pregnant. Nothing could have ever prevented that. It just might have happened a little later."

She drew a deep and shaky breath as he answered the question she'd never had the courage to ask.

His smile was sweet as he placed a kiss on her forehead and another on her lips. "I never had any question that you were the person I wanted to spend my life with." His smile grew, turning his brown eyes a warm whiskey color. "I hope when you've had some time to think everything through, that you'll still feel the same way about me."

# FORTY

"Miz Mickhels? Emma?"

Emma rubbed her sleep- and tear-caked eyes then looked up at the nurse who had crouched beside her. She had no idea how long she'd been sitting outside Zoe's bedroom door this time, but she had vowed that she wouldn't move until Zoe came out. And that somehow when this happened she'd find the right words that would make Zoe understand just how much Emma loved her.

Mostly Zoe had managed not to come out of her room when Emma was out of hers, but she'd seen signs of her down in the kitchen. Seen her lying on the swim platform one late morning. Sitting in an Adirondack staring out over the cove one afternoon. But each time Emma had approached, Zoe had stared right through her and refused to engage.

Yesterday, Emma had watched from her window as Ryan Richards pulled up to their dock, but by the time Emma had worked up her nerve and gotten downstairs certain that Ryan's presence would at least force Zoe to acknowledge her, they'd already left the cove and were picking up speed.

"You two need talking," Nadia said. "Or maybe some head knocking." Her tone and expression said she was just the person to do it.

"I know." Emma swallowed. "I want to talk to Zoe, to apologize. But Zoe's not interested in hearing it."

"Then you make her interesting. You're the mother." Nadia reached out a hand and helped pull her to her feet. "Is your job."

"It's kind of hard to do that through a door." Not that she hadn't already tried or had any real confidence that she'd do any better face-to-face.

"Then we open door." Nadia pulled a pocketknife from her pants pocket and flipped open the nail file, which she inserted into the center of the doorknob.

Before Emma could protest or prepare herself, the nurse twisted the knife. There was a click. Nadia pushed the door open. Emma shrank back.

"No. You not wussy out. Have talk."

Suddenly afraid, Emma tried to dig in her heels, but *she* was not the immovable force here. "But what if she won't talk to me?"

"Then you talk. Zoe listen." Nadia gave her another gentle, for her, push.

Emma entered her daughter's room on jellied legs. Zoe sat on her window seat in much the same position Emma had just been forced out of, knees to her chest, chin resting on her knees. She stared at Emma out of green eyes the same shade as her own. "I don't want to talk to you. I locked my door because I don't even want to have to look at you."

Emma kept walking, though the few feet past Zoe's bed and to the window felt like miles. She sat down on the opposite end of the window seat afraid that if she got too close Zoe might bolt.

"I just wanted to make sure you know how sorry I am." Emma's voice cracked on the apology, bending it all out of shape. "I never meant to hurt you. Or anyone else. I love you more than anything. I . . . I only wanted to protect you."

"Protect me? From what?" Zoe demanded. "From knowing who my father really was? From knowing that I was a mistake you wish you never made?" She buried her chin back in her knees. "Did Calvin know I'm not his?"

Emma nodded carefully.

"Well, at least now I know why he never acted like a father. I always thought there was something wrong with me that made him not be interested."

"Oh, Zoe." Emma's heart throbbed painfully in her chest. How had she made such an incredible mess of things?

"If I was such a bad mistake. So bad you didn't even want to admit it to anyone, why . . . why did you even have me at all?"

"But I did want you. I never once even considered not having you." The words she'd held back for so long rushed out. "You were unplanned, just like I was, but I wanted you. And I fell completely in love with you before I ever even saw you. I was just so worried about hurting Mackenzie."

"Yeah, well then maybe you shouldn't have slept with her boyfriend."

This was an undeniably good point. "That was wrong of me," Emma said. "Adam and Mackenzie were good friends of mine. If anyone knew that that shouldn't have happened, even after they'd broken up, it was me. I behaved so stupidly. I drank too much and I trampled all over my friendship with Mackenzie. That was the mistake I've regretted ever since. But not you, Zoe. Never you."

Zoe turned to look out the window as tears slid down her cheeks.

It was all Emma could do not to look away. But now with the scrim of fear and denial ripped away, Emma could see just how much of Adam her daughter carried. The man had a lot of good qualities. Enough for Mackenzie to have fallen in love with him and stayed married to him all these years.

"You're such a hypocrite. You've always told me to be honest," Zoe said. "To always tell you the truth. But you didn't tell me the truth at all."

"I know." The admission was painful. "And I — I don't even have a valid excuse. I was afraid to tell the truth. Afraid of losing Mackenzie's friendship. Afraid of how it would make me look." Emma saw it now for what it was. How selfish she'd been. Unable to accept the reality of what she'd done, she'd twisted it around and convinced herself that what she wanted and needed was what was best for others. *Just like Eve had always done.*

She'd not only lied to her friends and to her daughter, she'd lied to herself.

"I'm really and truly sorry," she said, meeting and holding her daughter's eyes. "I don't even know how to tell you how sorry I am." She dashed away tears with the back of her hand. "But I promise I won't lie to you again."

Zoe studied Emma's face long enough to make Emma squirm before she nodded. "And will you promise to listen when I tell you things?"

"Of course. I always listen to . . ."

"No." Zoe cut her off. "I mean really listen. Even if it's not something you want to hear."

"Like?" Emma felt the first stirring of hope. If they could talk this through, surely they could find a way to move forward, to put this behind them. If Zoe could forgive her maybe someday Mackenzie and Adam could, too.

"Like, just because you didn't want to act when you were a kid doesn't mean I shouldn't be allowed to. Acting does something to me. It makes me bigger, stronger. I don't know, just happier." Zoe's arms opened as she spoke. Her knees came away from her chest, her long legs crisscrossed on the cushioned seat as her face grew animated. "That's how I feel in front of an audience, or a film camera, or even a microphone."

Emma smiled at Zoe. "I feel the same way. It's in our blood. I just couldn't stand being forced to do it." By people who didn't seem to care whether she liked it or not.

"But you wouldn't be forcing me," Zoe said quietly. "You'd be letting me."

They studied each other for a few long minutes. Emma knew this was not the end of this conversation, but only the beginning. And it wasn't as if the hurt she'd inflicted was suddenly going to disappear. There was so much to atone for, so much lost time to try to make up.

"I'm not promising you a film with Eve. But I imagine we can find a way to let you get started in the business in a way we can both live with." Emma reached for Zoe's hand hoping that her daughter would allow it. "I might not have the right to ask it right now, but I need you to know how important you are to me. And I need you to forgive me."

She waited, barely breathing as Zoe accepted her hand.

"Did you ever forgive your mother?" Zoe asked.

She thought about Eve and then about herself. She had no idea why her mother had made the choices she had, had never asked a single question or even tried to understand her. She'd only nursed her own hurts and looked for a way to escape. She thought about her father and what his coming out would mean to Eve. How hard her mother had tried to pretend her marriage was something it wasn't and could never be. Who was Emma to say that her own reasons were purer?

"No," Emma said. "I never did." She grasped her daughter's hand more tightly. Zoe's fingers were longer and younger and in some ways even stronger than her own. She thought about what Eve was facing and how she'd chosen to try to use Zoe to soften it. She was not Eve, would never be. "But then I don't remember her ever asking me to."

As Serena drew closer Brooks Anderson unfolded his long legs, brushed off the seat of his dress pants, and stood.

Grateful for the years of acting under her belt, she squared her shoulders and raised her chin, moving forward without a single missed step. When she reached him she tilted her head and pretended to look behind him.

Reaching down deep she located a teasing tone. "You didn't bring your wife with you, did you?"

"No." He had the grace to look embarrassed. "But the old guy next door came out dressed in a really beautiful ball gown and invited me to wait inside."

"That's quite a compliment," she said, settling herself as she might in the first lines of a scene. "Jason Merrimen is a very well-known and highly respected drag queen. He doesn't invite just anyone in."

Brooks laughed and she saw him relax a notch.

"You see what you missed by not living in the Village?" she asked.

"I do." He reached for the grocery bag. "Here, let me take some of that." He hesitated. "Assuming you have a few minutes to hear an apology and don't mind if I come in?"

"Why would I mind?" she asked stepping past him. She would play this scene out and send him on his way. And then, well, no need to look any further than that. She took the steps lightly. As she opened the door she did her best to block her memories of the two of them standing in this spot drenched and eager to rip off each other's clothes. She blushed when she looked at the foyer wall he'd taken her against and thought she saw him doing the same.

She led him into the kitchen. He set the bag on the counter.

"I . . . I understand you spoke to Diana." His eyes sought hers and she met them evenly.

"Oh, yes. Because you were in the shower and couldn't come to the phone." She said this with a combination of wide-eyed innocence and the slightest of shrugs. She would not give him the satisfaction of knowing how much that had hurt.

"Just so you know. I wasn't expecting her. She took me by surprise when she waltzed into my hotel room."

She remembered her own surprise when Diana had answered the phone. How her heart had constricted. The agony of embarrassment as she'd realized that she'd fallen into bed with him without first finding out what was really going on. She managed to say nothing only by carrying the ice cream to the freezer then putting the few groceries away as slowly as possible.

She walked back to face him, careful to keep the island between them. She fished beneath the sink for a vase, which she filled with water. She was playing the part of a woman who is not surprised by betrayal. Even in this case it was not actually a stretch. "Imagine my surprise when she made it clear that your marriage was not actually 'finished.' I believe that was the word you used?"

He shifted uncomfortably and she wondered what he'd expected. Chest beating?
Wailing? "I thought we were finished," he said
a bit sheepishly as if he wasn't quite sure how
they'd gotten their signals crossed. "We
agreed to a trial separation. I was ready to
file for divorce."

She noted the word "was" as she reached
for the flowers and began to remove the cel-
lophane. She'd known that she'd "lost" if in
fact she'd ever been in the running, when
she'd heard Diana's smug voice on the
phone. "But you're not anymore."

He shook his head slowly. His eyes were
filled with what looked like genuine regret. "I
left you messages asking you to call me," he
said.

"I know. But there didn't seem to be any
reason to listen or call. It's clear that whatever
this *was* is over." It took all of her strength to
keep her voice even. She had to keep reminding herself that this was a part she was playing, not her real life at all. She found the scissors and carefully began to cut the stem of
the nearest sunflower.

"Before you toss me out, I want you to
know something," he said and she had the
feeling that he, too, had been rehearsing his
lines.

She nodded but held her features in check.
She was, after all, a professional. She was paid
large sums of money to do this.

"The choice was never Diana over you. It was what life I was brave enough to live," he said, taking her by surprise. "I handled it all so badly. Then and now. But I didn't start things up again in order to take advantage and I never meant to hurt you."

She closed her eyes for a brief moment under the guise of putting the trimmed flower into the vase. *Too late for that.*

"The thing is I've always admired you, Serena. You're one of the bravest people I've ever known." He spoke with an obvious sincerity that could not be shrugged off. She was grateful for the role she'd adopted. Because otherwise she might be launching herself into his arms and begging him to reconsider.

She picked up another stem and went about making it shorter.

"You've never let anything stop you," he said. "And even when you get knocked down you get right back up. You've never let anyone, not even me, get in the way of your dreams. While I . . ." Brooks gave her a rueful smile. "I didn't have the guts to turn my back on what was expected of me. Or to see how I stacked up here in New York. I chose the safe and the familiar. I did it back all those years ago." He shrugged, but not lightly. "And I'm doing it again now. I only wish I had half your courage."

She put the flower she'd been sawing on in

the water. And watched it practically disappear under the surface. "Well, I appreciate your honesty, Brooks. And your . . . admiration." She reached for another stem to keep her hands busy and so she'd have something else to look at besides the regret that suffused his face and the way he was looking at her lips. As if he was trying to remember how they tasted.

She felt herself begin to weaken. Felt the first prick of tears. *No.* She raised her chin and made a firm cut into the sunflower. This script might call for flower mutilation, but it did not call for tears. If she deviated she'd be doomed. She would not cry. Not now in front of him. And not later, either.

*Buck up,* she told herself. Then from what felt like nowhere, Maya Angelou's words floated into her head and filled her mind: *When someone shows you who they are, believe them.* The scissors slipped from her hands, clattering to the floor. As she bent to retrieve them it hit her: Brooks had shown her quite clearly who he was, not once but twice. Now he had come out and told her. How could she possibly ignore him?

"Are you all right?" he asked as she stood, frozen, trying to process this revelation.

Yes," she said as she studied him. It was almost as if she were seeing him for the first time. Brooks had never been the man who could share her dreams or think any bigger than what he'd grown up with. How tightly he'd clung to the life she'd been so desperate to escape.

Serena grasped another stem and began to hack it to bits. She'd spent so many years looking at what she'd lost that she hadn't paid enough attention to what she'd gained. Then she'd been so grateful that he'd "come back to her" and "chosen her" that she hadn't asked herself whether she should choose him.

She took a deep breath, felt her lungs fill with air. She imagined the bonds that had held her in thrall to Brooks and stuck in an endless stream of dead-end relationships, breaking apart and falling away.

"Are you sure you're okay?" He reached out and took away her scissors as if unarming a possibly deranged individual. "You're, well, are you sure you want those flowers so short?" He held up the one she'd just trimmed. It no longer had a stem of any kind. It was just one big yellow flower face. "I'm afraid if you put this in the vase like that it'll . . . I don't know; can flowers drown?"

"Oops," she said. But as she looked at him she felt freer and lighter than any flower, regardless of its height. For the first time, she saw what she'd never allowed herself to see. Brooks Anderson was not the great love of her life that had been unfairly denied her. He was just a really good-looking man she'd wasted decades pining for, but whom she did not actually love and who could never have shared the life she'd chosen. Like her role tonight, she had played her version of Scarlett O'Hara dreaming of Ashley Wilkes, who had far too little backbone for Scarlett, when there were probably scores of potential, and unmarried, Rhett Butlers who might.

"I kind of hope there's no flower abuse hotline." Serena felt almost giddy with relief as she shed all of the roles she'd been playing. She no longer had need of them. She did not understand how this had happened, but she was finally ready to escort Brooks Anderson out of her life, her heart, and her head.

"So," she said almost gaily as she took him by the arm. "I really appreciate you coming by to explain things to me." She brought them to a halt in the foyer then reached for the doorknob. "I hope you'll give my regards to your parents," she said as she pulled open the door.

"Thank you. I will." He blinked in surprise when he found himself out on the front stoop. Like someone who'd been watching a video he knew well but that suddenly fast-forwarded to a scene he'd never seen before and hadn't expected to watch. "Will you be all right?" he asked solicitously.

"Yes, I will," she said with absolute certainty. "You shouldn't have any trouble catching a cab over on the corner." She pointed him in the right direction.

She was careful not to smile too broadly at the relief that coursed through her. She still felt battered and bruised. But she was miraculously free of her obsession with Brooks Anderson.

She filled her lungs with another breath of heavy summer air and found it delightful. "You and Diana be sure and have yourselves a nice life, you hear?" she called after Brooks.

She stood on her stoop overlooking her neighborhood in the city that she loved. She was going to have that glass of wine in the garden. And then maybe the ice cream for dinner. After that she'd get a good night's sleep.

She'd think about Emma and Mackenzie tomorrow. After all, as Margaret Mitchell had once famously pointed out, "Tomorrow is another day."

# FORTY-ONE

The day was half gone, the air thick and sticky with humidity as Mackenzie emerged from the subway station at Sixth and Fourteenth and made her way toward Parsons The New School for Design. At the corner of Fifth she lingered in front of the University Center. At Thirteenth she peered into the lobby of the Sheila C. Johnson Design Center. New buildings dotted the historic Greenwich campus and she marveled at how much had changed. She'd attended her first classes weak kneed with fear and anticipation. To this day she did not understand how she'd not only made it into Parsons, but graduated from it. Graduates like Donna Karan, Marc Jacobs, and Tom Ford had left their marks on the fashion world. Mackenzie had spent the vast majority of her "career" designing shoestring costumes for a tiny theater in an even tinier town.

With no destination in mind, she wandered through Washington Square Park and the surrounding NYU campus, which was part and parcel of the historic neighborhoods it had been built within. She'd fallen in love with New York in those years and especially with the Village, which had been an intimate if grungier place back then filled with mom-and-pop stores, hole-in-the-wall restaurants, cafés, and clubs.

When they had the money they'd hit Cafe Wha?, the Village Gate, the Blue Note, the Bitter End. It had been a heady time. But as much as she'd loved living in the city that did not, in fact, ever sleep it had been the unlikely friendship with Emma — then Amelia — and Serena, both of whom were so much more beautiful and self-assured than Mackenzie had ever dreamed of being, that had made her feel as if she belonged there. *And now that friendship had been trampled. They were both lost to her.*

Her steps slowed in front of a small triangular-shaped garden at the apex of two sharply angled streets. She leaned against a section of wrought iron gate remembering how she had felt as a part of their inner circle, how accepted, how unexpectedly validated. Adam had been the icing on her cake of happiness.

Even the years of struggling to find a way to try to break into the fashion world, while Adam acted and directed plays in tiny theaters so far off Broadway that they might as well have been on the moon, had been invigorating. For a time everything had seemed so bright and possible. Once she had not only welcomed change, she had sought it out, done everything in her power to initiate it. And then she'd gotten pregnant and gone scurrying back to the small town she'd fought so hard to get out of. And she'd dragged Adam with her.

*The woman I fell in love with ran away from that kind of life. She even learned to trust in love at first sight. I'm not sure what's happened to that woman. I haven't seen her for a while.*

She pushed off the fence and let her feet lead her where they would, Adam's words filling her mind.

The next thing she knew she was standing in front of the basement apartment on Jones Street, staring at the double window that had provided the only daylight in the tiny studio apartment. Her drawing board/dining room table/desk had been shoved up against that window. Her bed had been a double mattress that sat on the hardwood floor. It was on that mattress that she'd first made love with Adam, the first male who had not found her too tall, too big, too awkward. He'd claimed she was "just right" for him. Had always said their bodies fit together perfectly. And yet he'd made a child with Emma — who was small and curvy and as opposite to Mackenzie as a woman could possibly be.

She felt a burst of pain. A yawning chasm of loss. A pulsing anger.

She turned away from the tiny daylight apartment where the life she'd once imagined had loomed so large, where each day had held so much promise. Where she'd believed she had the strength and talent to achieve her dreams, the courage to become whatever and whomever she wanted.

But she had only been fooling herself. She had not been certain or courageous. Not on the inside where it mattered most. Her steps slowed even as her thoughts raced. Adam's certainty had never wavered. His self-confidence, which had drawn her just as surely as his earnest brown eyes and lean good looks, had remained absolute regardless of the situation in which he'd found himself. And he'd been right to hold on, hadn't he? While she'd done nothing but despair over her childlessness and stake out her spot in his shadow.

Adam had said he loved her, couldn't imagine his life without her. Could she believe him? Should she trust him? And how could she ever trust herself when she'd failed so miserably to become the woman she'd meant to be?

She spotted the subway station ahead and picked up her pace. She didn't want to be somebody's helper, not even Adam's. And she didn't want to blog or write a book about the things she wasn't and didn't have. So many things she knew she didn't want. And no idea what she did want or what she was willing to do to get it.

She was almost to the station when the text dinged in. It was from Zoe. *It's mom. We need you. Please come!* An Upper East Side address followed.

"Your throat sounds practically back to normal," Wes Harrison said to Serena when they'd completed the first take. "What did you do for it?"

"Thanks." She cleared her throat noisily realizing that she'd forgotten how close to laryngitis she'd played it when she'd called in sick. She studied Wes, fighting back the urge to name some completely gag-inducing concoction of, say, equal parts urine and chopped-up cactus spine. "Oh, you know, just the usual." Which could be warm honey or hot tea with lemon or warm salt water or any number of fixes that people who relied on their voices for a living depended on. Even though in her case it actually involved shrugging off decades of ancient memories and wrongful yearnings, a cure she couldn't quite see Wes embracing. Lauri Strauss pouted over in a corner, an indication that Wes had already moved on.

Serena stretched happily while they waited for the next playback. She had, in fact, drunk wine in the garden and eaten ice cream for dinner then proceeded to have one of the best night's sleep she could remember. She felt light and untethered. Joyful. In fact, the only clouds on her lovely horizon were her former friends Emma and Mackenzie, who had once again ceased to be a part of her life.

"Let's try this one slightly bitchier," Ethan's voice rang out in the studio. "Even though you're not giving him the fan, you are extremely ticked off."

Ethan's concern over her health when she'd arrived that afternoon had made her feel slightly guilty. She'd seen his surprise when she'd accepted his hug and cheek kisses with a beatific smile. It was the first time since she'd known him that she hadn't been thinking about some other man in his presence.

Wes eyed her suspiciously. "Are you sure you're all right?"

"Right as rain." She smiled. She was still smiling when she let Georgia tear into him with a comedic intensity that had everyone in the control room gasping with laughter. Even Lauri's pout had tipped up into a smile. The take was, in fact, golden. Serena took an exaggerated bow and blew faux kisses into her microphone. "Gee, can I try that again?" she asked sweetly. "I think I can go a shade or two nastier."

Wes blanched but Ethan gave her the go-ahead. When the session was over Ethan met her out in the hallway, where they watched Wes stalk off. Lauri, who had apparently learned how to cut her losses much earlier than Serena ever had, walked up to the board engineer and batted her eyelashes at him. If the girl behaved herself perhaps she'd teach her how to use the fan.

"You were in great form this afternoon, Serena," Ethan said. His voice and eyes were admiring.

"Thanks, but I bet you say that to all your cartoon characters."

He laughed. "Okay," he said studying her. "What is it that's changed? You seem different somehow."

"Different?" she asked. "How?"

"I don't know exactly," Ethan said. "But I like it."

"Thanks." As they walked to the lobby she thought about the diversions he'd created when they'd needed to escape Mount Sinai and Le Cirque, the box of goodies he'd sent, his concern for others. He'd been great with Zoe, too. With a small sigh she shoved Zoe out of her mind along with her mother and Mackenzie. "I don't know if I've mentioned it lately, but I'm really glad to have you as a friend."

He stopped, turned. "I'm not really interested in being your friend anymore," he said.

Serena looked up wondering if he was teasing. But no, his expression was quite serious

— especially for Ethan. "Is it something I said or did?" Maybe he knew she hadn't really been sick. Or more likely, he'd finally noticed that she'd never really been a friend in return. She'd just enjoyed the attention, somehow coming to expect it as her due.

"No, not really," he replied.

Serena's good mood began to dissipate like an overfilled balloon that had sprung a small leak. Ethan was such a great guy, a real class act. Apparently his patience was not limitless. "I understand," she said finally. "It's been an awfully one-sided friendship, hasn't it? You've been so giving and I . . ." That's what she got for always being so distracted by men who weren't even half as interesting. She would have done better being friends with someone like Ethan than engaging in far too brief relationships with men who didn't give a flying fig about her. "I understand and I don't blame you one bit for . . ."

"Actually, I don't think you understand at all." The dimple in his cheek creased. His eyes behind the glasses were extremely twinkly. "What I'm trying to say, and none too suavely I might add, is that I don't want to be your friend because I want to be your . . . date. Main squeeze. To put this in casting terms, 'I'm tired of playing the funny, but geeky, guy friend. I want to audition for the lead male in your . . . life.'" He was smiling but there was no mistaking his sincerity.

"Oh." For the second time in less than twenty-four hours relief flooded through her as his words, and the way he was looking at her, sank in. She might not deserve Ethan Miller or his interest, but in that moment she recognized how lucky she was that he had not written her off, as he undoubtedly should have. A world without Ethan in it would have been considerably colder. "Hmmm," she said, as her lips twisted into a smile. "What kind of audition did you have in mind?"

"I'm not sure." He linked his arm through hers. "I didn't really expect to get this far before you shut me down and smashed all my hopes." He speared her with a look. "I'm not going to have to marry someone else to get my shot, am I?"

"Ouch! I totally deserved that. But, no." Her smile grew. She could actually feel it stretching across her face. "I think I've finally moved on from that."

"Thank God," he said as they strolled through the reception area. "Can I get back to you on the audition thing?"

"Sure." Her phone dinged. She glanced down at the screen then did an unintentional double take. "If you call me a cab you can skip right over the audition."

"All right, you're a cab," he said because it was expected of him, but he'd already moved to the reception desk. "Ask Paul to bring the car around, will you?" He took Serena's arm and walked her outside to the curb. "What's wrong?"

"The text was from Zoe. Something's happened to Emma. They're at an address on the Upper East Side." Her heart dropped. "Oh, God. I hope that address isn't Mount Sinai." She should have learned her lesson the first time. "She can't die now when I'm so mad at her."

"Do you want me to come with you?" Ethan asked.

She shook her head, began to refuse. "No, but . . ." Everything about him radiated concern for her and her well-being. She was finished pushing the right people away for all the wrong reasons. "Actually, if you don't mind riding along, I could use a little moral support."

"Done." He opened the limo door for her, handed her in, then slid in beside her. He took her hand as she gave the driver the address. For the first time she leaned against a strong male shoulder and knew that she could rely on it.

# FORTY-TWO

Mackenzie's cab pulled up directly behind a black town car just as Serena emerged from it. "Serena! What's going on?"

"I don't know! I got a text from Zoe about Emma. I was so afraid the address was . . ."

"Mount Sinai?"

Serena nodded.

"Me too." Mackenzie tried to get her breathing under control. The cab pulled off as she realized where they were. "Why are we at the Carlyle?" Mackenzie's heart was still pounding so hard it was hard to think. "What's going on?"

"Good question." They turned at the sound of footsteps and saw Zoe walking quickly toward them, her face creased with worry. "Thank God you came! This way!"

"What's happened?" Mackenzie asked even as they fell into step behind Zoe.

Mackenzie tried to brace for what they might see. *Had Emma had a relapse? Oh, God, had she died?*

Her heart in her throat, she picked up her pace to try to catch up with Serena, who was trying to catch up to Zoe as they raced through the entrance. Zoe stayed several steps ahead of them moving urgently.

Serena had her phone out as they followed her into Bemelmans Bar. "Have you called 911? We're not far from Mount Sinai; we can get Paul to drive us there," she huffed. They rounded the grand piano. Serena skittered to a halt. Mackenzie slammed into her back. They teetered briefly but regained their balance.

Neither of them were prepared for what they saw. And neither, it seemed, was Emma. Who even now was rising slowly from the banquette, the soft, yellowed light shadowing her face along with Ludwig Bemelmans's murals behind her. She looked even more shocked than Mackenzie felt. What she did not look was ill. Or anywhere near the verge of death.

Serena and Mackenzie turned on Zoe. "What is going on here?"

Zoe began to back away. "I thought it would be a good idea for the three of you to talk this out face-to-face. You know kind of a *Parent Trap* scenario. Like when Lindsay Lohan tricked her parents into being in the same place at the same time because she hoped they still really loved each other?"

"You're joking, right?" Mackenzie asked,

trying to slow her heart, which felt like it might beat its way right out of her chest.

"No. It's not a joke." Zoe continued to back away. "This is totally for your own good." She took another backward step. "If you want to go ahead and get started I, um, need to go to the ladies' room. But I'll . . . I can send over a waiter." She turned then and fled.

The three of them continued to stand where they were. Close enough to hear and be heard, not close enough to have committed to staying.

Mackenzie watched Emma's face. Even in the dark her eyes were tired and red, her face haggard, which seemed only fitting. Why should she sleep when Mackenzie couldn't?

A waiter appeared, noted that they were still standing, then asked, "Can I get you something from the bar?"

"I don't suppose you have arsenic on the rocks?" Serena asked. "Or an unregistered handgun or two?"

The waiter's gaze moved across all three of their faces before returning to Emma's and Serena's. Recognition dawned. He smoothed his hair as he glanced beyond them. "Is this like some new version of *Punk'd*?" he asked hopefully. "I don't see the cameras. But I do have some head shots in the back." He flashed a very nice set of caps. "Just leave it to me." He exited chuckling. "Poison and lethal weapons! Ha!"

No one moved. They looked, Mackenzie thought, like three adults contemplating an ugly game of Ring Around the Rosie.

"I had no idea Zoe asked you to come," Emma said. "But I am glad you're here."

"She didn't ask us to come," Mackenzie said. "She texted us that it was an emergency. That something had happened to you."

"Yes," Serena added. "We thought we might be on our way back to Mount Sinai. Somebody should explain to her what happens to little girls who cry wolf."

"But you came." Emma made no effort to hide her surprise or her gratitude. "Despite everything, you both came."

It was hard to argue with that one. Mackenzie flushed as she remembered just how quickly she'd dropped everything — including her anger — and raced to get here. Was it only a matter of emotional muscle memory? Blind panic? She'd felt just as frightened as when Emma had been in the coma and she thought she'd never hear her voice again.

"I got a message that Gran's apartment had come up for sale. And I . . . I think I'd like to buy it. I thought it might be good for Zoe and me to be bicoastal."

"So you and Zoe didn't plan this little get-together, together?" Mackenzie asked.

"We might have if she'd told me what she intended," Emma said. "Except that I'm done using lies on my friends."

"It sucks being left out of the loop, doesn't it?" Serena said.

"Yes, it does," Emma conceded. "But I'm so grateful that you showed up here for me. Even though I don't deserve it."

The waiter returned with a tray that held three pale green drinks in tall thin glasses. "I've brought you Gin-Gin Mules," he said, seeming unsure what to do with them. "One of our signature cocktails. They're on the house." He looked down at his tray. "Of course they would be easier to consume if you sat down." He looked around once again as if for a camera.

"You can leave the drinks here on the table," Emma said. "If they don't sit down I may have to drink them all myself."

The waiter did as requested then left them alone, but not without a splashy bow, no doubt meant for that well-hidden camera.

"What do you think, Mac?" Serena asked. "I'm still pretty pissed off at all that anger showered down on me just because I called a spade a spade. But other than Zoe, well, and Adam actually, you're the most injured party present. Shall we have a drink and get this behind us? See if there's anything left of our friendship?"

"I guess there's no harm in listening." Mackenzie took the chair, leaving Serena to slide into the banquette next to Emma. The room glowed in the artificial light that lit the

492

murals; heavy lamp shades inspired by the murals cast a similar glow on the wooden tables. The lush carpet muted the sounds as other tables began to fill. "Why don't you start with how you got Zoe to forgive you?"

Emma reached for her drink but didn't lift it. "I'm not sure she has, at least not completely. I'm just grateful that she's speaking to me again and . . . I don't know. I've been composing these huge apologies ever since the shit hit the fan." She smiled nervously. "And now that you're here I'm not sure I can remember a word of any of it."

"How odd," Serena said, her eyes on Emma's face. "I've seen you memorize pages of dialogue in a single sitting."

"That's because if you get it wrong on set or on a soundstage, you just do another take," Emma said. "If I screw this up I might never see you again."

Was that what she wanted? Mackenzie asked herself. To never see Emma again? To let go of their friendship once and for all?

Serena took a sip of her cocktail and sent Mackenzie a questioning glance. "What do you think, Mac? Are you ready for the apologizing to commence?"

"I think so." Mackenzie reached for her cocktail.

"Okay." Emma reached into her purse and withdrew a thick stack of handwritten sheets of paper. They shook slightly in her hand as she cleared her throat and prepared to speak.

"You're kidding," Serena said, eyeing the sheaf of papers. "That's . . ."

"Be quiet," Mackenzie said. "I want to hear this." She took a long sip of her drink, which had a gingery-lime flavor.

"I'm sorry, Mackenzie," Emma said prying her eyes from her notes and turning them on Mackenzie. "I'm sorry for everything. From that stupid, stupid night in LA to my inability to speak up, to . . ." The papers rustled in her hands and she put them down on the table in front of her, drew a fresh breath. "God, I really am sorry for everything." She glanced back down at her notes briefly before meeting Mackenzie's eyes again. "To this day I really don't understand how that night happened. I mean from the first time he met you, you were the only woman Adam ever talked about. And honestly, he and I . . . it wasn't as if we ever even looked at each other that way."

Mackenzie looked at the friend she'd always envied. With her small curvy body and beautiful face and that overabundance of talent, not to mention her famous name — who wouldn't choose Emma?

"I'm telling you, Mackenzie. Just in case you think Adam or I could have ever looked back on that night with any kind of fondness." A small smile tugged at her lips. "There's not enough tequila in the world to turn what happened between us into more than a sad and embarrassing memory."

"Really?" Serena shot Emma a look. "All that scribbling and this is the best you can do?"

"What are you, the apology police?" Mackenzie snapped. "Just let her finish."

Emma sighed, leafed through a few pages, then set them aside. "I promise you, if you could have seen Adam's face, both our faces really, when we woke up and realized what had happened . . ." Emma grimaced. "Well, I don't know which of us was more shocked or horrified. We couldn't get away from each other fast enough. Why . . ."

"That's enough." Mackenzie closed her eyes expecting to combat pain. Instead she felt a surge of relief at having this far less threatening image to replace the eager caresses her brain had been conjuring.

"And of course I know I should have told Adam that I was pregnant. It was wrong of me not to," Emma continued. "I just didn't want to complicate things when you and he were back together. And I was so afraid of losing you." She blew a bang off her forehead as she regrouped. "I would take every bit of it back," Emma said. "I'd wish it all out of existence. Except then there'd be no Zoe." Emma's eyes glittered with tears. "And no matter what, no matter how many stupid words I put down on stupid pieces of paper, I can't wish there was no Zoe."

Mackenzie nodded. She hated the circumstances, hated pretty much everything that had come to light, but she would never wish there was no Zoe, either.

"And that's the thing. I know the whole fairy godmother idea was kind of lame, but the longer I went without telling Adam or you the truth, the more impossible it became. And then when you lost your baby . . . I wasn't trying to hurt you. I just . . . I wanted to share Zoe with you. And it was the only way I could think of that would let me share her with both of you." Emma swiped at her tears.

Mackenzie felt tears of her own threaten. "I've loved being Zoe's fairy godmother. Even when it hurt, I loved being a part of her life. Right up until you pushed me out of it."

Serena nodded. "You pushed both of us out, without any warning or explanation. For five years. Do you have any idea what that felt like?"

"I do know. I have parents who did that to me my whole life. I'm sorry. It was just the older Zoe got the more I started noticing the things she'd gotten from her father. I guess I just panicked. I didn't know how to tell you and I was so afraid of losing you."

"So you just went ahead and got rid of us," Serena said.

Emma nodded, no longer trying to stop the tears. They dropped onto her notes, wetting

496

them and causing the ink to run and blur. "I pushed away the very people I was the most afraid of losing." She looked up at them through the sheen of tears. "How stupid and wussy is that?"

"Extremely," Serena replied, her eyes now glittering with tears. "I'd like to say I've never been stupidly wussy, but that would be a lie. And while we're at it, I'm really sorry I didn't process things a little bit before I accused Adam of cheating on Mac and ignoring the daughter he didn't even know he had." She picked up a cocktail napkin and tried to stanch the flow of tears. "Oh, God, this is pathetic. I hope that waiter/aspiring actor doesn't have any paparazzi on speed dial. I don't look anywhere near as attractive as Emma does when I cry."

"Who does?" Mackenzie sniffed. But for the first time she not only heard Emma's and Serena's apologies, she received them, felt them sink all the way in.

Adam had told her he loved her, had always wanted to marry her, and was eager to share what lay ahead with her. She could tell herself that he was lying because she was somehow unworthy or inherently unlovable. Or she could allow herself to believe that he'd meant what he'd told her. Allow herself to finally let go of all the insecurities she'd thought she had discarded but had actually clung to for so much of her life. The ones that had made her jealous of Emma, and uncertain of Adam, and sent her scurrying back to Indiana after all the effort she'd gone to to leave it.

"Are you okay?" Emma reached for her hand and squeezed it.

Mackenzie nodded though she wasn't a hundred percent certain it was true. Nothing any of them said or did would erase what had happened or make Zoe any less Adam's daughter. But the time had come to make the choices that would define her and determine her future. She could cling to the old hurts, walk away from the people who'd inflicted them — including these two women whom she'd loved practically from the moment she'd met them — and continue to live a small, safe life. Or she could choose to accept the truth, come to terms with what had happened, and find a way to move on.

She squeezed Emma's hand and reached for Serena's as the weight she'd been carrying began to lift. Even thirty minutes ago she would not have believed they'd ever find their way back. Now she prayed that they could. "I'm better than okay. And I appreciate your apology. And I — I hope we can move forward.

"But if we're going to be friends then I think we have to agree to complete honesty. I mean, I can see how a few lines got crossed, and I even understand how hard it might have been to speak up. But if we're going to be able to trust each other again, we're going to have to agree to tell the truth even when it's risky or inconvenient — or painful."

Serena felt both women squeeze her hands. Was she really sitting here crying in the middle of Bemelmans?

"I agree with Mackenzie. But I think we need to let go of each other right now. I'm not up for pictures of us blubbering and holding hands in the middle of a bar in the tabloids. Best-case scenario they think we've found religion together and are having a prayer circle. Worst case they think we're fruitcakes communing with spirits or having a séance or something." She smiled as they dropped each other's hands. "Though come to think of it, I feel like I might be sensing Gran's spirit telling us to have another drink." She raised her hand to get the waiter's attention.

"I know she'd be glad to see us getting our act together and our friendship back on track," Emma said. "Speaking of which, I hope you'll accept my sincere apology for blaming the blowup that night on you, Serena."

Mackenzie nodded. "Me too."

"That's it?" Serena motioned to the sheets of paper that still lay on the table, sodden though they were. "All these pages for Mackenzie and only one run-on sentence for me?" Serena sat back giving no sign of the relief she felt coursing through her. These two women could be a royal pain in the ass, but there was no denying how much she had missed them. "Good God, the injustice!" she proclaimed, her tone and accent pure Georgia Goodbody. "I was expecting a much larger apology than that."

"So you're saying size does matter?" Emma asked.

"Doesn't it always?" Serena shot back.

"I'll drink to that!" Mackenzie said as the waiter returned with three more Gin-Gin Mules and a head shot for each of them.

The tension eased further. It would never disappear quite as cleanly as Emma's memory of the accident and most of the coma, but Emma would have given up more than those few memories to have Serena and Mackenzie back and her secret finally shared, no matter how badly, with the people who needed to know it.

"Well, I think sincerity counts, too," Mackenzie added.

"All right, then," Serena countered. "I sincerely believe that size matters."

They smiled at each other. Clinked their glasses together. Took a long drink. Fingers tinkled on the piano keys and the hum of conversation rose as tables began to fill. It was said that confession was good for the soul. So was forgiveness. It seemed that Gin-Gin Mules didn't hurt, either.

500

A text dinged in on Emma's phone. She read it and looked up at the others. "It's from Zoe. She wants to know if it's safe to come back."

They considered each other over their cocktails.

"I don't know," Serena said. "I might need another mule and some lowdown on Jake Richards before I decide for sure."

"And I want to hear what Mac's decided about LA," Emma said. She especially wanted to know how Mackenzie thought Adam would cope with the whole fatherhood thing, but for tonight she just wanted to enjoy these women that she'd almost lost. "Because, well, I was thinking if you're coming out even to look around, maybe you guys would like to stay with Zoe and me for a while. You know, just till you find a place of your own."

Another text arrived.

"I say we let her sweat it out a little longer," Serena said as the pianist launched into a Gershwin tune. "Lindsay Lohan my ass." She raised her glass. "And FYI — I seem to be over Brooks Anderson — can you believe it? And, well, I was wondering . . . have either of you ever noticed how cute Ethan Miller is?"

"Wasn't that his car out front?" Mackenzie asked.

Serena nodded then picked up her cell phone. "Hold on, I'm texting Ethan to let him know everything's okay."

"Ethan's definitely cute," Mackenzie said. "And I'm glad to see you finally opening your eyes to the great guy under your nose."

"Agreed," Emma said. "And I'm not planning to tell Zoe yet, but I thought we'd try to work out the part on *As the World Churns* he offered her." She told them her plans to spend what remained of the summer at the lake. "And Nadia's going to stay on as caretaker."

"Edmund will be thrilled, I'm sure," Serena said drily.

The conversation ebbed and flowed without a stutter. There was so much to catch up on, so much to share. Emma told them about the call from Rex and the upcoming announcement of his and Eve's divorce and Rex's coming out.

"Oh, God, next thing you'll be telling us you've forgiven Eve," Serena said.

"Well, let's not get carried away," Emma said. "Though I was thinking that if Eve ever wanted to try to *be* Zoe's grandmother and not just 'act' the part in a movie, I'd ask Zoe if she wanted to give it a try."

They raised their glasses and took turns toasting. "To us."

"To friendship."

"To our week at the lake — however extended it may be."

Zoe came around the corner to join them, and Emma's heart filled with thanks and gladness.

*Cheers, darling. And hugs to all of you.*
Gran's voice sounded in her head.

"To our week at the lake!" Mackenzie said.

They raised their glasses and clinked to
that, Zoe's Coke glass added to the mix.

"I'm already looking forward to next summer," Serena said as they prepared to down
the little that remained in their glasses. "But
if you don't mind, next year I'd like to skip
the whole hospital/coma thing and head right
to the lake."

■ ■ ■ ■

# READERS GUIDE: A WEEK AT THE LAKE

BY WENDY WAX

■ ■ ■ ■

# DISCUSSION QUESTIONS

1. Did you identify with a particular character in the novel? Who and why?

2. Emma continues to hear her grandmother's voice, even though she is no longer a physical presence in her life. Do departed loved ones continue to influence your own thoughts and actions?

3. As the novel progresses, Mackenzie and Adam's relationship becomes increasingly strained. Did you want their relationship to survive or would they be better off apart?

4. Did Mackenzie harbor resentment toward Adam because he didn't want to adopt a child? Was the blog a way of concealing her true feelings from others or herself?

5. When Emma's betrayals are exposed do you sympathize with her? Who do you think was most hurt by her dishonesty? If a friend

kept something like this from you, could you forgive her?

6. Serena's therapist comments, "If you're going to expend time and energy imagining scenarios, you really need to allow for the positive." What does this say about Serena's personality? Do you tend to think for the best or the worst in difficult situations?

7. How does Serena use humor to dispel her discomfort? Why do you think she constantly makes light of difficult situations?

8. Were you upset with Serena for rekindling her relationship with Brooks? Can you understand her choice? Do you think it was necessary for her ultimate growth?

9. Emma comments, "She could see how much of [Zoe's father] her daughter carried." Do you think personality traits and mannerisms are genetic? Have you witnessed this within your own family?

10. Mackenzie is very blunt with Serena regarding her relationships with married men. Do you agree with Mac? Did you feel at all sorry for Serena?

11. At a very young age, Emma divorces her

family. What did you think of this extreme decision?

12. By the novel's end, do you think there was room for reconciliation between Emma and her parents? Did Emma's mother deserve a second chance or did she ruin it?

13. How does Zoe and Emma's relationship develop throughout the novel? What are some significant turning points in their narrative?

14. How does Emma's relationship with her own family affect how she parents Zoe? Were there moments when Emma was being overprotective of Zoe due to her own experiences?

The employees of Thorndike Press hope you have enjoyed this Large Print book. All our Thorndike, Wheeler, and Kennebec Large Print titles are designed for easy reading, and all our books are made to last. Other Thorndike Press Large Print books are available at your library, through selected bookstores, or directly from us.

For information about titles, please call:
(800) 223-1244

or visit our Web site at:
http://gale.cengage.com/thorndike

To share your comments, please write:
Publisher
Thorndike Press
10 Water St., Suite 310
Waterville, ME 04901